~ Look for these titles from Rhonda Laurel ~

Now Available

The Blake Boys Series

For the Love of the Game (Book One)
MVP (Book Two)
The Blake Legacy (Book Three)

Ebb Tide
Shutter
Star Crossed
"Masquerade" Halloween Heat IV

Print

The Rhonda Laurel Collection
"Masquerade" Halloween Heat MF
The Blake Boys Collection

The Blake Boys Collection

For the Love of the Game

MVP

The Blake Legacy

Rhonda Laurel

etopia
press

Etopia Press
1643 Warwick Ave., #124
Warwick, RI 02889
http://www.etopia-press.net

Previously published in digital format by Etopia Press

Print ISBN: 978-1-940223-81-0
Digital ISBN: 978-1-939194-16-9
Digital ISBN: 978-1-940223-15-5
Digital ISBN: 978-1-940223-61-2

First Etopia Press print publication: January 2014

~ Contents ~

For the Love of the Game

Morgan Reed was long overdue for a vacation. It occurred to her while doing inventory in her quaint bookstore last week that she'd read almost every book in the travel section, but she'd never seen any of the scenic places. Her world had never seemed quite as small as it did once she made the realization.

When she told Theresa, her travel agent, she wanted to get lost on an island, Theresa took her cue and began furiously tapping on her keyboard.

"I want to get lost at sea if possible."

Theresa's eyes narrowed as she read the screen. "There's a new destination, just started doing business with them a month ago. Very secluded. All-inclusive, the rooms are beautiful. They don't allow cell phones or newspapers. Just days of endless bliss on a deserted island."

"How deserted? I won't be seeing Gilligan and the Skipper, will I?" Morgan winced.

"No, silly. Deserted as in no obnoxious people standing on the beach gazing at a beautiful sunset with cell phones in their hands."

"I'll take it," Morgan said. The idea that no one could contact her was the most appealing part of the package. She longed for the days when cell phones were things you carried for emergencies only. Now it was a cure for boredom in most, and brought out bad driving habits in others. Paradise sans technology sounded like a good idea to her.

After tunneling through all the frivolous crap in her spare bedroom closet, Morgan finally located her suitcases. The large, pale pink suitcase and matching carry-on had seen better days; they looked like props from a seventies movie. She surveyed them and had to admit the style was a bit old-fashioned. An old airport luggage tag was still attached. When she leaned closer, she realized the tag bore a date from seven years ago when she went to Vegas. Seven years! What had she been doing for seven years?

Oh yeah, she'd spent the last seven years trying to keep her dream of owning a bookstore alive. The bookstore was her life. A quiet and organized life and she loved it, even though sometimes it was hard to keep afloat.

Whenever she got the blues, she would read one of the books in the travel section. She read about Fiji, the Cayman Islands, Australia, Hawaii, and Scotland. All of these places had rich histories set against the backdrop of a cinematic dream. It took a book about stress falling off the shelf and onto her head one day to make her take action.

Morgan walked to her desk in the living room and began jotting notes. First, she would get a new set of luggage. Then she would sift through her summer wardrobe and see what was salvageable. She wasn't much of a summer dress-up person, so maybe a visit to the mall was in order as well. She would have to go to her dad's house and get her passport. She was pretty sure it was still current. Now if only she could break in in the middle of the night and get the passport without having to inform her father she was going on vacation alone.

Morgan knew why they treated her that way. She had gotten lost during a family camping trip at Lake George when she was fifteen. After storming away from the family when one of her brothers had told her she was too young to get on a Jet Ski, Morgan had walked around for hours, refusing to admit she was lost. Finally she'd happened upon another family, who'd called the ranger's office to report she'd been found. Four hours later, a ranger dropped her off at the hotel. Her father's initial relief was followed up with the lecture to end all lectures. And to make matters worse, the brothers chimed in for good measure.

She kept her passport at her father's house not only because it would never be misplaced there, but because her dad was comforted by the idea that he would know when she was leaving town.

While writing all these things down, a wave of serenity washed over her. Ten glorious days on an island with nothing to do but watch the sun set while pondering the mysteries of life. She smiled and screamed into a pillow. *Oh my God! I am going on vacation!*

* * *

Morgan barely slept the night before her early morning flight. Her assistant manager, Michelle, challenged her to visit the place without doing any research on it beforehand, inspiring her to be surprised when she arrived. The problem was that she didn't like surprises. Her friends had called her a control freak on many occasions, but she preferred to think of it as someone who was prepared for anything. So she took Michelle's advice and was happy she did. The excitement was building in her so much she couldn't read the book she'd brought. Too excited to read a book? She found herself checking her watch every other minute, and clutched the handle of her new luggage so tightly her hand hurt.

* * *

Morgan stepped off the rickety single-engine plane and entered a tropical paradise. As soon as the balmy air encompassed her, she knew she would dread going back to the cold Philadelphia weather. The ocean breeze was blowing the palm trees in unison, as if welcoming the passengers. There were bright colors everywhere; even the airport workers' uniforms were a vibrant coral. As she climbed into the hotel shuttle cart, she smiled as the hostess greeted her with a mai tai. A postcard couldn't hold a candle to the island beauty that surrounded her.

The bookstore was in Michelle's capable hands. Morgan had called her father two days before her departure to inform him she was coming over to get her passport, and was not surprised to see her three surly brothers sitting at the kitchen table. She sat through three stern lectures from her family about traveling alone. Finally her stepmother, Sydney, had intervened and informed the men that Morgan was an adult who knew how to handle herself. Jason, the guy she'd been dating for six months, was out of town at a convention, so she opted to leave him a short voice mail. She'd considered telling him when she'd planned the trip, but she was afraid he would want to join her. Jason was a nice guy, but he wasn't the man of her dreams. She felt good about this vacation. But looking at that old luggage tag from seven years ago indicated that something was missing in her life. Had she been on a hamster wheel all this time spinning and spinning only to find she'd never left Philadelphia? Her life was good, but it was becoming a bit stagnant. She had nothing to get the blood rushing through her veins. Somewhere along the line, amid her comfortable existence, she'd lost her passion for life. Who knew, maybe she would find it here on the island? Her imagination was ramping up at the idea of finding what was missing in her life in ten days on a tropical island. Maybe that sort of thing happened in one of the books she read, but for her it seemed as likely as finding the Loch Ness monster in the hotel swimming pool.

* * *

Seth Blake had had all he could tolerate of paradise. What had begun as a low-key getaway after a hectic season became an after party for his Super Bowl win. Patton, a linebacker on his team, had let it slip that they were visiting a new, exotic locale, and the next thing he knew he was hosting a monster post-Super Bowl vacation bash for the team. He enjoyed bonding with his new team, but winning the Super Bowl and being the new superstar quarterback for the Philadelphia Titans was wearing him down. He ached to go home, even if it was still cold and dreary in Philly, and sleep for at least a week. Well, Philadelphia was his second home. The downside to the Titans making him an offer he couldn't refuse was that he'd had to leave Texas. He was born there. He had a sprawling ranch there. His family was there. But forty million dollars and a chance to cement the future of his family was worth living in a bustling city for a while.

The team had done nothing but party and play touch football on the beach since they arrived. Not one of them took a moment to explore the island or take in the awesome scenic view. The food was divine; the island was spectacular, and the beach bunnies were tanned and toned and all too willing to spend time with him. The days of endless partying were becoming stale to him, even at the ripe old age of twenty-eight. He'd dated plenty of beautiful women, but he wished he'd meet at least one that was beautiful on the inside as well. One could only talk about fashion, houses, and parties for so long. And every one of his cover girls were all too happy to share the spotlight the media kept trained on him.

He packed his bags and went to the small airport determined to get off the paradise isle without being missed. The booking agent at the counter, a tall, slender young man with dreadlocks, said he would have to wait for a private plane, but if he didn't mind, he could hop on a commercial flight that would be leaving soon. Suddenly another agent, a short, older, balding man, leaned over and whispered to the agent who was assisting him. The young man turned around and apologized profusely for suggesting he take a commercial flight. It amazed him people thought all celebrities were snobs. Not that he considered himself a celebrity. His fateful, glamorous die had been cast years ago when he went pro, and some national entertainment magazine had named him the most gorgeous man alive. He had a tough time living that down. There was the constant ribbing from his teammates for five months straight, and he'd had to change his phone number. He would get random calls in the middle of the night from women who also had some celebrity status and thought it was okay to call. His girlfriend at the time, Penelope, was a med student who'd become suspicious and insecure from the attention he was getting. In the end she dumped him, saying her studies were being affected by her involvement with him.

"That's fine," Seth said as pleasantly as he could so there wouldn't be a problem.

Besides, the commercial plane had come in and the passengers were exiting. He'd pass the time gauging how each would react to the scenery. Seth took a seat and watched as each person stepped off the plane and was captivated by the beauty of the airport.

He'd had the same reaction he arrived. His first thought was if the airport looked like a hidden oasis, the rest of the island was sure to be impressive. He hadn't been wrong. The bungalow he'd stayed in was magnificent. A picture-perfect ocean view from the deck. For the first time in a long while, he'd wished he had someone to enjoy that view with him. Loneliness was setting in and he didn't know what to do. He'd won the Super Bowl, for heaven's sake, and there was no one to genuinely share that moment of achievement. Sure, there were parties and plenty of opportunities to get laid, but no one to tell him that he'd done a good job, but now it was time to set new goals and achieve them.

The passengers all had looks of nervous excitement on their faces. He longed for that feeling again. That was the thing about accomplishing all your dreams at a young age. Cynicism became your new best friend. The plane passengers began to look the same, dressed in vacation battle gear. Sundresses and cabana shirts seemed to have the run of the island. Everyone fit that description except the last passenger to exit the plane. She was brown skinned and her reddish-brown hair flowed in the wind. The woman wore her sunglasses propped on her head, khaki cargo shorts, and a T-shirt that said, "Anywhere but Here." She had a sweet, girl-next-door look, not the model-of-the-week type he'd been dating for the past two years. When she smiled, something in him warmed inside. She stopped for a moment, surveying the airport with a hopeful look on her face. Suddenly Seth didn't feel the need to leave paradise after all.

* * *

Morgan stepped onto the white sand with her bag, ready for action. It was day three on the island, and it was finally time to test the waters. The ocean called to her, but the idea of putting on a bathing suit was more stress than she wanted on vacation. So she settled for the shortest pair of shorts she owned, a white T-shirt that bore the slogan "Down with Illiteracy," and a big, floppy hat. She brought her hat along as a deterrent from the sun, hoping to avoid sunburn.

There was a game of touch football in progress. As she got closer to the game she noticed the players were a bunch of tall, muscled guys showing off for the beach bunny cheerleaders screaming from beach chairs. What a shame that people had to resort to damn near stripping and flailing around in public to attract each other's attention.

Then another thought hit her—literally. A gorgeous man headed toward her at a million miles per hour, and all she could do was stop dead in her tracks and brace for impact.

* * *

For the third time that evening Morgan regained consciousness. The pain medication the doctor had given her made her euphoric and sleepy. When she'd come to, a nurse had informed her she had a bruised rib but nothing was broken. She lay in bed watching the white ceiling fan above her rotate, thinking of how quiet and sterilized the office seemed. She heard a sound from the corner of the room and turned to see the muscle head guy who had run into her on the beach, sitting in a chair opposite her, watching.

"Good evening."

"What are you doing here?" she asked, confused.

"I just wanted to make sure you were okay. I'm sorry about running into you like that. I didn't see you."

"I don't take it personally. Nobody ever does. Besides, you were too busy flexing for the beach bunnies," Morgan said, flashing a condescending smile. So what if he was six foot three and gorgeous? That didn't give him the right to steamroll over people on the beach.

"Was not," he scoffed.

"If you weren't, then you had a bad case of tunnel vision. Ever think of trying out for a team? I could be your reference to confirm that you could tackle someone pretty good."

"You know football?" he asked with an amused smirk.

"Steroid-pumped overgrown men on a field trying to throw a ball back and forth and scoring points."

"Well, that's the layman's explanation for it. It's more complicated than that, though. And minus the steroids." He coughed. "I can explain it to you."

Men and their posturing about sports. Morgan held up a hand. "No need. First you injure me; now you want to bore me to death. I have no need to fill my brain with random trivia about things I don't care about."

"Well, sports are a meaningful way of exercise, keeping in

shape, strategizing, and it has a place for those of us who weren't selected for the IQ Olympics." He chuckled as he leaned back in his chair, crossing his leg over his knee. "What slogan will tomorrow's shirt have on it? Your SAT scores? I've rather enjoyed reading your T-shirts the past three days."

"I wouldn't want to make the rest of the island feel inferior to me. Especially since they're a bunch of muscle head jocks running around. I would fear for my safety."

As he shifted slightly in the chair, she noticed how finely sculpted his body was and reaffirmed why he was out running around like an idiot. Every inch of exposed skin was muscled, well-defined, and lean. His shoulders were wide, but his waist narrowed, and he looked as if he ate five pounds of pasta for breakfast. But the face was in great contrast to the body. He had soft, striking features and piercing green eyes, giving him a hint of a boyish look, but she knew he hadn't been a boy in a long time. And his smile was perfect and rehearsed, like he'd practiced it a lot. It seemed more controlled than natural. Did he feel the need to put on a pleasant mask all the time? Smiling on command wasn't an easy thing. She'd ruined many a family photo because her two-second freeze frame would expire before the picture was taken. She wondered what would make him smile genuinely.

"Did you know that you moan in your sleep?" he asked in a low Southern drawl, surprising her.

"I do not."

"I was wondering if your husband told you that."

"I'm not married."

"Hmm. Then maybe that's why you moan in your sleep." He smiled.

Morgan returned the smile. "I think I know what tomorrow's T-shirt is going to say."

"What's that?" He leaned in closer to the bed.

"Up yours."

* * *

The next day she was released and was happy to be returning to her room. She had only seven days left in paradise and Morgan was determined to make the most of her time. As she gingerly put on her clothes, the nurse said someone had arrived to take her back to her room. She stepped out looking for a hotel employee, but instead saw the muscle head hunk standing near a golf cart.

"Your chariot, my lady." He motioned to the cart.

"I'm not going anywhere with you."

"It's the least I can do since it's my fault you got injured. I will be at your beck and call for the next few days."

"So what is this? Looking to finish what you started on the beach?"

"Please let me make it up to you," he said as he ran his hand through his short hair.

"No thanks."

"I'm gonna feel like dirt for the rest of my vacation if I don't at least help you get settled."

Morgan saw that the rehearsed smile from last night was gone. This one didn't seem to have a sales pitch lurking behind it. It was warm, genuine, and friendly. "Fine."

"My name is Seth, by the way." He extended his hand.

"Morgan." She met his hand and, to her surprise, his hands were almost as soft as butter. And those soft hands were attached to a deeply tanned muscular arm with a Rolex watch wrapped around the wrist. He helped her into the cart. As she slid into the seat the bottle of pain meds she'd gotten from the clinic fell on the floor. Seth immediately leaned over to retrieve the bottle; she leaned out of his way but not in time to avoid his lips brushing against hers accidentally. He lingered a bit before backing away.

"Sorry," he said with a lazy look in his eyes.

"So much for hand-eye coordination. You really shouldn't have been playing football yesterday." She glared at him, but her heart was almost beating out of her chest.

The ride back to the main tower was a mere ten minutes, but since Seth drove five miles slower than the posted speed limit, it was interminable. She wanted to be away from this guy in the worst way. During the course of twenty-four hours, he'd crashed into her, watched her sleep for God only knew how long, and kissed her. Morgan couldn't deny he was good-looking. If you went for that all-American, rugged, handsome type with a hint of Southern accent oozing out of his mouth every now and again.

"My room is in the main tower," she said as he approached the dividing road. He should have turned right to get back on the main path, but instead he made a left toward the ultra-exclusive bungalows. "Uh, you should have made a right."

"I know where I'm going." He stopped at the front gate to the private bungalows. He flashed a smile as the guard came out of the security shack. The guard leapt back in and opened the gate for him.

He stopped at bungalow twelve. "These are your new digs. On behalf of myself and the management for ruining your vacation."

"So basically you and the hotel don't want me to sue you." She laughed.

"Something like that. But I do feel bad. I would like a chance to make that up to you."

Seth smiled again, but this time it was a half grin and his eyes sparkled. This time the dimples in his cheeks deepened. If he was going to be sincere and sweet, Morgan would have no choice but to be civil to him. Hostility toward this man was helping her keep perspective on this wacky predicament.

The view from the pathway to the bungalows alone was more magnificent than looking out of the fourteenth story window in the main tower. The bungalow was on the beach, and it was beautiful. Felt like a home. The deck faced the water, which was a brilliant blue that beckoned closer and closer.

"Don't stare at it too long. The waves become hypnotic after a while. I stood on the deck for three hours the first day I got here," Seth murmured as he opened the doors to the deck.

"It is beautiful, isn't it? Morgan sighed.

"There's a bar and a kitchen. Two bedrooms and two baths. Big enough so we won't get in each other's way."

Each other? "What?"

"This is my bungalow. There weren't any more available. There's plenty of room, and you'll need someone to look after you."

"You've got to be kidding me." She put her hands on her hips. "I can take care of myself."

"Oh, okay. Think fast." Seth threw a pillow at her that hit her in the face, then fell on the floor.

She blinked. "Am I on Tropical Candid Camera or something? Do you lure women to your bungalow, then torture them?"

"You cannot take care of yourself. And this place is big enough for both of us."

"Like hell it is. I don't even know you! All I know is you hit like a Mack truck. And why would the hotel agree to this? Who are you?"

"I told you my name is Seth."

"Seth!" She snorted. "Sounds like you should be skipping down a dirt road in a pair of overalls with an ice-cream cone in your hand!"

"Really, Morgan? That's funny coming from a girl with a man's name."

"I haven't been a girl in quite some time, Seth." She folded her arms over her chest.

"Well, you're not acting like a woman right now."

"If I wasn't in such agonizing pain from being mauled by you, I'd deck you!"

Seth laughed and looked down at her small fist. "With what? Or were you going to borrow someone else's hand?"

Morgan lunged at him and knew immediately it was a mistake. The meds she had taken were beginning to take effect but not enough so that she didn't feel the pain of the sudden movement. He laughed at her as she hurled all the pillows on the couch at him, followed by the cushions, and finally as she turned to grab a coaster off the side table, he was in front of her and had her arms locked in his grasp. She looked up, glaring at him, only to see a green so sparkling it looked like someone had used a crayon to color his eyes, which were half hidden behind long lashes, too long and lush for a man to have. She'd never seen piercing green eyes up close and personal before. But his eyes reminded her of mint. The color of mouthwash? No, that was the smell of his breath as he closed in on her, his breath blowing ever so lightly on the bridge of her nose.

Morgan slowly raised her hand, touching his side, feeling every muscle along the way down to his waist and then down to the front of his pants. He was smiling at her, a devious smile like a cat that'd caught and ate a bird in the backyard. A satisfied smile, indeed. His smile vanished as she put pressure on his crotch.

"If you don't let me go, cowboy, you're gonna have a new career as an opera singer."

Seth laughed. "You could have just asked, you know. I think you just want to feel me up. Not that I mind the hand job."

Morgan refused to let him see her flush as she realized what she was doing. What started as a self-defense crotch grab had turned into a subtle caress. "Can you please let me go?"

"Are you hungry?"

She wanted to say no and storm off in some dramatic fashion, but she was hungry. He ordered room service while she changed her clothes in her new spacious room. By the time she came out—it took some time to maneuver because of her injury—lunch was waiting for her. Seth was sitting patiently at the table when she emerged from her room.

"Everything all right?"

"I got hit yesterday by some mammoth of a guy on the beach, and my rib is bruised. So it takes a while for me to do everyday things."

"You are not going to let that go, are you?"

"I'm like a dog with a bone," she said as she sat carefully in the chair.

He covered all the bases, ordering fresh lobster and shrimp and a gigantic plate of the fruits native to the island. They ate without saying too much, and afterward Seth told her he had to go out for a while. When he left she pulled out the book she'd been trying to read when the incident had occurred, and she enjoyed listening to the rumbling waves, drifting into a literary daydream. True, the book was fiction, but now she felt silly for overlooking paradise to delve into the book. She closed the book begrudgingly and made herself a drink.

* * *

Morgan was so serenely watching the sun set that she dozed off in the lounge chair. She woke a few hours later to find a blanket over her and Seth sitting in the opposite chair with his eyes closed. When she tried to get up as quietly as she could and return the favor with the blanket it only stirred him out of his sleep.

"Feeling any better?" he asked in a lazy drawl.

"A little."

He looked so innocent she didn't have it in her to trade barbs.

"You look well rested."

"I realized I was sitting in the middle of the pages of a book. Thank you for sharing your bungalow with me."

"You're welcome, ma'am."

"I'm turning in. It's been a long day." Morgan smiled. That Southern charm of his was growing on her.

Seth got out of his chair and ran a hand through his hair. "I guess I should too. Do you need any help getting ready for bed?"

"No. I can get ready for bed on my own. Good night."

* * *

Seth truly had good intentions when he'd offered to help her get ready for bed. But even as the words left his lips, images of Morgan naked began to float around in his head. When he came back to the bungalow and saw her sleeping so peacefully, he wanted to scoop her up in his arms and take her to his bed. But he did the gentlemanly thing and covered her with a blanket. He loved watching her sleep. Part of the reason he stayed so long in the infirmary with her was that he was captivated by the rhythms of her breathing. A slow inhale that made her breasts rise a little, followed by an exhale that seemed to cleanse her body. She looked so soft and sweet while she slept. But when she was awake she was a sarcastic spitfire. It seemed like she found peace when she slept.

He knew she would like the view from the bungalow. For the past few days, whenever he saw her on the island she was always gazing out at the water, watching wave after beautiful wave coming closer to shore. But not once did he see her actually getting in the water, or even in a bikini, for that matter. Maybe she was one of those intellectual women who thought it was offensive to put on a bikini and prance around the beach. She was short and petite and had curvy hips—baby-making hips, as his grandmother would say. She was soft and fragile, yet at the same time strong and powerful.

He hadn't planned past getting her to come to his bungalow. Now that she seemed resigned to the idea, he would have to strategize his next move. It would be much simpler if he was in the middle of a game; he fed off the raw energy of playing football. But he was in a bungalow with a woman he'd damn near crippled on the beach and was growing more attracted to as each hour passed. Holding her captive surely wouldn't turn out well; she'd demonstrated that afternoon she was willing to defend herself. He needed an incentive for her to want to stay with him. He could try to charm her, but she was leery of it. She seemed more open when he eased back and let the chemistry flow between them without him herding her in his direction. Slowly she seemed to be making her way there all on her own.

He headed off to bed too but didn't know how much sleep he was going to get with her in such proximity. He strained to hear through the wall as Morgan bustled around her room. He imagined her getting undressed and getting ready for a shower. The thought of soapy water cascading down her body made him hard. But this time he didn't have Morgan inadvertently stroking him. Yeah, he wasn't getting any sleep tonight.

* * *

Morgan woke with a new attitude the next morning. She mulled over her options: she could either complain about her injury to the guilt-ridden Seth, or she could enjoy herself and accept the situation as it was. She ordered breakfast and had it waiting for him when he came out of his room.

"I hope you don't mind." She removed the metal covers from the plates. "I ordered a little bit of everything to cover all the bases."

Seth picked up a piece of bacon and shoved it in his mouth. "Not at all. Thank you."

"So how long are you here on vacation?"

"Hadn't really thought about. As long as it takes to unwind." He winked at her.

"Must be nice." She sighed and played with her linen napkin.

"I don't vacation a lot. But when I do, I like to get my money's worth."

"This is my first vacation in seven years."

"Seven years." He raised an eyebrow. "Where were you? In prison?"

"Worse. Running a bookstore."

"I knew you were the reading type."

"The book in my hand was a dead giveaway?"

"No." Seth studied her face for a moment. "You look like a librarian."

"I've heard that one before."

"You know," he said with a slight gleam in his eye, "I've had librarian fantasies."

"You and every man on the planet." She giggled. "Let me guess. You're envisioning me with my hair in a tight bun, some nerdy glasses on the edge of my nose, and a tweed skirt with a long slit up the front?"

Seth had been eating a piece of toast. He took his time, finishing the toast, and took a sip of orange juice. "No. Just you. No bun, no glasses, and definitely no tweed skirt."

The temperature on the wall read sixty-nine degrees but to Morgan it was closer to a hundred and two. Those minty eyes of Seth's seemed more like an emerald green this morning. He looked quite refreshed while she'd tossed and turned all night. She had wondered if he would try to knock on her door but was disappointed that he had been a perfect gentleman all evening. But his comment made her believe he'd at least thought about it.

* * *

Seth took her parasailing. It took some coaxing and a trip to the boutique to buy a bathing suit, but she did it. Morgan was proud of herself. She was actually doing something instead of reading about it in the pages of a book. And having a handsome man to show her the way to pleasure and fun wasn't so bad either.

After the parasailing they decided to grab some lunch and wandered into a limbo contest. The bar manager asked them to be judges; they happily agreed.

As the contest was about to begin Seth whispered in her ear, "I bet you twenty bucks that the chubby guy in the Hawaiian shirt wins."

"I'll take that bet." She giggled.

And he was right. Louis Parsons, from Catontown, Oklahoma was indeed the winner. Morgan gave him his prize, a gift certificate to the spa and free surfing lessons. She couldn't help but ask Seth how he picked his winner.

Seth said, "Louis had something to prove because he was the most overweight and people snickered when he entered the contest. He wanted that victory more than everyone else; that's why he won."

Morgan smiled at his insightfulness. "Good call."

For the fourth time in an hour, a woman wearing a slinky red dress cruised their table. This time she pretended to drop something so she could conveniently bend down and give Seth a bird's-eye view.

"Can I help you?" Morgan said through her teeth.

"Excuse me?" the woman snapped.

"Can I help you? You keep coming over here." Morgan repeated, a little bit louder.

"Who do you think you're talking to, half-pint?"

"I'm talking to the piece of trash in a dress so short your vagina is going to catch a cold from the ocean breeze."

The sound of Seth's laughter made her turn her head in his direction. The woman gazed at Seth as if he was supposed to put Morgan in her place. "Sorry, sweetheart, but she's right on all accounts."

The vamp looked from Seth to Morgan and then back to Seth. After a moment she realized that almost every table had turned their attention on them, so she composed herself and mumbled, "Whatever."

"What did you say?" Morgan said, still fired up.

Seth jumped up in time to catch Morgan from leaving her seat.

He kneeled next to her chair and rubbed her forearm. "You won, champ. By a knockout."

She exhaled and rubbed her temples. "This has to be the most stressful vacation I've ever had."

"But you haven't had a dull moment since you stepped off the plane."

"You got that right." She laughed.

The simple motion of running his fingers up and down her arm seemed to calm her. Seth's touch warmed her skin. She glanced up to see the other patrons looking at them. "I take it that happens to you a lot?"

"Yeah. It does."

"I can't believe how she tried to dismiss me like that. I'm not chopped liver. There was a time when people had respect; now it's like the laws of the jungle to get a man. I'd like to leave now." Morgan stood.

"Okay."

"No, you stay. I'd like to be alone."

"I'm supposed to be looking after you," he murmured "How about a walk on the beach?"

They walked the beach until the sun set and when she said she was tired, Seth had her climb on his back, and he carried her to the bungalow. She was amazed that he seemed to do it with ease and never slowed his pace. He stopped once to pick up a beautiful seashell. He cleaned it off and handed it to her, and they were on their way again. When they returned to the bungalow, they sat on the deck again gazing at the moonlit sky while listening to sounds of the ocean. Morgan was fighting to keep her eyes open.

She didn't know how long she'd been out, but when she opened her eyes, Seth was placing her gently in her bed. She looked up and smiled at him. He simply kissed her on the forehead and shut her door.

* * *

Over the course of the next few days Morgan told him about her life and her bookstore, which was near ruins. The pipes leaked, the plaster was crumbling, and the place needed rewiring, but she loved her store. She told him about her wacky assistant manager, Michelle, who thought of promotions to bring customers into the shop. Morgan didn't have the stomach for it, but it seemed to give Michelle a sense of purpose. She admitted to him that, before Jason, she really hadn't dated that much. She and Jason had grown up together and ran into each other one day at the grocery store. After hanging out a lot it had only seemed natural that they make it official and call it a relationship. He was a nice guy who had a life plan that he was adamant about following.

"I think he thinks we look good on paper anyway," she quipped.

"How so?"

"I'm a small-business owner, and he's a marketing executive. We both have similar family backgrounds. He's knows I'm not the kind of woman who is a shopaholic or constantly craves attention. We've actually gone two weeks without seeing each other, and I didn't bother to ask where he'd been or what he'd been up to. And he didn't ask me either. I suppose it could be a comfortable arrangement."

"So what about love?" Seth smiled at her.

"I guess Jason thinks love is a sidebar to pursuing his life goals."

"And what do you think about love?" Seth asked as he tugged on the sleeve of her blouse.

Morgan really had to think about that one. "When it comes, you don't have to think about it. It's there and you embrace it."

Seth leaned in and kissed her. Morgan reached up and stroked his jawline.

"Is that what you're going to settle for? Jason's business proposal—I mean, marriage proposal?"

"I always thought I'd be a confirmed bachelorette." She laughed. "And have a ton of cats and chase the neighborhood kids down the street when they get too close to my house."

Seth took a deep breath. "Then marry me."

"What?"

"Well, let's get married. That way, when you go home, you can tell Jason you don't need his half-assed proposal because you eloped with a handsome stranger on the island."

She laughed at his lack of modesty, finding it comforting that the bravado wasn't really him. Her heart fluttered a little bit, suddenly feeling as if somewhere between all these lines it was real. In such a short time she had come to care for him, and she could feel the same energy from him. She looked into Seth's beautiful eyes, searching for…some semblance that his proposal might be for real. What would life be like with a man like that? She knew, without a doubt, that life with him would be sublime. "You are insane."

"Well, it would be a mock marriage. See that guy up on the pier?" He motioned ahead of them. "That's Alvin. He's a self-proclaimed minister. He's a nice guy, but a bit off his rocker. He's not really a minister, but he thinks he is."

Morgan smiled at him. "Let's do it!"

* * *

Alvin married them on the beach as the sun was setting. There were tiki torches placed sporadically in the sand for moonlight strolls. After they signed his register, Alvin began the ceremony in his native tongue. Seth and Morgan held hands and gazed into each other's eyes. When Alvin finally began speaking English, Seth reached into his pocket and pulled out the biggest rock she'd ever seen. She knew he'd snuck off to the hotel shop, but she didn't think he'd bought her a ring. Clearly it was a fake because she'd never seen a real ring that size. Seth placed the ring on her finger, and Morgan was amazed at how heavy costume jewelry could be. Alvin pronounced them man and wife, and Seth kissed his bride.

When they returned to the bungalow they both gave up the pretense that the attraction that had been mounting since the day they met didn't exist. As soon as he opened the door, Seth scooped her up and carried her over the threshold. What Morgan intended as a sweet, tender kiss between an imaginary husband and wife turned into a firestorm of pent-up lust. Seth laid her down gently on the couch, and then looked into her eyes for a while before he lay down on top of her. She finally realized how heavy he really was. His body was massive compared to her petite frame. While she briefly pondered how this all would work physically, she reminded herself that she read enough romance novels to know there was a certain finesse involved with two bodies connected. Seth had most of his weight on his elbows and his knees, clearly trying not to crush her.

He parted her lips and swirled his tongue inside her mouth, reminding her of licking an ice-cream cone. He then trailed his mouth softly down her neck as she tried in vain to unbutton his shirt. As she suspected, the man's body was worthy of a sculpture class. What she was surprised to find was there was more muscle tone and smooth skin than the bulging, raging muscles she'd anticipated. By the time Seth had made his way down to her navel, it hazily occurred to her to ask him if he had protection; he magically produced a box of condoms.

She chuckled. "A little ambitious, aren't we?"

"Nah. More like highly optimistic."

Morgan giggled so hard she began to hiccup.

Suddenly Seth looked and said, "Did I tell you how beautiful I think you are?"

Morgan shook her head no, afraid she would hiccup again and ruin the moment. Seth smiled and went back to the business of removing both their clothes.

* * *

Morgan smiled as she moved very slowly in the line at the airport on the main island. The memories of her wedding night still lingered heavily. She had to force herself to move and talk like a normal person. And if for some reason she thought last night was a figment of her imagination, the photo Seth took of the two of them together in bed with her camera phone was a nice reminder. In her trusty backpack, she carried a copy of her "marriage certificate" to Seth. It was just what she'd dreamed of in her secret, girly heart: getting married to a handsome man on a beach at sunset.

He was a nice guy, a gentleman with a heavy streak of devil in him. She'd never bothered to ask him what he did for a living; she'd bet whatever it was, he was successful at it. He'd told her to have faith that all her problems with the bookstore would work out because he could tell how much she loved it. She'd given him her business card and told him to stop by if he was ever in the area and wanted to read a good book. He'd looked at her for a long while, caressing her face with his gaze, sighed, and said he'd take her up on her offer.

"I'll even give you a twenty percent off discount." She grinned.

"Even to the man who bruised your rib?" He raised an eyebrow.

"I can honestly say I got a bruised rib and a new friend on this vacation. Those two memories will forever be intertwined."

"Well, if you ever need anything… If anything develops down the road and you incur any medical bills, just give me a call. Actually you can call me and tell me anything you want. I'm not particular." He'd turned over the wedding photograph Alvin had given them and wrote his numbers on the back of it.

They'd hugged each other for the longest time, each not wanting to let go of the time they'd shared. Seth had caressed her back and kissed her. Morgan pulled back after a while and asked, "Don't you think it's funny how we had so much fun together and we don't really know each other? I don't even know what you do for a living."

"Nothing you'd be interested in. It's a living."

"I don't think that anything you do is uninteresting."

As she took yet another step in the check-in line she noticed a man a couple of spaces ahead of her wearing a football jersey with the number twelve on it. At first she thought it was strange for the man to be wearing a jersey when it was so hot. Someone must have read her mind.

"Dude, isn't it a little hot to be wearing that jersey?" some smart-ass yelled from behind her. Everyone in the line laughed.

"I'm going to sleep in this jersey for the next week. Then I'm going to buy a glass case for it. Blake signed this himself!" The guy beamed back with a wide grin.

"No shit?" the other guy yelled back.

"Yeah man. He was on vacation on the smaller island. A bunch of the team was."

When she heard the name Blake, Morgan looked up to see the name, in fact, sewn into the top of the turquoise and white jersey. Her heart skipped a beat. Here she was thinking about him, and now she was inadvertently in the middle of a loud conversation about a football player named Blake. She often wondered about coincidences and how things happened that way.

"Excuse me," she said to the man in line in front of her. "Who's this Blake player?"

"Are you kidding me?" the seemingly nice man replied. "Seth Blake is a quarterback for the Philadelphia Titans. He's their golden boy savior."

"Is he any good?" was all she could say, although she'd personally attest to his tackling skills.

"He signed a forty million dollar contract last year. What does that tell you?"

It told her she was the biggest idiot on the small tropical island

and maybe even the planet. But she was still willing to hold on to denial. Morgan dug into her backpack, looking for the wedding picture Seth had scribbled his phone numbers on. Her heart thudded like a thoroughbred horse racing to the finish line in the Kentucky Derby. She clumsily pulled out the picture, then tried her best to get a close look at the jersey. She looked at the autograph on the shirt and then back to the picture where he'd scribbled his name at the bottom. It was a dead match.

"We are now ready to board." But she didn't want to leave. She wanted to go find Seth Blake.

And kick his ass.

* * *

Seth wondered how he had managed to spend seven days with the woman and not reveal to her who he was. It felt strangely good to know that Morgan liked Seth Blake, the man, and not the football star. That had been an upside to an exclusive resort that didn't allow any media. He hadn't had to pull out the charm to impress a woman like that since...well, maybe junior high? All his life he'd been the star and women had flocked to him. He looked over at the table and saw one of the cloth rubber bands she used to pull her hair into that cute little librarian bun on top of her head most days. He picked it up and rubbed it between his fingers. She was not the type of woman he'd been seen with in public and was perhaps the shortest woman he'd stood next to since the last time he'd visited his mother. Day after day he'd waited for her to transform herself into something a little more feminine...maybe? The attraction between the two of them grew each day, and he'd thought that maybe she'd feel sexy one day and put on a sundress or something. But it had never happened, and he'd decided he was happy she hadn't done that. If nothing else, she was true to herself. She didn't mind looking up at him to speak or getting on her tiptoes to kiss him, and he didn't mind staring at the top of her head, looking at reddish-brown hair that he loved the texture of.

He took the hair elastic and slid it onto his wrist. It was time to leave paradise. He was kind of glad her flight had departed before his, knowing he'd managed to keep his secret on the small island. By the time he and his teammates made it to the big island it would be another story entirely. His copy of the fake marriage certificate lay on the coffee table. He wanted to put it in his carry-on so it wouldn't get lost, and he wondered if he'd ever see his "wife" again.

Sam the bellhop knocked, then entered the bungalow, prepared to take all his bags to the car.

"Hey, Sam."

"Hey, Mr. Blake," the young man said.

"Sam, I told you to call me Seth. Remember?"

"Yes, so sorry, Seth."

"That's better. I hate to sound clichéd, but Mr. Blake really is my dad." Seth looked up to find Sam staring at the marriage scroll on the coffee table.

"Mr. Blake, um, Seth?"

"Yes, Sam?" Seth clasped his watch on his wrist over Morgan's hair elastic.

"Is that a marriage certificate?"

Seth laughed. "Not real. Alvin gave it to us when he married Morgan and me on the beach last night. The lady who stayed here with me. He's your uncle, isn't he?"

Sam stumbled. "Yes he is. Did he have you sign the registry?"

"You mean that scruffy leather book he carries around with him?" Seth asked, remembering Alvin had called it his trusty union record keeper.

Sam nodded. "Yeah. Did he perform the ceremony?"

"Yep, on the cliff not too far from here."

When Sam's questions suddenly dried up as Seth finished putting his wallet in his pants pocket, Seth looked up to see what was wrong. Sam looked a bit worried.

"What's wrong, Sam?"

"Oh dear, Mr. Seth. I have some troubling news."

* * *

Morgan stared at the numbers on the back of the picture so long they were etched in her brain. She went through the motions of getting off the plane, getting her luggage, and then going home to her apartment, not bothering to call any of her family to pick her up. She wanted to be alone.

Seth lied to her. Or did he? She remembered all the offhanded remarks she made about football and winced at the thought of the countless times she must have hurt his feelings. Now embarrassment was creeping in. Morgan tried to get a grip on the situation. She'd run through every emotion known to mankind since meeting that man. Now the run-in with the chick in the red dress was making perfect sense to her.

She still wore the fake diamond wedding ring he'd bought her at a gift shop. The fake diamond sparkled as the sun filtered into the room and hit it, and Morgan's hand began to feel heavy.

"Promise me you'll keep this as a memento of our time together," he'd said.

"Sure." She'd smiled, thinking the rock was so big she wouldn't want to wear it just for fun and have someone think she was loaded.

* * *

Morgan put her phone on speaker and dialed into her voice mail. There were a few calls from friends, a call from Jason saying he needed to talk to her, and a call from her assistant manager asking if she would be in the bookstore tomorrow. Of course she would. Getting back to her books, the feeling that rushed through her veins when she was surrounded by all that knowledge, aching to read everything in sight, was where she belonged. Maybe the world was too hectic and shallow and material for her. She would go back to the fort she'd built out of books, comfortable old leather couches, and lamps that made her feel like she was someplace elegant and scholarly. So what if the average customer wanted the latest trashy tell-all or something else she was forced to stock if she wanted to keep her store open? It was all in the name of reading, of appreciation, of taking in the knowledge of something one did not know before one cracked the spine of a book.

* * *

As the limousine glided smoothly away from the airport, Seth vaguely remembered getting into the thing. Dazed, he thought about Morgan and the revelation that Sam had dropped on him. Turns out the crazy uncle Alvin actually was a real minister who could officiate a real wedding, and that makeshift leather binder he carried with him was a record of all the weddings he'd done on the island for many years. So it was legal. The petite African American woman he'd slammed into on the beach and bruised her rib, better known as Morgan Reed, was really his wife. He chuckled, wondering what Morgan would say when he told her. They'd both taken what Alvin had said with a grain of salt, not knowing he had any officiating powers.

After the hotel manager had apologized profusely, Seth calmed him down and asked that he and Sam keep a lid on it. She lived in Philadelphia, and she owned a small bookstore, so she wouldn't be too hard to track down. It had only been two days, but he missed her. He thought about calling his agent and his publicist so they could be ready for the fallout once someone on that island was paid to talk. He didn't hold it against them. He was used to having people sell what they could about him to make a buck. But there was Morgan to consider; she was going to be bombarded and hounded. And he didn't want to see that happen.

For the moment he was content with the memory of her laughing in bed their last morning together, commenting about the gigantic fake diamond ring he'd bought her. She would kill him if she knew how much that ring really cost. Ironically, it was worth much more than the amount she told him she needed to fully renovate her bookstore. He'd known she would never take any money from him so, in his own way, he'd given her what she needed. She'd promised she would never throw it away, and if she ever found out its true worth, maybe she would pawn it and get the repairs done to the bookstore.

He could only imagine what she would say if some reporter walked into the store asking her to comment on her marriage to him. She would be shocked and hurt, and he didn't want that for her. He'd have to find her himself and break the news that she was indeed legally Mrs. Seth Blake.

* * *

Morgan's reality of being a small-business owner had returned. Her assistant manager, Michelle, had kept everything running smoothly, but there were promotional opportunities for the store that Morgan had to deal with. After two days, her family collectively got over the fact that she'd taken a cab home from the airport. She gave her friend Theresa a glowing review of the island, minus everything that had transpired with Seth. She managed to successfully dodge Jason, not looking forward to seeing him. She didn't love him and she suspected he didn't love her either, not in the way that mattered. His male biological clock had begun ticking and she was the closest woman in the vicinity.

"Hey Morgan," Michelle said as she peered between an empty spot in the bookcase.

"Yes?"

"You never mentioned your vacation. Did you like the island?"

"It was nice."

"Just nice?" Michelle huffed. "For a person who hasn't been on a vacation in years I thought I'd get a better reaction than nice."

The door chimed, which meant they had a customer. In an effort to end the conversation with Michelle about the vacation, Morgan scooted to the back room. She heard animated voices and Michelle was becoming louder and almost purring like a kitten. *Must be a male customer.* Michelle was an outrageous flirt, but Morgan couldn't blame her for wanting someone in her life. Michelle even devised their latest promotion at the store—speed dating for speed readers. The concept was more than a little wonky, but she decided it didn't hurt that they'd turned the small café area into a dating venue on Friday nights, hopefully joining the hearts of fellow bookworms.

"Morgan, can you please come to the front? There's someone here to see you," Michelle said via the intercom.

She sighed, hoping it wasn't one of her brothers complaining because she took a taxi home from the airport. Good grief, were they ever going to let her grow up? Morgan pushed past the double doors from the stockroom and walked, with heavy steps, to the front of the store. What she found was a vision, standing quite handsomely in denim jeans that fit his body perfectly and a blue shirt. He may have been out of his element but she would know that body anywhere. Seth.

"Hi Morgan."

"Hi." She beamed a bright smile, then it faded when she remembered his secret.

"Can we talk?"

"I'm not sure I want to talk to you, Mr. Blake."

Michelle chimed in. "Of course you want to talk to Seth Blake! We just got in a box of his biography. I was going to unpack them today. Maybe you could do a book signing here! That would help us out quite a bit."

"Michelle." Morgan cut her eyes at Michelle in an effort to

silence her. "Mr. Blake is not welcome here."

"Are you kidding me? We have the Golden Goose right here in our bookstore and we're not going to ask him to lay one egg? No offense."

"None taken." He laughed.

"What do you want, Seth?" Morgan said.

"Well, I was in the area and I thought it would be nice if I took my wife to lunch," he said with a great big smile as he held up the marriage certificate.

"You've got to be joking."

Seth sighed. "Apparently Alvin wasn't as crazy as he seemed to be."

* * *

Talking to Morgan in between her ringing up customers was getting him nowhere. And if she wasn't helping a customer, she would dash off and do anything but address what he'd told her. So he left to give Morgan some time to process the bomb he'd dropped, but he came back after closing, hoping to take her to dinner.

"Sorry, I have to get ready for the festival tomorrow. But thanks anyway," she said, not looking at him.

"I can help, and we can order in."

"Not busy tonight? It is Friday."

"And where am I supposed to be on Friday night?"

"I don't know. Don't you have some bimbos on-call or something? I saw that picture of you with Melanie Leighton in the paper. She looked like she didn't mind your company."

Melanie Leighton was a supermodel he'd dated off and on and he had run into her at a benefit he'd attended the other night. A photographer had taken their picture, hence the rumors that Melanie was Seth's new bride.

Seth laughed. "That picture was taken out of context, and I am a married man. I don't date anymore."

"You two make a good-looking couple. What is she? Five-ten?"

"Five-nine."

As soon as he'd heard that camera flash, Seth knew he'd have some explaining to do. The benefit had been on his calendar for months, and it was for a good cause, so he'd attended. The benefit was scheduled when he and Melanie were dating so she'd decided to keep her ticket. The breakup had been slightly messy, but he was happy that she had moved on; she was even cordial to him. When the cameraman appeared she was actually telling him about some rich businessman she'd met in Milan named Jean Paul. She'd said she was happy, and he was happy for her. His attempt to give her a friendly congratulatory hug captured on film had them back in the limelight as a reconciled couple.

Morgan grabbed her list and walked to the back room. She began pulling books off a shelf and placing them on a rolling cart. There was a title on a top shelf she needed to get, and she craned her neck back to see it; she turned around, looking for the ladder.

"I'd like to see you reach those." Seth's voice boomed from the doorway. "I can reach it, you know, without a problem."

"And all I have to do is ask?" she said grumpily.

"Nope. My mama raised a gentleman." He casually reached up and took down the books. "I'm starving; you want to order something?"

"There's an Italian place around the corner. They have really good food."

"So Italian it is. What would you like?"

"Surprise me." She went back to her list. She handed him her door keys so he could let himself back into the store.

"Okay. I'll be back in a little bit."

Morgan was so immersed in gathering her list and tidying up she didn't notice the time. The smell of — spaghetti, or was it chicken parmesan? —took her over as the back room began to fill with fragrant aromas of garlic and tomatoes. She looked up and noticed the overhead lights of the store were off, but the lights from the lamps she had placed sporadically near armchairs were lit.

It gave a cozy and intimate feel to the store.

Then she heard the violin. A violin? A violin softly played a heavenly serenade as she walked slowly to the front of the store. She did have a sound system, but the clarity of the violin was too crisp to be a recording. She approached the door and opened it to find a table for two set with a nice white linen cloth and dinnerware, another table holding a variety of foods, and a violinist playing passionately in the corner.

"Dinner is served, madam." He winked at her.

"I thought you were going for takeout?"

"I did. You didn't tell me what you liked, but luckily for me everyone at the restaurant adores you. So I spoke with the owner, Anthony, and he helped me out a bit."

"I thought you were going for takeout," she repeated like a drunken parrot.

"And you also said to surprise you."

"I did say that." She smiled. "Thank you. It's beautiful."

Seth held out a chair for her. He sat as a waiter served them. "I ran into Melanie at that benefit. It wasn't intentional."

"And it's none of my business," she said quietly.

"Well, I wanted to explain. We've been getting along great, and I don't want you to think I was being duplicitous or something."

"Fair enough."

He coughed. "I did have an ulterior motive for coming here tonight."

"What's that?" She swirled spaghetti with her fork.

"I was wondering if I could have my book signing here."

"Why on earth would you have it here?"

"This is a bookstore." He looked around. "I thought it was kind of a no-brainer."

Morgan took a sip of her wine. "I can't believe a bigger bookstore isn't vying to have your signing with them."

"I did have a contract with Montgomery Swift Books, but there was a snafu, and I am now looking for a place to hold my signing."

"The largest bookseller in the country has a problem hosting your book signing?"

"Yes, ma'am." His eyes twinkled.

"I'm afraid I can't offer you anything on the level they would."

Seth glanced around the store. "This place is intimate, so I would have more control over who my publicist invited. And it would be good publicity for your bookstore."

Morgan wrestled with the idea of hosting his book signing. It would generate business for the store. But it would also get them closer to being found out by the media.

Seth continued to talk. "Morgan, please don't over think this. I promise it will be a good experience for both of us."

"All right. You have a deal." She smiled and held out her hand for a handshake.

He took her hand and kissed the back of it. "My publicist will have a contract delivered on Monday."

* * *

Morgan loved attending the festival every year. She would set up her booth early, nearly in the same spot every year for five years running. She didn't normally bring anyone with her from the store, but she knew she would see people she knew.

By early afternoon the festival was packed, with people strolling from booth to booth. As usual she was asked if she had the five latest best sellers, which she did, and was glad to see them sell. She'd also brought books about travel and political commentary and hoped some of them would move too. She noticed while unpacking her merchandise that her assistant manager, Michelle, had packed some of Seth's books.

The evening with Seth had been almost perfect. He'd dropped her off at her apartment around one in the morning but she was too wired to sleep. She'd decided to make a cup of tea while processing the events of the night. Morgan hummed as she mulled around the kitchen while waiting for the teakettle to whistle and decided to turn on the news.

There was a special news segment in progress. "We at WQTE have just confirmed that quarterback golden boy Seth Blake has a married a local woman. It was first speculated that he'd married on-again, off-again model girlfriend Melanie Leighton, but Ms. Leighton's people have denied these rumors..."

As the report continued Morgan stood frozen by her kitchen sink, hoping they wouldn't mention her name.

* * *

The title of his biography was *Love of the Game*, and they couldn't have selected a better cover. It was a picture of Seth after he'd lost one of his games. She could see the devastation and the humility in his eyes. The words tugged at her heart. This was no biography about a rise to fame and glory. It was an in-depth analysis of loss and failure, and from reviewing his mistakes, he became a better football player and human being. Seth was very careful to speak plainly and succinctly about his life. He told the story about how he'd become interested in football and how his destiny was spelled out for him at an early age. There was a chapter in which he stated that he'd thought about giving up and pursuing something else, to have some semblance of a normal life, when he realized he'd become a corporation. He eloquently ended that chapter saying that once a person has set something big into motion, he has an obligation to the world to see it through to the end.

There seemed to be something happening at the end of the line of tables, but she couldn't see. She heard someone say, "Is that really him?" The ruckus seemed to be moving its way down toward her station. *Oh well*, she thought, it would make its way to her anyway, so she picked up the book she was reading and sat back in her chair. Then she remembered she'd forgotten to put out the bookmarks she had in the plastic bucket and turned to look for them.

"Miss, can you recommend something to read?" a deep voice asked as she bent over the plastic storage tub.

"Sure. I'll be right with you. Is there a particular genre you like?" She turned to see Seth with a big grin on his face. He was standing there with three of the biggest men she'd ever seen in her life. She knew one of them was Patton Hawkes, the linebacker for the team. The other two guys looked vaguely familiar as well.

"How about romance?" Seth grinned.

"You don't strike me as a romance kind of guy," she said. "What are you doing here?"

"I missed you," he drawled, those green eyes burning right through her. "This is Patton, Terrance, and Dante." All of the men stepped into her space and kissed her on the cheek.

"Did you sell any books yet?" Patton asked, looking around.

"Just a few. The festival is going on until seven. There are really good food vendors here if you guys are hungry."

"Smells good." Patton laughed and rubbed his stomach. "We're going to educate Seth here on soul food."

"Good luck with that." She laughed. She turned to see where he'd gone, but he'd parked himself in the chair she'd been occupying.

Seth glanced into the tub and saw his face. "Why isn't my book on the table?"

"Uh…there was no room."

"Huh," he grumbled.

"Please, like me selling your book here is going to put a dint in the already skyrocketing sales."

"No, you've done that all by yourself." Seth gave her the once-over. She looked refreshed. One would never be able to tell they'd stayed up half the night talking and packing books. Or that she'd talked until she fell asleep in his arms on the long leather couch in her store.

"How did I do that?"

"People are interested in why I would put a book out, disappear for a few months, then pop up married before the season started. Like there's some big puzzle to solve in the last chapters of the book. Or at least that's what my publicist said. And besides, you're hosting my book signing. That could be good publicity for the bookstore."

A crowd started to form around Seth and his teammates. Seth casually reached into the bucket and pulled out his books and signed the copies. He then passed the books to the rest of the team, who also signed, and, what do you know, people were lined up to buy his book. The books went like hotcakes, with Seth and the boys putting on a little show for the fans, answering questions and playing with some of the kids. While they did that, some people actually wandered past to buy a book. As Seth signed the last copy of the book, which he gave to one of the kids he'd been chatting with, he stated, "For anybody who wasn't able to purchase a copy today, you can get autographed copies at my book signing next week at my wife's store, Reed Books. It's a lovely little bookstore; feel free to come down and browse. I bet she's got whatever book you're looking for. I know she has what I need."

Seth winked at her, then turned to the crowd. A few of the ladies sighed. All eyes were on Morgan. Then someone yelled, "Can I get a picture of you and your wife?"

"Sure," Seth said. He slid his arm around Morgan, thinking about the bruised rib. She was tough. She bounced back in no time.

"Couldn't come by yourself? Had to bring reinforcements to

the African American Heritage Festival?" she asked as they posed for the picture.

"No, I was on my way when Patton called, and I told him where I was going. He wanted food," he said with his movie-star smile.

"I read your book."

"Did you? What did you think?"

"Thought it was weird at first that you wanted to discuss in great detail every game you've blown in your entire career, including the peewee league. But then I realized after every failed game, you grew as a person somehow. Defeat taught you how to be a better player."

"Where you were you when I was trying to explain that to my biographer? He fought me tooth and nail, but I won." He laughed.

She was getting used to hearing that laugh. "A great man revels in his victories and defeats with the same measure."

"You are absolutely right. Where did you hear that?"

"Just in one of many books I've read." She smiled. "I can see why these people adore you."

Seth glanced down at the gold chain that gleamed against her brown skin. The chain seemed to be holding something heavy as it disappeared down into her T-shirt. He then glanced at her hands. With his smile still in place he asked, "Morgan, where is the ring I gave you?"

She reached up and touched her collar. "I know it's silly, but I wear it around my neck."

"About the ring. I know I told you I got it from the gift shop, but that wasn't exactly true. I actually went to the jewelry store in the hotel and bought it."

Morgan gulped. "So what are you saying?"

"Let's just say it cost more than my parents' first house," he drawled. Seth found that even more amusing. If his father found out how much money he'd spent, he would have gone bonkers.

"I've been letting this thing hang off my neck for days. Someone could have taken it!"

"Well, if you'd kept it on your finger you wouldn't have to worry about it."

"I don't want to put on this ring until I know what it means. I've been waiting for you to bring up an annulment."

"I've been thinking about that too." Seth moved her over to the other side of the tent, away from the ears of the crowd. "What if we don't want to get an annulment? I've been meaning to ask what you thought about it, but I was afraid you would say something I didn't want to hear. Maybe we can continue…dating?"

"You don't date your wife."

"Sure you do. My dad always told me that's how you keep a relationship alive. You can't let little things or everyday living wear away a relationship. Romance is eternal, he says."

"Did your daddy also tell you to marry virtual strangers you meet on islands?"

"No." He laughed. "But he did tell me to keep my eye out when miracles come my way. I had a good feeling since the day I met you. And I take pride in my gut feelings. The last time I made a decision off my gut, I got a forty million dollar contract."

She let out an exhausted breath. "All that money you have. I am a pauper compared to you. It's not right. It's not fair. I wouldn't feel right being with you."

"Since when does money have anything to do with how you feel about a person? I know you don't care about my money. You never bothered to ask me what I did for a living when you met me."

"And I insulted your livelihood countless times."

He laughed again. "Well, that was definitely an exercise on my ego, but I lived. It felt good not talking about houses, yachts, and my career for a while."

Morgan closed her eyes and took a deep breath.

"Morgan, what do you want?" he asked.

"I want you to invite me to dinner."

"My place tonight."

"Um, tonight's not good. The festival doesn't end until seven."

"Okay, I'll buy the rest of your inventory." Seth reached into his back pocket and pulled a black credit card out of his wallet with a logo she'd never seen before.

"There has to be at least two thousand dollars' worth of merchandise here."

Seth arched his eyebrow but didn't comment.

Morgan laughed. "Let me guess. This has a hundred thousand dollar limit?"

"You could probably buy a plane with it if you like." He grinned.

"Well, I'm lucky if I can get a tank of gas with my credit card."

"If you need anything, I would be happy to—"

Morgan put her hand up to his chest in an attempt to stop him from finishing his sentence. Seth put his hand over hers.

"Morgan. Don't over think this. I'll send a car to get you at eight." Seth's hands fell to her waist; he pulled her against him. His mouth covered hers, his tongue pressing lightly for her to open, and Morgan's tongue met his. She glided her hands up his back and caressed him under the polo shirt he wore. For a moment the world faded out and it was only the two of them. It wasn't until Patton let out a loud whistle that they realized they were in the middle of a festival. They broke apart, both breathing heavily.

"Eight o'clock," Seth said with a wild look in his eyes.

"Yep," Morgan breathed.

"What are you doing to do with the merchandise?"

"You bought it. What do you want to do with it?"

Seth stepped forward to address the crowd. "Can I have your attention, everyone? My wife, Morgan, has been gracious enough to donate the remainder of her merchandise. Anyone interested can help themselves to what's on the tables."

Morgan's tables were clean within fifteen minutes.

* * *

Morgan was getting ready for her date when her doorbell rang. It was her driver for the evening, who introduced himself as Oscar, handed her a dozen roses and informed her he would be waiting for her outside whenever she was ready to go. Oscar opened the car door for her when she emerged from the apartment building. She climbed in to find a bottle of champagne waiting for her.

The ride to Seth's penthouse was sublime. Oscar had classical music pumping through the speakers, and Morgan even poured herself a glass of champagne. She peered out the dark window, watching the scenery. Philadelphia seemed majestic to her at night. Oscar finally stopped in front of the Ashcroft Building, an old historic landmark that had been turned into luxury condos about twenty years ago. The lobby of the building looked like a museum. She remembered a newspaper article that said it was being listed as a stop on a tour schedule for its architectural history. She even had a book on the history of the Ashcroft at the bookstore.

Oscar escorted her in and handed her over to a surly man named Eli. Eli smiled politely at her and informed her that Mr. Blake was waiting for her. He escorted her into the elevator, entered a key and pushed the penthouse button, then stepped out.

Butterflies invaded her stomach as she ascended higher and higher. She played with her ponytail and suddenly felt underdressed. She'd opted for a nice pair of gray slacks and a blue cardigan. She'd even managed to put on some lip gloss. She'd seen him in cargo pants, a speedo, and even jeans. She wondered what the superstar football player dressed in when he was lounging around his penthouse apartment in a building that had been featured in several style magazines. She got her answer when the elevator doors opened and Seth stood in his doorway waiting for her in a pair of black slacks and a black silk shirt. Although it kind of looked like bed head, his hair was perfectly moussed, and she could tell he'd shaved. The only thing missing was a ten-gallon cowboy hat and a pistol on his side.

"Morgan," was all he said.

"Hi, Seth."

Seth took her hand and guided her into the penthouse. "Did you enjoy the car ride?"

"I-it was excellent," she stuttered, distracted, as he caressed the back of her hand.

"Welcome to my humble abode. Let's get the tour out of the way. Shall we?"

Seth kept a firm grip on her hand as if she was going to break loose and make a run for it. Not that she didn't think of it. Every room he navigated her through had something eloquent, exotic, or sophisticated in it. There was rich black leather in the living room, an elegant marble dining room table with place settings for eight, and several flat screen televisions bolted to the walls of a room he called his strategy den. Each television was tuned to a different sports program. There was a wall with glass shelves that housed all his trophies. His bedroom was just as she'd imagined it. It looked like a man lived there. He had a king-size sleigh bed draped in a bluish-gray bedding. There were two huge plasma televisions positioned on the wall opposite the bed.

Two huge balcony doors led to a terrace lit softly with white decorative lights. When she peeked in the bathroom, she was amazed to see not two, but three sinks, a Jacuzzi, a shower fitted with ten strategically placed showerheads, and a claw-foot tub. In the center of the room was a fabric-covered bench with a magazine laying on it. So this was how the rich and famous lived?

When they returned to the living room, she was at a loss for words. She knew it was rude the way she kept quiet, but she was still taking it all in. There seemed to be never-ending contrasts and layers to this man. The simple, sweet, anonymous Seth she'd met on the island was getting further and further away from her, and she missed him. But was it really fair to make him some one-dimensional character in her mind? Perhaps if they'd never seen one another again she could have lived with that perception of him. And now that she was crawling out on the other side of her romantic dream getaway scenario, it was a bit overwhelming.

"You look very nice tonight." He smiled. "I forgot to tell you that when you got off the elevator, I was so happy you didn't cancel."

"Thank you," she said she as wrapped her arms around her stomach. "I had no idea I was coming to... I would have worn something else."

"Nonsense. I only dress up when I'm networking. I would rather be back on my ranch at home with a pair of dirty jeans on and taking a stroll with Iris."

"Iris?" She bit her lip, hearing another woman's name.

"Iris," he repeated and brought her over to a photo. "Iris is one of the best things in my life."

Morgan reluctantly honed in on the picture only to discover that Seth was in it standing next to a horse. A beautiful horse, but nonetheless a horse. She let out a chuckle. "Iris is a horse."

"Not just a horse." He grinned and grabbed her hand. "A good friend. But admit it. For a minute you were jealous."

Morgan suppressed a grin. The man wanted her to admit being jealous over what had turned out to be a horse. "You really are a cowboy, aren't you?"

"I'd love to take you to the ranch. We could ride together."

"I don't ride, Seth."

"I don't believe that." He smirked.

"Where exactly have you seen a slew of horse stables in Philly?"

"They're around. And you have the rest of the state of

Pennsylvania."

"I'm a city girl. And no matter what I'm surrounded by, I've always remained within my urban perimeter."

"I could teach you to ride," he said in a husky tone. "Riding a horse is all about finding a rhythm. It's like making love. When you find that right person, you develop a rhythm with them. It's all about moving together and keeping a pace."

She hadn't realized it, but Seth was putting his own words into practical application. He placed his hands on her waist and drew her closer to him. As he pressed her against him, she thought maybe he did have a hidden gun somewhere on him because she could feel a bulge in the front of his pants. Seth leaned down and moved his mouth against hers; it only took Morgan a second to let him slide his tongue into her mouth. He sucked on her tongue and ran his fingers through her hair, stopping at the clip holding her ponytail in place. He opened the clip and slid it into his pocket. His skin warmed every place Morgan's hands glided on his body.

Seth was pretty sure he was getting another hand job from her, but this one was on purpose. He started his journey from the living room to the bedroom. With each step they took, a piece of clothing was removed. By the time they reached the doorway of his bedroom Morgan was wearing a fancy black lace bra and panties and Seth was naked. He couldn't kiss her enough, caress her enough, or love her enough. That was what he was feeling—love for his petite, feisty, stubborn bookstore owner. His heart began beating faster as the word *love* bounced around inside his head. Seth pulled back his sheets as best he could while liberating Morgan from her bra. He immediately cupped her breasts. She moaned in appreciation of his thoughtfulness. Everything about her body was smooth and soft. Nothing in his life could compare to the feelings this woman evoked in him. He reached in his nightstand and pulled out a condom. If Morgan had given the slightest hint that he didn't need to use it, he would have happily hurled it over the balcony. But for now being responsible won out over throwing caution and common sense to the wind.

Tomorrow he would tell her his true intention for inviting her to his house. Tomorrow he would give her a heartfelt speech about how he was falling in love with her and wanted to share his crazy Seth Blake, the Quarterback Corporation life with her. Tomorrow he would tell her the book signing at Reed Books was a ruse to let him pay for her repairs so she didn't have to worry so much about keeping the store afloat. Tomorrow he would tell her he'd had his entire staff in Texas looking for a stallion for her so she could learn how to ride with him. Tomorrow they would figure out how to integrate two very different lives in a happy living arrangement. Tomorrow he would give her keys to the penthouse, hoping like hell she'd say she'd move in with him. Tomorrow.

* * *

Seth Blake might have been the pride of Philadelphia right now, but his greatest test was going to be surviving meeting Morgan's family. After spending almost every day together for three weeks, she told him she would be busy the following Saturday.

"Family thing. I promised my dad I would a while ago. But we could meet up afterward." She smiled and gave him a kiss on the cheek.

Seth started the blender again, mixing his daily ritual breakfast energy shake. Morgan winced at half the things he put in there, but he was convinced he could get her to try it.

"Uh, Morgan honey, did it ever occur to you to invite your husband?"

"Hey, Seth, did you know your Southern comes out of you when you are trying to be charming or mildly pissed off?"

"Is that right?" He winked at her.

"That's right."

"Why didn't you invite me?"

"I wasn't sure if you wanted to go. We've been doing a good job dodging the press, but my family is another thing. I'm not sure you can handle it."

"I can handle it." He patted his chest. "Me strong like bull."

"Do you bring your equipment home? You may need it."

* * *

After summoning them all to her father's house to tell them about her marriage and wading through a myriad of arguments with her family, she finally called Seth over. Four grown men waited on the porch for Seth like he was coming to pick her up for her first date. She had to hand it to Sydney, her father's wife, for stepping in and calming everyone down. She and Sydney had never had very much to say to each other, but she was thankful her father had waited until Morgan was sixteen before he started dating again. He had been alone for a while; Morgan's mom had died from pneumonia when Morgan was nine. By the time Curtis and Sydney were getting serious, Morgan was on her way to college.

She could see Seth getting out of his Range Rover and thought how incredibly brave or brain damaged he was for coming to her father's house. But he was serious about his intentions.

"I don't know who's crazier, you for having the guts to face your family, or Seth for walking into the lion's den," Sydney said as she watched the debacle unfolding.

"Would you believe I had no idea who he was?" Morgan asked.

"I can believe that. If it weren't for your father and brothers you probably wouldn't know what a football looked like." She snickered. "Good gracious, he's even better-looking in person."

Morgan went for the door but Sydney put her hand on her shoulder. "I know you are a grown woman and can make your own decisions, but those men on that porch care about you in their own obnoxious, overbearing way. They've never really met anyone you've dated before, and they have to feel like they didn't just give you to Seth. I know it sounds silly, and it is, but that's what they probably feel."

Morgan turned around, amazed at the quiet wisdom of her stepmother. All those years she'd been avoiding her like the plague, trying to keep clear on her feelings for her mother. So she followed Sydney into the kitchen and they fixed something to eat and some iced tea in silence. Eventually the men came in the house, and if she was correct, she even heard some laughter.

"All clear?" Morgan yelled from the kitchen.

"Really, Morgan," her brother Robert said, "you would think we were animals or something. We just had to check Seth out. MVP last year or not."

All the men seemed to get a chuckle out of that. It seemed being the MVP had once again been an asset to Seth. A few hours later she gave him a tour of her dad's house and they ended up in the backyard on a swing.

"So this is where you spent your summer days?"

"Yeah. Must seem really small compared to the sprawling ranch you lived on."

"Not really. In Texas there's just a lot of land."

"Yeah, but still."

"Morgan, I know you look at us and see so many things that are different. And in this world today people make sure they stick with their kind and promote separatism. I can assure you we have more in common than the things we don't. And just to let you know, I've dated all kinds of women before. But I've never dated a bookstore owner."

"Well, I've never dated a jock."

He made a coughing noise. "I will have you know that I am more than a jock. I got my college degree, and I'm currently taking courses online for my master's. It fits into my schedule and cuts down on the hysteria sometimes, staying in the shadows."

"So what are you getting your master's degree in?"

"Psychology," he said. "I'm a good player, because I look at all aspects of the game. And a bulk of the game is played in your head before you hit the field."

"Well, well." She chuckled and gave him an appreciative look. "You've met the immediate family. How do you feel about meeting the rest of them?"

"Anything you want to do is fine with me."

"I want to go back to your apartment and let me show you my appreciation for putting up with my family." She waggled her eyebrows.

Morgan let out a giddy yelp as Seth picked her up and threw her over his shoulder and headed for his Range Rover.

* * *

The family party was the following weekend, and Seth had not wavered about wanting to attend. Morgan thought it was sweet he wanted to meet her family and have a public relationship. This would be the first of many steps of acknowledging to the world that they were a couple. She only wished her family wasn't so outlandish. There was no doubt in her mind that something wacky would happen; she'd had a knot in her stomach all morning. But when Seth grabbed his car keys and her hand and headed for the elevator, she began to feel at ease. She was a nervous wreck and he seemed cool as an ice cube.

By the time they arrived, the family barbecue was in full swing. Morgan held Seth's hand and made her way to her father and brothers. She gained confidence when she was around those burly, meddlesome men. Some of her cousins came over, and just like she'd imagined, word was spreading that Seth Blake was here with her. Her father made a stern yet friendly quip that Seth was there to spend time with his daughter, not sign autographs or give mock interviews. It all seemed to be going nicely until trouble arrived. Her brother Charles was the first to spot them coming up the driveway to the backyard.

"Well, what do we have here?" Charles said in a thick voice. "Seth, my man, you are in for a treat today. 'Cause this barbecue is about to get interesting."

Morgan turned around to see why Charles was pointing. Her cousin Charisma had just walked into the backyard with none other than Jason—her Jason—on her arm. Jason must have felt a chill as cold as the Grim Reaper's hand on his shoulder because his gaze flew up and locked onto hers.

Morgan had gone silent, but her brothers and her father were grumbling something about whooping the guy's ass. As if they knew they were the center of attention, the guy and girl slowly came their way, with all eyes following them.

The woman spoke first. "Hey Morgan. I know this is awkward and embarrassing as hell, but Jason and I have been trying to tell you for weeks about us. We didn't know if you would come today, but frankly I'm tired of putting my life on hold for you. We are happy." Charisma took a step back and rubbed Jason's arm. "And I am sorry you didn't satisfy him or he wouldn't have come to me."

Morgan stared at both of them in disbelief. Charisma stood there with her arm around Jason like someone had just given her a new puppy. She had to get her bearings. A part of her wanted to ask the outraged questions and let the family drama play out, but she knew in her heart, no matter how it had happened, that she wasn't terribly upset that someone took Jason. Though her family probably still reeled from the fact that superstar Seth Blake was at their barbecue, she thanked God he was there. First, it took a sting out of this moment of humiliation. Secondly, she also realized Seth was standing behind her with his hand at the small of her back, and she found that very comforting. She would do damage control later. Right now she had to deal with the two would-be conspirators in front of her.

"And what am I supposed to say, Charisma?" Morgan said, musing to herself that the plot just thickened when she said the name Charisma, knowing her cousin lacked any ounce of charisma. "Am I supposed to thank you for taking Jason off my hands?"

"No, I expect you to be a lady and leave us alone," Charisma said loudly.

Jason decided to speak. "I've been trying to tell you. For months now."

"And when was that? Before or after you proposed we get married? Settle down?"

Jason lowered his eyes. "I wasn't thinking straight then, and a part of me knew you'd never really consider it. You know, I tried, but you are a hard woman to love."

"She's not hard to love. I'm doing just fine." Seth's deep, soft, yet firm voice crackled through the air like a cherry bomb on the Fourth of July.

Jason looked up, clearly angry. "Man, who the hell are you? Morgan, who the hell did you bring?"

Seth stepped forward and extended his hand. Jason looked at Seth's hand, which was damn near double the size of his. "My name is Seth Blake, and I'm Morgan's husband." He gave Jason a big ol' country boy smile.

The barbecue suddenly went silent. People were in corners whispering and Jason looked like he'd just seen his dearly departed grandmother.

Someone yelled out, "Oh, hell no!" and someone else burst into laughter. Morgan knew it was time for this travesty to end.

"It's rude not to shake my brother-in-law's hand, Jason," Charles yelled. "So I guess my sister doesn't need your half-assed breakup speech anyway!"

Morgan took a step back, resting on Seth a bit. He put his arm around her waist.

Suddenly Charisma went off topic. "You're Seth Blake. The quarterback for the Titans?"

"Yes, ma'am."

"Charisma, you don't have to worry. I found a man who could handle all of my needs. So you and Jason have my blessings," Morgan said.

"When did all this happen?" Jason barked.

"Oh, we got married on the island you let her go to all by herself," Seth said.

"Morgan?" Jason looked at her.

"Jason, you have no right to pretend to be hurt. You've got to be kidding me. What you and my half-assed cousin did was months in the making."

"So you're leaving me for Seth Blake?" Jason said Seth's name with such wonder in his voice she wasn't sure exactly which gambit of emotions he was processing at the moment. He kind of sounded like he wanted an autograph.

"No. Actually you left me. And we're both better off. Maybe we can both find the happiness we obviously weren't getting from each other."

"Seth Blake or not, I'm gonna kick your ass." Jason lunged closer, but Morgan took a few steps and kneed him in the groin. Jason went down with a loud groan and fell upon his knees. Seth went to intervene, but her father said, "Seth, she got it." Not one of her brothers moved.

"Jason!" Charisma yelled and bent down beside him. "You bitch!"

"Seth, I think the party is over," she said as she took his hand in hers.

"You okay?" He kissed her hand.

She nodded. Morgan kneeled down and spoke softly to Jason. "Jason, do everyone a favor and stay down. I didn't see the Super

Bowl, but the man didn't win MVP for nothing. And you have four very angry men behind him. Do the smart thing for once in your life."

* * *

Seth was on the phone talking to his publicist. Even though he was pacing up and down the corridor of the private plane, she could hear his responses. He said he was in charge of his personal life. He finished the call and sank down in the white leather chair opposite hers.

"So how bad is it?" she asked.

"Not bad at all. Certainly not anything I wasn't already expecting," he said, smiling at her. "Someone called my publicist and asked for confirmation that I broke up your engagement to Jason and stole you from him."

"Engagement?"

"Yeah."

"It was probably—"

"No matter who said what, it was going to become public knowledge anyway, Morgan. I don't want to evade questions any more. I want everyone to know we are married."

"Won't this hurt your career?"

"I like to call moments like these media speed bumps." He laughed.

She smiled in response. "Not that I don't appreciate it when you said you wanted to cheer me up after that fiasco of a barbecue, but where are we going?"

All she'd been able to see was the plane ascending from the private airport and was now headed in some unknown direction.

"We are going to my ranch in Texas."

Morgan's eyes almost bugged out of her head. "Don't you have to shoot a commercial in a few days?"

"Yes. We will be here three days max, and then we go back."

"I can't take off like this, the bookstore..." She huffed.

"I called Michelle and asked if she would do me a super huge favor in return for tickets in my box this season."

"You are slick, Seth Blake."

"I prefer the words crafty, spontaneous, and good under pressure."

"No, slick aptly describes what you did."

"If you say so, Morgan Blake," he said as he gazed into her eyes. "That name growing on you yet?"

"I'm warming up to it."

"Good." Seth leaned forward and kissed her on the mouth.

* * *

The Twelve Horseshoes ranch was a huge piece of land. Morgan fell in love immediately with the house and the stables. The staff welcomed her and, to her surprise, she didn't get one strange look. She got a few howdy ma'ams and the house staff addressed her as Mrs. Blake. Again she was in the center of contrasts. His Philadelphia penthouse life was nothing like his ranch life. She wandered around as Seth made phone calls. He seemed busy so she found her way down to the stables on her own.

She walked through the barn, acclimating herself to the smells. This was Seth's world. Not playing football in some city no matter how much they paid him. She felt his soul resonating on the ranch.

As she walked through the stables, she saw a short, older woman coming her way with a horse. She was dressed in dusty jeans, a red long-sleeved shirt, and had a cowboy hat pulled closely over her eyes. She appeared to be one of the ranch hands. The woman stopped in front of her.

"Hi, there. You must be Morgan," the woman said.

Morgan peeped under the woman's cowboy hat and replied, "Yes, it's nice to meet you. That is a beautiful horse."

The horse was a lovely brown color with a white patch near the center of his head. He looked serene but feisty at the same time.

"Yes, he is. He's a new addition to our family. Seth got him last week."

"I don't know much about horses, and I certainly haven't been up close to many, but he's magnificent." Morgan breathed as she reached out and stroked his mane. "Have you known Seth long?"

"All his life." The woman smiled enigmatically.

"What's his name?"

"Reed's Fire," Seth said from behind her.

Morgan turned around and smiled. "Odd name for a horse."

Seth came behind her and put his arms around her waist. "Reed's Fire is much like his owner. Sweet and tender one minute and hell on wheels the next. I think you two will get along great."

It took a moment for the words to sink in. Seth then lifted the older woman, twirled her around, and let out a yell. "It's good to be home! I missed you, Mama."

"I missed you too, baby."

"Morgan, this is my mom, Teri Lyn Blake." He smiled sweetly.

"No need in running now, honey, you've already married my son," Teri Lyn said with a hearty laugh.

Morgan didn't realize she'd begun backing slowly out of the barn after Seth's declaration. "Oh! I didn't mean…"

"Don't worry," his mother drawled, "I'm familiar with the fight-or-flight syndrome."

"Mama has a wicked since of humor." He winked.

His mother turned to him. "She is exactly as you described her. I think she and Reed's Fire will get along great."

* * *

After two hours of goading and encouragement, Morgan was finally on Reed's Fire. Seth had saddled up Iris and they were taking a leisurely stroll. As the sun began to set behind a clearing, Seth stopped.

"I have a confession to make. I crashed into you on the beach. I was trying to get your attention. Actually, I'd been trying to get your attention for three days, and I was getting desperate. I had Patton throw a long pass but I underestimated how far he'd throw after having six of those Tropical Depression drinks. It was either you get hit in the face with the ball or get tackled by me."

Morgan smiled but remained silent.

"I love you, Morgan. I think I fell in love with you that day I saw you getting off that plane on the island," Seth declared.

"I love you too, Seth." She leaned over and kissed him on the mouth. "But I'm gonna tell our kids that you ran into me accidentally."

"Is that right?" he drawled. "And how many kids are we going to have?"

"At least three. The accidental thing is more romantic, I think."

"You think so?" He kissed her hand.

"Trust me. I'm an avid reader and a bookstore owner. People love a juicy plot like that. It was fate. Blah, blah, blah." She laughed.

"About your bookstore. My business manager has a talent for finding rare business opportunities. I told him about your store, and he thinks there's good potential for expansion. He's thinking a bigger place at a building downtown, and then within six months you can open your second store."

"Seth," she said, exasperated.

"Who knows where it will lead? You could expand on your children's section. I'm sure Michelle will come up with more crazy promotional ideas. But you wouldn't lose sight of that atmosphere you want for your customers. Cozy and intimate without being too commercial. A home away from the public library."

She laughed.

"I may one day be that guy who's married to Morgan Reed of the national chain Reed Books. I just want you to be able to pursue your passion in life. I have football and the ranch. You have your books. With any luck we'll have brainy, athletic kids."

"Sounds good to me, number twelve." Morgan leaned forward and kissed Seth. She could see in his eyes the children they would have running around the house. And she didn't worry about how they would manage to have lives in between his football career and her building a media empire. As long as they made a pact that family came first, the rest would be easy. The sun was saying its final good-bye for the day, but not before it blanketed Seth's land with a golden hue. She felt much like she did that day when she'd stepped off the plane and into paradise. But this time she was hopeful about her future with the man who had been taking her breath away since the day he ran into her on the beach. All she had to do was look up from her literary fantasy to see it was time to start filling in the pages of her own book.

MVP

~ Dedication ~

To Morgan and Seth, thank you for turning a short story into a romantic adventure.

Chapter One

Morgan Blake took one more sip of her wine before placing the glass back on the silver tray. She looked out across the five-thousand-acre ranch from her seat on the veranda, but her view was suddenly obstructed by two strong hands covering her eyes.

"I've got another surprise for you," Seth purred in her ear.

Another surprise? They'd only been in Texas for six hours but she'd taken a tour of the Twelve Horse Shoes ranch, met Seth's mom, Teri-Lyn, and got her first riding lesson on her new horse, Reed's Fire. Then Seth had suggested they stay for the rest of the week. What more could he give her?

"Will it be better than finding out the ranch hand I was talking to earlier was actually your mother?"

"Don't worry, you're gonna like it," he drawled, as he led her into the bathroom.

Candles surrounded a huge claw foot bathtub that sat in the middle of the room, filled with bubbles and rose petals.

"Want to take a bubble bath with your husband? Take your mind off lunch with momma tomorrow?"

"Only if you wear the hat." The minute she had seen him wearing that Stetson on the ranch, her heart had skipped a beat.

"Yes, ma'am."

Morgan shivered at the feel of Seth's big, strong, calloused hands as he undressed her. Seth took his time removing each piece of clothing from her body before removing his own. He then gathered her into his arms and placed her into the tub, without getting a drop of water on his Stetson.

The hot bath felt like heaven, soothing her aching muscles and washing away the dirt from touring the ranch. But it was all worth it, especially getting to ride her brand new horse for the very first time.

"Reed's Fire is a beautiful horse. I think we made a connection."

"Well, that's what I was going for, a love connection between you and the horse."

"I read this book…"

Seth's chest rumbled against her back. "What a surprise."

"About animal totems." Morgan flicked bubbles onto his nose. "It was interesting. Animals come into our lives at different times as a way to teach us a life lesson. It's a very interesting and spiritual topic. I'll bring a book home for you to read. Your bookcase could use a little diversity."

"Hey! I have some pretty good biographies."

"And they're excellent reads, if you want to be a general in the military or a pro athlete." Morgan rolled her eyes at him.

"I can't remember the last time I had the time to just read a good book." He kissed her shoulder.

"Well, you could read at night before you go to sleep."

"Reading a book is the last thing I think about when I'm in bed with you."

"Good point. But when you come to the bookstore, you browse around and I never see you reading anything."

"That's because I'm distracted by the owner. She's really hot. Can't take my eyes off her."

"I'm serious. There's so much we don't know about each other." Morgan sighed. She had agreed to give their relationship a chance but the nagging doubt still lingered in the back of her mind that she would wake up one day and it would all go away. Seth didn't want to talk about their differences and insisted their whirlwind romance wasn't a flash in the pan. She wished she had his unwavering confidence in their marriage.

Seth nibbled on her ear. "We have plenty of time to learn those things about each other."

"What genres do you like?"

Seth thought about it for a moment. "Hmm. I like spy thrillers. And I am a history buff. What about you?"

Morgan picked up her wine glass and took another sip. "Spy thrillers, absolutely. History, yes. I also like horror but it scares the crap out of me."

Seth chuckled. "So why read it if it scares the crap out of you?"

"Because a good horror book is supposed to do that." She shrugged.

"Well, those nights you get scared, I'll make sure to check all the closets and under the beds."

"Deal."

"What did I tell you? We have a lot in common."

"I'm glad you like taking baths but I never pictured you as a claw foot bathtub kind of guy." Morgan put the glass back on the tray and relaxed against Seth's chest.

"I am not a claw foot bath guy. You love the tub in the penthouse so I had one installed here."

"You what?" Morgan splashed water on the black marble floor with her lightening quick turn.

Seth assailed her with kisses to mute her practical protests about the tub. His hands ran along her rib cage, palming her breasts, then torturing her with his thumbs making lazy circles around her taut nipples.

"Why did you do that?"

"Because I knew it would make you happy." Seth held her in

place so she'd stop squirming.

"It did but—"

"Morgan Blake, are we going to fight every time I try to do something nice for you?"

"No."

"You finished fussing with me, woman?"

"Yes," she sighed. "That was very nice of you to have the tub installed."

"Glad you're beginning to see things my way," he drawled as he continued his sensual exploration of her body.

* * *

The sunlight filtered into the big picture window, jutting Morgan out of her cozy slumber. She nestled closer to Seth in the king size bed as he ran his hand along her ribcage and settled on her butt. Just as she curled against his body, the phone rang.

"Hey, Bodine." Seth rubbed his chest while someone talked on the other end. "No, I don't know what time it is." He yawned then paused, casting a sidelong glance at her. "She did? I'll be there in half hour." He hung up the phone and looked at Morgan. "Baby, Bodine said you put your name on the work roster for today."

"Who's Bodine?"

"He's the ranch manager and a good friend of the family."

"Oh." she yawned. "Yes, I did."

He chuckled. "Why did you do that?"

"Because you did."

"I always work when I come here."

"I thought you said the work ethic around here was everyone helps out."

"It is. But that doesn't apply to you."

Morgan sat up. "I want to do my part, whatever it may be."

"I know you can and then some. You could probably march out right now and milk a cow." He laughed.

"I wouldn't go that far. The only thing I plan on pulling on this week is attached to your body." Morgan flashed a devilish smile.

"Besides you have a lunch date."

She groaned. "What time is your mother taking me to lunch?"

"Around noon."

"Why did I agree to have lunch with her alone? Can't we reschedule when you can come with us?"

"She just wants to spend some time with you."

Morgan pulled the bed sheet over her head.

"I know we made magic happen under these sheets last night, but I don't think they have the ability to render you invisible today."

"Smart ass."

"You've met my mother. What was your first impression of her before you knew who she was?"

Morgan lowered the sheet. "Before I knew who she was I thought she was a nice lady and we were on our way to having a lovely, polite conversation."

"Momma only has one face. What you see is what you get."

"Sure I can't help on the ranch today?" Morgan ran her hand over his bedhead. He always looked sexy when he woke up. His green eyes sparkled in the morning.

"Take one of my credit cards and have a good time with Momma." Seth took his wallet off the nightstand and opened it for her to pick one.

"Is that what you do with all your women?" Morgan raised an eyebrow.

"Nope. Just my wife. And before you ask, you are the first woman that's ever been to the ranch." Seth gave her a quick kiss.

"Good to know. What time do you have to report for duty?"

"According to Bodine, I should have had my narrow ass down there by now."

"You tell Bodine I said there is nothing narrow about your ass."

She slapped his butt and followed him into the bathroom.

* * *

The ride into town with Teri-Lyn was relatively quiet. Morgan hit the scan button on the car's radio, searching for a tune to diffuse the silence.

When Seth had kissed her then hopped into a pickup to head to the stables, Morgan had contemplated jumping in front of it. He had assured her repeatedly that she and Teri-Lyn would get along great, but she still would have felt better if he were there too. But if he had been brave enough to meet her dad and crazy brothers, then she could muster up some courage to have lunch with his mother.

The ranch seemed never ending as Teri-Lyn drove around the property. Morgan had assumed they all lived in the same house because Seth's was huge, but his parents and his brother JJ had their own homes as well on the property. After twenty minutes Morgan finally saw the entrance to the Twelve Horseshoes Ranch. Once they were on the road and away from the lush greenery of the ranch, signs of a bustling city came into view.

"We're here." Teri-Lyn pulled into a parking spot.

The restaurant she had chosen was very chic and trendy. A huge brick fireplace sat in the middle of the floor. The walls were painted bold, bright colors and abstract paintings draped the walls. The hostess seated them immediately and a waiter took their order. Morgan looked at the menu, her cell phone, anything to avoid eye contact with Seth's mom. Morgan gripped a blue linen napkin like her life depended on it.

"What did that poor napkin ever do to you?"

"I'm afraid the napkin is a casualty of my nerves."

Teri-Lyn reached over and gently prodded the napkin out of Morgan's hand. "Take a deep breath and relax. I'm your mother-in-law, not a prison warden."

"Sorry. I'm just anticipating the third degree that should be coming." Morgan grabbed the glass of water in front of her and took a big gulp.

"I was surprised when Seth called me and told me he got married. Women have been trying to get their hooks into him all his life. And he fell for you so fast." Teri-Lyn's eyes fixed on Morgan.

"Is this the part where I try to convince you that I am worthy of your son's love? Or maybe I should apologize for not being what you expected in a daughter-in-law?" Morgan could imagine what she was thinking. Terms like *impetuous, ill-advised,* and *lapse in judgment* were all swirling in her head. She'd been thinking the same thing too. The lunch was a ruse to figure out if she was with Teri-Lyn's son for the wrong reasons. She felt like she was caught in the crosshairs of Teri-Lyn's intense gaze.

"Well, to be honest, you are a bit shorter than I expected," Teri-Lyn drawled.

Morgan tried her best to suppress a smile. "Sorry. I've been this height since I was thirteen."

"Good to know. How about we don't make any assumptions about each other? I am not one of those mothers who don't want her sons to find happiness."

"But you do want to make sure they've found the right person?"

"Of course I do."

"What kind of woman did you want for Seth?"

Teri-Lyn looked at her for a while before she answered. "Someone who is kind, sweet, and knows her own mind. Seth has a pretty strong personality but there are moments when he's relaxed and happy, he's more like the good natured boy he used to be before football became his life. I've been seeing the old Seth since the two of you met. He's driven, but he never slows down to enjoy what he's accomplished. He's always on to the next quest."

"When we met, he was trying to unwind. He didn't tell me

who he was or why he was on that island." Morgan sighed and graciously sipped the glass of wine the waiter placed on the table.

"He was wired about the Super Bowl. I told him to take a vacation. Didn't tell him to take his whole team." Teri-Lyn laughed.

"I think they followed him there."

"He's always been a leader and a good one. People follow his lead because of the conviction he has for what he does. You'll see a change in him when the season starts. He gets a little cranky and very focused. You just let him go through his paces."

Morgan couldn't imagine that side of him. He had to be one of the most easy going men she knew.

"Why don't you tell me something about yourself?"

"Do you want the CliffsNotes version? Well, I own a bookstore." Morgan started to tick off the basics of her life on her fingers like counting titles in a series. "I have lived in Philadelphia all my life. I am the youngest and the only girl in my family. I have three brothers. My mom died when I was nine. And my dad and my brothers can be a bit stifling sometimes, but I guess that's because my mom wasn't around."

"But it made you tough. Seth told me you don't take any crap and you know how to handle yourself."

Morgan blushed. "I promise you I'm not some hot head."

"Seth needs someone in his life that has a backbone and isn't playing the damsel in distress card all the time. Because he'll spend all his time rescuing you. That is what my husband taught all my boys. You take care of your woman. End of story."

"He is very protective."

Teri-Lyn snorted. "My husband and those boys are chivalrous to a fault. When John and I first got married, we had the most terrible fights. He didn't want me working. He thought I was supposed to sit in the house and tend to the hundred kids he planned on having. Boy did we have some epic fights." She laughed.

"Seth and Bodine seemed to get a kick out of me signing up on the work roster. I mean, I've never worked on a ranch but I thought I could help out in some way."

"Then you must be going bonkers in that penthouse. His staff in Philadelphia is pretty intense."

Morgan laughed for the first time that afternoon. "The cook won't let me cook. I tried to wash a load of clothes and the maid almost hyperventilated."

Teri-Lyn nodded in agreement. "One night when I was visiting I made myself a turkey sandwich. What a mistake that was. I thought the cook was going to quit on the spot."

"We both knew it was going to take time for us to find a way to make it all work. It's hard to simply let someone do something for you that you've been doing for yourself your whole life."

"Seth and his dad are cut from the same cloth. All you have to do is firmly let him know there has to be some balance, and he'll come around. I haven't been married for thirty-five years because it was easy. The best things in life take effort, time, and nurturing so it can become something wonderful."

"I'm glad we had this talk…" Morgan didn't know what to call her.

"Teri-Lyn is fine. JJ's wife, Eden, calls me Mother Blake. I want to punch her in the nose every time she says it."

Morgan laughed. "He told me about his brothers. No luck in the daughter department?"

"The harder I prayed for a girl, the more boys popped out. I think John was praying louder than me. He said he wanted a football team. I feel sorry for you, hon. You have three brothers at home and three brothers-in-law down here. There is no shortage of men in your life."

"Tell me about it." Morgan sipped her wine.

Teri-Lyn smirked. "My son is head over heels in love with you."

Morgan paused, at a loss for words. The term "head over heels" always sounded crazy to her. Who would be that slap happy and idiotic over another person? That was exactly how she felt about Seth and to hear another person say it, his mother no less, gave her a warm feeling inside. If someone else could see the love they had for each other, then it was not a hopeful figment of her imagination anymore.

"The feeling is mutual."

"So what are your plans for the future? Now that Seth is in your life, they had to have changed."

Morgan laughed to herself, thinking Seth must have inherited his diplomacy from his dad because Teri-Lyn didn't mince words.

"Seth has his football career and I have the bookstore. I am very active in the community and have been trying to get funding for a reading initiative that would go to services like the reading hour for the kids in the library and teaching illiterate adults to read. Seth and I have talked about having kids. When we get into the groove of our busy lives, we can start a family."

Teri-Lyn smiled. "I have a good feeling about the two of you. Who knows, maybe I'll get some grandchildren this decade. Eden keeps stalling when JJ talks about starting a family."

"A family sounds nice. But to be honest with you the idea of motherhood scares me. Before I met Seth I didn't think about having kids."

"No one is ever ready to be a mother. One day it happens and boom, you're changing diapers and wondering why you didn't have a baby sooner."

"Seth would be a good father," Morgan sighed.

"Yes, he would." Teri-Lyn smiled. "How about we do some shopping after lunch? He told me your trip down here to Texas was kind of spur of the moment. We can get you some things from this boutique down the street."

Three hours later, and inundated with shopping bags, Morgan

was ready to tell Teri-Lyn she was done for the day when she saw something in the next store window display that made her stop dead in her tracks.

* * *

Seth lifted a bale of hay and tossed it aside when he saw his mother's car coming up the drive. He walked down the trail to meet her and Morgan, pulling off his gloves and patting down his clothes as he went.

"Did you two have a good time?"

Morgan jumped out of the truck and into his arms. "Your mom bought me cowboy boots!"

He looked down to see a pair of pale pink cowboy boots on her feet. "They look good on you, baby."

"Whew! You smell like you've been digging a ditch all afternoon." Morgan tried to wiggle out of his arms.

Seth tightened his grip. "I've been doing manly work all day. I think Bodine is trying to kill me. Wait till you get a whiff of me after a game."

Seth looked up and saw his mother smiling at him. Teri-Lyn nodded her approval, and he smiled back, relieved that their lunch date had gone well. Then Seth glanced in the truck and saw the array of bags.

"What did you two buy? Half of Texas?"

"And my boots." Morgan grinned.

* * *

Word was spreading like wildfire that Seth was home for a visit. A barbeque on the ranch had been planned and Seth's attendance had become mandatory. Teri-Lyn assured him that the guest list would be modest and that he'd be able to slip away with Morgan at the first sign of a mob.

"You really like those boots." Seth chuckled as she walked the room, trying to break them in.

"Yes, I do. But what I really liked was my conversation with your momma. You were right, Teri-Lyn shoots straight from the hip."

"Told you."

"So" — she stopped in front of the mirror to brush her hair — "what is the rest of your family like?"

"Let's see. JJ is named after my dad, John Jacob. He's the oldest. He's married to Eden, the meanest woman in Texas. She won the Miss Texas title seven years ago and has been impossible to live with ever since. JJ used to play pro ball too but got injured his third year on the team. After he accepted football wasn't in his future, we became partners in a land development company."

"And your other brothers?"

"There's Tyler, he was born right after me. Tyler is a bit of a...free spirit. He thinks it's his mission in life to sleep with every woman on the planet. Momma calls him the one card that keeps her from having a royal flush. And Channing is the baby. He's the brain of our brood. He's goes to Georgetown Law."

Morgan chuckled, shaking her head. "You have an interesting family."

"They're your family now too." Seth waggled his eyebrows at her.

Chapter Two

Morgan had a death grip on Seth's hand as they waded through the sea of people who greeted them at the barbeque. The effortless way he charmed the crowd amazed her. Seth steered her toward a hulking, imposing man with graying hair. Seth and the man shook hands, beaming at each other, then Seth slung an arm over the man's shoulders.

"Bo, I want you to meet my wife, Morgan. Bodine has been working with my dad for a very long time. Everyone just calls him Bo. He was kind enough to take over the ranch when I started traveling for work."

Morgan extended her hand. "Nice to meet you."

"You're the same little lady that put her name on the work roster?" Bodine looked her up and down and chuckled. "What exactly did you think you were going to do?"

Morgan huffed. "I'm stronger than I look."

"I'll take your word for it. It was the thought that counted. But I must say you certainly pretty up the place." Bo grinned.

Seth glared at him. "Down boy."

* * *

The afternoon seemed to fly by as Seth entertained the crowd, after being prodded by Bo, with stories of his Super Bowl win.

"Seth, is there another Super Bowl win in your future?"

someone yelled out.

"Third time's the charm." He grinned and the crowd laughed.

"If anyone can do it, this man can," another voice yelled out in the distance.

A hush fell over the crowd when up walked none other than country singer Tate McGill. Morgan recognized him immediately and felt like an idiot that she hadn't correlated that when Seth talked about his friend Tate. He stood taller than she had imagined, his curly blond hair tucked beneath his hat. He had piercing, ice blue eyes that seemed to hide storms behind them and a mega watt smile just like Seth's.

"McGill! I thought you were on tour!" Seth hugged his friend.

"I thought you were in Philadelphia."

"You know how it is when home is calling."

"I hear that. And you brought back a wife this time." Tate winked at her.

"I sure did." Seth put his arm around Morgan's waist. "Morgan, this is Tate McGill. My oldest and dearest friend."

"Oh, I know who he is. I love your songs." Morgan beamed as she shook Tate's hand.

"Thank you. Always nice to meet someone who appreciates my music."

"So what are you doing in town, Tate?" Seth asked, a confused look on his face. "I thought you were on tour."

"The Cinnamon Festival is this weekend. I'm headlining." Tate gave him an expectant look.

"I forgot about the festival." Seth sighed.

"How could you forget all those good food vendors?" Tate raised an eyebrow and looked at Morgan. "Oh, you've had more important things on your mind."

Seth laughed. "You can say that again."

"Morgan, the festival has the most delicious food you will ever taste in your life. Seth and I ate something from every vendor one year."

Morgan gasped.

Seth laughed at that. "Morgan hasn't adjusted to my healthy appetite yet."

Tate pointed at Seth. "This man will eat you out of house and home. I hope you know how to cook or he's going to get pouty quick."

Morgan folded her arms across her chest. "As a matter of fact, I am a good cook."

"Yes, she is." Seth nodded.

"That's a good start to a marriage." Tate chuckled. "Blake, we doing a bonfire tonight?"

"Hell yeah."

"Good, I'm going to grab some chow. Where's your momma?"

"Over there talking to Bodine."

"First, I kiss your momma, then I'll grab some grub. Morgan, how about I sing you this new song I've been working on around the bonfire tonight?" Tate flashed a pearly white grin.

Seth shook his head. "You ain't serenading my wife, McGill."

* * *

Most of the party goers from the barbeque had gone home; only about a dozen people remained. As promised, Tate was sitting by the bonfire with his guitar in hand, ready to entertain. Ray and Josh, two of the ranch hands, worked on the fire while Bodine poured some mysterious contents into jelly jars.

"Here you go, Morgan." Bodine handed her a jar and gave her a thumbs up.

Morgan, who was on the phone with Michelle, her assistant at the bookstore, took a sip of the contents and winced. She ended the call thanking Michelle for taking over while she was away and told her she'd make it up to her.

"Everything all right?" Seth dropped a few logs on the bonfire.

"Michelle is just curious about what's going on down here. And she wants me to bring her back a hunky Texas man like you." Seth rubbed her shoulders.

"Is this moonshine or bathtub gin?" Morgan took another sip from the jelly jar. "It tastes awful."

"Something like that. Bodine, don't give my wife that swill. You'll rot her insides." Seth took the glass out her hand.

"Trust me, you'll thank me in the morning." Bodine laughed.

The stars illuminated the night sky. Morgan leaned against a fence, counting as many as she could. Seth retrieved blankets from his truck, insisting she put one on to fend off the night air.

"Your mother warned me about your over protective nature." She grinned slowly at him as he draped the blanket over her shoulders.

"I got it honest. My father taught me many things about women."

"Yeah, like what?"

"That the stubborn ones need the most attention."

"I think I like the word feisty better than stubborn."

Seth kissed her. "Look it up in the dictionary some time, your picture is next to both words."

Tate's hand slipped off the guitar and Bodine burst out laughing. Seth put a few more pieces of wood on the bonfire before pulling Morgan down with him to sit on a blanket.

Morgan stole his Stetson and placed it on her head. "So can we play hot cowboy when we get back to Philly?"

"The hat stays here. So, if you want to see Reed's Fire, this hat, and those cowboy boots, you have to come here to the ranch."

"That's not fair, we play naughty librarian at least twice a week."

"The things I do to avoid a library fine." Seth grinned. "Come here."

Morgan purred like a kitten when Seth pulled her onto his lap and wrapped his arms around her.

Tate laughed. "Oh yeah, she's feeling it."

Morgan looked at Tate. "So you two went to high school together?"

Seth brushed a stray hair out of her face. "Actually, Tate and I have known each other since we were five. We did everything together. He even lived with us the last two years of high school. He's a pretty decent football player, but he turned down a college scholarship to pursue music."

Tate cleared his throat. "My best friend is exaggerating. I was OK on the field but nothing compared to the feats he performed. Sometimes I think he has a robotic arm. It was clear which one of us was going to take it all the way to the NFL."

Seth scoffed. "That's not true."

"It is. If it weren't for him I would have been cut from our high school team the first year. Seth told our coach if I didn't play, neither would he. Can you believe that?"

Seth leaned in close to Morgan's ear. "He just needed a little direction."

"I knew the best thing to do was to get him the ball."

Morgan smiled. "So singing was your true calling?"

"Yeah, I've always been good with a guitar. Besides, with all the girls falling all over him, I had to come up with a gimmick."

Seth laughed. "You definitely got more action than me, Tate. He'd whip out that guitar and girls would be all over him. He was having concerts in high school."

"I remember one time when that cheerleader Rebecca tried to date both of us." Tate howled with laughter.

Seth put his hand over his face. "That was a nightmare. Thank goodness we found out before either of us sealed the deal. We always had one rule: no fighting over women."

Morgan nodded. "That was a good rule."

Tate paused, but his fingers remained on the guitar. "Rebecca figured neither of us would tell the other. But we'd compare notes to make sure we weren't crossing over into each other's territory."

"We both dumped her on the same day." Seth raised his beer bottle in salute.

"And then there was this time I saved his ass."

"When did you save my ass, Tate?" Seth crinkled his brow, puzzled.

"That time I uncovered the plot the cheerleaders had to kidnap you. I don't know how twelve dainty girls did it but they somehow kidnapped my boy and had him tied up in the girls' locker room. They all got tired of fighting over him and decided that it was only fair that he deflower all of them at the same time."

Seth let out an exaggerated sigh.

"Luckily I caught wind of it and told the principal. They found him backed into a corner fighting for his life." Tate laughed. "They all got suspended for a week and couldn't cheer for three games. The whole high school was in an uproar."

"Those girls were aggressive and had a thorough plan. I'd never done that much talking in my life." Seth ran his hand through his hair.

Morgan gave Seth a suspicious look. "Being trapped in a locker room with a cheerleading squad didn't appeal to you?"

"Men have the right to say no too."

"Seth has always been a one woman at a time kind of guy," Tate said. "He was hung up on Penny at the time. I tried hostage negotiating and taking his place but they wouldn't go for it."

"Penny was your high school sweetheart?" Morgan asked.

"Something like that," Seth mumbled.

When Seth wouldn't elaborate, Morgan just smiled. "Sounds like friendship is important to the two of you?"

"Good friends are hard to find." Tate nodded.

"Amen." Seth raised his beer bottle in salute again. "But it did give you a lot of song writing material."

"Hey McGill, I thought you were singing me a song?" Morgan murmured.

"Your husband doesn't look like he's in the mood for another man to be singing to his woman. But I will be thinking about you while I sing it." Tate winked at her.

Morgan erupted in a fit of giggles.

The sweet sound of Morgan's giggles sent waves of pleasure to Seth's heart. He loved her carefree laughter, a close second to the soft feel of her skin. The first time they had made love after their wedding ceremony, the feel of her skin was burned onto his hands, every part of him aware of the silky feel of her.

As Tate sang his sweet love song, the words echoed what Seth felt. Morgan stretched her legs and crossed them, her pale pink cowboy boots catching the light of the fire. She had been so excited when she had gotten out of the truck, showing them off.

He wished they could stay like this, by the fire, under the stars at the ranch with those he loved around him. He was finally ready for love, ready for the children Morgan told him she wanted. She surprised him with that one. He thought he'd have to convince her to have at least one child, but she was open to a litter of kids. He didn't have the heart to tell her that the Blake men had a long line of boys in the family and the chances for a girl would be slim. He remembered how rambunctious he and his brothers were and how they drove his mother crazy.

Morgan looked up at him, studying his face. "I love you, Seth Blake."

"I love you too." Seth placed a gentle kiss on her lips.

"Are we going to go riding tonight?"

"I'm afraid it's too dark. We can go out in the morning after breakfast."

"Can you teach me how to ride bareback?" she whispered in his ear.

Seth rose to his feet with Morgan in his arms. "Gentlemen, we are turning in for the night."

Bodine laughed. "I told you. One sip of that and a woman is putty in your hands. Why do you think Bonnie is still married to me?"

"Because you knocked her up twenty-eight years ago." Tate plucked one of his guitar strings.

"Goodnight, everybody," Morgan murmured, her eyes on Seth and Seth alone.

"Good night, darlin'." Tate raised his jelly jar in salute. "As usual, I sing the love songs and Blake gets the girl. Brings back memories."

* * *

When Morgan woke the next morning, she felt like a jack hammer was going off inside her head. Seth was still sleeping peacefully beside her with his Stetson covering his face. She tried to turn in the bed but her legs felt heavy. Morgan peeked under the covers to find she was still wearing her cowboy boots. What the hell were they doing last night?

She lifted the Stetson and put it on the night stand. Seth didn't make a move until she pulled back the covers to remove her boots.

"Morning." He her gave a lazy smile.

She winced. "Please don't shout."

"I'm not. It's that damn whiskey you drank last night." Seth held up the jelly jar that was on the night table.

"Why didn't you take it away from me?"

"I did. You grabbed another one on the way back to the house. Then you threatened to divorce me if I took it again." He shook his head and chuckled.

"And you believed me?" She laid her pounding head on Seth's shoulder.

"There was a lesson waiting to be learned. Listen to your

husband and you won't get hangovers from illegal whiskey."

Morgan ran her hand through Seth's hair. "Why do I still have my boots on?"

"Because you gave me the ride of my life last night." Seth flashed a devilish grin.

She groaned. "I don't remember what happened after we left the bonfire."

"Did you, by any chance, take any gymnastics classes when you were in school?"

"Two semesters in high school. Why?"

"I'd like to make a donation to your high school's athletics program. Your dismount is of an Olympic caliber." He leaned in to kiss her.

"Exactly how much fun did we have last night?" Morgan moved away, shooting him a suspicious look.

"Well, we stopped short of you taking pictures of my 'hot body' and sending them to Michelle." He waggled his eyebrows.

"I don't care how drunk I was, I never would have done that."

"Don't worry, baby, your super freak status is safe with me."

Morgan gasped as she spied bruises on his chest. "Oh my goodness, did I bite you?"

"Yes." He laughed. "This one is my favorite." Seth turned over onto his side, displaying his back.

Morgan searched his back, arms, and shoulders. "I don't see anything."

"That's because you're looking for New York when you should be looking for Florida."

Morgan's eyes drifted lower until she reached his ass. There were two distinct bites marks. "Why did you let me bite you?"

"We were trying something new. I went with the flow. You don't hear me complaining. Any other sports you took up in high school?"

"Fencing." She smirked. "Let's see you turn that into

something dirty."

"I can lunge at you with my saber any time you like."

"You know fencing?"

"Good for hand-eye coordination. I like to watch if I catch it on TV. Besides, you never know when sword fighting will come back in style."

She laughed while rubbing her temples. "Do you have something for a hangover?"

"I don't know if you deserve it." Seth tickled her sides.

"Ouch! Don't make me giggle, it makes my head hurt."

"Damn. I suppose I can mix up something I call the Morning after Mixer. I make it for the guys when they party too hard when we're on the road."

She peered from behind the pillow. "What's in it?"

"You don't want to know."

"Raw eggs?" She shuddered, remembering the concoctions he made daily.

"And tomato juice, some lime, a little cooking lard—"

Morgan clamped her hand over his mouth. "Just bring the drink."

* * *

Seth kissed his mom when he entered the kitchen. "Good morning, my beautiful mother."

"Good morning, baby. Where's Morgan?"

"Upstairs. I have to whip her up a patch of my hangover cure. She drank some of Bo's paint thinner last night." He looked through the window and saw the landscaper outside looking at sketches. "What's going on out there?"

"I was thinking Morgan might like to change some of the flowers. Maybe we can plant some things she likes."

"That's a great idea. Thank you for making her feel at home."

"I like Morgan. She's not one for wasting words. She says

exactly what's on her mind."

"Reminds me of another woman I know." He chuckled.

"I always knew you'd end up with a fireball. But can I ask you something?"

"Anything." Seth perused the fridge for the ingredients for his hangover concoction.

"Did you tell Morgan about Penny?"

Seth froze while moving aside a carton of milk. He hadn't thought about Penny in a long time. The day he had seen Morgan on that island, his daily thoughts of his high school sweetheart had diminished. *I want to be more than Mrs. Seth Blake,* were the last words she had ever said to him.

Seth continued his rummaging. "Not much to tell."

Teri-Lyn sighed. "You are a generous man but now it's coming back to bite you on the ass no matter how noble it was."

"Momma…"

"Don't Momma me. You wrote a pretty big check so Penny could start that clinic. How are you going to explain that to Morgan?"

"Penny and I went our separate ways when being with Seth Blake became too much for her. The money for the clinic was a friendly gesture and a sound investment."

"But you were still hung up on her for a long time."

"Penny was my first love." He shrugged.

"And you thought she'd be your *last*." Teri-Lyn raised an eyebrow. "A part of you was biding your time with those skinny celebrity hussies until Penny decided she wanted you again."

"No, I did not."

"Sure you did. Take my advice, son. The quicker you rip this Band-Aid off, the less Morgan will feel like you were hiding it from her. Or even worse, think that you still have a torch for Penny."

"Yes, ma'am."

Seth put together his drink and walked back upstairs, trying to figure out his options. His mother was right about his motives for the clinic. He just hoped he could explain it to Morgan.

* * *

The Cinnamon Festival was in full swing by the time they arrived. Morgan had to admit Tate didn't exaggerate about the numerous food vendors who attended each year. There were rides and games that seemed to span for miles. She didn't have the guts for the wilder rides but when she saw the Ferris wheel, she grabbed Seth's hand and dragged him over to it. He helped her into the seat and nestled close to her.

The view of the fairgrounds from the Ferris wheel was spectacular. Morgan could see the stage that Tate was to perform on in a few hours. It was a beautiful day and Seth was showing her a great time, but she could tell something had changed in him this morning. The drive there had been nearly silent, with him occasionally glancing over at her.

The wheel stopped, and Morgan could see the attendant letting more people on the ride.

Their seat moved a little bit, and Seth put his arm around her. "They're just letting some people on."

"I know. I wasn't scared."

"Then maybe I just wanted to put my arm around you." He kissed her.

"Are you pulling out your cheesy high school moves on me?"

"Is it working?"

"Maybe." She laughed, caressing his cheek. "You want to tell me what's going on with you?"

"Why do you think something's going on with me?"

"You can flash that superstar smile at everybody else, but I see can past that particular defense mechanism."

Seth sighed and shifted in his seat. "I have to tell you something that I don't want to and I need to tell you now."

"Why the urgency?"

"Because part of what I need to tell you about is right there. I am one of the chief contributors of the Main Street Clinic." Seth pointed across the fairgrounds at an RV with a big banner on it advertising free wellness checkups.

"OK."

"The person who runs it is Penelope Winterbourne. She's a doctor..."

"Your high school sweetheart." Morgan bit her lip. Seth's jaw had tensed, his brows furrowed. A feeling of melancholy suddenly washed over her. She didn't want to hear what he was about to say.

"We dated in high school and through college."

"So what happened?"

"When I went pro, Penny and I split up for good. Fame was too high a price for her. She said if she stayed she would always be in my shadow. That nothing she would accomplish as a doctor would mean anything because she would be the quarterback's wife."

"How did you feel about her leaving you?"

"She made her decision. I went on with my life. It's all in the past."

Morgan's heart sank. "Why do I get the feeling it's not that simple? She dumped you and you gave her money to help her dream come true. That doesn't sound like the past to me. It sounds more like the future deferred."

Seth clenched his jaw. "The clinic was a good cause. I knew it meant a lot to the community."

"It meant a lot to Penny. You sprang into action to help her because you still have feelings for her."

"No. Penny meant a lot to me at one time—"

"You didn't want to talk about her when Tate mentioned her the other night."

"No, I was more focused on having a pleasant evening with my wife."

"Yeah, but—"

"We both had a past before we found each other. I don't want to look back. I want to move forward. With you."

"Your past is filled with glamorous women and a high school sweetheart that you helped to start a clinic. Maybe if mine were more colorful this wouldn't be an issue."

The ride came to a stop. The attendant asked if they wanted to go again but Morgan blurted out, "No," and tried to climb over Seth to get out of the seat.

"Want to get something to eat?" Seth helped her climb down.

"No. I want to be alone for a little while. I'll meet you at Tate's concert." Morgan started to walk away.

"I'm not letting you wander around by yourself." He reached for her arm.

"I'm a big girl. I think I can manage my way around a fair ground." She tried to get out of his grasp.

Seth didn't let go. "I'm not going to let you out of my sight."

"Can you just give me some time to myself?" Morgan reached up and pried his hand off her arm. She didn't want him to touch her or for her to get roped into hearing him explain his actions to help Penny. Right now she just wanted to work through the waves of anger rolling through her.

"Morgan." He reluctantly let her go.

"I'll see you later." Morgan disappeared into the crowd.

* * *

Seth called Tate and told him to look out for her, so Tate was able to catch up with her by the tilt-a-whirl. Seth could have made a big deal about it, but he opted to give her the space she said she wanted. Trying to explain about the clinic sounded cut and dry when he said it in his mind, but when the words came out he had no easy defense for giving Penny the money she needed to start the clinic. He was grateful she hadn't asked how much he'd donated, knowing the amount seemed enormous, but it was just a drop in the bucket to him. Knowing Morgan was in the capable hands of Tate did not ease his mind. He wanted to settle this Penny business once and for all.

Penny leaving him had nearly killed him. Seeing her every once and a while normally stirred up feelings, both the good and the bad, but he didn't feel that way today. He felt surprisingly neutral about it all and a little pissed he even had to bring it up to her.

The last thing he wanted was for the ghost of a dead relationship interfering with his marriage. Seth glanced at his watch, wondering if enough time had passed so Morgan wouldn't think he was being pushy. He wasn't good with sitting around stewing about a problem. He was a fixer. He got paid very well to be a fixer on the field. Damnit. He missed her already and it had only been an hour. He had a feeling that coming to the festival was a bad idea but Morgan got excited about the prospect of cotton candy. Seth headed toward the stage. An hour was long enough to give her time to get her thoughts together.

* * *

Morgan didn't believe for a minute that, while standing in a massive crowd talking to some of his fans, Tate just happened to run into her. After talking for a few minutes she tried to make a run for it, but he offered to buy her a lemonade. Once her drink was gone, he took her to a corn on the cob vendor, then to a hot dog truck, all the while telling her stories about his and Seth's boyhood escapades. Every time she tried to leave, he'd give her something else to eat. Tate was a nice guy, and she liked how surprisingly down to earth he was despite his musical success. He and Seth were best friends, and she wasn't surprised when Seth told her that Tate had a cabin on the ranch. But at the rate he was going, she'd gain ten pounds going down memory lane with him.

"Tate, how long are you going to keep me busy? We've stopped at every food vendor at this fair." Morgan eyed him suspiciously.

"Until I'm sure you won't bolt." Tate handed her some cotton candy on a stick.

"Shouldn't you be rehearsing?"

"I will do a sound check after you eat that cotton candy."

"I know you're trying to be a good friend to Seth but—"

"He's my best friend and I would do anything for him." Tate furrowed his eyebrows at her.

She couldn't help but laugh. "So this is the kind of interference you used to run for him when you were kids?"

"Yep." Tate tipped his hat at her. "You know he called me and told me about meeting you on that island. He told me he knew that you were meant to be his wife."

Morgan took a deep breath and exhaled. "You were there, Tate. How was it between Seth and Penny?"

"You know how first loves are."

"Actually, no I don't. Seth…" Morgan closed her mouth to force herself from continuing the embarrassing truth.

"Oh, Morgan." Tate put his hand on her shoulder.

"I sound like a naïve idiot, don't I?"

"No, not at all. As a matter of fact I think that's the sweetest thing I've ever heard. How often can a man find a woman who hasn't loved anyone else but him?"

"It never occurred to me to ask if there was someone out in the world he still loved."

"If you don't mind me saying so, Seth and Penny was a million years ago."

"Tate," she sighed.

"Now just hear me out. Penny always had a way of yanking his chain, even back in high school. She had these dreams of being this big time doctor and, in my opinion, she never believed Seth would go pro."

"There you are," said someone from behind them.

Morgan turned to see Seth walking toward them.

She whispered to Tate, "Please don't tell Seth what I said."

"Your secret is safe with me." Tate winked at her, then patted Seth on the back. "I'll see you two at the concert."

Morgan turned to Seth. "What part of I'll see you — "

Seth took Morgan's face in his hands, but she pulled back. It felt unnatural not wanting to kiss him. What the hell had she gotten herself into? A few months ago she could live without a man for the rest of her life, now she was at a fair grounds in Texas conflicted because she was denying herself the pleasure of being kissed by the man she was pissed with right now.

"You're not kissing your way out of this one, Blake."

* * *

Tate's concert turned into a reunion of sorts. Every time Morgan turned around, out sprang another person who'd known Seth his whole life. The group moved their impromptu party to the Bright Star saloon, a bar the gang used to frequent in college. Morgan slid into the booth; Seth sat next to her and grabbed her hand. She tried to pull away a few times but his grip would grow tighter.

After yet another old friend piled into the already cramped booth, Morgan excused herself to go to the ladies room. She washed her hands twice, checked her phone messages, and contemplated calling Michelle. Finally she opted to sit at the bar. People were dancing, the music pounding, and everyone seemed to be enjoying themselves. Morgan ordered a beer but when she tried to pay the bartender leaned over and said, "Your husband has already taken care of it."

"Well, I can at least tip you."

The bartender refused, shaking his head.

"That's one of the perks of being Seth's girl, you never have to pay for anything," a voice said behind her.

Morgan turned as a woman slid onto the stool next to her. She didn't need anyone to tell her that was Penny. She had noticed the woman had been watching her and Seth from across the room for the last hour.

Penny Winterbourne was a beautiful woman. She had long, flaming red hair tucked neatly under a cowboy hat. Her eyes were green, just like Seth's, and she had a near perfect smile that revealed every straight tooth in her mouth. She was five foot six but the heel on her boots added another inch or so. Seth would have no trouble kissing her. Morgan wondered if it was a coincidence that Penny picked today to wear what were probably the tightest pants in her closet. Blue designer jeans gripped every curve and turn of the good doctor's body and the blouse she wore tied at the midriff left little to the imagination.

Morgan took a sip from her beer. "Sounds like you've had some experience."

"You could say that. I'm Penny Winterbourne." She extended her hand. "I hear congratulations are in order."

Morgan shook her hand. "Morgan. I hear you're still reaping the benefits by way of past association."

"So Seth told you about the clinic." Penny flipped her hair over her shoulder.

"The man is honest to a fault. That's one of the things I love about him."

"He does have a way about him." Penny let out an exaggerated sigh. "I can say I am surprised our Seth got married. He was dating glamorous models, partying all the time, and jet setting around the world. I thought for sure he'd be an eternal bachelor."

"Did you really? Beneath that confident, playboy exterior, I've found that *our* Seth is a nice guy who just wants someone to love him. Not all the things he can give them."

The crowd erupted in applause as Tate took the stage. Morgan could feel heat on her back and knew Seth was now standing behind her.

"Hey, Blake, it's good to see you." Penny flashed a warm smile.

"Good to see you too, Dr. Winterbourne. I see you've already met my wife, Morgan."

"Yes. Congratulations on your marriage. This is quite a surprise. When did you two get hitched?"

"Three months, six days ago." Morgan took a swig of her beer.

"Wow. Why so secretive? I always imagined you'd have a big soiree at the ranch."

Seth took the bottle of beer out of Morgan's hand and took a swig too. "I thought so too, but I enjoyed the privacy we had. It was just the two of us, standing on a cliff at sunset with a very eccentric minister. It was perfect." Seth turned to Morgan. "Dance with me?"

"I'm afraid I don't know how." Morgan held up her hands in defeat.

"Just follow my lead." Seth took her by the hand and led her onto the dance floor.

Morgan remained rigid as Seth moved to the rhythm of Tate's song. She didn't want to feel the comforting warmth of his body right now, she wanted to get away and clear her head.

Seth caressed her back and settled his hand on her butt. He tried to lift her chin with his other hand, but she tucked it to her chest to avoid looking at him. A loving, simple gesture turned into a contest of wills.

"If you don't relax, I'm going to pick you up and carry you out of here."

Morgan's eyes widened. "You wouldn't dare."

"Try me." Seth looked her right in the eye.

"Only if you get your hand off my ass." Morgan tried to reach back to move his hand.

"Nope." Seth pulled her closer.

She sighed. "Let's negotiate."

He kissed her on top of her head. "I'm listening."

"We finish this dance like civilized adults, then we leave. I don't think I can take any more of your trip down memory lane."

"Agreed." Seth twirled her around.

Seth led her out of the bar as Tate started an encore. He didn't have to look back to know Penny was watching them leave. He put Morgan in the truck and drove off. For a few miles there was silence.

"Morgan—"

"She's pretty. You two must have made an adorable couple in high school. Don't tell me, you two were the king and queen of the prom?" Morgan put her finger up to her lips.

He didn't answer. He knew a verbal minefield when he heard one.

"Don't answer. I already know. You were Mr. All American and the two of you were voted most likely to get everything your perfect hearts ever wanted?" She reached to turn on the radio, but he caught her hand.

Seth gave her a sideways glance. "Are you just letting off steam or deliberately trying to hurt my feelings?"

"I honestly don't know." She exhaled, slow.

"When you know which direction you're taking this conversation, we'll continue it."

"OK, I'll take the category Hurt Blake's Feelings for a thousand." Morgan hit the dashboard as if it were a buzzer.

Seth slammed on the breaks and pulled off the road. He unclipped his seat belt and pulled her to him.

"I'm not getting murdered on the side of some Texas road by a serial killer. Can we go home please?" Morgan tried to squirm out of his grasp.

"There's nobody out here but us," He murmured as he kept her still in a bear hug.

"Yeah, the boyfriend always says that in slasher movies right before the maniac jumps out of the bushes. Home, please."

"Not until you tell me why you're acting this way. This is not my Morgan."

"We don't really know each other that well. Do we?"

"Don't give me that crap. We know each other. The day I met you, I felt like I'd known you my whole life."

"Then why don't you know I'm feeling…vulnerable right now?" Her gaze drifted down, away from his. "I don't know how other women handle meeting a husband's ex flame but it's a first for me. So much of what I feel for you is a first for me. To know you loved someone and you did an incredible thing for her, that just tells me how much she still means to you."

"My generosity to Penny in the past can't hold a candle to the love I feel for you. I hope you don't hold that against me. And I love you too much to let you think otherwise." Seth ran his hand through her hair.

"There are times when I think this is all so crazy. How we met. Why we stayed together."

"You said you would give us a chance."

Morgan looked back up at him, her gaze wary. "I did."

"Did you mean it?"

"Of course I did. Especially after I saw my horse." She laughed.

"I knew that would seal the deal."

Morgan's face softened. "No, the endless nights of bliss in bed with you is what sealed the deal. And you're kind of cute in a cosmopolitan cowboy way."

He smiled. "So we're leaving the past in the past. Right?"

"Yes. I just hope it stays there."

Chapter Three

Seth was delighted that Morgan was in better spirits by the time they headed back to Philadelphia. He credited her change in mood to one last ride on Reed's Fire before they drove to the airport. Morgan bid Reed's Fire a woeful goodbye and promised to come back soon. Teri-Lyn drove them to the airport, gave them both a bear hug, and made them promise to come back soon so Morgan could meet the rest of the family.

The stillness in the penthouse was welcoming to Seth. He noticed the relief on Morgan's face that she wasn't accosted by the staff asking her if she needed any help. As soon as they stepped off the elevator Seth wanted to go straight to bed but ringing phones and Morgan's tummy had other plans. He'd turned on his business cell phone when they landed in Philadelphia and was bombarded with seventeen messages. Most of the messages he assumed were about the commercial he was shooting in a few days for a new endorsement deal he had with a sports drink company. He made calls while Morgan went into the kitchen to fix them dinner.

* * *

Seth placed his iPhone in the docking station on the kitchen counter and put on one of Tate's songs. Not a bad way to end the day, a quiet dinner at home. "Sorry about all those calls."

"I know it comes with the territory." She smiled as she hugged him. "Is everything good with you rescheduling the commercial?"

"Perfect. What's for dinner?" He reached in the fridge for a bottle of water.

"I was thinking a nice piece of grilled fish with asparagus and a salad? Just have to check and see what's in the fridge. I have to balance out all that rich food you fed me this weekend. Your stomach is a bottomless pit." Morgan rubbed his belly.

"My brothers and I have eating contests."

"I wanted to ask your mother what she fed you all. How did all you giants come out of such a petite woman?"

"Momma says we all got daddy's genes. Although, we did all have red hair when we were born." Seth ran his hand through his hair.

Morgan laughed.

"God's honest truth. Our hair darkened around age three."

"Your mom showed me your baby pictures. You were adorable. By the way, I have to work tomorrow. I'll try not to wake you when I leave." She pulled out the asparagus from the vegetable crisper.

"I thought you had the day off?" He scratched at his five o'clock shadow.

Morgan shrugged. "I do but every other Sunday I volunteer for story hour in the children's room at the library. It's my turn tomorrow and I forgot to reschedule when we left town."

"Nice." Seth opened the fridge and retrieved some veggies to make a salad.

"It's one of the programs I rallied for in the community and the kids are so cute at that age."

"What age is that?"

"Right before they discover television and the internet," she said with a laugh.

"What time is story hour?" Seth took the vegetables over to the sink for a rinse.

"Ten o'clock. About three kids show up despite the mailers and posters. Two of them are my customers' kids from the bookstore. They come as a show of support." Morgan chuckled.

"I'll be ready at nine."

She waved her hand at him. "Oh. You don't have to come."

"And what if I want to?" He looked at her.

She shrugged, prepping the hollandaise sauce. "Sure. Of course. I just thought you'd be a little bored."

"Not at all. In fact I'll be your assistant." He smiled sweetly.

Seth came up behind her and wrapped his arms around her waist while she stirred the sauce.

"I appreciate the enthusiasm but you haven't tasted the food yet."

"I'd rather taste you right now." Seth turned off the fire under the pot and lifted her onto the island counter.

"We can't have sex near the food."

He trailed kisses down her neck while unbuttoning her jeans. "I won't call the board of health if you won't."

Morgan reached over and picked up a whisk out of the caddy. "I could teach you this whipping technique I learned in home economics class."

As Seth pulled Morgan to the edge of the counter, something vibrated between them.

"Take it easy cowboy, that's just my cell phone." Morgan laughed and reached into her pocket. "Damn it, it's my brother Robert."

"Maybe you should answer it. You didn't call anyone and tell them we were back." He kissed her nose.

"I thought I gave up my four wardens when I introduced them to you."

"They'll never stop worrying about you. I know how they feel. I'm sure Robert will spread the word that you're home." He played with the buttons on her blouse.

"Hey, Robert, someone better be dead or at the least in a diabetic coma," Morgan said into the phone.

He pulled at the snap on her jeans and slowly pulled down her zipper until she stopped him.

She smirked and held out the phone. "He wants to talk to you."

"Hey, Robert, what's up?"

Morgan reached for the phone, but Seth moved out of her way.

"Sure, that sounds great. See you then." Seth ended the call. "He said to tell you he misses you."

"No, he did not. Where is my brother taking you to?"

"I was invited to dinner by all three of your brothers."

"Are you going?"

"Of course. Your brothers are nice guys. It wouldn't hurt to have a relationship with them."

"Robert has a man crush on you. You're always his fantasy football quarterback pick."

"I'm sure after a while I'll just be that dude that's married to their baby sister. We should have your family over for dinner one weekend."

"If you let them see those flat screens in your strategy den, they'll never leave."

* * *

Morgan touched the chrome knob on the bookstore door and felt like a piece of herself had been restored. Every time she went away Michelle would take the opportunity to put her own decorative mark on the place. A colorful piece of art on the wall, new throw pillows for the couch, or a new gourmet coffee flavor would be added to the menu.

"Hey boss!" Michelle shouted from an aisle.

"Don't call me boss."

"Chick who owns this store?"

Morgan put her bag down on the counter. "Somewhere in

between those two extremes is a happy medium. Let me know what you come up with. How are things?"

"Rome did not fall while you were gone." Michelle took a bow.

"Good to hear."

"You look radiant, by the way, now that you've been getting the *quarterback sack* on a regular basis. I meant to tell you a few months ago."

"I wonder if they make human muzzles," Morgan wondered aloud.

"How was Texas? And please if you say nice, great, or good, I am going to hit you."

"How's wonderful?"

"I accept that. Elaborate."

"Met Seth's mom, some of his friends, and my new horse, Reed's Fire." Morgan rifled through her bag, looking for her phone.

"How sweet is that?" Michelle squealed.

"Yes, and guess who was there?" Morgan held her hand over her mouth to suppress a smile.

"Somebody frickin' famous I bet."

"That country singer Tate McGill." Morgan handed the phone to her to show her a picture of Seth and Tate.

Michelle tried to speak but the words wouldn't come out. Her mouth fell open so wide Morgan noticed she'd gotten a new filling.

Morgan shook her head. "Well, I'll be damned. Something shut you up. Yes, before you ask, Tate McGill is just as sexy in person. He even sang a new song he's working on by the bonfire."

"I hate you."

"I know."

"Please send me that picture. I need it."

She picked up her cell phone and sent the picture to Michelle's phone, shaking her head. "Fine, there you go."

Michelle picked up her smart phone and sighed. "Holy cow. Tate and Seth shouldn't take pictures together. That's too much sexy in one concentrated area."

"We had a great time all week until we went to the Cinnamon Festival. Met his old high school sweetheart. She's a doctor and runs a clinic."

"All I heard you say is that you met the bitch that isn't married to Seth. How's Seth's mother? Did she tell you that you weren't good enough for her quarterback son and try to pay you off?"

Morgan laughed. "You watch too many soap operas. She's pretty, shorter than me, and has a beautiful head of red hair. We had a very frank discussion."

"So no...keep your hands off my son?"

"No. Seth spent so much time in the dating pool I think she genuinely just wants someone who's a good person for him."

"Well, that you are and then some honey."

"Thanks, Michelle."

Michelle bit her lip. "I didn't tell you before, because I didn't want to ruin your good time down there..."

Morgan rolled her eyes. "Spit it out."

"Jason stopped by the other day." Michelle winced.

Jason, her ex-boyfriend Jason? The same Jason who dumped her for her cousin, Charisma? Just great. "What did he want?"

"Don't know. He asked for you, I said you weren't here. He said I was lying. I told him that your rich, quarterback husband whisked you away to his ranch in Texas and I didn't know when or if you'd be back."

"He has a lot of nerve. Seth's publicist told him someone went to a newspaper and said he'd stolen me from Jason."

"I saw that sound bite. The press didn't play it up this time. It sort of came and went."

"Well, that's good."

"Yeah, but I can't believe they paid Charisma and Jason for that lie. Because you know it was Charisma, it had to be."

Morgan sighed. "You know Seth wants to drop it. He said he

doesn't take it personally any more. I still want to choke the shit out of Charisma and Jason."

"Yeah. Your cousin does seem driven though. Didn't you say she only dated basketball players?"

"She's an NBA groupie."

Michelle shook her head. "By the way, you also got a call from some woman named Whitney. She said she was the administrative assistant for Dana Schmidt, the head of the Reading Rainbow Initiatives committee."

"Really? I've been trying to get in touch with her for months about the library's reading hour."

"Whitney said Dana would like to make an appointment with you and to call her back as soon as you came back to town."

"Maybe my luck is changing for the better."

"Also, here's a list of the inventory that needs replenishing. I had to order another case of Seth's biography. I think people stop by hoping to get a glimpse of him in the store." Michelle handed Morgan a clipboard.

"Did you read it?" Morgan scanned the list.

"Yes, I did. That dude is so humble it's painful."

"Humble was the last word I would have used when we met."

"We got a package in the mail for the upcoming booksellers' convention. If you want one of us to go, you need to send in the registration form as soon as possible. If you fill it out now, we can have it ready for the mailman today." Michelle shooed Morgan toward the back of the store.

Morgan went to the back room in search of the package and found a copy of the book she'd ordered for her father's wife, Sydney, on her desk. The book Sydney wanted was out of print but Morgan had worked her magic and found a copy. It was her way of saying thank you for the talk they had the day Seth came over to meet her father and brothers. The idea that she'd missed out on having a relationship with her all those years would cross her mind every now and again. Spending time with Teri-Lyn in Texas reminded her of the absence of a mother figure in her life.

Sydney really wasn't a bad person or a terrible stepmother. Morgan did, however, still feel like she'd replaced her mother in a way but how could she begrudge her father the right to be happy? He'd even waited until she started college to seriously start dating someone. His marriage to Sydney was Morgan's incentive to get her own apartment when she graduated from college.

Sydney's advice and Morgan's willingness to listen had changed both of them that day. She didn't know what kind of relationship she wanted with her stepmother, but she could start with the peace offering of the book. It was the perfect excuse to drop in and out without too much fuss.

Morgan finished the form and brought it up to the counter. She took a look at the work schedule for the week. As usual, everything was running like clockwork while she was away. The day was getting off to a good start. She'd just been talking to Seth last night about her plans and something positive seemed to be happening. Of course she would call back and make an appointment with Dana Schmidt. She'd been trying to get in touch with her for over six months.

The doorbell chimed as a customer entered the bookstore. Morgan flipped through the stack of mail, anticipating the customer bringing a book to the register eventually.

A trendy-looking woman walked up to the counter. "Hello, are you Morgan Blake?"

Morgan hesitated for a moment, holding back the response that her last name was Reed. Didn't the sign outside say Reed Books? But she wasn't a Reed anymore, was she? The thought of hyphenating her name didn't sit well with her either.

Morgan smiled, putting on her best customer service face. "That's me. How can I help you?"

"My name is Chandra Passatore, a reporter for *Philadelphia Style* news magazine. I would love to do an article on the woman who finally snagged Seth Blake."

Morgan's smiled faded too fast to recover. "Surely you have better stories to investigate, Ms. Passatore. I married Seth Blake, I didn't capture Bigfoot."

"Surely you know being married to the Titan's gorgeous, eternal bachelor and MVP is newsworthy?"

"I think it's more like intrusive gossip. He's entitled to his privacy."

The reporter's nasally, condescending laugh made Morgan tense. "Seth Blake is the property of the Philadelphia Titans and by default property of this city that adores him. So, technically, we own you too. I can do an interview on your new lives together and put a good spin on it."

"You sound like we're trying to get over some scandal."

"Seth did steal you from your fiancée." The reporter raised an eyebrow.

"In case you haven't been told, Pennsylvania is a free state and no one *owns* me. Seth didn't steal me from anyone. And if this sad attempt to nicely coerce me into doing an interview to cover up some nonexistent scandal is all you've got, I hope you have a backup career choice on the ready."

The reporter's face twitched. "I won't be the last reporter to try and get a scoop from you. I thought you'd be amiable because your bookstore places ads with us, so you'd be comfortable with someone you already have a business relationship with, but I guess the bigger mags have gotten to you already."

"I suggest you buy a book. That's the only way you're going to leave this store with any information."

"Let me know if you change your mind." The reporter put her card on the counter and walked out.

"What happened?" Michelle hurried to the front of the store.

"Some reporter bitch just tried to hit me up for an interview."

"Maybe you should hire a publicist?"

"For what?"

"To navigate these situations from time to time."

Morgan crossed her arms. "I don't need a publicist."

"I bet Seth has a publicist."

"Yes, he does. He spends a lot of time arguing with her on the phone."

* * *

It had been three weeks since Morgan had moved all her things out of her apartment and became fully invested in living with Seth. She had to admit it was fun waking up to him every morning, fending off enticing advances so she could make it into the bookstore. It was all too easy to get lost in those sleepy, lust-filled eyes and decide to take a vacation day or two, or twenty. Seth's time was not as structured during off season even though he had other commitments. She didn't realize how involved he was with his other business ventures. He especially liked talking to his father and brother JJ on a daily basis about their latest land project. She'd listen as they joked and insulted each other for a good half hour before they got down to business.

She knew he was smart, but she hadn't realized the scope of his business ventures. She had assumed when he didn't play football that he and some bikini clad plaything just frolicked around the world until it was time to play football again. Little did she know when he wasn't trying to get her to play Marco Polo under the covers, he was stapled to his desk.

Things were going well at the bookstore, the repairs had been made and there was no problem in the foreseeable future. She was free to continue her quest to get funding for the reading hour at the library. Her goal was to have a daily reading hour as well as other interactive programs that would help people of all ages. She'd finally synced up with Dana Schmidt from RRI and had a meeting with her next week.

A note from the cook said the lasagna was in the oven and still had an hour to go. Morgan had managed to ease up on her discomfort about the staff and just let it be. It occurred to her that having the older women around, cleaning and cooking, reminded her of her brief time with her mother. Kara, the cook, hummed while she worked and it reminded Morgan of mornings with her mom.

Coming home to a tidy house always filled with something fragrant coming from the kitchen was beginning to feel normal to her. Morgan was on her way to the bedroom to change for dinner when she heard the doorbell ring. Seth hadn't mentioned he was expecting anyone so she went to the living room to find him escorting a man with a briefcase into the penthouse.

"Sam, good to see you." Seth led the man into the living room.

"Anything for you, Seth, you know that." Sam turned and held out his hand. "You must be Morgan. I'm Sam Tulliver, Seth's business manager."

Morgan shook his hand. "Nice to meet you."

Seth nodded at him. "Sam looks out for my financial interests, and he's very good at it. I wouldn't trust anyone else with my portfolio."

Sam shifted his briefcase from one hand to another. "I promise not to take up too much of your time."

"It's not a problem," Seth said. "We were just sitting down to dinner. Care to join us?"

"Thanks for the offer but I'm having a late dinner with Erica tonight. I have to be at the restaurant in a half hour. All the figures are up to date." Sam took a thick file out of his briefcase. "I included the information on that resort property your brother and dad looked at in Arizona. From what I've researched so far, this will be a good investment."

"Good to know."

"I'll get back to you with my final analysis by the end of the week. When you have the time, my friend Shane Bracht would be delighted to help you look at commercial properties. He can meet with you whenever you like."

Seth thanked him for coming by and walked him out. When Seth returned he handed Morgan the file. She scanned the documents and a huge lump formed in her throat as she read. Morgan knew he had an expansive portfolio but to see it on paper, neatly itemized, was mind blowing. In addition to his business investments, football salary, and endorsement deals, he owned three more houses in California, Colorado, and Montreal.

"I want to you to have full disclosure about everything in my life."

"Except ex-girlfriends," she mumbled.

"Morgan, I didn't tell you about Penny or my donation right away because of exactly what happened. You'd try to find a way to diminish what I felt for you."

Morgan gave him an expectant look.

"But I do apologize for not telling you sooner. What you are looking at is just what I am worth on paper."

"Don't get me wrong, it's impressive, but I can assure you that you are worth so much more than numbers on a page."

"We need to start taking steps to consolidate our lives. If something were to happen to me, you —"

"Why are you talking like that?"

Seth caressed her arms. "I'm just being realistic. I could easily be taken out by a runaway golf cart or some freak accident. If something were to happen to me you need to know what we have, so no one can take advantage of you. I'd like to start by paying off any debt you may have."

Morgan shot him a look of indignation.

"What?" Seth asked.

"You are incredible."

"That's not the first time you've told me that." He tried to kiss her but she pulled back.

"This time incredible means impossible."

"What did I say?"

Morgan took a seat on the couch. "I know you mean well but I won't let you pay down my debt. I was doing OK with the bookstore. Well, before all that business with the repairs, but it was comfortable. I have you, it's more than enough."

"Does this mean you won't let me help you with the bookstore expansion?"

"When the time is right, we'll negotiate. I'll draw up a business plan on my own and we can have Sam take a look at it. Then I will ask for a loan with a low interest rate."

"Do I get to dictate the default terms?" Seth smiled wickedly.

She raised an eyebrow. "That depends. If it involves that jar of chocolate sauce and those strawberry preserves in the night stand next to your condoms, I want no part of it."

"That's not fair."

"Tough. I had to shower for an hour to get that sticky mess off my body."

"It was worth every glorious minute it took to scrub your body clean." He smiled as he looked her up and down with a devilish glint in his eye.

Morgan shook her head at him. "I'd like to make some progress getting the reading programs off the ground at the library first. Then I can focus on expanding the bookstore. In the meantime, I could use all the emotional support I can get."

Seth sat down next to her and put an arm around her shoulders. "You got it."

* * *

Morgan's confession that she'd never been to the Titan's stadium nearly killed him. All her years of living in Philadelphia and living with her football fanatic family, she'd never set foot in the stadium. Seth informed her it was time for phase two of the football lesson he'd been giving her and that included a personal tour from him.

She marveled at that sharp memory of his, knowing the name of each person they encountered, from the executive office to the maintenance staff. They made their way to the stands and Morgan stopped, in awe, as she surveyed the bleachers and the massive land that composed the football field.

"This is amazing," she whispered.

Seth squeezed her hand. "Wait until you see the view from the field."

"We can go down there?"

He smiled.

"Silly question, I know."

Seth squeezed her hand again and they made their way onto the field.

"It all seems so much smaller on television. How do you run around on this field with all that padding on?"

"Lots of practice. You wanna throw the ball around?" He waggled his eyebrows.

She laughed. "Are you kidding me? Pass on a football fan's fantasy of throwing the ball around with the star quarterback? My father is somewhere with the hairs on the back of his neck standing straight up, and he doesn't know why. I'll take a shot."

Seth called out to one of the workers at the other end of the field to get him a football. He caught the ball and instructed Morgan to move back about ten yards and tossed the ball softly to her. He whooped when she caught the ball the proper way.

"Good catch."

"Three brothers, all played football in high school. They practiced in the back yard. The front yard. In the house. In the kitchen. During dinner."

He laughed. "You ever think that maybe some cosmic force was grooming you for something like…being married to me?"

"No, I thought they were repeated attempts on my life and one day I'd get taken out with a football and it would be ruled an accident." Morgan threw the ball back to Seth with a little power behind it.

"Clearly you learned something while ducking for cover. You have a nice little technique."

"Then stop throwing like a girl and show me a real pass." Morgan stuck her tongue out.

"We've had enough football related injuries haven't we?"

"You did save me from a getting a nose job."

"I'm glad. You have such an adorable nose. I would have missed it." Seth walked toward her.

She looked around the stadium. "How does it feel when you're out here? When all those seats are filled with screaming fans? We're here alone, and the magnitude of all this is overwhelming. I can barely breathe." Morgan sighed.

He shrugged. "Focus."

"And the cameras are always on you. Don't you ever want to pick your nose or something?"

"You get used to that too. And my momma would kill me if I picked my nose on national television."

"I could see that being played on every sports show in America."

"That would be something."

"So." Morgan crossed her arms over her chest. "You gonna throw me a real pass?"

"OK. I want you to go down to the twenty yard line. I'll throw it to you and we'll see if you can get to the end zone before I catch you."

Morgan rolled her eyes as walked past him. "That shouldn't be a problem. We're already on the thirty yard line."

Seth caught her hand. "The other twenty yard line."

She squinted down the field. "You've got to be kidding me."

"I would never kid a beautiful woman, especially if she's my wife."

"I'm going to call a cab because it's going to take me some time to get down there."

"I have all day. Besides I get to watch you walk all the way down there."

She turned and reluctantly started walking. "You know –"

"It's good exercise. One of these days I will get you to jog with me."

"Yeah, if I grow another five inches."

Morgan didn't have to call a cab, but she felt like she needed one. She called a time out every ten yards to catch her breath while Seth stood there laughing at her. She looked back at the end zone. Didn't look too far away. She could do this.

"OK, big boy, give it your best shot," she shouted down the field. "And remember I know how to catch so don't chicken out and go limp noodle on me."

"OK." He nodded his head. "Why don't we make it interesting?"

"What do you have in mind?"

"I win, you have to get a tattoo just like mine." He pushed up his sleeve to display his number twelve tattoo.

"Did you have any head injuries last season?"

Seth tapped on his head. "All marbles are in there and accounted for."

"So, if I lose I get branded like one of the animals on your ranch?"

"I prefer to think of it as a beautiful soulful expression of our love in permanent ink on your body."

"And what do I get if I win?"

"What do you want?"

"If I win, I can give you a full body wax. Everywhere. Maybe we can give you a Brazilian down there." Morgan smirked.

"Not on your life."

"What's the matter, pretty boy? Scared to take that last step into metrosexuality?"

"Just for that, I get to pick where you get the tattoo." He grinned like a shark.

"Quit stalling and get ready for the hot wax I see in your future."

Seth sent the ball soaring through the air like a little brown heat-seeking missile. Morgan kept her eye on the ball and anchored herself so she could firmly catch it and still have enough energy to run. She let out a celebratory yelp when she made contact with the ball, tucked it in to her arm and ran. She remembered what her brothers said about running with the ball. *Don't look back unless you feel the heat on your ass.* She was mere inches from the ten yard line when she felt Seth closing in on her. She managed to make it to the five yard line before Seth scooped her up and carried her into the end zone.

Applauding erupted from the stadium, the employees cheering in the distance.

"Show off," she managed to get out between pants.

"I know exactly where I want that tattoo on you." He threw the football down and kissed her.

"Can we negotiate?"

"OK." Seth reached into his pocket and pulled out a ring box. "How about you wear this instead?"

A lump formed in Morgan's throat as she gazed at the black velvet box. "What did you do?"

"It took the jeweler a while to get the detailing right but I wanted them to be perfect. Two vines entwined for eternity." Seth opened the box to reveal platinum wedding bands.

Morgan's heart skipped a beat when she saw the etching on the rings.

"They're beautiful."

"I had yours inscribed."

She smiled when she read the inscription. It read *Morgan, best tackle of my life.*

"I love it. I almost forgot how you almost mortally injured me."

"Bruised rib."

"Held me captive in your bungalow."

"Romanced you until you saw things my way." Seth slipped the band on her finger.

"You sure know how to put a good spin on things." Morgan pulled him down for a kiss. He met her half way and picked her up, wrapping his arms around her.

* * *

Seth arrived early for the commercial shoot, anxious to get it over with. This would be his fourth endorsement deal and they were paying him a pretty penny. He liked that he believed in the product and had been drinking it for a while before they approached him with the deal. Things went much easier when he had practical knowledge of the product he was going to attach his name to, and he was a fan of FitPro sports drinks.

He had wanted Morgan to come with him but she'd been fortunate enough to get that meeting with the woman at the Rainbow Reading Initiative. He admired her tenacity and her commitment to literacy. He had gotten a kick out of seeing her strut around on the island wearing those catchy literacy slogans. She was, by far, the hottest nerd he'd ever seen in his life.

The setup crew was pretty laid back. No one accosted him for an autograph and everyone was very polite. The change in the air came when his publicist Vivian arrived. Vivian marched in and was sprouting orders like she owned the place, all without removing her sunglasses.

"So happy you could make it," Vivian said in a clipped tone.

"Of course I would. You sent me twenty-four reminder emails."

"I wouldn't have to email you if you answered my calls."

Seth took a deep breath and exhaled. He was not in the mood for Vivian's theatrics today.

"Why didn't you return my calls?" she repeated.

"You know I don't answer calls when I'm at the ranch."

"And I suppose doing damage control to salvage your reputation isn't a priority?"

"There's nothing to salvage. I told you Morgan's ex-boyfriend and cousin were behind that story and it was no truer than Big Foot being spotted by the Liberty Bell."

"And what about Melanie?"

Melanie? They hadn't dated in months. Seth rolled his eyes. He had known right from the start that Melanie and Vivian were friends, but he hadn't cared at the time.

"Melanie is in love with some European banker who is more than delighted to fork over his fortune to her. When I saw her at that fundraiser she looked happy. We wished each other well."

"Are you sure you know what you're doing? You know I'm just looking out for you, gorgeous. Four months ago you were dating models. I never thought when you finally got married you'd be settling for something a little more…home grown."

Seth's face burned and he clenched his hands into fist. "Home grown?"

"Don't get me wrong, she's not an unattractive girl but she's hardly worth a second look. You need somebody who's suited to your glamorous lifestyle. You need someone who is worthy of your image, not some common nobody who runs a small bookstore."

"Vivian, you're fired."

Everyone around him stopped what they were doing and stared. He and Vivian had been together for many years. They'd had their fair share of disagreements in the past and they'd always patched things up. But Vivian's remark about Morgan hit a nerve.

Vivian clutched her pearl necklace. "Seth! You'd pick some woman you just met over me?"

"Save it, Vivian. You don't tell me who to love or who to marry. That's not what I pay you for."

Vivian stalked off in a fury. Seth looked at his entourage and decided it was time some boundaries were set.

"Everybody listen up, because I am only saying this once. Anybody who has a problem with my wife or how I live my life, I am happy to accept your letter of resignation right now. If I find anyone is responsible for spreading hurtful gossip about her, you will be terminated immediately."

* * *

Morgan arrived at her appointment with Dana Schmidt early, eager to have no reason for the woman to reschedule. The Reading Rainbow Initiative had a far reaching hand in the community and would help tremendously to get the ball rolling again on the reading hour at the library. With funding getting cut left and right for city programs, Morgan prayed that the library would be spared and it had suffered several near misses in the past two years. But now, the reading hour for the toddlers and the book club for the young adult readers were on the chopping block.

She smiled, remembering the look on Seth's face when she had emerged from the walk in closet in her power suit. Her best effort to look professional was met by a horny football player who wanted to play hide and seek before she left this morning. After promising to pick up where they left off, he had wished her luck and told her he loved her.

"Ms. Schmidt will see you now," the receptionist said.

She escorted Morgan down a long corridor, the clicking of Morgan's heels echoing through the sparsely decorated hall.

Dana waved them in when they reached the open door of her office. "Morgan, come in!"

"Thank you for meeting with me, Dana."

"Thank you for being so committed. My goodness you're not a teacher and you have this tenacious drive about the library's programs."

Morgan tried to hide a smile. "As a bookstore owner, I am still vested in education. Just like I am vested in this community."

"Of course. I think it's admirable that you want to keep programs going for our youth."

Morgan handed her a proposal. "Not just our youth readers. Although, I do think it's crucial to get them interested at a young age. My youngest attendee at the reading hour is two years old. But there are still a number of adults who do not know how to read because of things like learning disabilities that weren't detected when they were younger and they're too ashamed to admit it. And people who are new to this country that have difficulty learning English. There should be an outreach to people of all ages who want to read."

"So what do you propose?" Dana flipped through the file.

"Keeping those programs funded at the library is a start. Then we could have other outreach organizations build a small platform within their community."

"We need something to spark an interest. How would you feel about incorporating a celebrity to endorse this?"

"That would be great. It definitely wouldn't hurt."

"You're married to Seth Blake aren't you? Do you think he would consider being our celebrity endorser?"

Morgan shifted uncomfortably in her seat. "My husband and I don't get involved in each other's work lives."

"But surely he would do it for you. The two of you being married must have been the best kept secret in this city. I met him a few years ago at a charity event, and he is off the charts gorgeous.

He said hello and I got heart palpitations."

Morgan's fingers itched to grab the proposal out of Dana's hand and cram it down her throat. She didn't know what enraged her more, the fact that Dana talked about Seth like he was a piece of meat or that he would readily be the poster boy just because she was married to him. And Dana's transition to girlfriend mode so swiftly while Morgan was trying to achieve something good was unprofessional.

"I'm afraid coming here was a mistake, Dana. I had assumed after many months of trying to contact you that you wanted to talk about something more worthwhile than my personal life." Morgan jabbed her proposal back into her briefcase and walked out.

* * *

Seth wanted to be in a better mood before he went home to Morgan after the commercial shoot, so he dropped by to see his friend Patton. Seth was still seething from Vivian's remarks. When did he hand over control of his life to people like Vivian? Between pushy publicists and old flames popping out of the woodwork, he was praying none of it scared Morgan away.

"Thanks, man." Seth took a swig of the beer Patton had handed to him.

Patton gave him a friendly punch in the arm. "You know Vivian is crazy. She was always pimping girls to you."

Seth chuckled. "You would think that."

"It's not like you can't pull the ladies by yourself. But she pretty much wrapped Melanie up in a bow and handed her to you."

Seth nodded in agreement. One day Melanie had appeared at his front door wearing a slinky black mini dress, with a bottle of champagne in her hand. "Yeah that was creepy."

"But you hit that anyway."

"I said it was creepy but it worked."

Seth and Patton both erupted in laughter.

"Now, look at you a year later." Patton took a sip of his own beer. "Married."

Seth smiled. "Yeah. I didn't see that one coming."

"I think you did. One minute you're trying to sneak off the island, the next I see you two parasailing."

"The minute I laid eyes on her getting off that plane I knew…"

"I'm happy for you man. When you were with Melanie, you did not look as content as you are right now. I hope you and Morgan have a great life together."

"Thanks, man."

Patton nodded and took a swig of beer. "Did she like the ranch?"

"She loved it, especially the horse I bought her. I think she loves him more than me." He laughed. "So where is the lovely Nina?"

"She's out shopping. Retail therapy is her way of dealing with the baby thing." Patton sighed.

"Still having a hard time?"

"Yeah, that last miscarriage just before the Super Bowl took her over the edge. She refused to go on the team vacation. She couldn't possibly redecorate one more inch of this house, and she's booking party planning events every week."

"It'll happen soon for you two. She just needs some time to grieve."

Patton took another swig. "What about you? Plan on making me a godfather any time soon?"

"I can't wait. As soon as Morgan says the word, I'm ready. In the meantime we're getting in a lot of practice." Seth smirked and waggled his eyebrows.

Patton spit out his beer. "Oh shit!"

"What?"

"You play like my grandmother when you get laid on a regular basis."

"That's a damn lie, Pat."

"Why do you think we've won two Super Bowls?"

Seth thought for a moment. "Shit. Very hard work and determination?"

"And…you always break up with a woman just before the playoffs! Think about it. We've won two Super Bowls because you be all twirped up over not getting any and you funnel all that energy into the game."

He ran his hand over his face. Was Patton right?

"Don't worry about it man, just tell Morgan you can't have sex during the season." Patton chuckled.

Keys jingled in the lock, and he turned to see Patton's wife, Nina, come in the door with ten bags in her hand.

"Seth!"

"Hey, Nina." He climbed off his seat to hug her.

"Congratulations on the wedding." She gave him a leering look.

"I know."

"You know what?"

"I am in the dog house with you and most of the planet about my marriage. But I do want all of us to get together for dinner. Soon."

Nina set down her purse. "I'd love to meet the woman who could snag the bachelor of the century."

"Morgan's a sweetheart," Patton said.

"You two look good together. Patton showed me that picture of you and Morgan at the festival. She owns a bookstore?"

Seth grinned. "She does. She's very dedicated to literacy and is even involved in some community programs."

"Like what?" Nina removed her high heeled shoes and took a seat next to her husband.

"She does story hour at the public library for the kids a couple of times a month."

"Wow, that sounds cool."

"She's looking into organizing programs to raise literacy awareness. When Morgan gets something in her head, nothing stops her."

"Sounds like you two have a lot in common." Nina smiled.

Seth scratched at the label on his beer. "Yeah, she worries we don't. I try to reassure her that this limelight on our lives is just temporary. Another story will come along and people will lose interest in us."

"Seth Blake, you've been voted sexiest man alive twice, bachelor of the year four times, and harder to hog tie than a bull at a rodeo. Whatever the hell that last one means. Your singleness is legendary. People are going to want to know what exactly Morgan has that persuaded you to give all that up."

"What are you, keeping a scrap book on him?" Patton huffed a laugh.

"No, but I have some friends that have one. You know how many times some desperate chick has played nice with me because they knew you and Patton were friends?"

Seth's eyes widened. "I'm sorry about that."

"Don't be. I am good at putting bitches in their place. Tell him, baby."

Patton took a swig of his beer. "Yeah, man. Nina has a talent for insulting a large group of people at one time."

Seth couldn't help but laugh. "Damn, Nina."

Patton nodded his head in her direction. "Maybe Nina can help Morgan through the viper pit."

Seth and Patton looked at Nina.

Nina shook her head. "You two don't even know if Morgan and I will get along. That's wishful thinking that we'd hit it off like best buds because you two are friends."

Seth chuckled. "I have no doubt you two would get along. You both have that brutal honesty thing going on but you carry it off in a classy way."

"It couldn't hurt to pay her a welcome," Patton said.

Nina bit her lip. "OK, I'll do it. Partly because I'm nosey and partly because you're family, Seth."

"Thanks, Nina."

* * *

By the time Morgan reached her father's house, some of the disappointment from the disastrous episode with Dana had faded away.

"Hey, Dad." Morgan kissed her father on the cheek.

"How's that husband of yours?"

"Good. We had a great time on his ranch. He bought me a horse."

Her dad's eyes widened in awe. "The Twelve Horse Shoes is an impressive ranch. That journalist lady did an interview with him on his property last year."

"Why is it that everyone in this family knows more about that man than me?"

"Defiance."

"What?"

"How many times did I try to teach you about football?"

She grinned. "Too many."

"And you end up marrying a football player. Do you see the irony in that? Because I do."

Sydney entered the room. "Hi, Morgan. Is that my book?"

"Yes." Morgan smiled and handed it to her.

"How was your meeting today?"

"How did you know I had a meeting today?"

"I called the bookstore and Michelle said you were out wheeling and dealing. So how did it go?"

"No dealing, but I wish I'd had a wheel to roll over her neck."

Sydney sucked in air between her teeth. "That bad?"

Morgan shook her head. "I don't want to talk about it."

"I still keep in touch with a few of my sorority sisters who are pretty active in the community center. I could shake a few trees—"

"Thanks, but I'd rather do it on my own," Morgan said quietly.

Sydney smiled. "OK."

Morgan was having a hell of a day. She immediately regretted how curtly she answered Sydney. Here the woman was trying to help her cause, and she slipped back into treating Sydney like an enemy. She'd just left the office of a woman whose help she needed but was ambushed by a hidden agenda. What she needed was a dose of the past to soothe her. The box in her father's attic usually did the trick. She'd moved all her things from her place into Seth's penthouse. Maybe it was time to take her box of memories to her new home too.

"Dad, I have to go into the attic and get a box I left up there." Morgan excused herself and headed upstairs. She didn't have a lot of stuff left at her dad's house but there were still a few boxes that remained. She spotted the taped up box nestled in the corner. It had been moved from her secret hiding spot but it hadn't been opened. Taking her keys out of her pocket, she used one to cut through the layers of tape.

A floorboard creaked behind her.

Her brother Robert had walked into the attic. "Hey Squirt, Dad told me to come up here and help you look for a box."

"Hey, it's my husband's new best friend. You two going steady yet?" Morgan stuck out her tongue at Robert.

"You're jealous I want to spend time with your husband?" Robert kissed her on the cheek.

Morgan pushed him out of her way. "No, curious though. Why do you want to spend time with Seth?"

Robert parked himself on a chair. Morgan looked over at her brother and tried not to smile. They'd been bickering all their lives.

It was more off putting when they were getting along.

"He's a nice guy and my brother-in-law. Besides, I know you can't wait to get away from all of us. Like it or not we're still your family. Sometimes I think you forget. But Seth won't let you forget about us. Family is important to him."

"What do you mean forget about you?" She scowled at him.

"I think you want to be part of Seth's life and distance yourself from us."

She couldn't pretend they had a lot in common or that she visited them on a regular basis. All her brothers were married and had lives of their own, but they all seemed to make time to butt into her life.

"I'm not trying to forget anything. As a matter of fact, I'm trying to remember." Morgan pulled a picture of their mother out of the box.

"You look like her, you know."

"Do you think so?" She scrunched her nose.

"Yep. I've always treated you like a child and you're now closer to middle aged than an adolescent — "

"Watch it."

"But occasionally I spend time with my baby sister and, for a little while, I get to see my mother's face again."

"So all that bossing me around and never letting me do anything was out of love?"

Robert grinned. "I have to admit we were obnoxious about it. But it was all in the name of looking out for you."

She smiled back. "I do admit you did teach me some great self-defense moves."

"Self-defense? You could be a street brawler. You got Jason good in the chestnuts after he dumped you in front of everyone. I was almost hoping Charisma would do something stupid so you could kick her ass. Did you tell Seth you know how to shoot a gun?"

"No. I was saving that for later. You should see his gun collection at his ranch."

He laughed. "I want to tell you he's not good enough for you but he's my idol. So I'm a little conflicted."

"Can you take the box downstairs for me?" She batted her eyes at her brother.

Robert sighed but picked up the box. "No problem."

She kissed her brother on the cheek. "Thank you."

"For what?"

"Looking out for me. I couldn't imagine your intrusive ass being out of my life."

"Good, because Seth invited us to dinner next Sunday." Robert gave her a cheesy grin.

"Yay," Morgan said in a droll tone.

Chapter Four

Seth felt much better after leaving Patton's house. There were some things that couldn't be helped, and he felt certain he'd made the right decision with Vivian. There were enough external factors in their lives that they couldn't control, he wasn't going to have someone on his payroll making negative remarks about Morgan.

The ride home gave him time to think about how his public image had been perceived the last five years. The women in his life had known he wasn't serious about them. He would meet one of them after a game or at an event, and it was clear what they both saw in each other and how long it would last. He and Melanie had stayed together so long because they had a crazy relationship. Melanie went from hot, to cold, to lukewarm constantly, and he found her erratic behavior exciting. They broke up just to have great marathon makeup sex. It was fun and he liked that her modeling jobs and his schedule kept them apart a lot. When they were together for too long they ran out of things to talk about.

Was it possible that maybe people didn't believe he could be with someone as sweet and down to earth as Morgan? She didn't like to party, and he almost had to beg her to go out to dinner. Many a night they fell asleep on the couch, her in his arms, while watching television. But soon he'd be on the road and those quiet evenings at home were going to become scarce. Tonight he looked forward to shrimp scampi and hearing about her meeting.

Hmmm…sex or food? The elevator couldn't ascend fast enough to the penthouse.

Seth opened the door and walked inside. "Hey baby! I told you I'd be home on time! I have an idea for some predinner entertainment." Seth unbuttoned his shirt as he walked through the house.

Seth opened the terrace door to find Morgan sitting in a lounger, looking out at the city.

She turned to him and smiled. "How was your commercial shoot? And why are you half naked?"

"Commercial went well. Was on my way to seduce you." Seth took a seat on the lounger and laid back into her arms. "How was your interview?"

Morgan sighed. "Dana wanted me to dangle you like a publicity carrot. I declined. I have a feeling her interest in returning my calls began when she found out we were married."

"Is there anything I can do?"

"You're doing it right now." She wrapped her arms around him.

"What's your action plan?"

"I keep going until I achieve my goal. Failure is just an opportunity to exceed your limitations to succeed."

"Wow, you did read my book. But seriously I would love to help." What was the harm in a little push?

"You want to help, then you can boil the linguine and maybe give me a nice back rub after dinner."

* * *

The Main Street Clinic's main number illuminated the display on Seth's cell phone. Penny had called him three times in the past month. Each time he saw her personal number he'd sent it to voicemail. There was a time when he would have been elated to see her face pop up on the display screen. But he had long since deleted her picture. He wondered if it was the happiness she had sensed when she'd seen him that motivated her to call. She had never bothered to call when he was dating Melanie or the two women that preceded her. They had crossed paths at the banquet fundraiser last year, and she'd made a snide comment about his latest dish de jour. He had taken pleasure in her obvious jealousy, but she always had the upper hand, knowing someone like Melanie became his type after the fame took over his personal life. Her place, in what was left of his trampled heart, had always been secure. When he saw her that night at the Bright Star, that confident expression she usually wore was absent. Morgan was not some model or actress. She was a natural beauty and utterly real. That was what he loved about her.

He ignored Penny's call once again. And he did a pretty good job of avoiding talk of Penny and the clinic. Until the invitation to the annual Main Street Clinic banquet in Texas arrived via messenger.

He had been certain, after the Cinnamon Festival, he wasn't going this year. But Morgan would surely see the invitation, and he didn't want to hide it from her.

"Did you get the package the messenger dropped off?" Morgan said as he walked into the kitchen.

"I did." Seth casually placed the invitation on the table.

"Fancy." She examined the invitation.

He fidgeted and crossed his arms. "The clinic has a fundraiser banquet every year."

"Do you want to go?"

"No. I can just send a check." He reached out and touched her hand.

"It says here you will be there and that you will be part of the bachelor auction." Morgan showed him the bottom of the invitation.

"Damnit, I forgot all about that."

"What services were you offering at this auction?" She smiled sly and winked at him.

He laughed and pulled her close to him. "Usually a date with the winner."

"I've been to one of these. It's usually a candlelit dinner or something romantic."

"I've been to a few of these too and one year a guy named Reynard outbid all the women at the event."

"Oh my." She laughed. "What did you do? Take him out for a beer?"

"No, he still wanted to go out for the romantic candlelit dinner."

She giggled. "Well, it was in the name of charity."

Seth shook his head. "I can't participate this year. I am no longer a bachelor. I am happily married." He waved his wedding band at her.

Morgan clasped his hand within hers and held it to her chest. "It's to raise money for the clinic. I wouldn't mind a lunch in the middle of a crowded restaurant. And if the winner is eighty-nine, even better."

He couldn't help the start of a smile. "I'm sure Momma would love to have us visit again. And you get to see Reed's Fire."

Morgan glanced back down at the invitation. "And Tate. Looks like he's on the menu too."

"Tate loves these events. Last time we did an event together, a group of his fans pooled their money. He went missing for two weeks." He laughed.

"What happened?"

"Listen to his third CD. There's a track on there called 'I Lost My Soul at the Candlewood Hotel in Houston.' He was being literal."

Morgan gasped. "That sweet, handsome, blond-haired angel?"

"Hey, I forbid you to call another man handsome. Especially if he's my best friend. I could tell you some stories about Tate and that guitar."

"It sounds like the two of you are neck and neck with the infamy. Wild parties, hot women. How you two managed to have successful careers is incomprehensible."

"My dad always said it was OK to play hard as long as I worked even harder."

Morgan looked down at her hand meshed with his. "You didn't always play hard. You had Penny."

He pulled her closer. "Believe me, being with Penny was harder than sowing my wild oats with Tate."

"I thought the hard relationships were the most passionate." She looked up and searched his face.

"No, the hard relationships are just exhausting and lead nowhere."

She held his gaze. "I'm OK with going to the banquet. I know Penny's going to be there. And I also know that you love me."

"And I always will, Morgan."

Seth knew, after that statement, his plan to tell her about Penny's phone calls was shot to hell.

Chapter Five

Morgan's cell phone rang as she was shelving inventory in the stockroom. She hit the call button so fast on her phone she neglected to look at the caller ID.

"Morgan!" a shrill voice yelled her name like it was a disease. Shit. "What do you want Charisma?"

"I want you to stop telling the family I sold my story to a tabloid to make money off you."

Morgan climbed down the ladder in the stockroom. "I did no such thing. And it wasn't a big stretch the family figured it out. Everyone knows how money hungry you are."

"That's not true!"

"Sure it is. Didn't you brag not too long ago about having a ball player in your pocket and you were planning to get knocked up with his baby so he'd marry you?"

"I don't know what the hell you are talking about."

"Sure you don't. I think grandma even threw out her turkey baster because of you. Everybody knew you'd do whatever it took."

"I'm tired of hearing about the legend of the great Morgan. I can only imagine what you did on that island to trick Seth Blake into marrying you."

Morgan scoffed. "So that's what's bothering you. That must sting. Your bookworm cousin usurped your ass and you can't stand it."

"You're trying to ruin Jason's reputation. People are calling him a chump for losing you to Seth Blake. Rob's cop buddies keep giving him traffic tickets for no reason."

Morgan wanted to laugh at that but her blood pulsed hot fury through her veins. "Were we not at the same party? Jason dumped me, in front of our whole family with you, my cousin, happily in tow. What I'm hearing is that the humiliation you thought you were going to inflict on me didn't quite pan out. We've been doing this all our lives, Charisma. You were always somewhere trying to steal a boy or sabotage me in some way. Now you're mad because everybody knows how nasty you've always been to me."

"You little bitch, you need to stop spreading lies about me or you may find some more unflattering information about you in the media again."

Morgan exhaled. "Luckily for me I've led a relatively boring life. Seth's been living his life on the front page for years. There is nothing you can say that's going to change what you did or how you did it. But I do have some advice for both of you. If you ever want to have kids with Jason, keep him away from me."

Morgan jabbed at her phone and ended the call.

"Charisma?" Michelle leaned in from the doorway. "You don't really think she knows what the word 'usurp' means, do you?"

Morgan and Michelle both erupted in a fit of giggles.

Morgan shook her head. "What was I thinking? I wasted a good word on that bitch."

Michelle shrugged. "She may have stolen Jason, but you stole her moment and in a very public fashion. For somebody as self-centered as her, it's gotta sting."

"She's tried crap like this all our lives."

Michelle sighed. "Family."

"Yeah, family."

Michelle motioned to the front of the store. "By the way, boss, there's someone here to see you."

"Who is it?"

"I don't know but whoever she is I feel like a rich billionaire is going to come through the door looking for her with a marriage proposal."

Morgan raised an eyebrow, intrigued. "Looks that good?"

"Fresh off the page of a fashion magazine."

Morgan located her mystery guest in the health section. "Hello, I'm Morgan. And you are?"

"Hi, I'm Nina Hawkes, Patton's wife."

Morgan agreed with Michelle, Nina Hawkes did look like she'd just stepped off the pages of a haute couture magazine. Her long, curly brown hair lay perfectly over her shoulders. She wore a chic black form fitting dress that showed every curve she had. Her skin was a smooth creamy caramel color and her makeup was flawless. She stood at least five seven with her three inch heels and had the posture of a supermodel. Nina was the kind of woman Seth had been seen with often. Sometimes, when Morgan was alone in the store room she would do an internet search on him. Partly to see if any pictures of the two of them had surfaced yet. There weren't any of them but there were plenty of former girlfriends and most of them looked like Nina.

Morgan managed to smile. "Pleasure to meet you, Nina. Seth speaks very highly of you. We're going to have you and Patton over for dinner soon."

"I'm looking forward to that."

Morgan escorted Nina to the café and gave her a coffee. Visions of Seth and Patton conspiring to find her a friend danced around in her head. She loved Seth and thought Patton was the sweetest man she'd ever met, but she knew men thought women becoming friends was as simple as how they did it.

The conversation started a bit awkward at first but once they got going, Morgan relaxed and Nina's shoulders lost their tension.

She listened to Nina talk about Seth, and she could feel Nina's genuine, friendly interest in him. It was obvious they spent a lot of time together, but she had already known that from when Seth had come to the African American festival with Patton and two of the other players from the team.

"So did Seth and Patton lay it on thick to get you to come here?" Morgan laughed.

Nina smiled and sipped her coffee. "Not really. I would have done it anyway. But those two think the world is a football field. They create a play then yell out for someone to execute it."

Morgan shook her head. "I thought it was just me. Seth isn't good with letting the pot simmer." A customer walked up to the counter and Morgan stood. "Excuse me for one second."

"Sure. Go ahead." Nina waved her off with a smile.

She left a moment to help the customer, then returned. When she sat back in her seat, she caught Nina staring at her. "Something wrong, Nina?"

"Forgive me for being blunt, but you were not what I imagined."

"Oh. What were you expecting?"

"Some uptight, middle class, bourgeois, social climbing, prissy bitch."

Morgan smirked. "You must be thinking of Seth's ex-girlfriend."

Nina laughed. "Well, since I've narrowly escaped insulting you, how about lunch sometime this week?"

Morgan gave her a genuine smile. "I'd like that."

* * *

Morgan opted to skip the run with Seth before going to the library. Well, he ran and she walked. He asked if he could go with her to the library again, and she happily said yes. They'd spent the day before in a shopper's warehouse, getting supplies for the bookstore and snacks for the kids for the reading hour. She had a feeling it was his first time shopping in a bulk warehouse because every time she turned around he'd put something in the cart he had absolutely no use for. The staff did the shopping and she'd never seen them run out of anything. Finally she had to tell Seth to pick one thing he wanted to buy. It took him fifteen minutes to decide between a fifty pack of tooth brushes or a case of ink cartridges.

She turned on the television in the walk-in closet while she searched for something to wear. She thought she heard his name, so she turned up the volume. The one morning she decided it was OK to watch the news, Seth's face jumped off the screen.

A reporter spoke while the camera focused on pictures of Seth. "Sources report that this is another surprising turn of events for the Super Bowl champion. Vivian Carbone has been Blake's publicist for more than five years now. Sources say they split after Vivian made some disparaging remarks about his new bride in public. Blake fired her. He then issued a warning to his employees: talk about Morgan and you'll get the axe."

She stood there for a moment, almost not believing what she'd just heard. Seth hadn't mentioned it to her.

"Just give me a half hour and then we're off to the library." Seth peeled off his clothes as he headed for the bathroom.

"Did you fire your publicist?"

He stopped. "How did you hear about that?"

She shook the remote in her hand. "Made the mistake of turning on the television."

He sighed. "Yes, I did."

"The news report said she made disparaging remarks about me so you fired her."

Seth's jaw clenched. "Disparaging is a polite word but yes, she did. I didn't need her approval to marry you, and she forgot which one of us was the client. I'm not doing business with anybody who thinks they can say whatever they want about my wife and there not be consequences."

"What did she say?"

"It doesn't matter."

Unfortunately, for some reason it mattered to her. "Vivian has been with you for a while right?"

"There is no choice between you and a misguided employee." Seth reached out and rubbed her cheek.

"Do you ever wonder—"

"No."

Morgan's next question was smothered with a tender kiss. Seth's attempts to quell her questions worked. By the time Morgan had run out, she was enjoying a shower with him.

* * *

Morgan normally made her way into the children's section of the library without a fuss but today a crowd blocked her path.

Seth followed her, carrying her bags. "Looks like you have a big turn out today."

"No, there must be another event." But there was indeed a line forming at the children's room door. Confused, Morgan waved over one of the librarians. "Hey, Harriet, what's going on?"

"These people are here for story time. There's a photographer and a reporter from the *Philadelphia Style* and I think a news crew has set up. Isn't this exciting?"

Morgan looked at Seth, who took her by the hand and led her around the corner.

"Breathe."

She took a big gulp of air then exhaled. "I think the reporter that came to the bookstore that day is in there."

Seth nodded. "I told my new publicist, Daniel, about you being accosted at the bookstore. After he called and ripped *Philadelphia Style* a new asshole, he made a deal with them. He told them you're a passionate community advocate who reads at the story hour at the library and that's where their story is."

"Daniel, huh?" She smiled.

"He has an outstanding reputation. Vivian was jealous of him."

Morgan wrapped her arms around her middle. "I hate being in the spotlight."

"I know you do. From time to time we will be in front of cameras, part of my life dictates that. But the good news is it sounds like you won't want to do a reality show. The wife of one the guys on the team is on that NFL Wives show."

She laughed. "I wouldn't presume I'd be that interesting."

"It's just another Sunday. The kids are waiting for you to read them a story. You really get them involved when you read to them. Nothing else matters but spending time with them."

"OK." Morgan exhaled. "Team Blake is ready to go."

He looked at her, his eyebrow raised.

"I just imagine you saying something like that when you're in a huddle."

"I'd like to believe I'm a little more eloquent than that. As a matter of fact I've been known to give moving speeches."

"Just kiss me."

He took her face in his hands and kissed her hard. Morgan waded through the crowd and found her three faithful patrons and about twenty more kids. She took her seat in the old red beanbag chair and pulled out the latest book.

"Today we are going to read about Benny the Bunny and his trip to New York City..."

When the kids started clapping, the reporter, photographer, and the camera crew faded away. Seth was putting out juice and graham crackers on a nearby table. Morgan laughed to herself, thinking how long she'd tried to get people to bring their kids to the library.

* * *

Seth stayed in the back, trying not to divert the attention away from Morgan's reading to the kids. When he had told Daniel about the incident with the reporter at the bookstore, he had been impressed by Daniel's ability to make it work in her favor. He worried about her being ambushed or thrust into the limelight. All she wanted to do was raise money for the library programs and it was clear she didn't want to take any from him.

Out of the corner of his eye Seth spotted Harriet, the elderly librarian, coming in with a stack of trays, so he greeted her at the door and placed them on the table next to the snacks.

"Thank you, dear."

"My pleasure, ma'am. Is there anything else I can help you with?"

"Yes, there's a box of flyers I wanted to give Morgan before she left today. Can you help me with them?"

"Show me the way." He smiled at her.

They slipped out of the room and walked toward the administrative office.

"Morgan is such a sweetheart. I would hate to think what would happen if the library couldn't continue the reading hour. She loves it more than the kids." Harriet laughed.

"She does get a lot of pleasure out of it."

"She's very good with kids." Harriet winked at him.

"She is an excellent story teller."

"Well, it's in her genes. Her mother would pack a crowd in here when it was her time to read."

"Her mother?"

"Yes, Elizabeth Reed was a librarian here many years ago. She would bring Morgan to work with her. Elizabeth would read to Morgan on her breaks and the kids in the library would flock around her. Pretty soon it became a ritual. We had an unofficial reading hour for a long time before someone took notice and decided to give us funding for it." Harriet led him over to a wall covered in framed photos. "Here's a picture of the two of them."

Seth looked at the picture Harriett pointed to. Morgan must have been about five years old and sitting in the lap of a woman who looked just like her. They had the same sweet smile and bright eyes. They were sitting on a bright red beanbag.

"Would you believe that's the same beanbag she's sitting on now? Morgan insists on keeping it. Whenever it tears she takes it home, repairs it and brings it right back. Elizabeth would have been so proud of her. Morgan fought to get her bookstore off the ground. She even fought with herself to come back here to the library. She stayed away for a long time after her mother died. Sometimes I would see her sitting outside on the steps, but she would never come inside. Then one day, she walked in and declared she wanted to volunteer here. Of course I said yes. She's been crusading ever since about the importance of reading and how it sparks the imagination."

Seth and Harriet made their way back to the reading room just as Morgan was getting to the end of the book. Now he knew why she didn't talk about her mother that much. The pain of losing her mother was infused with her crusade. If only she'd just take the money he would readily give her. There had to be something he could do to make her see she didn't have to fight all the time.

Chapter Six

The team was holding a party to kick off the new season. Seth informed Morgan that his attendance was mandatory, but he assured her it wasn't a big deal. It was a chance for the team to catch up with each other and toast the coming year. After she settled her nerves she'd decided to ask Nina for some help. They'd been out to lunch a few times after their first meeting and Nina seemed to pop up at the bookstore every so often. Morgan reached for her phone and called her.

"Hey, Nina. I hope I didn't catch you at a bad time."

"You didn't. I have a few minutes before my next appointment and this client is never on time." Nina laughed.

"Your client?"

"I own an event planning company."

"Oh. Wow." Morgan bit her lip. She didn't mean to sound so surprised that Nina had a job.

"I bet you thought I just flitted around town spending Patton's money?" Nina cooed.

"Well, yes, to be honest, and quite fashionably in your Christian Louboutin's." She laughed.

"Patton gave me the money to start up and after some networking it paid off. I developed a little client base after the people who were trying to be nice to Patton sloughed off. You know, I envy that about you. You had your bookstore and your community projects going before you met Seth. No one is ever going to think he did anything for you."

"But like you said, you've made it into something of your own." She didn't want Nina to think she was judging her.

"Patton would have bought me a rocket to get to space if he thought it would take my mind off my obsession with babies. That's the only thing he can't give me. Nothing on his part. My body won't cooperate."

Morgan fumbled for a way to respond. "I'm so sorry to hear that."

"You did not call to hear about my fertility issues. What's up?" Nina's voice picked up.

"I was hoping you'd have some time to help me shop for a dress for that team party that's coming up? The last thing I want is to be the laughing stock on some gossip show."

"So you want to make a stunning debut?"

"I don't want to end up in somebody's what not to wear column." Morgan laughed.

"When I'm finished with you they're going to send you to Milan for a fashion shoot."

* * *

Nina picked her up the morning of party, stating they were going to make a day of it. She insisted on getting Morgan a full spa treatment to relax her nerves. They had lunch and talked for a bit before going back to Nina's house to get dressed.

"How long does it take you to get ready every morning?" Morgan joked as she squirmed in her chair.

"My husband would say too long, but he never complains about the finished product. There." Nina applied the last bit of mascara to Morgan's eyelashes.

Nina slid the mirror to Morgan, who was at a loss for words.

"If you're speechless imagine how Seth's going to react."

Morgan eyed her reflection in the mirror. "I don't know if he's going to recognize me."

"Great!"

"Not great. You're good Nina but this isn't me." She sighed.

Nina put the mirror down. "Can I be honest with you?"

"More so than the past two months?"

"Yes."

Curiosity got the better of Morgan. "Go ahead."

Nina grabbed a few of her makeup brushes and placed them back in the case. "I learned the hard way about all this fame shit. Being the spouse that's not in the limelight is hard. The key is to let all the garbage in the media fall away and concentrate on your marriage. You know Seth. He's a good man. Just have faith in the vows you took and ignore the rest of it."

Morgan frowned. "Nina, how bad is it? I don't think you're telling me this as a public service announcement."

Nina fiddled with her makeup case. "I've seen the wives of some of the other players say things to him you wouldn't hear in a porn movie. You have an opportunity tonight to let everybody know that Seth's off the market and it's a bad idea to mess with your marriage."

"Thank you for the advice." Morgan hesitated but then lifted a gift bag and placed it on the table.

"What's this?"

"A thank you for helping me get ready." After spending some time with Nina and a few prodding questions to Seth, she had a good idea of the hell Nina was going through miscarrying those babies. "There were three great books on difficult pregnancies that I thought you might like to read. In this book" — Morgan pointed to a book titled *Late Bloomer* — "the woman tried to get pregnant for fifteen years and then boom; she got knocked up at age forty two. Go figure. But it's about the spiritual journey she took as a result of not being able to have a baby exactly when she wanted one. She said when she finally gave up on her dream, a miracle happened. Maybe you can get your miracle someday."

Nina's jaw had dropped open. "Thank you, Morgan." Tears glistened in Nina's eyes and then she hugged Morgan. "I can't believe you are making me cry and we are on our way to a party."

Morgan laughed but hugged back.

* * *

Seth didn't usually mind the team parties, but he was not looking forward to this one. The subtle snipes, the fake smiles, it was all part of this world when he was in front of the camera. He had managed to have an intimate book release party; they had a good time with family and friends. But this crowd of brazen jug heads could break up a marriage easily. Hell, it already had. Tim Seaver's wife had thrown a chair through a glass door last year when she caught some groupie giving him a hand job in the bathroom. Elton Chatz had to have physical therapy for months after trying to intervene in a cat fight between his new girl and his baby momma at one event. Seth did not want reality entertainment becoming part of his life.

Patton greeted him with a hug. "Hey man, you nervous?"

"Nah, I'm just curious where our wives are. I thought I'd get to talk to Morgan before this evening started. Wanted to tell her to just ignore anything stupid she might see or hear tonight."

"I wouldn't worry about it. Nina will be around. I think they're becoming friends." Patton smiled.

Seth smiled back, happy to know Morgan and Nina were developing a friendship of their own. Patton waved over a few of their teammates. They joked and talked about the upcoming season, all of them anxious to get back to work. He grabbed a mini quiche on the serving tray as it went by and a glass of champagne. Suddenly his teammates went silent except Lamont Brayer.

"Damn. Who is that?"

Seth didn't bother looking up but Patton's nudging implied he should. They were surrounded by beautiful women all the time but it never stopped them from checking out fresh meat. But it was Morgan's entrance that was causing a ruckus. His mouth went dry when he saw her wearing a beautiful black, one shoulder dress that hugged her frame all the way down to the short hemline that stopped just above her knee. The black, three inch open toe heels she wore showcased her pretty toes and brought attention to her well defined legs. Her skin had a silky glow to it. Her hair was blown out, with a few scattered curls, and she'd done something to her eyes, because they looked more dramatic, her long lashes more pronounced. Red lipstick adorned her full, pouty mouth.

"I'd like to lick those candy apple lips," Lamont Brayer said.

Seth snapped out of his daydream. "What did you say, Brayer?"

"I said—"

"That's my wife and if you go anywhere near her, I'll kick your ass."

Patton put a crushing hand on Lamont's shoulder. "I think you owe the man an apology."

"Shit, Blake, I didn't know. Sorry. No disrespect intended but I didn't know your wife was that damn hot."

Patton squeezed harder. "Lamont, you were almost home free."

* * *

Morgan shook so much from nerves walking through the room she grabbed Nina's hand. "See, he looks confused."

Nina laughed. "No, that's not confusion getting bigger in his pants."

Morgan made her way over to Seth, who looked good enough to eat in his charcoal gray suit. It fit him like a second skin, like most things did over those defined muscles. He had his hair spiked up a little tonight and he'd shaved. Clean shaven or with a five o'clock shadow, it didn't matter to her. His scent was the combination of body gel, shampoo, and cologne. It melded into something utterly masculine and only he smelled that way.

He stared at her but didn't say a word. Patton did the introductions of their teammates. Not that she heard the names, but she managed to shake hands. Her gaze was glued on the only man who remained silent within the group. Those green eyes seemed to be getting darker by the second as he kept his gazed fixed on her. At some point Nina turned Morgan's hand loose and grabbed Patton's, and everyone eventually scattered, leaving her alone with her mute husband.

"Now is not the time for you to go silent on me. What do you think?"

Morgan tried to do a discreet turn to show him her dress but Seth caught her mid turn, slipping his hand around her waist and pulled her against him.

"Don't make another move or this is going to be the most embarrassing night of my life," he drawled into her ear.

Seth stood at full attention between them.

She grinned and slid her arms around him. "Does this mean you like my dress?"

He looked down at her and swallowed hard. "You're killing me, Morgan."

"You look…incredible in that suit." She played with his tie.

"I look like a vagrant compared to how beautiful you look tonight. I already threatened Lamont for making a crass remark about you."

"This outfit comes with a hitch I'm afraid. I will need a huge favor when we get home."

Seth looked like he would fight an army for her. "Anything."

"I am going to need a really good foot massage. These heels are tortuous."

He smiled. "I can't tell by the way you gracefully floated over here."

"I got a crash course at Nina's charm school." Morgan laughed.

* * *

As Nina navigated Morgan through the party, introducing her to some of the player's wives and girlfriends, a stunning woman in a silver gown, her blond hair perfectly coiffed on her head and a diamond necklace hanging around her neck, glided up to them.

"Morgan Blake, right?" The woman extended an elegant hand. "You're the talk of the town these days. I'm Jocelyn Fontane, pleasure to make your acquaintance."

Morgan shook hands on autopilot. She had read articles about Jocelyn Fontane. Not only was she wife of the owner of the Titans, but she was pretty active in the community. Jocelyn Fontane was just the person who could open doors to help her with her literacy campaign but it didn't feel like the right time to talk about it.

"It's a pleasure to meet you, Mrs. Fontane."

"Please, call me Jocelyn. Morgan, tell me more about yourself? Seth told me you have quite a few irons in the fire."

A golf ball-sized lump formed in Morgan's throat. Nina made eyes at her to answer Jocelyn.

"Well, I own Reed Books. It's a small bookstore but we have a huge inventory. I read in the children's room at the library every other Sunday. I would like to start up a reading initiative again. There are still a lot of people out there who cannot read, even in this day and age."

Jocelyn tilted her head and gave Morgan a different look from before. A little surprised perhaps, and more than a little impressed. "That's a noble cause you have, Morgan."

Morgan shrugged, the lump in her throat still refusing to budge. "I like to believe it's my responsibility to do what I can."

Jocelyn extended her hand again. "It was a pleasure meeting

you. I knew when Seth finally settled down he'd find a woman of great character."

Morgan swallowed. "Thank you."

She and Nina watched as Jocelyn Fontane floated away.

Morgan palmed her face but then remembered she shouldn't smudge her makeup. "Oh god, I was rambling like an idiot." Morgan felt eyes on her. She looked over to a crowd of women who were giving her the once over.

Nina looked too. "They're jealous. Getting close to Jocelyn Fontane is not easy. She hates phony people."

Morgan felt her heart slowing from high gear back to normal. "She's a nice lady. I think she actually cared about what I had to say." She shot a glance back at the crowd of women who were still glaring at her. "Unlike them, I imagine."

* * *

Morgan and Seth left the party not much later. As soon as the driver closed the limousine door, Morgan straddled Seth and planted a passionate kiss on him.

Morgan sighed. "I think instead of the foot massage, I'm going to need a full body massage."

"Is that right?"

"That's right." She purred as Seth pulled her closer until she sat over the big bulge in his pants.

Morgan began to grind against him as she slid his suit jacket off his broad shoulders. The smooth motion of the limousine coupled with Seth's deliberate movements was sending sensual shock waves to her system. The sensations came in crashing waves as Seth manipulated her clit, rubbing her in small clockwise circles, suddenly stopping then resuming counter clock wise. It was hard for her body to keep up with his teasing rhythm. Her body would build up only to have to wind down and adjust to the new direction he was taking her in. Damn, he knew how to play her body like a harp, strumming and picking at the right spots to hit the right chord. She tugged on his belt, then unbuttoned and unzipped his pants, liberating his massive erection from his designer boxer briefs.

She groaned. "Your hand should be a registered as a lethal weapon."

"So should your—"

Morgan slapped his arm before he could finish.

She could feel her whole body blush, a warm tingly feeling that began in her toes, traveled up her legs and settled at the center of her body. Her skin felt like a live wire, each nerve ending open and gearing up for the climax that would eventually come when he finished having his tortuous way with her. When he lovingly nipped at her skin while making a sensuous trail of moisture down her breasts, she shuttered and started to whimper. In her heated frenzy, she still managed to remove his tie and unbutton his shirt. She wanted to see his tanned skin, to see those chiseled pecks and granite abs. It was hard to admit looking at his body made her feel like a school girl who'd never seen a man before. He had a raw, smoldering sexual appeal that was never lost on her. Whenever they gave in to the libidinous aspect of their connection, that was when she was glad there was more to them than an intellectual relationship. She appreciated a smart man, and thank god he was, but she was fortunate enough to get the extras too.

Seth pulled her onto his lap, slid his hand under the hemline of her dress, and made his way underneath her lace panties. He slid two fingers inside her, while his thumb ran slowly across her clit.

Seth reached over and hit the intercom button with his free hand. "Charlie, why don't you take us on a tour of the city? We're in no rush."

Charlie laughed. "No problem, Mr. Blake."

When Morgan liberated him from his trousers, Seth gripped

her hips and lifted her up and slowly lowered her onto his penis. His body convulsed from the skin to skin contact. She was always so tight and fit him like a glove. Each time he made natural contact with his wife, the world faded away. The first time had been in Texas, the night she had gotten drunk off Bodine's bathtub whiskey. Morgan had stripped off everything except those cowboy boots and rode him au natural.

His body rocked in rhythm with Morgan's riding motions, the muscles in his legs and thighs becoming taut. Making love to her was more intensive than his football training. How such a petite woman was able to elicit such arduous performances from him was amazing. He'd never worked so hard or so tenderly to please a woman in his life. There was always something new to learn about her. When she rocked forward Seth caught her breasts in his hands, taking his time licking and sucking on each nipple. Her body began to tighten around him and Morgan reached up for the closest thing to her, his hair. Seth didn't mind the death grip or the sheen of the sweat forming on her skin. Hell, droplets were forming on his as well.

"Seth," she moaned.

"I love you, Morgan."

The explosion between them ignited, and she collapsed on top of him.

"I love you, too."

* * *

Morgan shifted the stack of books in her hand and wandered down the aisle to find the right section. She started shelving the books when a familiar voice spoke behind her.

"I stopped by a few times but Michelle said you weren't here."

Morgan turned around to see Jason standing at the other end of the aisle. "What do you want Jason?"

"I thought we needed to talk. Just the two of us with no

audience."

"Why do I get that consideration now? You should have done that months ago. Instead of selling your story to the highest bidder." Morgan rolled her eyes and wondered why she was standing there listening to him.

Jason shook his head. "That wasn't me. I can now admit that Charisma and I were a mistake. I didn't want to tell you about us at the barbeque like that, Charisma insisted, saying you spent your whole life acting like you were better than her. I guess she was looking for payback."

"We have been at odds for a long time but if you were listening to me when I complained about her; you would have stayed away from her. Instead you decided to help her humiliate me. I think you should ask yourself why you were willing to do that. I've never done anything so horrible to you to warrant the treatment I received from you."

Jason averted his gaze. "I've been thinking about that. You are always so…aloof. It's off putting sometimes. There was a part of me that was angry with you and wanted to see you hurt. To see that other people around you were capable of making you feel something."

"Even if those feelings were anger and shame?" Morgan clenched her fists.

Jason hung his head. "I didn't say it was a well thought out plan. I saw your picture in the paper. You were at some party. You looked beautiful."

Morgan shifted the books in her arms. "Thanks, I guess. Why did you come here?"

"I'm leaving town. I found a job in Michigan. Being the punch line with my friends and my family is getting old. I need some space."

"I don't know if Michigan is ready for you and Charisma." She laughed.

Jason shook his head. "I'm not taking her with me. I may be a little self-centered but Charisma thinks the sun revolves around her. I was furious when she sold that story to the tabloids. That was the last straw. I don't know what she was trying to accomplish but I figured the two of us had done enough damage to you already."

"That sounds like a good move for you."

"Yeah." He looked at the door. "Morgan, I just wished I could bring out in you what Seth Blake did. His being famous is a sting but it isn't the reason I hate the dude. I would have hated anyone who could pull you out of the shell you were in and make him love you."

"Seth didn't *make* me do anything. You just know when it's the right person to let into your heart."

"Like I said, he was able to do what I wasn't." Jason shrugged.

She waved at him. "Good luck in Michigan."

"Good luck to you too. I wish you and Blake nothing but happiness." Jason hesitated but then walked out of the bookstore.

Morgan stood there for a moment trying to collect her thoughts. Jason hadn't sold her out to the tabloids.

Michelle walked through the front door. "Was that Jason?"

"Yeah."

"What did he want?"

"Maybe forgiveness. He's moving to Michigan without Charisma."

"The state of Michigan dodged a bullet."

Morgan bent down to pick up some bookmarks that had fallen on the floor and a wave of nausea hit her. She groaned in response to her churning stomach.

"Morgan, you all right?"

Morgan excused herself and bee lined it for the bathroom. A half hour later she emerged from the bathroom with a cold compress on her head. Michelle was waiting for her in the office.

"This would be the third time you've hurled in a week,"

Michelle mused as she ate her salad.

"Is not."

"Yes, it is."

Morgan thought about it and realized Michelle was right. She had probably been working too hard, juggling so many projects. She made a mental note to slow down, and failing that, to buy some antacids.

* * *

Morgan had just reached her wits end after yet another failed meeting. The latest person cited budget cuts and there was no money to start another program. At least she didn't ask about Seth. The woman did refer to her as Morgan Blake, but Morgan didn't remember telling the woman her new last name. It was on to the next phase of her plan, if only she knew what it was.

She walked into the stylish boutique to pick up the dress she planned to wear to the banquet. It had taken an afternoon of shopping with Michelle and Nina and threats of wearing a burlap sack if she tried on one more dress until she had found the right one. It was a pink strapless gown with an elegant corset and a long, flowing skirt. Morgan also got a matching shawl in case she lost the nerve to show all her assets that night. When she tried on the gown, she had to go up a size because her normal size six felt snug. She had been feeling a little bloated lately, but she attributed that to all the salty food she'd been craving, probably thanks to Seth's crazy diet.

The sales clerk recognized her immediately and hustled into the back to get her things while another thrust a glass of champagne into her hand and had her sit in an oversized leather chair.

"Morgan?" someone said from the direction of the fitting room.

Morgan got up and peeked around the corner. It was Jocelyn Fontane.

"Jocelyn, hello."

Jocelyn came out in a stunning gown. "What do you think?"

"You look fabulous. As usual." Morgan smiled at her.

"Thank you."

"What's the occasion?" Morgan asked.

"Dinner with the governor." Jocelyn played with the skirt.

"It looks fantastic on you."

The sales clerk brought out Morgan's gown and took it out of the dress bag so she could look it over.

"Morgan, that's beautiful. That color will look stunning on you. Where is Seth taking you?"

She sighed. "To a banquet in Texas."

"Well, you will definitely turn heads in that dress." Jocelyn smiled. "How's the fundraising going for your literacy campaign?"

Morgan sighed again. "Not as quickly as I'd like. But I'm still trudging along." Morgan motioned to the sales clerk she was satisfied with the alterations.

"Did you ever consider starting your own charity?"

Morgan stammered, searching for an answer.

Jocelyn smiled. "When you have the answer to that question, why don't you give me a call?" Jocelyn reached for her purse on the table and pulled out her business card.

Morgan stared blankly at the card in her hand. Jocelyn's sales clerk appeared and told her she had a few more gowns for her to try on. She told Morgan to have a fabulous time at the banquet and disappeared back into the fitting room.

Morgan's own salesclerk walked over. "Mrs. Blake, you're all ready to go. I found some nice barrettes to go with the gown."

"Thank you." She walked out, her mind still far away, thinking about what Jocelyn had said.

Chapter Seven

They arrived at the ranch a few days before the banquet so they could spend some time with Seth's family. As soon as they arrived Morgan climbed over Seth, out of the truck, and headed immediately to the stables to see Reed's Fire. She brushed his mane and fed him carrots, even though Bodine said he'd just eaten. She was having a lovely chat with the horse when out of the corner of her eye she saw Seth. She turned around to find the entire Blake family smiling at her. Morgan hugged Teri-Lyn and apologized to everyone as Seth introduced her to his father, John Jacob, and his brothers, JJ, Tyler, and Channing. Every last one of them was big, handsome, and downright charming.

Bodine asked Morgan if she wanted Reed's Fire saddled so she could ride him, and she happily said yes. Seth was getting ready to ride Iris when his father asked if he could join him. Morgan rode ahead while the two men trailed behind and talked.

"Good to have you home son. We don't see you nearly as much as your mother would like." John Jacob patted his son on the back.

"It's good to be back."

"Ready for the new season?"

Seth smiled but remained silent.

John Jacob let out a hearty laugh. "You got it bad boy. You're usually bouncing off the walls when it's this close to the season starting."

Seth looked on at Morgan, who'd learned how to get the horse to stop for her. She was sitting with her eyes closed, soaking in the sun's rays. "There are worse things that could happen to a man."

"Indeed, there is." John Jacob nodded his head in agreement. "There were some things I wanted to tell you before you got married. I had the same talk with JJ before he got hitched."

"I guess I robbed you of having that talk with me." Seth grimaced.

"It's never too late. We have plenty of time." John Jacob smiled.

* * *

Morgan looked around the dinner table, hoping the Blakes wouldn't notice her exit. Tonight's dinner, Tyler's Fire in the Hole chili was more like a raging inferno in her stomach.

"Excuse me," she said as politely as she could. Then she dashed to the bathroom.

By the time she finished puking her guts out, Morgan was sure she'd had a near death experience. She sat on the floor of the bathroom with a wet guest towel on her neck. There was a light tap at the door, then Teri-Lyn entered.

"Are you OK?"

Morgan smiled. "I think that chili was a little spicy for me."

"Would you believe Tyler turned it down a notch for you?"

"I appreciate it but I think my stomach is no match for the Blake digestive tract."

Teri-Lyn looked Morgan over. "There's something different about you."

"I haven't been getting enough sleep. I've been campaigning for funding for the library and it hasn't been going well. Not to mention the bookstore has been busy and I promised Seth I'd be home at the decent hour every night. We were talking on the way down here and I don't even remember falling asleep halfway through the conversation. He woke me up to tell me we were landing."

"No, that's not it." Teri-Lyn looked her right in the eye.

Morgan tried to shrug but was too exhausted. "I'm sure this country air will put me back on track."

"I'm sure it will. Maybe you should see your doctor about some vitamins or something when you get back."

Teri-Lyn helped Morgan get up from the floor.

"Did someone mention apple pie for dessert?" Morgan asked.

Teri-Lyn smiled. "Sure did."

It startled Morgan when her mother-in-law touched her cheek and laughed at her request for pie. They rejoined the family in the kitchen. Seth seemed so content laughing and joking around with his father and brothers. His smile faded, replaced with concern when he saw Morgan coming back into the kitchen with his mother. Morgan countered Seth's worried look by sticking her tongue out at him. Teri-Lyn cut her a big chunk of pie, so Morgan took a fork out of the drawer, sat on Seth's lap, and shared it with him.

"I think your brother tried to kill me," she whispered.

"Babe, I forgot how Tyler is with the spices." He rubbed her belly.

"I should have known something was awry when I saw him pouring that bottle of Jack Daniels into the pot." She grimaced. She'd actually seen Tyler put at least twenty ingredients in the chili but didn't want to chicken out in front of her burly in-laws.

"I guess I'm just used to his cookin'."

Tyler apologized repeatedly while Channing assured her his turn at the stove would be much better. JJ admitted he couldn't boil water, but he could whip her up a mean peanut butter and jelly sandwich if she was ever in the mood. Her stomach flutters had calmed down by the time she and Seth had finished the pie. But they would return whenever she caught Teri-Lyn smiling at her.

* * *

The ballroom of the Crystal Lily Hotel was nothing short of spectacular. Every fat wallet in Texas was there and that meant the clinic would get more hefty donations. Regardless of why he had become involved with it, Seth was happy the clinic was there for people in need who couldn't afford proper healthcare.

"Seth, good to see you!" Dex Montgomery, the director, shook Seth's hand.

"This is my wife Morgan."

"So good to meet you, Morgan!"

Morgan shook his hand with a smile. "Nice to meet you too."

"This is going to be an epic fundraiser. Tate is here as well. Dear, I hope you don't mind us auctioning off your husband?"

"Not at all. As long as he's returned untouched and in one piece. It's all in the name of charity."

"Good." Dex Montgomery scurried off to tell the auctioneer that Seth had indeed arrived.

"Morgan, you look absolutely ravishing," a familiar voice said behind them.

"Thank you, Tate." Morgan gave him a hug.

"Blake, I can't believe you made it." Tate laughed.

"Morgan suggested I attend." Seth shrugged his shoulders.

"It's a good cause and I get to see you two handsome devils in tuxedos." Morgan smiled.

"Morgan, I won't be offended if you bid on me tonight." Tate winked.

"She's not spending one dime on you, McGill," Seth drawled.

"Gentlemen, we're ready to start the auction." The auctioneer motioned for Seth and Tate to follow her.

* * *

Seth and Tate stood next to the curtain backstage waiting for their cues.

"Is my bow tie straight?" Tate asked.

Seth repositioned it. "Now it is. You look more nervous than when you're performing."

"How'd you get yours so straight?"

"Morgan tied it." He smiled.

"It was very cool of her to let you do this. You hit the jackpot with her."

"I know. I'm going to take her on the date with me. I hope the winning bidder doesn't get upset about it. Are you going to write another song about this auction date too?"

"That's the plan." Tate winked. "Have you seen Penny tonight?"

"No, I didn't but then again I wasn't looking for her." That was true. He'd made up his mind that he was staying as far away from her as he could.

"Oh yeah?"

"Tate, she's called me several times but I didn't answer."

Tate whistled at that. "Our pretty Morgan must have struck a nerve. Penny never could stand to see you happy. That's probably why she stayed with you so long." Tate laughed.

The lights dimmed and the crowd started applauding. It was time for the auction to start.

* * *

Morgan thought she'd seen Penny in the crowd but couldn't be sure. When the lights dimmed and the auctioneer took the stage, she saw Penny, looking radiant in a crimson dress, scooting closer to the front of the stage. The auction began and the crowd went wild. The bidding went by fast; bachelor number five was already on the stage. It was obvious they were saving Seth and Tate for last.

When Tate finally took to the stage, Morgan got to see just how dashing he looked in his tuxedo. Hands flew up so fast the auctioneer could barely keep track. The bid was up to a whopping ten thousand dollars. Morgan was standing next to a group of ten women who were trying to calculate how much money they had all together. The last she heard they were up to thirty-five thousand dollars total but then an argument broke out about how they were going to share Tate. She never did get to listen to that infamous song Seth told her about, but now she was dying to hear it. The bidding slowed down to fifty-five thousand until Tate grabbed the microphone.

"Now ladies, I know you can do better than that. We're trying to make sure the Main Street Clinic has another successful year. I tell you what, I'll even bring my guitar on the date."

There were a few cat calls and someone by the stage made a racy comment about how much fun Tate was bound to be. That fueled Tate's fire and he began to sing *a capella*. The bidding finally ended at eighty thousand dollars. Tate grinned and strode off the stage.

"Our last bachelor for the evening is none other than Texas' favorite football son. For those of you who didn't get to see the cover of the last *Gentlemen's Monthly*, I suggest you take a sedative before you look. Cause that man nearly burned up the pages. Give a warm welcome to Seth Blake!"

Seth walked on stage looking like a hot combination of a cowboy and a secret agent. The auctioneer was smiling so hard she didn't even notice he'd taken the microphone out of her hand.

"Ladies," his deep voice reverberated through the speakers, "I have a confession to make. Many of you don't know that I got married recently and my beautiful wife, Morgan, insisted I do this event because she knew it was for a good cause. Now I can't show you as good a time as Tate can, but I would love to have lunch with one of you."

Morgan thought that would have put a damper on the lust riddled crowd but there was so much yelling and shoving going on, someone nearly knocked her down. Suddenly her consent to send her new hubby up there as fundraiser bait was getting irritating.

"We'll start the bid at a thousand." The auctioneer blushed as Seth draped his arm around her.

Morgan shook her head at him. He winked at her and the crowd went wild again. She found it hard to believe that every single woman in there thought he was winking at them and not his wife.

Paddles started flapping in the air as the bidding quickly catapulted into the ten thousand range.

Suddenly a voice shouted out, "Twenty thousand."

Morgan knew that high pitched twang from the Bright Star: Dr. Penny Winterbourne.

Oh, hell no.

The other bidders remained engaged and the price kept climbing. Penny would not be out done and waved her paddle.

"Eighty thousand dollars."

The look Seth directed at Penny was not a happy one, but he didn't lose his cool. The auctioneer continued but no one else answered when she asked for eighty-five thousand. Morgan stood there, trying to get a grip on the situation. Penny was sticking it to her, in public, because she was mad that Seth wasn't sticking it to *her* anymore.

"Excuse me ladies, can I borrow your paddle?" Morgan said to the group of ten deflated women who couldn't match Penny's bid.

One of the women sadly turned it over. "Good luck, sweetheart. The crimson queen up there looks like she's loaded."

Morgan held up the paddle. "Ninety thousand."

Penny looked back at her but held up her paddle again. "Ninety-five thousand."

"One hundred thousand."

"One hundred twenty thousand."

The auctioneer's repeat of Penny's bid boomed in Morgan's

ears. Penny turned and gave her a small smirk. Seth looked like he wanted to jump off the stage and throttle Penny. Morgan's heart was beating so hard she could hear it in her ears. It wasn't about the fact that her husband was standing up on the stage about to fall into the evil clutches of an ex-girlfriend, it was about how all of it made her feel. The only thing she could compare it to at the moment was getting a favorite toy taken away when she was a child. That was ridiculous because Seth wasn't a toy. He was a man. The same man that had purposely run into her on the beach to get her attention. He wanted her. She didn't have to spring some trap to lure him her way. She felt silly for getting into a bidding war with Penny. It was time to put an end to her civilized battle.

"One million dollars," Morgan said, trying to sound as casual as possible. As soon as she said it her stomach started doing flip flops, but the look of horror on Penny's face was worth the million bucks already.

"One million going once, going twice, sold to the pretty lady in the pink dress."

* * *

Morgan wrote a check to the auctioneer. There were plenty of people crowding around her, now that everyone knew she was Seth's wife. She had a new fan club made of the ten women whose paddle she had borrowed. She graciously thanked them for lending her the paddle then informed them that they were going to spend the day with Seth.

When she was finally able to get away from the crowd, her hands were shaking.

"Baby, what's wrong?" Seth asked.

"I just wrote a check for a million dollars." She breathed heavily.

"Feels good don't it?" Tate smiled.

"I think I'm going to be sick." She looked at Seth.

The room was getting stuffy, and she felt like she was swirling about on a carousel. Morgan high tailed it to the ladies' room just in time to get to a stall and save her lovely pink dress from being ruined. She leaned against the door afterward, her skin feeling clammy. Had she eaten today? Preparing for the banquet had taken all day. She had wanted to look her best, especially knowing Penny would be there.

The click of the restroom door gave her hope the ladies that had been in there when she had sprinted in had left. She just wanted to splash some cold water on her face and find Seth. Morgan clutched her rumbling stomach. That wasn't going to happen any time soon.

"Are you OK? Someone said you were in here throwing up?" Penny said as she walked toward Morgan.

"I'm fine. What are you doing?" She backed away.

"I just want to take a look at you." Penny still came at her.

"I don't think so. You couldn't diagnose a hang nail for me." Morgan held up her hand.

"I told Seth and Tate I would come in and make sure you were OK." Penny hunched her shoulders.

"That must have been painful for you." Morgan smirked.

"I take my oath as a doctor very seriously. And the way both men were concerned about you, I had to see for myself if you were all right." Penny put her hand on her hip.

"Bet you were wishing I was dead, right?"

Penny clutched her throat. "What a horrible thing to say."

"Not as horrible as pretending to be the pious doctor. I did outbid you after all."

"Oh that? This is a fundraiser. I was trying to get the crowd hot and bothered so they would bid high." Penny turned to wash her hands.

Morgan dug her nails into her palm. "You keep telling yourself that."

"I don't have to explain myself to you. Besides you were the one who outrageously drove up the bidding price." Penny smirked.

"I would think, since the money will be going directly to the clinic, you wouldn't consider it outrageous."

"Of course the donation means a lot. But you didn't have to let the world know how insecure you are. If I had won, what's the harm of one date with an old friend?"

"If your old friend Seth was still so accessible to you then you wouldn't have had to bid for a date." Morgan leaned on the wall for support. The nausea was coming back.

"He loves me. He always has. He goes off and distracts himself with women, but he always comes back to me. You remember that while you're biding your time until he leaves you." Penny dried her hands with a paper towel and threw it in the trash.

"If you really loved him at all, you would have never left him. But the real question is, if he still loved you, why did he let you leave and didn't try to win you back?" Morgan retrieved her purse off the sink and pushed past Penny. As she moved along the corridor she saw a chair at the entrance. It was only a few feet away but her feet felt like lead and the clamminess returned. Now dizziness was setting in and the corridor spun. Morgan collapsed before she reached the chair.

Chapter Eight

Morgan's eyes opened to find a very weary looking Seth sitting on her hospital bed. His bow tie was missing and his five o'clock shadow was beginning to show. The room was quiet except for the thunderous sound of the intravenous drip echoing through the room. The memory of their first meeting flashed in her mind but this time there were no sandy beaches and palm trees dancing in the wind.

She smiled. "Déjà vu."

"Morgan," was all Seth was able say as he leaned in and kissed her.

"This is so embarrassing." She blushed. She was in a hospital gown and her pretty pink dress was hanging in the open closet.

"You scared the hell out of me." Seth cupped her face in his hands.

"Sorry. I've been burning the candle at both ends. Where's your family?"

"In the waiting room. Aggravating the hell out of the hospital staff."

"I see they're giving me fluids." She took a look at the label on the IV bag.

"Yes, they said you were dehydrated. They also ran some tests. The doctor will be in any moment."

Morgan took his hand and brought it to her heart. "Hey, you

look shaken. I just passed out. Unless I did it in an undignified way. Did my dress fly up in the air?"

"No. But you did look like Sleeping Beauty." He smiled.

"I can live with that."

A big bearded man entered the room wearing green scrubs. "Mrs. Blake, so glad to see you're awake. I'm doctor Engle. Don't mind me, I was finishing up in surgery when the nurse told me she heard you talking to Mr. Blake. Thought I'd pop in to give you the results. We took blood and had it rushed to the lab."

Morgan smiled. She wondered which Blake had insisted her blood work be rushed. "Thank you for taking such quick action."

"No worries, dear." Dr. Engle grinned. "Now I have the results here. It's pretty big news."

Morgan felt her heart clench. What had she done to herself, running ragged, trying to do too much at once?

"You two are going to be parents."

She gasped, then laughed. She was pregnant? That explained a lot.

"A baby?" Seth grinned as he squeezed her hand.

Morgan smiled, still in shock. "A baby."

Dr. Engle couldn't stop grinning either from the looks of it. "That's right. I am very proud to say I told Seth Blake he's going to be a father. Wait until my golf buddies hear about this." Then he cleared his throat. "But in all seriousness, your husband was telling me you had an issue with chili the other day. And you haven't been eating well. You were a bit dehydrated. I want to start you on prenatal vitamins immediately. From now on you have to eat well, the baby will be cravings those nutrients as well. I'll have the staff bring you in a big breakfast and I want you to continue the IV until tomorrow. So, I would like you to extend your stay for another day. I will be back in two hours to go over a few more things with you. I will send my notes to your OB-GYN in Philadelphia." Dr. Engle zipped out of her room as fast as he'd entered.

"Dr. Dynamo didn't tell us the due date." She turned to Seth as she recovered from the shock of the news to find him with a big, goofy grin on his face.

"Morgan, you don't know how happy you just made me." Seth touched her nose with his.

"I know we just got married and—"

He silenced her with a long, sensuous kiss.

"It looks like she's feeling better or he's giving her mouth to mouth resuscitation," Tate said as he and the whole family filed into the room.

"Leave them alone, boy." Teri-Lyn smiled. "They're celebrating."

"Celebrating what?" John Jacob said.

Seth beamed. "Morgan and I are having a baby."

Between all the hollering, hooting, and hugging, Teri-Lyn made it to the side of the bed and hugged Morgan.

"Honey, I didn't have the heart to tell you that although Tyler's chili can take the paint off a car, you were having classic pregnancy symptoms."

"I must have sounded like an idiot to you."

"Denial is the first stage of pregnancy for new mothers," Teri-Lyn said with a laugh.

"Morgan, honey, any special cravings you been having?" John Jacob asked. "We have to feed my grandson right."

"Or granddaughter," Morgan said.

"Seth, you didn't tell her?" John Jacob glared at him.

"Tell me what?" Morgan looked at Seth.

"Well, baby, boys tend to run in the family. There is probably a girl born once a generation. And your dad had three boys before he had you, so the odds are in the male favor."

She huffed. "Well, there's always a possibility of a girl. None of us here are doctors."

"Sure," all the Blake men said in unison.

* * *

Seth convinced Morgan to stay at the ranch a few more days after she was released from the hospital. He didn't want to take any chances she would get sick on the plane. She wanted to go to the stables to see Reed's Fire, but he had forbidden her to go.

"Did you just ban me from going to the stables?" She clutched one of his trophies in her hand, threatening to throw it.

"Yes, I did. It's dangerous for you to be down there."

"Are you going to be an overbearing daddy during this whole pregnancy? Cause last time I checked you have a job. And it starts in a couple of weeks."

"Yes, ma'am. If I have to bubble wrap you every day before you leave the house, I'll do it."

"If you tried something that idiotic, no more sex for you."

He chuckled. "We both know who'd crumble first."

Morgan yawned. "I'm tired just from arguing with you. I am going to take a nap."

"That sounds good." Seth grinned. "A nice nap."

"First, you have to go and check on Reed's Fire." She folded her arms over her chest.

Seth snorted. "That horse lives in a five star stable and has round the clock care."

* * *

Seth made his way down to the stables after Morgan ran out of steam and finally succumbed to sleep. The doctor had told her it may be a few days before she was back to her normal energy level, but she didn't want to listen. One look in her eyes and he knew she was more tired than she was want to admit. He knew fussing with her would accelerate the process.

He'd been hearing congratulations the last couple of days but each time someone new said it, a sense of happiness filled him again that he couldn't describe.

"He is a beautiful horse," a familiar female voice said from the other side of the stables.

Seth's back stiffened. "This is Morgan's horse."

Penny's lips twitched. "You sure are spoiling that wife of yours."

He nodded. "She's worth it. What are you doing here?"

"I hear congratulations are in order."

Seth laughed. "How did you find out about that?"

"I went by the hospital this morning. I thought I would check up on Morgan, see if she's doing OK."

"She's fine."

"How long do you think that will last? Do you think a baby is going to keep you together? The two of you have nothing in common." Penny walked around the barn, looking at the horses in their stalls.

Seth gritted his teeth. "Forever, if I'm lucky."

Penny sighed. "Are you really happy without me?"

"Things happen for a reason. Everything turned out of the best."

"Did it?"

Seth looked her right in the eye. "I love Morgan."

Penny held his gaze. "You're settling for her and when she finds out it's going to break her heart. Then you're going to have a baby to share."

The blood pounded in his ears at that. "Now wait a damn minute. I didn't *settle* with Morgan."

"Do you forget I've known you all your life? I know being with this woman is different but it's not you."

"You have no idea what I want or need in my life. Not anymore. People grow up and want different things for themselves."

Penny scoffed. "Well, I hope you don't think Ms. Priss is going to move back here on the ranch when you retire from the NFL. You hate Philadelphia."

"I do not hate Philadelphia."

"You would write long emails about how it was so far away and the people were rude. You said you missed home and couldn't wait until you could come back and be on the ranch full time."

Seth glared at her. "I don't think I was giving living in the city a chance because I was so convinced I'd be happy living here with you. What a mistake that was. And you don't get to talk about Morgan like she's some insignificant play thing. She is going to be the mother of my children. She deserves more respect than that from you."

Penny folded her arms. "Why don't you just admit that you still want me? You've always wanted me."

"You always wanted me to want you. We were playing a game and only you had the rulebook." He laughed bitterly.

"It was hard to see you plunged into the limelight and knew it was only a matter of time before someone took you from me."

"I never understood why you didn't give me more credit as a man who loved you. Why would you think it would be so easy to tuck away my feelings for you?"

Penny flipped her hair over her shoulder. "You know how hard I had to fight in high school? Every girl in the school wanted you. The cheerleading squad kidnapped you for heaven's sake and some of those girls were my friends. How long could I expect you to resist temptation at every turn?"

"All you needed was a little faith in me."

"I never stopped loving you, even when I was pushing you away."

"Penny, stomping on my heart was the best thing you could have done for me. It's in the right hands now. I don't worry about Morgan throwing it away. I have found a sense of peace I never had with you. Nothing you can say about the past could make me derail my future."

Penny blinked her eyes rapidly like she was trying not to cry. Seth didn't want her to cry or to even hurt anymore about their relationship. It simply just wasn't worth it.

"Will you continue to contribute to the clinic?" Penny said quietly.

"That clinic is the one thing we didn't manage to screw up. Believe it or not I was proud of you when you opened it and I respect and admire what you've done with it. You did it. You made your dream come true. That reminds me of that little girl I used to know who wanted to save the world. *That* Penny Winterbourne will always be my friend."

"My, my Seth Blake. Look at the man you turned out to be. Love does agree with you. I know you'll be a great father." Penny ran to Seth and hugged him.

"Thanks, Penny."

Seth walked Penny to her car. As she drove off a sense of relief flooded him. This was the closure he had needed so many years ago.

Seth froze when he saw Morgan walking toward him. "Aren't you supposed to be taking a nap?"

"I came down to see what was taking you so long."

"So how much did you hear?"

"Enough." She smiled at him.

He smiled back. "Since you won't be riding for a while, let's take a walk."

Seth and Morgan held hands as they walked around the ranch. Finally, she stopped and rested in Seth's arms under the shade of a huge oak tree not too far from the house.

Seth tucked her head under his chin. "What are you thinking about at this very moment?"

"It's good to be back here. I like cowboy Seth. He's very sexy."

"Is that right?" he drawled.

"That's right. One look at that Stetson and I'm ready to get naked." She giggled.

"You are something else, Morgan Blake." He kissed her.

"It's so beautiful here. You want to move back here permanently someday. Don't you?" She up looked at him.

"I've been thinking about it. Hard. I know it's a lot to ask. But we have plenty of time to talk about it."

"I don't care where we live. I just want to be with you, raising our kids." Morgan leaned into him and squeezed him.

Kids? That sparked something inside him. Seth scooped her up and carried her back to the stables. He locked the door to his office, carried Morgan over to his desk, and placed her on it, but not before he wiped it cleaned of everything, including two trophies.

"Did they break? I'm pretty sure those were important." She looked down on the floor.

"I'll win new ones." He pulled off her jacket and blouse.

Seth ran his hands along her arms then slid down the straps of her bra. It didn't matter what bra she wore, the swell of her breasts falling lusciously out of the soft fabric always sent shivers down his spine. He'd dated women who'd had surgery to look this way. But not his Morgan. She helped by wiggling out of her jeans and panties as he made a slow trek down her hips to remove them.

"You know these are going to get bigger?" she murmured.

"I'm not complaining." He took her nipple into his mouth and suckled it while Morgan unbuttoned his shirt, but she took her sweet time with his jeans. Seth ran out of patience and pulled off his jeans, boxers, and boots all at the same time.

And there they were skin against skin, making contact and promising sensual friction. Her skin a few shades darker than his tan, he imagined the baby's complexion being a culmination of that, and he sighed. His children were going to be the perfect mix of the two of them. He climbed on top of the desk and slid into her.

Seth stilled, barely able to contain the pleasure rippling through his body. "I'm not hurting the baby am I?"

"The baby is fine."

Morgan wrapped her legs tight around his waist and they quickened the rhythm. It was moments before he remembered to breathe. Morgan's moans brought him back to the matter at hand as she began to squirm and grab hold of his back. Seth buried himself deep inside her, then pulled out and plunged back into her over and over. Morgan tightened around his penis and ran her hand down to the small of his back, a particularly sensitive area of his body. As soon as her hand traveled down to his ass, he couldn't stop the build up from erupting. He'd done a good job until then of keeping his weight off her. Seth eased onto her and laid his head on Morgan's chest, but he didn't pull out of her. She ran her hands through his hair.

"We have had one hell of a week," Morgan mumbled.

"Yes, we have." He kissed her hand.

"So how many babies do you want?" She tugged on his hair.

Seth propped himself up on his elbows, still covering her. "I was thinking…ten."

"Ten!"

"OK, seven. Is that a better number?" Seth arched an eyebrow at her.

"No." She shook her head.

"Seven is a good number."

"It's an obscene number." She rolled her eyes.

"Let's negotiate." The corners of Seth's mouth turned up.

"I'm listening." She tried to scowl but couldn't suppress the smile forming on her lips.

Seth ran his hand through her hair and pulled her close for a long, hot kiss. "We'll keep making babies until we get a baby girl."

Morgan giggled. "That may take a while."

"Hey, I'm fully committed to doing everything I possibly can to get you a girl. If we happen to have six boys while we're waiting, no harm, no foul."

She opened her mouth to protest but Seth ran his tongue down the side of her neck. He started to harden inside her again.

Morgan moaned. "Deal."

Epilogue

Time had flown faster than Seth had wanted when the season had started. The excited rush he normally felt when he suited up and went onto the field was replaced by melancholy. He was focused on the season but the comfort of waking up in the morning with his hand over Morgan's growing belly made it more than tempting to hibernate until the baby was born. He hadn't anticipated the connection they already had would deepen and expand. He wanted to be with her all the time and let the rest of the world fade away. Love was no longer a feeling but a state of being for him. He was happy all the time and had even forgotten to be tense and cranky about his work goals. In a matter of a year his outlook on life had changed and so had his future. Prospective fatherhood had a calming effect on him.

Each time he went away for a game and returned, Morgan seemed to blossom more into her pregnancy. Her hair grew tremendously, her skin always had a natural sheen, and she'd become very amorous. Seth didn't complain that his wife had the hots for him on a nightly basis; he wanted to keep the momentum going so she'd be agreeable to having another baby in the near future.

* * *

Seth had orchestrated a detailed schedule of visitors at the penthouse while he was at away games. Morgan had figured out his brother Tyler's surprise visits weren't much of a surprise at all. She'd forgiven Tyler easily, and he'd go out and get her a greasy cheese steak from a restaurant she liked. From that moment on Morgan didn't mind the babysitters as long as they brought good food with them.

For Christmas, Seth surprised her with a project that began when they returned from the ranch after the banquet. For months Morgan brimmed over with curiosity as she saw contractors remodeling one of the rooms in the penthouse. Morgan burst into tears on Christmas day when she saw Seth had a new library constructed with floor to ceiling bookshelves and attached rolling ladders. The room was furnished elegantly, including a fireplace, but he'd added a special touch and placed that red beanbag from the library in the corner. He told her that she could read to the baby on the beanbag, just as her mother had done with her all those years ago. He also had a copy of the picture of her and her mom from the library made and it hung on one of the walls. Morgan wouldn't leave the library for the entire day and even missed Christmas dinner at her dad's house.

They bickered from time to time about how long she spent at the bookstore and working on her nonprofit organization, Reading Builds Bridges. Morgan's fundraising had taken a strange and interesting turn. She was furious when he offered her the money to start it. She was even madder when he orchestrated a way for her to get it. Morgan caught on quick to his attempts to introduce her to people who would be able to help her. It never occurred to him that Jocelyn Fontane would be the person to mentor his wife. Jocelyn and Morgan seemed to run into each other on their own and finally the two of them began putting a plan together. He couldn't take any credit for that and Morgan appreciated that his influence wasn't the reason for Jocelyn's help. Turned out Jocelyn believed in Morgan's cause all on her own. In the end, he made her realize how much he loved her and he just wanted her to be happy. She was able to convey to him why it was important to her to do it on her own. Making sure the library had what it needed was a way for her to keep her mother's memory alive in her heart. Seth apologized for trying to solve a problem that had a specific solution she needed to find for herself.

He took her to the ranch often, and his mother loved helping them get the house ready for the baby. He enjoyed knowing their children would have the best of both worlds: the hustle and bustle of Philadelphia living with Morgan's family and the mellow, slow paced life on the ranch in Texas with the Blakes.

* * *

It was the fourth quarter and Seth was doing his best to keep his head in the game. He couldn't shake the feeling that something was wrong. With twenty-eight seconds on the clock, Seth threw one hell of a pass to Lamont, who caught it in the end zone and scored a touchdown. The game ended with a score of thirty-four to twenty-six.

The crowd roared. They had done it again—he had done it. The field flooded with people in celebration. Reporters swarmed the team.

"Seth Blake, you have done it again!" one of them yelled over the crowd. "Third year in a row as a Super Bowl champ and MVP! How do you feel right now?"

Seth took off his helmet and wiped the sweat from his face. Before Seth could respond someone tugged at his sleeve. His agent, Luke, whispered into his ear.

Wide-eyed, he turned back to the reporter. "It was a great game, but I gotta go. My wife is in labor."

Seth took off toward the exit, running so fast the security detail escorting him couldn't keep up. Someone asked if he wanted to change before he left, and he stopped for a second to give them a menacing scowl. Then he continued his trek to the front of the stadium. A limo stood waiting for him with a police escort to the hospital. He hoped he hadn't missed it. This Super Bowl wouldn't mean shit if he missed seeing his son born.

* * *

The limo driver made it there in record time and as soon as he pulled up to the hospital, Seth's brothers, Tyler and Channing, stood outside waiting for him.

"Congratulations, man, she hasn't delivered yet." Tyler smiled at him as they ran into the lobby.

The ride up to the seventh floor was interminable. Seth paced in the small space of the elevator as it slowly went floor to floor. Seth finally remembered where he was when he caught an elderly woman looking at him like he was a Martian. Then he remembered he was still wearing his football gear.

Seth opened his mouth to explain but nothing came out. Channing ran interception.

"Ma'am, this is my brother's first baby. So he wanted to be prepared for anything."

The woman smiled and everyone on the elevator laughed, including Seth. Finally the elevator stopped and his whole family sat waiting just outside it. His parents, JJ, and Morgan's family had commandeered the waiting room.

The nurse put a gown on him and led him into the delivery room.

"Morgan," he breathed once he saw her.

Morgan smiled but spoke through clenched teeth. "We wouldn't start without you. Did we win?"

He laughed. "I don't think that's important right now."

"I told the baby to please wait until his father won the Super

Bowl. Did we win?"

"Yes, we won."

"I think I may have broken JJ's hand. I grabbed it when I felt my first labor pain, and he screamed." Morgan exhaled as she breathed through the passing contraction.

Seth laughed. "Probably not. I've seen him arm wrestle Patton."

"Right now, I feel like I could arm wrestle Patton. They glossed over the labor part in that pregnancy book I read. This is not slight discomfort."

"You look beautiful." He touched one of her ponytails.

"I'm sorry I couldn't stay and see the rest of the game. My water broke in the third quarter."

"I love you so much, Morgan." Seth kissed her senseless.

Morgan let out a blood curdling scream and gasped. "I love you too. I know you had a long day but I need the MVP to coach his son out of my belly."

Seth looked at her for a moment, amazed at how well she was doing despite the unbelievable pain she must have been in right now. This by far, was the most magnificent thing he'd ever done in his life. Creating a life with the woman he loved. He kissed her long and hard. "You don't know how happy you've made me."

"I have an idea." She smiled, tears falling down her cheeks.

"Morgan." Seth touched her nose with his.

Morgan let out another cry.

* * *

Three hours later Seth Jacob Blake Jr. let a healthy scream rip as he came into the world. As the nurses took him to clean him up, Morgan grabbed Seth's hand.

"We did it. A healthy baby boy. He's beautiful," she choked out as the nurse put her son in her arms. The moment Morgan saw her son, who had piercing green eyes just like his dad, she knew life would never be the same.

Seth smiled. "Of course he is. His father is handsome and his mother is gorgeous. That kid didn't stand a chance."

Morgan shook her head and tried not to laugh along with the nurses. She looked up at him and realized he was still wearing his uniform.

"You didn't change?"

"I ran off the field so fast I think I broke my own yardage record. I was not missing one moment of this."

"I knew you would get here in time. We knew it." Morgan kissed the baby. "But we're going to plan the next baby. No more down-to-the-wire deliveries."

"You got it." He laughed. "SJ's brother will be planned from conception to birth. And delivery will be in the off season."

"Why don't you tell your son all about the game?" Morgan gingerly moved the baby into his arms. When Morgan handed the baby to Seth, a current of energy flowed between the three of them.

"SJ, daddy played a hell of a game today," Seth said softly.

"Language, Blake."

"This is from the woman who cursed like a sailor for nine months."

"That was the baby talking. I'm normally a lady." She flashed a cheesy smile.

"SJ, you're momma is one of the feistiest women I've ever met in my life. I knew the minute I saw her getting off that plane that she was the one for me. One day you're going to meet someone like her and come to me dazed and confused."

Morgan laughed. "And what are you going to tell him?"

"Don't ever let her go."

Morgan smiled, thinking how much their lives had changed in such a short amount of time. Last year they were virtual strangers and now they were a family. She heard the bustle outside her hospital door, the rest of the family anxious to see the baby, but she wanted just a few more moments alone with her two most important people. She looked forward to the next chapter in their lives.

The Blake Legacy

~ Dedication ~

To Morgan and Seth — thanks for the dance.

Chapter One

Seth Blake begrudgingly prepared for the impromptu press conference in the hospital amphitheater. He didn't know how his publicist, Daniel, had managed to organize it, but there was a media circus waiting down stairs to interview him. After he'd won the Super Bowl, Seth had found out his wife, Morgan, had gone into labor, and he'd run out of the stadium so fast there had been no time for interviews and congratulatory fanfare.

Now he held his son, Seth Jacob Blake Jr., in his arms, celebrating his third win in a row was the last thing on his mind.

Morgan assured him that she and the baby would be fine for an hour without him. Despite the fact that their entire family stood outside in the hallway, he took the quickest shower of his life, peeking out of the bathroom from time to time to check on them. Morgan looked radiant, despite not having slept the past seventeen hours. The nurses wanted to make her more comfortable, but she wasn't interested in anything that required taking the baby out of her arms.

Seth changed and shaved, but he still wasn't ready to go. As far as he was concerned, seeing his son being born was the most exciting and fulfilling thing that had happened all day.

He sighed. "This shouldn't take too long."

Morgan smiled at him. "Take all the time you need. You did it. You're a third time MVP and Super Bowl champ. This is your moment."

"*This* right here is my moment." He leaned in and kissed her and the baby.

"The sooner you leave, the sooner you'll be back." Morgan shooed him out of the room.

Seth stepped out into the hall and came face to face with the Blake and Reed clans.

"Congrats again, baby." His mother, Teri-Lyn, gave him a big squeeze. "Sydney and I will go in with Morgan while you do your press conference."

"I went back to the hotel and got her hospital bag." Michelle, who was standing next to Seth's brother Tyler, pointed to the bag in a chair. "Thank goodness my neurotic friend packed one just in case."

Tyler smirked at him. "If he picks up a football while you're down there, I promise I'll come and get you."

"That's not funny, Tyler." Seth punched his brother in the arm.

"I don't know about a football, but maybe he'll pick up a guitar," Seth's best friend, Tate McGill, said behind them.

"You're both wrong," Channing, his youngest brother, said. "One look at him and you can tell he's a genius. It's clear he wants to study law."

Seth shot all of them evil looks, but he enjoyed the endless possibilities for his son's life. He and Morgan had talked about the dreams they had for their child before he was born. Morgan had assured Seth she was OK with his secret desire for his son to one day be a football player in his own right. Both agreed as long as he was happy and healthy, Seth Jacob Blake Jr. could carve out whatever life he wanted for himself.

* * *

As soon as Seth stepped into the crowded amphitheater, his team began chanting their battle cry. Cameras started flashing and reporters fired questions at him from around the room. He moved toward the stage and was greeted by his good friend and team mate Patton Hawkes. Patton gave him a hug and took a seat next to Seth at the center table.

"Seth, how's your wife?" a reporter yelled from the back of the room.

"She's fine. The baby's fine. I couldn't ask for a better day than this." Seth ran a hand over his face.

"Boy or girl?" someone else shouted.

"A boy. His name is Seth Jacob Blake Jr. And before anyone asks, he will be a quarterback." Seth grinned and winked.

The room erupted in laughter. Technical questions about the game began to flow, and he was grateful he could answer on autopilot. He congratulated the team and reinforced the group effort involved to win, thanking each of them for playing their best. Everyone agreed that his fifty-five yard pass to Lamont to score the winning touchdown was the greatest play of the game.

"How does it feel to achieve three Super Bowl wins in a row, something no team has ever achieved before?" The million-dollar question came from the back of the room.

Seth tugged on his ear. "It feels great, but it's also a humbling experience. This achievement shows how dedicated every player was on the team to doing our jobs, and in the process we made a little football history."

"Being three time MVP ain't bad either, is it?"

The crowd roared.

"The honor of being named MVP is never to be taken lightly, and I have much respect for it. Somebody thought I was doing something right, and I appreciate that. But if I didn't work with exceptional people, there would be no title."

"Seth, what were you thinking when you threw the ball to Lamont?" a sports reporter for Sports Now yelled out.

"I was thinking, Lamont, if you never catch another pass I

throw you, this is the one you should catch." Seth laughed.

"Were you aware your wife was in labor during the game?"

"No. She told my family that under no circumstances was anyone allowed to tell me she was in labor until the game was over." He shook his head, smiling.

Patton grabbed the microphone off the stand in front of him. "And before anyone asks, I am the godfather to his son."

There was rumbling among the team about why Patton should have the honor. Seth covered his mic with his hand, leaned over, and whispered to Patton, "Thanks, man."

"They'll get over it," Patton spoke into his microphone.

Damn. The rumblings grew louder. Seth had to defuse the situation before it blew up in his face. "Our wives are good friends. Nina was always there to help Morgan during the pregnancy."

His teammates kept grumbling but gradually went quiet, and Seth tried not to wipe sweat off his brow. Questions about the game resumed, and Seth fired off responses as quickly as he could, anxious to get back to his family. He didn't want to miss a minute of the first day of his son's life. He did his best to be polite, but after forty-five minutes, he informed everyone he was headed back upstairs. After a brief conversation with Daniel and his agent, Luke, Seth slipped out a side door and headed for the elevator.

"Great game today," a familiar voice said from the direction of the reception area.

Seth turned to see T.K. Holbrook, a friend of his father's and one of the richest men in Texas. T.K. was also the owner of the football team the Texas Tomcats. T.K. had courted Seth throughout his football career to play for him, but timing was never on their side.

"Thanks, T.K." Seth shook his hand.

"And congratulations on your baby boy. John Jacob let me get a peek at him; he's a handsome little devil. I see a Super Bowl in his future."

Seth laughed. "I'm hopeful."

"If he does, then maybe a Blake will finally play for the Tomcats." T.K. winked at him.

The elevator door opened, and Seth held out his hand to keep it ajar.

T.K. hitched up his pants. "I knew you could do it. I knew you would take the Titans to glory when you signed that contract. I regret I couldn't get to you first."

"Well, the timing wasn't right. Things seemed to have fallen into place for a reason." Seth smiled.

T.K. nodded at Seth's sentiment. "You've given them three Super Bowl wins. I knew you were a champion the first time I saw you play in grade school. Your father and I would talk about that all the time when you were a boy. We both knew you'd be in the Hall of Fame one day."

"It's a little early for that. But everything I've done in my career was to work toward being an exemplary player and to make my family proud." Seth held out his hand again when the elevator door began making a jerking movement.

"Well, you've definitely done that. Listen, I know you want to get back to your family. Congratulations again."

"Thank you for stopping by, T.K. I appreciate it." Seth nodded.

"Your contract with the Titans is up in a year, right?" T.K. rubbed his chin.

Seth had to think about it for a moment. There had been so much going on he'd forgotten about his expiring contract. "Yes," Seth said as he stepped inside the elevator.

T.K. smiled and tipped his hat.

The elevator doors closed, leaving Seth alone to process T.K.'s surprise visit. A few years ago the possibility of playing in Texas would have been his biggest dream come true.

The elevator opened again, and he was surprised to see the corridor leading to Morgan's room empty. Seth gently opened the door to her room to find her nursing the baby.

Morgan looked up when he walked in. "We were just talking about you."

"Is that right?" Seth sat on the bed and caressed her cheek.

"I was telling Jake about what a great game his dad played today."

"Jake? That's a nice nickname."

"It was not my idea. The family got together and decided that S.J. sounded pretentious. Your father said he looked like a Jake. After that decision was made, they shifted to where he would go to college. I kicked everyone out." Morgan flashed a cheesy smile.

Seth shook his head. "You didn't."

"I love them all, but they were driving me crazy. I threatened to institute a demerit system on visitation tomorrow. How did the press conference go?"

"I told everyone you were holding the next Blake quarterback in your arms."

Morgan giggled. "No pressure on your son at all. Your dad brought in this man he said was an old friend of the family. His name was T.K. Holbrook. Did you see him?"

"I ran into him downstairs." Seth moved her bangs out of her eyes for her. Her hands were a bit full after all.

"Good. He seemed anxious to talk to you. I got the feeling it was about more than a congratulatory chat. What did he say?" Morgan furrowed her eyebrows.

"He wanted to congratulate me on the baby and the win today."

The sound of Jake's suckling noises echoed through the room. Seth couldn't help but grin. "Boy is he hungry."

"He's going to have your big appetite."

Seth kept watching, entranced. Morgan had to cough to bring his attention back to her face.

"Yes?"

"You do know my breasts won't remain this size?"

He smirked. "They might."

"Well, if I go back down to my normal cup size, maybe you'll start looking me in the face again." Morgan arched her eyebrow.

Seth held his hand to his chest, feigning indignation. "I beg your pardon. I was just admiring the luscious view."

"Well, I got a spare tire to go with the bigger boobs." She groaned.

"Morgan Blake, you are beautiful, right now, just the way you are." Seth kissed her tenderly on the lips.

* * *

Jake finished nursing, so Morgan hit the call button and a nurse responded immediately to assist her. The nurse told them what to expect throughout the night from their newborn and that she'd check on them in an hour. Teri-Lyn was able to barge back in for a few minutes to unpack the dinner she'd brought them from a nearby restaurant. She kissed them both goodnight and said she'd be there bright and early tomorrow.

"This was so sweet of your momma to get us dinner." Morgan scooted over as Seth climbed onto the bed with her.

"Comfortable?" He nestled closer to her, putting his arm around her.

"Yes." She kissed his cheek.

"Am I hurting you?"

"Not possible." Morgan placed a hand on his thigh so he would stop moving. "I'm tough, remember?"

Seth held the steamed asparagus spear to her lips. "Eat."

Morgan took a small bite. "The nurse said I could be out of here as early as tomorrow afternoon."

"We'll see about that. I don't want you released until the doctor is sure you and the baby can travel."

"Women don't stay in the hospital very long after deliveries anymore." She sighed. "I can't wait to get Jake home."

Seth took a sip of his water. "Jake is a pretty tame nickname. I'm surprised Tyler or Channing didn't come up with something crazy like Switch or Buckeye."

Morgan covered her mouth to muffle a hearty laugh. "Nothing crazy about the name Jake Blake. Sounds like a poker player who's running from the law."

Seth snorted. "I see your point."

His cell phone pinged. Morgan picked it up from the nightstand and checked the display. "You forgot to hit confirm on the six-week countdown you started. What exactly are you counting down?"

"Nothing." Seth swallowed.

Morgan moved the phone out of his reach and smirked at the title of the countdown. "Back on Morgan's Field."

He shrugged. "I was just setting a reminder for your check up with the gynecologist."

"What a dutiful husband." Morgan sat up. "So, about these brothers for Jake. I think we should lay out a plan right now."

"I'm ready." Seth sat up too.

"Hold on, cowboy. I'm aware of your diabolical plan to have your own football team. We will discuss having another baby when Jake starts showing some independence."

Seth nodded, accepting the challenge. "I'll have that boy doing our taxes by the time he cuts his first tooth."

"Leave him alone. I'll be happy if he can find his own foot and knows who Mommy and Daddy are."

Seth scratched at his five o'clock shadow. "At eight months, I was already riding my first horse, Lucky."

"And bench pressing one-fifty?"

"Hell yeah. Would I lie to you?" He leaned in for a kiss, his eyes twinkling.

"No, but your bravado is legendary. You know I can confirm

all these tall tales with your mother." Morgan moved away from him.

Seth planted a tender smooch on her cheek. "What are we going to do about our nanny situation?"

They'd interviewed at least two dozen nannies when Seth was home between games. Nightmarish scenarios had run through Morgan's mind about some super sexy, nubile nanny that would come in and try to steal Seth and the baby from her. After waking up screaming one night, she'd stopped the interviews and prayed a better solution would appear.

"Is there another reason why you don't want to get a nanny?" Seth searched her face.

She shrugged. "I didn't have a nanny. My mom took care of me before I started school. If she was busy, my grandmother watched me."

"I didn't have one either. Momma stayed at home and took care of all of us." Seth nodded in agreement.

"And I don't need some hot young thing coming into my house under the ruse of taking care of the baby but secretly trying to seduce you and kill me." Morgan laid her head on his shoulder.

He chuckled. "Baby, I do love that wild imagination of yours, but that scenario will never happen."

"I know it will be hard work, but I'd like to raise Jake on our own. I'm sure there will be times when we need a sitter, but we have plenty of family and friends to ask for help when we need it. I don't want to hear about my son's childhood through a re-cap from someone we hired."

"If that's what you want, that's what we'll do." Seth kissed her on top of her head.

Morgan closed her eyes. "Did I tell you how much I love you today? How much I love our son?"

"You did, but I never get tired of hearing it." Seth nuzzled her neck.

* * *

It was time for Jake's first visit to his pediatrician after
returning to Philadelphia. Morgan was a nervous wreck, but Seth
was a quiet comfort. It seemed like he was handling everything
better. She was too anxious to sleep, keeping a watchful eye over
the baby and feeling emotional all the time. Seth had made her
some toast and she'd cried because he'd put butter on it, touched
that he remembered how she liked it. But then he teased her to
make her smile. He assured her that everything would be fine.

She'd noticed Jake's stool was dark when she'd changed his
diaper, so she'd taken a picture of it and sent it to everyone in the
address book on her cell phone. She'd finally gotten an answer
from Teri-Lyn, who said it was probably meconium and that it was
normal for a baby only a few days old. But she wanted the doctor
to verify it. Her brothers had sent her a few choicely worded text
messages, thanking her for ruining their appetites. After several
calls begging Seth to confiscate her phone, she'd promised not to
send any more pics of Jake's bowel movements.

"Seth Blake Jr.," the nurse called out from an open door leading
to the exam rooms.

"You ready?" Seth squeezed Morgan's hand.

"Yes." Morgan rose, and they followed the nurse down the hall
to the first room.

Dr. Fenwick came in and examined Jake while talking to Seth
and Morgan. The exam looked more like playtime, but she was
very thorough. Jake responded to Fenwick's prodding with ease.

"Seth Jr. is doing great. His responses to the reflex tests are fine
and his stool is normal. Morgan, thank you for showing me that
picture." Dr. Fenwick laughed.

Morgan shrugged. "I sent it to everyone I know. I'm shocked it
hasn't gone viral."

Dr. Fenwick studied them both for a while before speaking.
"Seth, you went from the adrenaline rush of the Super Bowl to the

high of being a new father without a break. Try to get some rest if you're feeling tired. It was a great game by the way."

"Thanks, doc. We've been taking it easy since we've been home." Seth beamed.

"Morgan" — the doctor removed her glasses — "you look like shit."

Morgan folded her arms across her chest. "Is that an official medical diagnosis?"

"I've got three kids myself. I was so riddled with worry about my first son, my husband found me passed out from exhaustion in our kitchen. Just breathe, and if it makes you feel better, staple the baby monitor to your forehead. You won't be any good to your son if you run yourself into the ground."

"I don't know if I can simply unwind like that." Morgan exhaled shakily.

"You have this big, strong man to help you. If he can throw fifty-five yards to his wide receiver for a game winning touchdown, he can help you take care of his son." The doctor smiled wryly.

"Being good under pressure is a job requirement for him."

"I know I can say only so much to soothe you. It doesn't seem that way, but instinctively you know what to do. You've already read every good baby book I could suggest. In no time you'll be ready for the next one."

Morgan looked at Seth, whose eyes lit up when Dr. Fenwick mentioned the next child. Dr. Fenwick couldn't resist asking him more questions about the Super Bowl, and Seth answered fervently while rocking Jake in his baby seat and caressing Morgan's hand. His touch had a calming effect on both of them.

* * *

Seth untangled himself from Morgan, careful not to wake her getting out of the bed. The sound of her snoring was music to his ears. After weeks of insomnia, she was finally getting some much-needed sleep. He showered, brushed his teeth, and dressed then headed for the baby's room. Jake was still asleep so he parked himself in the white rocking chair he'd had custom made in Texas and covered himself with Morgan's old baby blanket that her mother had crocheted when she was born. It smelled like the mixture of mother and son. He wished there was a way to bottle the smell to take it with him when he was on the road during the coming season.

The toy stuffed nursery was in pristine order. Morgan made sure all of Jake's clothes were folded, diapers were on the ready, and all of his baby things were in their place. Teri-Lyn and Sydney had helped her decorate it months ago. Large letters spelling out Jake's name, accompanied by the pale blue painted walls and alphabet wallpaper, made the room feel cozy.

Seth smiled, eyeing the unopened presents in the corner of the nursery. Well-intentioned friends had sent zany gifts that Jake was definitely too young to play with right now. Seth's friend Derek Popovich, the goalie for the Philadelphia Pirates, had sent over a hockey stick and puck. One of his teammates had sent a ninety-inch flat screen television.

Morgan found most of the gifts obnoxious, but what she really loved was Tate's present to Jake. The guitar sat on a stand against the wall as if it were patiently waiting for Jake to be able to do something besides drool on it.

There were so many things Seth wanted to teach his son and the importance of family, friendship, and loyalty were on the top of his list. These were the things he'd learned from his father. He felt fortunate to have had a good relationship with his dad growing up. Following his father's advice had led him to a professional career in football and getting married to the woman of his dreams. John Jacob had taught him a lot about listening to gut instincts and following his heart. His father had told him that the hardest part about being a man was the ability to be vulnerable to someone.

That advice had echoed in his head the day Seth had met Morgan, and it'd led him to the kind of happiness he'd only seen between his parents. His father never pushed or intimidated, he simply let Seth be his own person. Seth would be damn lucky if his relationship with Jake was like the one he had with his dad.

Like clockwork, Jake came out of his slumber the same time every day. The second he opened those green eyes and focused on Seth, it was show time. Something tugged at his heart every time he looked at his son. Sometimes it overwhelmed him, thinking about how awesome it was that he and Morgan created a life together.

"Good morning, Jake." Seth picked him up and cradled him in his arms. "I know you were expecting Mommy, but we're going to let her catch up on her sleep. So I'm intercepting. I'm going to give you a bath and then your momma can feed you. Today I'm going to teach you all about Uncle Patton's position. He's a linebacker..."

* * *

"Let's go, Blake! Give me twenty!" Seth bellowed above her.

Morgan looked at Seth, angry that she was too weak to throw anything at him. When she'd asked for his help getting rid of the baby weight, she had no idea he'd turn into a drill sergeant. Seth couldn't contain his enthusiasm as he constructed a workout routine for her and ordered workout gear and all kinds of electronic gadgets for her to monitor her progress. He was even hopeful that she would start jogging with him.

Her favorite pair of jeans was hanging in their walk-in closet, silently mocking her. Her futile attempt to get into them last week had resulted in near paralysis. She'd lain on the bed and pulled up the best she could until she'd reached her hips, where they remained stuck until she swallowed her pride and asked Seth to come take them off. It wasn't fair that after having a baby, he still looked ripped and sexy as hell and the only thing she felt comfortable in was one of his jerseys. After hearing a reporter call him a "hot dad" on a morning news program, she was determined to return to her petite frame. She may not have been as smoking hot as he was, but she was determined to achieve lukewarm status, at the very least. She was living with a man who had fitness down to a science. Why not ask for his help? Today's torturous workout included sit-ups, and she was failing miserably.

She grimaced. "If I do five, can I have a cookie?"

Seth leaned down and got in her face. "If you want a cookie, you have to do ten sets of five."

She did three more crunches, then collapsed on the floor. "Stomach cramp."

Seth reached for her belly, but she pushed his hand away.

"No touching the jiggle."

"If you do two more crunches and your cool down stretches, you can have that protein shake I made you." He smiled.

"Do I want to know what's in that shake?"

His smile widened. "No, you don't."

Morgan followed him into the kitchen and planted herself on a stool. Seth hit the blender to meld the contents he had waiting and poured the shake into a glass. She took a deep breath before swallowing. A delightful strawberry flavor overpowered the unidentifiable healthy ingredients in the drink.

"This tastes good." She licked her lips once she'd downed the rest.

Seth turned off the second blender, which contained his daily protein shake. "I know you like strawberries, and you didn't have to sacrifice any calories."

"Thank you, Sergeant Blake." Morgan saluted him.

"You're doing great, babe."

"You think so? It feels like a waste, getting up early, twisting my body into a pretzel, and not getting any cookies." She huffed.

"Think of it as training for chasing after Jake when he starts walking."

"That's true. He's going to be all over the place."

"Soon he'll be moving out of his crib, making room for his brother."

Morgan raised an eyebrow. "Renting out his crib already? I don't know if he'll go for that. It's a nice crib."

"If he won't go willingly to make room for his sibling, I intend to bribe him with a big racecar bed. Already have it picked out." Seth devoured the rest of his shake.

"Devious man." She shook her head. "I have a new appreciation for your workout routine. Why do you do it every day?" She tapped her fingers on the counter.

"When someone twice my size is coming at me on the field, I don't want to get squashed like a pancake." He snickered.

"Right. Then you wouldn't get to hear sound bites of your wife calling an opposing player a son of a bitch for hitting her husband. We only heard about that quote for about a month." She grimaced.

"Well, you were pregnant and your filter was nowhere in sight. Besides, I love it when you defend me. It's sexy. According to my countdown app, there's three weeks to go." Seth leaned over the counter and swept his tongue into her mouth.

Morgan let out a low groan in appreciation. Seth rounded the kitchen island and pulled her to the edge of the stool, positioning himself between her legs. He deepened the kiss as she grabbed hold of his shoulders. Just as Seth slipped his hands under her T-shirt, Jake let out a cry on the baby monitor. Seth sighed and pressed his forehead against hers.

He uttered a curse. "How does he do that? Every time I touch you, he wakes up."

"Language, Blake," Morgan whispered. "I think he knows about your plan to kick him out of his crib soon."

Seth chuckled. "You may be right."

"Welcome to fatherhood." She laughed as she disentangled herself from him and headed to the nursery.

* * *

Morgan was changing Jake's diaper when the reminder beeped on her cell phone that her anniversary was in a week. *If you ever need someone to watch the baby, I'm just a phone call away.* Sydney's words ping ponged around in her head. Did her stepmother mean it? Morgan wondered, but the sincere smile that had accompanied the statement meant Sydney wasn't just being polite. Sydney's kindness over the past year had taken Morgan by surprise on more than one occasion. Sydney had even thrown her a baby shower. It was a nice surprise, walking into the house after her reading hour at the library to an intimate celebration with a few close friends and family.

"What do you think, kid? Want to spend time with Sydney while Mommy goes shopping?" Morgan blinked when she saw the faint traces of a smile on Jake's face. She dialed Sydney's cell phone number while slipping Jake's adorable chubby legs back into his jumper. On the third ring, Morgan contemplated hanging up. Maybe it was a sign it wasn't a good idea. She'd just about given up when she heard her stepmother's voice.

"Hello, Morgan. How are you and the baby?"

"Hi, Sydney. We're fine."

Sydney chuckled. "That's good. I was thinking about you this morning."

"It's going well, but I'm afraid I'm going to break him or something." Morgan tapped Jake's nose with her finger.

"Nonsense. You can't break him. He's a tough little boy. He's part cowboy and part Reed."

Morgan smiled. "I know it's just first time mom nerves, but I still worry."

"The worrying will never stop. The trick is to get a handle on it early before you're hiding behind fire hydrants and garbage cans, stalking him for the rest of his life. You're doing a great job. Your mom would have been so proud of you."

Morgan went mute waiting for the golf ball size lump in her throat to budge. Hearing Sydney mention her mom felt odd to her. Finally she eked out, "Thank you."

"How does Seth like fatherhood?"

"He's over the moon about it."

Sydney began rattling on about Morgan's father, Curtis, taking an interest in golf. Which brought Morgan back to her reason for reaching out to her.

"Sydney, I know it's a lot to ask, but would you be able to watch Jake for me? My anniversary is next week, and I wanted to go shopping for Seth's present."

"I'd be delighted to watch him," Sydney bubbled into the phone.

"Well, you pick the day—"

"Tomorrow is fine. I have a few things I wanted to bring over for him anyway."

Morgan exhaled. "I think this family has bought everything in the city of Philadelphia for a baby. What else did you find?"

"He's too young for half of it, but in a few months he'll be the sharpest dressed baby in a hundred mile radius."

"OK, how about you come by at ten? He usually takes a nap around that time, and he won't be too much trouble."

"Sleep. Awake. It doesn't bother me. I just want to spend time with him."

Morgan looked at Jake and waggled her eyebrows at him. He gave her a curious look. "We'll see you tomorrow at ten. Thanks so much."

"Anything for you. You know that."

Morgan hung up, surprised at how well that had gone. She'd never asked Sydney for anything and now she was asking to watch her son. The pregnancy had changed so many of her relationships. She felt closer to her entire family. Seeing one of the Reeds walk through the door of the bookstore no longer made her tense up.

Robert dropped by the bookstore often for lunch, she was helping Jared, who was recently divorced, decorate his new bachelor pad, and she talked to Charles, who was in the military and currently stationed overseas, all the time. She was even spending time with her niece Avery. She credited her niece's newfound interest in her to Seth. Avery was thirteen and had a not so secret crush on him. Whenever he came into the room she would blush and go mute. Morgan sympathized with her niece's plight and prayed the family wouldn't catch on and tease her about it.

* * *

Morgan couldn't wait another minute. After poking him and sprinkling cold water on his face, she still couldn't get Seth to budge. In a last ditch effort to wake her husband, she slid her hand under the covers and caressed him.

"Good Morning, Mrs. Blake," Seth cooed and reached for her.

"Happy anniversary!" Morgan straddled him and planted kisses all over his face.

"Is it our first anniversary already?" He opened one eye.

Morgan went still. "Don't even joke about that."

"I'm just pulling that terribly cute, short leg of yours. How could I forget the day I married you?" Seth kissed her and rolled her onto her back.

Morgan was so engrossed with his sensual caresses she didn't realize he'd fastened a diamond tennis bracelet onto her wrist until they came up for air.

The bracelet sparkled against her skin. "It's beautiful."

"You're beautiful." Seth placed a trail of kisses along her collarbone.

She glanced over at the alarm clock on the nightstand. "We have exactly seventeen minutes before your son wakes up."

"What do you have in mind?" He tugged at the lace strap on her nightgown.

Morgan pushed him off her and went to one of the guest rooms to retrieve his present. She'd wanted to build up to the big gift but now she said screw it, he could open the smaller gifts later.

When she returned with his new set of golf clubs in a bag with a big red bow wrapped around it, he started to laugh.

"What's so funny?"

"Great minds think alike." Seth went into his office and brought back a set of clubs in a bright pink bag with plaid trim. "I thought we'd play a round when the new golf resort opens in Arizona. I can teach you how to play."

"You're on." Morgan checked out her brand new clubs.

Seth stretched his arms above his head. "How about we start practicing today at an indoor driving range?"

"Sounds good to me. I'll see if Sydney can come over for a couple of hours." Morgan reached for her phone.

"I already asked her. She said yes." His green eyes twinkled with mischief. "And I have one more present for you. But I'll give it to you later." Seth kissed her hard.

"OK." Morgan shook her head, wondering what outrageous thing he'd done now.

* * *

Morgan was in the process of giving Jake his fiftieth kiss goodbye when Sydney kicked them out of the house and told them to have a good time. Clubs in hand, Morgan and Seth got on the elevator and headed for the lobby. Morgan didn't think anything of it when Seth declined the doorman's offer to bring his car to the front of the Ashcroft. He smiled and said they'd be going to the garage to get it. Morgan followed him through the parking deck, stopping dead in her tracks when she spotted a new Firenze red Range Rover with a big red bow on it in the parking spot next to his.

Seth spoke first. "Before you say anything about it being too extravagant, I want to remind you that it's my anniversary too, and I get to do what I want for my wife."

"What kind of logic is that?" Morgan glared at him.

"It's not logic. It's heartfelt emotion." Seth took a deep breath. "It's fully loaded. I took your brothers to the dealership with me, just in case I missed anything you would want."

Morgan laughed. "You don't take kids to a candy store. Those idiots like tricked out cars almost as much as they like football."

She opened the car door and flipped through the manual on the seat. The SUV looked just like Seth's with a few modifications. She inspected the vehicle, impressed with the shadow walnut console and the supple ivory leather. The new car smell was intoxicating.

"We did have a good time. My salesman Peter ordered lunch for us. We watched a hockey game."

Morgan put a hand on her hip. "Was that the day you told me you had to go to the stadium?"

"Yes, I wanted it to be a surprise. I just want you and Jake to be safe."

Morgan closed the door and walked to the front of the car. The license plate caught her eye. It read M BLAKE. "Very subtle with the vanity plates."

Seth looked at the plates and grinned.

"Thank you. I love it." She hugged him.

Morgan fielded happy anniversary calls via her blue tooth in her new SUV as Seth directed her out of the city to the driving range. She had to admit her new car was a smooth, elegant ride. It had plenty of room for Jake's things and all of her work stuff. She was going to miss her old car; it was only a few years old. She pondered if she could talk her brother Robert into letting her give it to Avery when she started driving in a couple of years.

The golf lesson began with a detailed explanation of the game. Morgan loved how intense Seth got when he talked about sports.

She slipped on her new gloves and grabbed a club. He helped with her stance, explained to her the difference in the clubs, and told her to try them out until one felt right in her hands. Hitting those balls was more therapeutic than she'd imagined. Seth, impressed with her swing, let her be and started hitting a few balls of his own.

"Hey, you want to have a wedding?" Seth said.

Morgan kept her eye on the ball. "I love the thought of the sublime redundancy of it all, but I thought we had one already."

"Did you want a formal wedding?"

Morgan glanced up at him and then back. "Uh oh, what brought this on? Have you been watching those reality wedding shows in the middle of the night again?" She laughed.

Seth sighed. "OK, I will admit that I watched a few of those shows and the women seemed super excited about getting married. A big, splashy wedding in front of family and friends. Hell, even in front of a few enemies. I don't want you to feel cheated years from now when you look back on how our married life began."

Morgan broke her putting stance and looked him in the eye. "OK, let's do it. We'll go back to the island and find Alvin. He can perform the ceremony again. I'll go dig out my wedding attire. I believe it was a pair of carpenter shorts and a T-shirt with blue flowers on it. Jake can be the best man. Maybe Reed's Fire can be my maid of honor."

Seth raised an eyebrow. "That sounds more like a circus. And your wedding T-shirt had pink flowers on it."

"You remembered." Morgan kissed him.

"It sounds very animated, but—"

"Did you enjoy our first fake wedding?"

When it looked like he was contemplating it, she hit him in the stomach.

"Ouch." He clinched his abs. "Yes."

"The only thing that was missing was family, friends, and much fancier clothes. Those carpenter shorts cost me fifteen dollars.

A nice wedding dress would have cost at least ten thousand dollars."

"Ten thousand? Wow, I have no concept of what things cost." He smirked.

"True. But remember, I'm friends with Nina, who is my part time fashion consultant. Nina would make sure I find the most exquisite and expensive gown your money could buy."

"A small price to pay to give you the wedding you wanted."

"And the wedding cake. Five obnoxious tiers of bland cake covered in Teflon icing with a little bride and groom on top. I think the elaborate show is for the guests. I don't feel cheated in any way. I got the best part of the deal."

"OK, if you're sure about this." Seth pulled her into his arms and kissed her.

Morgan and Seth hit a couple dozen more balls before they decided to grab lunch at his favorite restaurant. Morgan liked the cozy, intimate environment of Rockford's steak house. They were always seated in a booth that had maximum privacy and the wait staff treated Seth like a regular customer. No one ever asked for his autograph or interrupted their meal to chat him up.

"Did you like your presents?" Morgan smiled at him.

Seth put down his menu. "I loved each and every one of them. I didn't know you'd gone shopping."

"Ha! I went shopping when you had lunch with Luke. Sydney was kind enough to babysit."

"I think it's nice how the two of you have grown closer. It's about time." Seth looked at her.

"I wouldn't say we got closer. My hormones had me on emotional overload. I told my brothers I loved them all the time. One day I drove to Bryn Mawr after work just to give my father a hug. I'm sure I won't live that sentimental crap down." She threw her napkin on the table.

"Well, I think it's nice that you did it." He caressed her hand.

"You think it's nice I ravaged you every night in bed." She smirked.

Seth put his hand to his chest. "Well, I did whatever I could to keep my pregnant wife happy."

"You were a good sport about letting me make a human sundae out of you. Where is that ice cream scoop by the way?" She tapped her lips with her finger.

"In the nightstand. I had Kara replace the other one. You should have seen your face at the baby shower when I scooped that ice cream to go with the cake." Seth burst out laughing.

Morgan shuddered. "I will admit I said a silent prayer over that ice cream."

She glanced at her phone for the twentieth time. Sydney hadn't called. She put it back in her purse when she caught Seth looking at her.

"I'm glad you liked your golf clubs," she said.

"I can't wait to show my dad and J.J. when we go to Arizona."

Morgan laughed. "You're talking about your monogrammed bag, aren't you?"

"Yep. I'm a Sr. now."

Morgan couldn't resist pulling out her phone again. "Sydney hasn't called."

"Which means everything is OK." Seth took it away from her and slid it into his shirt pocket.

"Since you got to use a get out of anniversary jail free card with the SUV, I get to use one. But you have to tell me the truth."

Seth smiled. "OK."

"Do you want to go to the Tomcats?" Morgan searched his eyes.

"Morgan," he sighed.

"Don't 'Morgan' me. Answer the question. Honestly. It's important."

Time stood still for Morgan as she waited.

"Yes. I would consider it," Seth said.

"Was that so hard?"

Seth stared down at the table. "The simplest things are often the most difficult."

"Not today. It's our anniversary." Morgan leaned over and kissed his cheek.

He took out his wallet to pay the bill. "So what do you want to do now?"

Morgan shrugged. "Want to go the movies and make out?"

"Yes," Seth fired off.

"What do you want to see?"

Seth grabbed her hand and headed for the door. "I don't care. I have no intention of watching the movie."

* * *

Seth and Morgan returned home from their date to find Sydney reading a book to Jake in the library.

"He was such a good boy. No fussing." She smiled fondly down at him.

"That's because he loves his grandma," Seth said as he picked up Jake.

Morgan shot Seth a dirty look. Luckily she was standing behind her stepmother. Sydney, on the other hand, beamed and practically floated out of the door.

Seth glanced at Morgan once Sydney had left, and she shook her head.

"I don't want to talk it about."

Before he could say a word, Morgan was off putting away their golf clubs. When she came into the baby's room, he suggested she take a relaxing shower and he'd put Jake to bed.

An hour passed. He knew Morgan liked to take her time in the bathroom, but it had been a while since he'd kicked her out of the nursery. Confident that Jake was sleeping soundly this time around after a few false starts, Seth adjusted the volume on the baby monitor and went in search of his wife.

He made his way through the steam-filled bathroom and reached the stall door. He opened it and found Morgan leaning against the wall.

"Baby, are you OK?" Seth decreased the water pressure.

"I'm just tired. All the activity of the day is finally catching up with me." She tried to give him a smile.

"Let's get you out of there." Seth reached for her.

"No, I need to shave my legs. They feel prickly," she mumbled.

"No, they don't."

Morgan rolled her eyes. "You're sweet but a bad liar."

Seth held up his hands. "Honest."

"Just give me a minute. Or ten. I'll shave my legs then I promise I'll get out." She closed her eyes again.

The hot water felt good against Morgan's skin. A sleepy feeling had come over her when she'd first stepped into the shower. Now moving wasn't an option. It felt so good to stand there, letting the steam cleanse away the exhaustion that had crept up on her. The opening of the shower door again brought her back to reality. She opened her eyes to see Seth standing there in all his delicious nakedness.

"What are you doing?" she asked.

He was holding a can of shaving cream and one of his razors in his hands. Seth got down on his knees, the water cascading down and plastering his short hair to his head. Those sexy green eyes of his peeked up at her through wet lashes. Morgan's eyes widened as his huge hand engulfed her ankle, not sure what he was doing or if she'd be able to participate. He placed her foot on the center of his chest then reached for the shaving cream. Starting at the top of her leg, he released a jet stream of the pink gel from the top of her hip to her ankle. He made sensual circles on her legs until the lather became foamy and white. With each touch, it sent a deep, pulsing sensation to her clit. She was exhausted, but she wasn't dead.

"You have such pretty toes," he said.

She laughed and wiggled them in response. He'd used that chocolate sauce he kept in the nightstand one night, pouring it on top of her foot and ascending her body until he reached the center of her breasts, spending hours licking her clean.

Seth reached up on the shelf in the stall and retrieved his razor. The first stroke on her flesh felt like heaven. How a man so powerful and athletic could deliver such a light, tender, and loving a touch was beyond her. And the most endearing thing of all was that he was using one of his razors. Even her fanciest disposable paled in comparison to the smooth precision of the ones he used. Seth continued his downward strokes, careful to follow the ridges and curves of her legs with one hand while his other remained around her ankle.

When he finished both legs, he kissed her on each thigh, gathered the shower water with both hands, and rinsed her off. He stood and pressed her against the wall with a searing kiss. An eternity seemed to pass, wedged between that wall and his hard body, as he delivered the most sensuous and heart-pounding kiss he'd ever given her. When they finally broke apart, Seth's penis was at attention between them. They both knew it was too early to be intimate, but she appreciated the closeness without needing a release. He turned to cut off the shower, but she stopped him. Morgan came up behind him and wrapped her arms around him. One hand encircled the base of his penis while she moved the other one slowly up his shaft. They hadn't made love in a while, the daily exhaustion of being new parents left little time for intimacy, and she needed to let her body heal. She shuddered at the feel of him, thick and hard in her hands, wishing he was inside her now. Seth's head fell back when she gently skimmed her finger over his tip.

"Morgan," Seth groaned.

She applied a little more pressure, pretending she was playing a flute, his groans like a melodic overture to her ears. She could tell by the tightening of his shoulders that he wasn't ready to give in to the building climax so quickly. She often marveled at his stamina in bed, and he had a level of self-control she could only attribute to being a professional athlete. She could feel the tension rising in his back; he was trying to hold off the inevitable. She moved the hand that was on the base of his shaft and slid down to massage his balls. She then slid one fingertip down and between his perfect ass. He jerked at the unexpected touch, releasing his pent up passion in her hand.

Seth turned off the water, grabbed a towel, and began to rub her dry. He looked at her for a long time with a goofy grin on his face. "I think you may need to carry me to the bed."

"Two more weeks." She ran her tongue over his nipples.

"Two more weeks." Seth kissed her. "Happy anniversary."

Morgan laughed as he scooped her up instead and carried her into the bedroom.

Chapter Two

"The soon-to-be free agency status of Philadelphia Titans quarterback Seth Blake is the hot topic today. Blake's contract will expire with the Titans next year, and the rumors are rampant. It is speculated that an opportunity has arisen for him to play for the Texas Tomcats, the team Blake has mentioned in past interviews as his fantasy team. From what I understand, this has been a long-time dream of his, but his recent four-year relationship with the Titans has flourished into something remarkable. It's hard to believe he would leave the team and the city that loves him, but we know in the world of professional sports that sometimes platitudes and assumed loyalty is not a motivating factor to remain with a team. I'd like to place bets on the estimated new salary for the quarterback when the bidding war for his talents begins…"

Seth turned off the television and willed himself to get back to work. He wouldn't have known about the broadcast had Patton not sent him a text and told him to turn on the Sports Network. Now was the time for quiet reflection about his future, not listening to hypotheses by sports analysts. It was the off-season, for heaven's sake, and he should get a lengthy reprieve before shifting back into strategy mode.

The plans for the new golf course and spa were draped over his desk, waiting for his final approval. His dad, never insistent about too many things, had asked that he review them and give him a call. When he'd unrolled the design sketch, he knew why his father wanted him to examine every detail. Leave it to John Jacob Blake to show you something when a simple statement could have sufficed. Seth smiled and dialed his dad.

"John Jacob Blake speaking. You've got ten seconds to speak fast or not at all," his father said into the phone.

Seth laughed. "Hey, Daddy."

"Hi, son. You looked over those blue prints I sent you?"

"Yes, sir. Everything looks great."

"Are you OK with the final decision?"

"As—as long as it's OK with J.J.," Seth said, taken aback that his father asked for his approval.

"Then it's agreed. Where's my boy?"

"Morgan is feeding him."

"Is she still planning to go back to work?"

"Yes."

"I suppose you didn't bother to tell her that she didn't have to go back to work." John Jacob laughed.

"That's like telling Momma to do something." He sighed.

His father chuckled. "When you coming down here?"

"Next month."

"I'll see you then. Love you, son. Give Morgan and Jake my love. Your mother is going to be so excited to see them." With that his father ended the call.

Seth rolled up the blueprints, blown away by his dad's decision. He'd always viewed him as a strong, silent type. He wanted to tell Morgan what a generous, heartfelt thing his dad was doing with the land development project, but he'd save it as a surprise.

Seth's cell phone rang. He was surprised by the name on the caller ID display. "McKinney, how the hell are you?"

Ross McKinney was an old college friend and a running back

for the Texas Tomcats.

"I'm good, man. Congrats again, on the win. Listen, I'm in town for a few days. You want to go out for a beer?"

"Out for a beer? Are you kidding me? Dinner here, I insist. You can meet my wife and son." Seth beamed.

* * *

Ross arrived at six o'clock with a baby gift. It had been ages since Seth had seen his old college buddy. He was a native Texan as well and had boyhood dreams, just like Seth, of being part of the Tomcats football dynasty. Fate had led Ross to the Tomcats during the draft, and he'd been playing for them ever since. Seth had played against friends on other teams before, but each time he played Ross and the Tomcats, he felt like he was doing something sacrilegious.

Ross entertained Morgan during dinner with tales of his and Seth's college life, but Seth stopped him short at some of his racier escapades. It was fun reminiscing with him, but he knew that wasn't his friend's real reason for visiting. Whenever Ross wasn't telling the truth, his eyes moved faster than a camera shutter. When Morgan went to check on Jake, the other shoe dropped.

"Thank you for inviting me to dinner." Ross drank back the single malt scotch Seth poured for him.

"Anything for an old friend. But I know you came here for another reason."

Ross laughed. "You could always see right through me. That's why I hate when we play the Titans. OK, I'm not going to lie, I think it would be great to have you come to Texas when you're contract is up. Hell, you're in the state half the time anyway. We could put the Tomcats back on the map. The last five years have been hard on us, but I know if you were our quarterback, we'd be back on top."

Seth sighed. "The Tomcats have a lot offense issues."

"Ed Worthy, our head coach, is working on that. There's going to be a lot of shuffling around next year."

"Have you been talking to T.K.?"

"He's very interactive with the team. Some would say too interactive. We chat all the time. When he asked me what I thought the team needed to change our luck, I told him we needed you."

Seth ran his hand over his face. "T.K. came to the hospital the night of the Super Bowl."

"That should tell you how serious he is about you." Ross chuckled into his drink.

"Do you think we could turn the Tomcats around?"

"I know we can."

Seth swirled around the scotch in his glass. "I'll think about it."

* * *

When Morgan had excused herself to check on Jake, she'd bid Ross a goodnight, anticipating she wouldn't be returning to the living room. She knew the baby was sleeping, but the neurotic side of her wanted to check and make sure Seth had everything he needed his first day on his own with Jake. He had good instincts with the baby and was a natural at soothing him so that Jake wasn't much trouble—he just soaked in all that was going on around him with a smile—but she still worried.

She'd passed Seth's study today when he was listening to the segment on the sports show about his possible career change. He'd never said it to her, but she knew something was on his mind. She'd asked Teri-Lyn who T.K. Holbrook was one day during her daily call from her mother-in-law and learned that T.K. owned the Tomcats. After that all of the pieces fell into place. T.K. was a family friend who'd made a special trip to see Seth under the guise of congratulating him about the baby. He wasn't allowed to court him publicly; there were rules of engagement in the NFL that had to be followed when trades and free agency matters came into play.

Jake's birth was the perfect time for T.K. to drop in and plant a seed in Seth's mind about his team. She'd read *Love of the Game* cover to cover and one of the most touching chapters was Seth's realization that he wanted to be a professional football player after visiting the Tomcats stadium with his dad. She wanted to bring it up, but she also wanted him to talk openly about it first.

Satisfied that Jake's baby arsenal was fully stocked, Morgan went into the study to pack her work bag. Thanks to Michelle, there were no fires to put out while she was away. Her friend and assistant manager would stop by with Chinese food and give her weekly recaps. They would gossip and work on her latest project: a young adult book club that would meet in the lounge area of the store every Saturday afternoon.

Morgan had visited a few schools with flyers and talked to some of the teachers, but she'd hit pay dirt when she asked her niece Avery for her opinion. Robert's daughter jumped out of her chair, started sending text messages to her tween friends, and came back with a list of twenty members for the first book club meeting.

Morgan had a meeting with Jocelyn next week. Their mentoring relationship had blossomed into a great friendship. Jocelyn had told her she had a natural poise and eloquence that was perfect for engaging with the public. Morgan may have resisted being a football player's wife but Jocelyn assured her she complemented Seth's public image. Her guidance and encouragement was proving to be priceless.

Her cell phone rang. Morgan answered, but she didn't recognize the number. "Hello."

"Hi, Morgan. How are you?"

Morgan took a deep breath. It was her aunt Debra, Charisma's mother. "Hi, Aunt Debra. I'm good. How are you?"

"I'm a little irritated with you. First you get married to that football player and don't tell anyone. Then you have a baby and don't bring him around for me to see."

"I've been busy."

"Too busy for family? Charisma said you'd changed, but I didn't want to believe it."

Morgan's jaw clenched. "It would be hard to see the family and not see your daughter."

"I know you and Charisma never got along, but I'd hoped you two would have a better relationship as adults."

"We never got along because your daughter was always doing something to me when your back was turned. She sold that story to the tabloids and put my private life on display. Does that sound like mature adult behavior to you? This wasn't something like her wearing my clothes without asking. She was deliberately trying to derail my life."

"I'm sure we can work past this. I don't like that my two favorite girls don't get along. I'd like to talk to both of you. How about we have lunch?"

"Aunt Debra, I appreciate you trying to play peacemaker, but I think Charisma and I are way past waving white flags at each other. If you'll excuse me, tomorrow is my first day back to the bookstore since having the baby, and I have some things to do. You take care." Morgan ended the call.

Finished in the study, she made her way to the bedroom and got ready for bed. Seth's friend Ross had left a half hour ago, and she could hear Seth in Jake's room on the baby monitor. She closed her eyes for what she thought was a moment and woke when Seth kissed her.

"My aunt Debra called me," she said.

Seth furrowed his brow. "Charisma's mother? What did she want?"

"She said she wanted to sit down with me and Charisma and talk things out. I declined." Morgan rubbed his cheek. "Did you enjoy seeing your old friend tonight?"

"It's always good to catch up. He gave me a recruitment speech on the Tomcats." Seth kissed her again.

"Little does he know you're already halfway there. Did you tell him you were interested?"

"I never said that."

"Yes, you did. In your biography. You said going to the Tomcats stadium cemented your decision to become a professional athlete."

Seth thought about it for a moment. "So I did."

"Did T.K. send him?" She pulled back the covers, motioning for him to join her. Once he did, she nestled into his body.

"Ross came here on his own accord." Seth stroked her hair.

"He seems like a nice guy."

"He is. Ross and I played well together in college. We were good friends off the field."

"Like you and Patton are now?"

"Yes." Seth lightly ran his fingers up and down her arm. A soft caress was always the best way to get her to go to sleep. "You ready for your first day back to the bookstore?"

"As ready as I'll ever be," Morgan said, her speech slurred. "Seth?"

"Yes?"

"Do you think I'm a bad mother for going back to the bookstore?"

"Of course not. We both have responsibilities. And we've worked out a system. Jake won't be neglected in any way."

Morgan nestled closer to him. "Seth?"

"Yes?"

"I love you."

"I love you too."

* * *

Michelle leapt out of an aisle to greet Morgan as she entered the store. "Welcome back, Momma Bear!"

Morgan jumped and dropped her bag. "Michelle, you scared the shit out of me!"

"Just trying to keep you alert. New mothers have to be ready for anything." She giggled.

"Well, if I count the years I've known you, I've been a mother for a very long time." Morgan gave her a hug.

"Where's Jake?"

Morgan smiled. "He's home with Seth."

"I wanted to see him." Michelle stomped her foot.

"I think he's a little young to be on the payroll. Now, to business. What's new? What's old? Any good gossip?"

"The throw pillows are new—one of our patrons decided to have a clumsy moment on the way out of the store with an iced coffee. What's old? Me! My twenty-sixth birthday is next week." Michelle lay on one of the couches and put her arm over her eyes.

"I know about your birthday and have your not-so-surprise party scheduled in the backroom on Wednesday at four. I was thinking of just shooting off a flare gun instead of getting you all those damn candles." Morgan laughed.

"Thank you for being so sensitive to my fragile state."

"You get no pity from me. I'm a year older than you. If you're old, I should be someone's grandma."

Michelle lifted up suddenly. "Speaking of grandmas, Sydney's book came in the other day."

"Sydney's not Jake's grandma," Morgan blurted out.

Michelle's eyes widened. "OK, still working on your Sydney issues. How's everything else?"

Morgan sighed. Did everyone know Sydney was her sore spot?

"Come on." Michelle tugged on her arm. "Let's catch up on the gossip."

Morgan greeted the rest of her staff as they made their way to the office. In appreciation for all their help the last year, she'd given everyone a generous pay increase. Michelle deserved a medal for all the duties she'd taken over while Morgan was out on maternity leave. She'd also helped out with some administrative duties for Reading Builds Bridges. When Michelle had offered to help, Morgan must have hugged her for ten minutes.

"So how's Tyler?" Michelle murmured as she leafed through a pile of invoices on her desk.

Morgan stumbled trying to sit in her chair. "Tyler who?" Michelle asking about Tyler was not a good thing.

"Tyler Blake. Six foot two, gorgeous, looks just like your husband but with a hint of devil in him."

Morgan shot Michelle a deadly look. "Why do you want to know about Tyler?"

"We got to know each other Super Bowl weekend." Michelle blushed.

Morgan shook her head frantically. "This is not happening. It's almost incest."

"How so? We're two non-related, consenting adults."

"Sure it is. You're my best friend. He's my brother in-law, who looks eerily like my husband. This is wrong on so many levels."

"It's only morally wrong in Morgan's book on strict propriety in her social circles. I think there are monks who would tell you to loosen up. I do admit Seth and Tyler look alike, but I've long since given up my crush on Seth since you married him. I thought it was wrong to want to spread him like jelly on a piece of toast when he was my best friend's husband."

"I appreciate you releasing the raunchy hold on Seth in your mind. But that doesn't mean you pick up the torch with the next Blake you see."

"Being around those men is like being around too many attractive men in a sex club. The possibilities are endless. Channing is so sweet you can eat him with a spoon. If I were five years younger, I'd get arrested just so he could be my lawyer. J.J. has the most intense eyes I've ever seen and is too damn sexy for his own good. He's perfected that quiet, brooding thing. Or maybe it's his obnoxious wife, Eden, that has him brooding. And then there's that slice of heaven, Tyler. I bet he tastes like—"

"Michelle, tell me you did not sleep with him?"

"What kind of girl do you take me for?" Michelle balked.

Morgan shot her a dirty look.

"OK, we were flirting a bit during the game. And let me tell you, it took some work. His eyes were glued to the field. By the time we got back to the hotel from the hospital, I was too tired to be seductive."

"Where was I when you were surveying the land?"

"Going into labor. You are a booty-call blocker." Michelle stuck out her tongue.

Morgan sighed. "What a shame."

"Tyler Blake is one hot piece of Texas. I wouldn't mind getting my hands on him for a long weekend."

Morgan rubbed her temples. "Tyler Blake is a bad idea. He chases women like it's a professional sport."

"Still, that's one fine looking bad idea."

Morgan just shook her head and walked away.

After showing everyone in a five-mile radius every picture she'd taken of Jake, she returned to her desk. She sent a quick text to Seth to see how they were doing. He replied that he was teaching the baby how to read football stats. Checking inventory, returning phone calls, and approving Michelle's promotional ideas all seemed rather pedestrian when her son was at home and could be doing something amazing that only his mother could appreciate.

* * *

Morgan was glad Nina had made it tonight. Seth and Patton were having a guy's night out at the Slap Shot Bar, so it was a good time to catch up over the box of cupcakes Morgan had picked up from Nina's favorite bakery.

"So glad you could make it. I got cupcakes from the Sugar Express." Morgan rubbed her hands together in delight.

Nina groaned. "I'm big as a house, and you go out and get the greatest temptation in Philadelphia."

"Is this the same woman who told me not to worry about weight gain and just enjoy being pregnant?" Morgan gave her a skeptical look.

Nina shook her head. "Well, that was different. You weighed about fifty pounds before you got knocked up."

"Nina, please. You're thin as a rail, and you work out almost as intensely as Seth does, don't give me that crap."

"Says the woman who does a swan dive under the bed every time her husband walks into the room to avoid him seeing her naked."

Morgan sighed. "I think we've reached a stalemate in this baby-weight-gain bitch fest."

"Good, because you look great. Look at those big boobies; you must have gone up two cup sizes. You could work at a strip club." Nina tapped Morgan's breast.

"Hey! I could have worked there before. I would have been the bookkeeper in the back room, but I could have worked there."

Both Morgan and Nina giggled.

"Jake asleep?" Nina asked.

"Down for the count." Morgan waved the baby monitor in her hand.

"You keep him on that schedule, don't you?"

"I try. Seth sneaks in his room at night. I sneak in after Seth. It's no wonder he sleeps."

"Can I take a peek at him? He was asleep the last time I was here. I'll be quiet."

Nina couldn't resist touching Jake's hand when they went into the nursery. Morgan pulled her out before Nina poked him one more time, trying to get him to wake up.

"Are you trying to screw up my schedule?"

"I just wanted to spend some time with him." Nina pouted and followed her into the kitchen.

Morgan plated the cupcake and passed it to Nina.

"You are in for a world of trouble when he gets older." Nina chuckled.

"Why do you say that?"

"He's such a cutie already. He's going to look like Seth with a deep tan."

"Don't worry, I've already put in an order for a skank-o-meter. I'm going to keep him innocent as long as I can before some trollop gets her hands on him."

Nina took a bite of her cupcake. "How was the return to the bookstore?"

"Great. Michelle is the best. Store runs like clockwork when I'm not there. Are you still working part time?"

Nina nodded. "I'm micromanaging my staff. I have two more jobs then I'm hanging up my event-planning shoes. Unless you want me to organize a fundraiser for you."

"Baby steps, Nina. I just got over my fear of speaking in public." Morgan licked at the icing on her cupcake.

Nina pulled Morgan's hand to her stomach. "Can you feel that karate chop?"

"Your baby girl likes sugar."

"I don't know if I'm ready for a girl." Nina groaned.

"No? I would have thought you'd have her enrolled in the divas training academy already. If there's one person I know who should have a girl, it's you. You have that femininity thing down to a science." Morgan batted her eyes at her.

"Patton is talking about buying guns and building a fortress somewhere. He's going nuts."

Morgan poured them both a glass of milk. "I think it's nice he's becoming psychotic in the name of protecting his daughter. I've been on the receiving end of that psychosis. You bitch and fight, but you feel safe too."

Nina looked at Morgan for a while then finally said, "Thank you."

"For what?"

"For giving me that *Late Bloomer* book by the woman who had trouble conceiving. I did the things she suggested and it worked. I have my baby now and everything is fine. Thank you for helping me believe in miracles again." Nina burst into tears.

Morgan rounded the island and gave her a tight squeeze. "You're welcome, you big ole cry baby."

Nina laughed through her tears. "I'm going to miss you if Seth decides to leave the Titans."

Morgan sighed. Suddenly Seth's impending career decision was on everyone's mind. Nina had called her that afternoon after the sports show, and they'd talked for a long time about the prospect of Seth going with another team.

"I don't think we're friends because of proximity. We would keep in touch and visit, no matter what happens." Morgan handed her a box of tissue.

"Do you want to go to Texas?"

"Am I ready this very minute to transplant myself there forever? No. My family is here. The bookstore is here. I've been making progress with my non-profit."

"Then tell him you don't want to leave." Nina pouted.

"It's not that simple and you know it." Morgan sighed. "These cupcakes are making me hungry. Want to get Chinese food?"

Nina patted her pregnant belly. "Yes."

Morgan retrieved the menu from a draw and gave it to Nina. "I like everything on their menu."

Nina looked it over. "By the way, a friend of mine from *New Day* magazine reached out to me. They want to do an article on you. She asked if I would run it by you. I told her I would only mention it if it was a real interview and not some puff piece like how it feels to be the quarterback's wife. I know you hate superficial bullshit like that."

"Really? What does she want to talk to me about?"

"*New Day* magazine focuses on modern family living. Interracial marriages, same sex unions. Stuff like that."

"And again, why does she want to talk to me?"

Nina chuckled. "I don't know if anyone has told you, but you and Seth are an interracial couple."

Morgan put her finger to her lips. "Why am I always the last to know everything?"

Nina hunched her shoulders. "You get a chance to plug your non-profit. So, I can give her your number?"

"I'll talk to your friend then make my decision about the interview."

* * *

The Slap Shot bar was owned by one of Seth's dearest friends, Derek Popovich. After Patton had informed Seth he'd all but disappeared since becoming a parent, he felt guilty about ignoring his friend. He wasn't proposing a wild night out, simply a few drinks and maybe a meal at Derek's bar. Morgan didn't mind; she'd readied for some girl time with Nina.

A few of the guys from the team were at the bar, not to mention a few basketball and hockey players he knew. The most interesting thing about the establishment was that Derek didn't allow any televisions, which proved to be stressful for the clientele who were mostly self- centered professional athletes who loved to see themselves on sports commentary shows.

Derek offered a lavish décor as a great consolation prize. The bar was furnished with leather couches, fine art work, and a space design that maximized the comfort of a large crowd. Soft music played through a premium sound system, but never so loud you couldn't hear your dinner guest. Patton and a few of the guys from the team had hated it the first time he'd brought them but eventually appreciated the serenity of getting away from the spotlight.

It was usually crawling with beautiful women who were looking to bag themselves a rich athlete. Seth had learned a long time ago not to dip his toe in this particular dating pool, and he was damn glad he was out of the dating game all together. What had once seemed sublime — finding a gorgeous woman to spend some time with until they both tired of each other — now left a bad taste in his mouth. He definitely wouldn't have met Morgan there.

Sheena, the bartender, made her way over to Seth and Patton with a drink. "Seth, a woman at the end of the bar bought you a drink."

An *expensive* drink. The generous lady had sent over a glass of the best top shelf single malt scotch Derek kept in his inventory.

"Sheena, please send it back. I'll reimburse you for the drink and the tip."

Sheena nodded and took the drink away.

"I bet it's that chick that's been gawking at you for the last hour," Patton said. "The stink of wedded bliss has made you more attractive."

Seth shook his head. "Pat, it's getting better. My neighbor Svetlana knocked on my door a couple of weeks ago."

"Damn, I remember Svetlana. She's the one who walks through the lobby of the Ashcroft in a bikini."

"Yeah."

"Did you two ever…?" Patton waggled his eyebrows.

"No. Whenever she was in the country, she would drop by to see if I was finally ready to 'taste the nectar of her sweet fruit.' Her words, not mine. But this time, she rang the doorbell, and Morgan answered. Svetlana had on a full-length mink coat and a bikini underneath. Svetlana said she's hot and needs to see me." Seth's cheeks reddened.

"Oh, shit! What did Morgan say?"

"She threw the bottled water she was holding in her hand on Svetlana and said, 'That should cool you down.'"

Patton burst out laughing. "I think Morgan and Nina were separated at birth."

Seth couldn't help but laugh with him.

"Seth Blake, you handsome devil." The owner of the feminine voice behind him placed her hand on his back.

He moved out of the way and turned around, shocked to see Morgan's cousin Charisma. Her hairstyle had changed since he'd seen her at the barbecue, but he knew it was her. She was dressed like she was on the prowl, and her tight white dress accentuated every curve she had. The expensive heels she wore gave her some height, but she wasn't that much taller than Morgan.

Seth tightened his jaw. "Charisma."

"What a surprise seeing you here. I thought Morgan kept you tied up in that penthouse of yours." She gave him a wicked smile.

"What can I say? I love being in the company of my wife." Seth smiled sincerely back at her.

Charisma seductively ran her finger around the rim of her wine glass, but he kept his eyes fixed on her face. Surely she knew that he knew what she was trying to do. Thankfully Patton didn't move from his spot on the stool. Seth just stood there, not encouraging any further conversation.

"Jake is a beautiful baby," Charisma said. "Has those green eyes of yours."

"I think he looks like his mother."

Charisma sucked her teeth. "My little cousin sure lucked out with you. It's amazing how she blossomed after that awkward bookworm stage of hers. She was a tomboy for years."

"Lucky for me I think nerdy women are hot."

"I've seen the women you dated before you married Morgan.

There was nothing nerdy about any of them." She cackled.

"All of those women were a dime a dozen; that's why I never proposed to any of them. Even in this bar there are plenty of beautiful women here on the hunt looking for a man with money. I don't have to worry about that. Since the day we've met, Morgan's only wanted me."

Charisma pouted at Seth's constant rebuttals. Whatever she had set out to do when she came over, it was obvious it wasn't working. To make matters worse, a small crowd was starting to form, listening to their conversation. He wondered if she'd learned anything from that confrontation at the barbeque. He didn't want to humiliate her, but she wasn't getting away with throwing digs at his wife.

"It was good seeing you again." Charisma leaned forward to kiss him on the cheek.

Seth moved out of the way. It was getting awkward. "You have a nice night, Charisma."

She pivoted on her stiletto heels and walked over to a table where a group of women sat having drinks.

Patton whistled. "Who was that?"

"That was Morgan's cousin. She's the one who sold that story to the tabloids."

Patton shook his head. "She was pushing up on you hard, man. She's lucky Morgan wasn't here."

Chapter Three

Seth's suggestion they take a road trip to Pittsburgh to see Tate's concert instead of flying was a welcome surprise. They were both in a celebrating mood after getting the green light from her gynecologist to resume intimate activities. Her six-week checkup after delivery had gone quite well. The doctor said she was physically in good shape and told her not to worry so much about those pesky few pounds that lingered. Morgan looked at him like he was crazy. A few pounds were pesky, but she felt like the remaining eight were enough to sink a tugboat.

After loading up her new SUV, they dropped Jake off with Sydney and Morgan's dad. She and Seth had had a long talk the night before about taking the trip. He was OK if she didn't want to leave Jake, but he pointed out that Sydney and her dad were looking forward to keeping the baby for the weekend. Guilt hit her the minute she left her father's house, but she kept marching on to the Range Rover.

"I like the way your SUV handles." Seth maneuvered effortlessly onto the highway.

"I have to admit it has a lot of room." Morgan sighed. "But I do miss my old car."

Seth laughed. "I could fit that thing in my pocket."

"Stop exaggerating. It was a cute car," Morgan said as she spied the display on her cell phone.

"He's OK." Seth squeezed her hand.

"I was just making sure I could get a signal out here in the country."

Seth gave her a sideways glance.

"Honest." She held her hands up.

"So, what's new in your world, Mrs. Blake? Besides being a kick-ass mother and wife?"

"I had a chat on the phone with a reporter from *New Day* magazine yesterday. She's a friend of Nina's."

"What did she want to talk about?"

"She wants my opinion on being in an interracial relationship in this day and age."

"Are you going to do it?"

Morgan looked at him. "Before I made that decision, I thought we'd talk about it first. We've never really talked about..."

Seth smiled. "How much we love each other?"

She laughed. "That's never been an issue for us."

"Exactly."

"I agree, but you're a high profile celebrity. Sometimes you become a poster child and don't realize it. We may be two evolved people, but I'm afraid our children will still have to deal with it."

Seth squeezed her hand. "And we'll be there to help them through it. Look at the two of us. The biggest difference between you and me is that you were born in the city and I'm a country boy."

"You know if this were the not so distant past, loving each other would have been socially unacceptable and even criminal. We would have been ostracized." She gazed out the window at the greenery on the side of the highway, not really seeing it.

"And I would have fought for us, Morgan. I'll always fight for us. No matter what comes along, we will face it together." Seth kissed her hand.

"Damn right."

"Sounds like you're going to do the interview then?"

Morgan smiled. "I'll ask Daniel to contact the magazine and hammer out the details."

* * *

Tate didn't disappoint with his performance. Morgan couldn't tell which heated up the stage more: the elaborate lighting or Tate strutting around with that guitar like it was a sex toy. He possessed energy like no other musician she'd seen in a live venue. When he wasn't flirting with the women in the crowd, he was flirting with his female band members. In one of his calmer moments, he gave a shout out to Morgan and Seth, whom he introduced as his brother and sister-in-law. He then introduced a new song he'd written titled, "A Man's Glory," citing the couple as his inspiration for writing it. Morgan was so touched by the song, she cried.

As soon as the concert ended, four surly looking bodyguards came to the front row and retrieved them. They could have watched from backstage but Morgan enjoyed being among the crowd. They were escorted through a maze of amped-up people and finally led to Tate's dressing room. Tate was taking a shower and yelled he'd be right out.

"Come in here with all your clothes on, McGill," Seth said as he and Morgan took a seat on the couch.

"Scared I might take your woman?" Tate emerged from the bathroom dressed in jeans and a white T-shirt.

"You'd have to do a lot more with that guitar—"

"Seth!" Morgan put her hand over his mouth.

Tate came over and kissed her on the cheek. "I love driving him crazy. How are you, darlin'?"

Seth ducked when Tate tried to kiss him too.

Morgan snickered at that. "I'm good. Great concert."

Tate gave her an appreciative once over. "Well, you look great. I can't even tell you had a baby a few months ago."

"Did Seth tell you to say that?" She squinted her eyes at Tate.

"Seth didn't tell Tate to be looking at his woman," Seth grumbled.

"He can get so sensitive." Tate laughed.

"Your backup singers are very sexy," Morgan said.

Tate laughed again. "Those are Tate's Angels. Did you see the one in the middle?"

"Yes, she set off my skank-o-meter." The singer in the middle was the one whose skirt was dangerously short.

"That's Misty. She used to have a thing for your husband. I told her three times today that he was happily married with a child." Tate smiled widely at Seth.

Morgan looked at Seth, who shook his head.

"How's my nephew?" Tate walked over to the bar to grab two beers.

"He's fine. I put the Future Country Western Singer T-shirt you bought on him once a week." Morgan grinned.

"Please." Seth huffed.

"But I especially like the My Daddy's a Cowboy shirt." She scrunched her nose at him. "So what's new with you, Tate?"

"After the tour is over I'll be headed to California. I'm thinking about signing with a new record label. I have a meeting with Kate Garrison at Atlantis Records."

"You're a busy man. Teri-Lyn told me you're doing some redecorating at the cabin to make it more woman-friendly. Is there a particular woman you're making these changes for?" Morgan smiled.

"It never hurts to be prepared in case the day hell finally freezes over." Tate winked at her.

Morgan saw the flicker of emotion in his stormy blue eyes. Tate looked like he was at odds with himself about something. Seth wouldn't go into detail whenever she asked about Tate's past. He simply said that a man shouldn't have to carry around as much baggage as he did.

"So what made you think about one day settling down?" Morgan asked.

"When I was writing that new song, it made me think about much happier my friend has been since he met you. Contentment can do wonders for a man's soul. I've been thinking about being open to finding some of that myself."

"You may find it sooner than you think." Seth looked his friend in the eye.

Tate held up his beer bottle. "I'll drink to that."

* * *

Morgan and Seth got on the road after a big breakfast with Tate. Morgan saw a sign for an outlet mall and asked Seth to stop, hoping to add some essentials to her wardrobe. She was making steady progress with her weight loss but still felt uncomfortable in her old clothes. They walked around until a pretty dress in a boutique window caught Morgan's eye. But it didn't fit, so she tried another one. Then another one. After about an hour of nothing fitting right, Morgan sat on the bench in the fitting room, suppressing the urge to cry.

Sure her breasts were bigger, but her waistline had expanded, and her arms were fuller. Fitting into her normal size six seemed like an impossible dream these days. How she looked had never occupied her mind so much before because she'd rarely changed. She owned the same pair of perfect jeans since high school. They accentuated all the right places and were very comfortable. Last week she'd tried them on again but this time Seth didn't have to help her out of them. That was some progress.

Morgan leaned her head back and closed her eyes while she waited for the salesgirl to come back with another pair of jeans.

"Is this some kind of shopping meditation that women do?"

Morgan opened her eyes to see Seth standing there. "Praying

for the next pair of jeans to fit. What are you doing back here?"

"I intercepted the grandma clothes Tiffany was bringing you and picked out some things for you to try on."

"You didn't." She sighed. The clothes he held in his hands—tops with deep V-necklines and soft fabrics meant to cling to the skin—were not meant to hide post-pregnancy fat.

Seth entered the small dressing room and yanked on the thick silk cord holding the curtain in place. "What is going on with you and clothing lately?"

"In case you haven't noticed my body is going through some changes. The exercises are helping, but I'm still not where I want to be." Morgan pouted. "And please don't say one nice, sweet word to comfort me."

"Is that what the shrine to your favorite pair of jeans in our closet is all about?" Seth laughed.

"It's not a shrine."

"Really? I don't know how many people put a pair of jeans on a gold hanging rack and shine a spotlight on it."

Morgan crossed her arms. "You are such an exaggerator."

Seth turned her to face the mirror. "In Texas, we specialize in tall tales and short, fiery women."

"Well, I've had those jeans since high school, and I am determined to wear them again."

"Morgan…"

"Not a word." She closed her eyes and bit her lip.

"Morgan, open your eyes."

Seth wrapped one arm around her waist as he slowly liberated her from the blouse she'd thrown on when he came into the dressing room. Morgan was wearing a purple bra and panty set; he loved how the vibrant color accentuated her brown skin. Her breasts were fuller, giving her already ample cleavage the appearance of two sensual globes barely being contained by the satin and lace. Seth started with a kiss behind her ear, then slowly slid his tongue down the side of her neck and continued down the slope of her shoulder, removing the strap with his teeth. Her breast spilled out of the bra even more, and he reached up to gently roll her erect nipple between his fingers. Morgan gasped, so he whispered in her ear the necessity for quiet, so they wouldn't get busted in the dressing room. She smiled at that, then pressed herself against him, rubbing until his cock twitched and was at full attention. She turned her head to meet his mouth, their tongues entwining in a sensual kiss. Seth reached up, unsnapped the bra, and threw it on the floor. He covered her breasts with his hands, giving them the full attention they deserved. With each tender stroke, Morgan became more pliant in his arms, leaning back for support. She reached behind her and pulled at the zipper on his jeans. He broke the kiss and let her go, amused at the pouty glare she gave him.

Seth got down on his knees, pushed her against the wall, and gave her panties a good tug. He put his hands on her hips and trailed kisses down her stomach, paying special attention to the small paunch that remained from her baby weight. Morgan's soft exhale encouraged him to go further, so he took her leg and propped it up on the wooden bench attached to the wall. Before she could protest, Seth spread her open with two fingers and a long gliding movement, then dipped his tongue inside her folds. He leaned closer and deepened his connection until Morgan was grabbing his hair, pulling him to her. He loved imposing the erotic torture on her. He would pleasure her this way for hours at home, coaxing multiple orgasms from her. But he also knew that when she reached her boiling point, everyone in the boutique would know what was going on in there. He rose and pulled down his jeans and boxers.

She came toward him, but he shook his head and stopped her, turning her around to face a wall with a bar attached to it. He put her hands on the bar and stood back a bit, resting his cock on her ass. Seth pushed her legs apart, then slid into her from behind, in one swift move. He grabbed her hips, which helped him control the slow, sensual rhythm they created. The heat from their bodies connecting was making him sweat, but he'd be damned if he let go of her to take his T-shirt off. Morgan pushed back to meet his thrusts. As quiet as they both were, the sounds of ecstasy began spilling from them. Seth bit down hard on his lip to quiet himself. He took one hand off Morgan's hip to cover her mouth while caressing her clit with the other. His thrusts became frantic as he held back as long as he could. Finally, he lifted her off her feet with the final thrust, his mind going blank from the intensity of his orgasm.

He stayed connected with her for a while, until their panting returned to normal breaths. Seth, drenched with sweat, pulled up his boxers and jeans and took a seat on the bench, then pulled Morgan onto his lap.

"You do know we're going to have to buy one of everything in my size in the boutique," Morgan mumbled as she kissed his jawline.

Seth chuckled. "A small price to pay to show my wife how hot she is."

Morgan cleared her throat. "What are the chances we can walk out of here like nothing happened?"

"Baby, I don't think that's possible, but we can try not to blush at the register." Seth kissed her nose.

Tiffany, the sales woman assisting Morgan, gave them a sly, knowing grin when they came up to the counter. She carefully wrapped Morgan's items and asked the fateful question: was he Seth Blake. Morgan looked like she wanted to go through the floor but Seth defused the situation by giving the woman an autograph and showing her a picture of Jake. Tiffany nodded that she understood how difficult it was to have time alone with a baby and showed them pictures of her son. Morgan smiled when Seth remarked that they weren't so different from any other couple.

They picked up Jake at her dad's house early in the afternoon. Morgan confessed to Seth that the few days away from Jake had passed like an eternity. They got back to the penthouse in time go to through his daily routine of feeding and a bath. Morgan told him all about Uncle Tate's concert well after his bedtime while Seth watched them. When Jake was finally down for the night, Seth and Morgan picked up where they'd left off in the dressing room.

Chapter Four

Morgan grabbed the mail from the counter and took a seat on one of the couches in the bookstore. Her hand began to tremble as she read the letter from the library. She read it twice. The library had accepted her proposal for an internship program to keep a steady flow of readers in the library. Morgan took out her cell phone, took a pic of the letter, and sent it to Seth. A minute later his ring tone played on her phone.

"Hey baby, congratulations!" Seth said.

"Thank you. Can you believe this letter?" She sighed, looking at it again.

"I am so proud of you. Enjoy this moment."

"I'll be home around four."

Morgan was getting ready to get back to finalizing details for a book signing to be held later that week when Michelle hustled into the store.

Morgan handed Michelle her letter. "Look what I got in the mail."

Michelle skimmed the letter and started bouncing around like her shoes were on springs. "Congratulations! I can see college kids jumping all over that as course credit."

"Thanks."

"Oh, I forgot to tell you I made some progress with scheduling the book fair at the assisted living facility near your dad's house."

"Great. Did you send them the questionnaire on the types of books they want us to bring?"

"Yep. They emailed it back today." Michelle reached behind the counter to retrieve it.

Morgan pinched herself. "Is this really happening?"

"It's really happening. Reading Builds Bridges is taking flight." Michelle smiled and gave her a pinch too, for good measure.

* * *

Seth carefully removed Jake from the rear of the Range Rover so he wouldn't wake him and walked into the building. Father and son had developed a rhythm when traveling and it was now a natural thing to take Jake wherever he went. *Sports Page* magazine had been gracious enough to push back his interview a week, and he didn't want to put them off any longer.

Morgan had volunteered to reschedule her meeting at the library to stay home, but he'd refused her offer. The decision not to get a nanny often made her wring her hands with guilt when situations like this arose, but he reminded her that they both agreed to juggle responsibilities as working parents. He enjoyed the time he and Jake spent together and was grateful for the experience.

As soon as the elevator doors opened on the fifth floor of the building, he could hear the music pulsing. That normally wouldn't have bothered him, but Jake was taking a nap, and he couldn't risk him getting off his schedule. Seth whipped out his cell phone and dialed Celine, the contact at the magazine that was waiting for him.

"Celine, this is Seth Blake. I'm down the hall, but I need a favor…"

Two hours later Seth was posing, in an elegant suit, for his cover photo. Celine had graciously transformed the atmosphere from nightclub to nursery. When the music had died down and he'd made his way to the loft, a nursery rhyme was playing on the sound system and the usual titillating honeys that always seemed to be in the vicinity of places like this were walking around in respectable clothing. Seth found a good space for Jake's car seat and didn't have to worry about him for long. The women surrounded him and *oohed* and *ahhed* for at least a half hour before they began shooting. Jake continued to sleep while his fan club kept watch over him. That time gave Seth a chance to talk to Celine about the photo shoot. Instead of a salacious cover, he thought he'd take a different approach. Celine looked a little disappointed but Eddie, the photographer, assured her that, clothed or not, Seth was still hot.

It surprised him too that he didn't want to show some skin. He was proud of his body. He stayed in shape for work, and he took pleasure when Morgan stared at him with that hungry look in her eye. But there were greater things to consider now. Did he want his kids to pick up a magazine and see Daddy half naked on the cover? The perception his children would have was now important to him.

Eddie cursed under his breath about the nursery rhyme music.

"You can change the music if you like. I just don't want to wake him from his nap. His momma would kill me." Seth smiled.

"Any special requests?" Eddie perused his iPod.

"He's partial to jazz and some of his uncle's songs. Do you have any of Tate McGill on there?"

"Do I? I'm his biggest fan! I absolutely love his track from his third CD, 'I Lost My Soul at the Candlewood Hotel in Houston.' Tate McGill has inspired many a sleepless night for me." Eddie fanned himself.

Seth laughed.

He had brought a few props with him: the suit, his championship ring, and some of his football gear. Eddie's work impressed him. He saw a few of the test shots and was confident it was going to be a cover he could show his kids. Everything was moving along at a good pace. He glanced at his watch. Jake would be up soon. As soon as those words entered his mind, Jake took his cue and began to move in his car seat.

"Eddie, give me a minute, he's been in that for a while. I don't want him to get cranky." Seth put his football helmet on the table and unsnapped Jake from the seat.

Jake wasn't fully awake, letting out a big yawn as Seth propped his head on his shoulder. Seth knew with a few animated words and a kiss Jake would slowly come out of his sleepy state. But if the room stayed quiet and Seth rubbed his back, Jake would sleep a little longer. He nestled closer to Seth's body and went back to sleep.

"You are a natural." Celine beamed at him.

"He's easy to please," Seth drawled.

Eddie continued snapping pictures. "This is too precious. If you don't mind, I'd like to snap a few of you and Seth Jr. to take home to your wife."

"Sure."

Seth tuned out the camera clicking and Celine's chatter and listened to the sound of his son's even breathing. There he was posing for yet another magazine cover while looking after his son. So much had changed in his life in such a short amount of time. Holding a trophy used to be the most important thing to him. Now, he was holding his son, his true legacy in his arms, and it made him feel better than football ever did. His love for the game was being overtaken by something more powerful than he'd ever imagined: fatherhood.

* * *

Seth whistled as Morgan walked into the kitchen wearing the dress they'd picked up at the boutique on their way back from Pittsburgh. The black cocktail dress had a plunging neckline and clung to those hips of hers he loved so much. She wore her hair down, the soft curls lying on her shoulders. Morgan was slimming down from exercise, but she hardly mentioned losing the weight anymore. Who knew hot dressing room sex would make her realize how sexy she was post-baby?

"You like?" Morgan twirled around.

"I have good taste." Seth pulled her into his arms for a kiss. "How's the champ?"

"Out like a light. He should sleep through the night. How's my rack of lamb coming along?"

"I just checked it. It smells divine."

"Kara's recipe was easy to follow. Did you see the way she was looking at me when she left? That look did not inspire confidence." She laughed.

"Kara is very protective of the kitchen." Seth chuckled. "I wonder if we can blend—"

Morgan gave him a disapproving look. "You are not pureeing lamb for Jake."

"Hey, he was eyeballing that pork chop I had the other night." Seth raised an eyebrow.

"I saw you. You were taunting him with that bone."

"Blake men don't eat no mashed up bananas. We go from breast milk to ribs," Seth bellowed as he retrieved a serving platter from the top shelf of a cabinet.

"If it were up to you and your crazy brothers he'd take a slab of ribs, a flask of whiskey, and a good cigar for his first day of pre-school."

"Man's got to start somewhere." He shrugged.

"I am keeping you grubby cowboys away from my sweet-cheeked, red haired baby." She stuck her tongue out at him.

"I noticed his hair color changing the other day." Seth smiled at her.

"The baby book said his changing hair color was normal. Much like yours, when you were young. Damn strong Blake genes, I bet he's going to look like a carbon copy of you. He's going to be taller than me by the time he's seven."

"I see you too when I look at him." He kissed her on top of her head.

"Do you think we have enough wine?"

Seth laughed. There were three cases of wine on the kitchen table. "More than enough."

"You do remember who we invited?"

"Let's see, Patton and Nina. Elton and his fiancée. Mike and his wife Krista. And Lamont and his new mystery woman."

Morgan folded her arms across her chest. "We should have uninvited that jailbird Lamont."

"Don't worry." Seth kissed her. "Lamont won't be a problem tonight."

It was just his luck that after an attempt to bury the hatchet with Lamont and get to know him better, Lamont got arrested for fighting in a nightclub. There had been a picture of him on the front page of the newspaper last week, after the brawl. A mystery woman was shielding him with a gaudy, gold purse.

Patton and Nina were the first to arrive. Elton, Tricia, Mike, and Krista arrived together. Nina offered to help but Morgan insisted she stay put while Morgan served the guests appetizers. Patton reminded the guys that they were each scheduled to appear at his football camp for kids this summer. Seth and Patton joked about their upcoming joint endorsement deal. After the Super Bowl, the true scope of their friendship had become visible to the world, and they had been approached about shooting a commercial together for a footwear retailer. Morgan gave the ladies a tour of the house while Seth mixed drinks. After an hour, it looked like Lamont and his date were going to be a no-show. The evening was going well until Elton asked about Seth's impending free agency status.

"I haven't made any decisions yet." Seth shook his head.

"We have a great team; surely you don't want to break that up?" Elton said.

"Elton, any statement I make about it right now will feed a firestorm of rumors. I don't think it's fair to the team for the sports world to cover whether or not I'm staying with the Titans when there are a lot more important things at hand. The coming season. A new strategy. Winning three times has put a target on our backs. Every team out there will want to be the team that stopped our hot streak."

"But—"

Patton spoke up. "Elton, the man answered your question honestly. I know you don't think he's going to tell you anything that would jeopardize his family's future or the team's."

"How can you be so calm about it, Pat?" Mike asked.

"When he came here four years ago, remember how pissed everybody was that Boyd left and we got the new dude? Even with all the doubts and non-support, he did his job. He committed himself to the Titans in spite of all the bullshit. I don't believe that a man like that would leave without thinking everything through."

"Thanks, Patton." Seth nodded.

Morgan rose. "Shall we all move to the dining room?"

The doorbell rang. Seth went to the door while Morgan went into the kitchen and, with Krista's help, brought out the side dishes. She returned to the kitchen and sliced the rack of lamb. She placed it on the silver serving platter Seth had retrieved for her earlier. Morgan was quite happy with herself that she hadn't burned anything. She turned the corner with her plate of lamb to see Seth's pleasant expression had changed to a frown. Lamont Brayer stood behind him with none other than her cousin Charisma in tow.

Morgan set the tray carefully down on the table and saw Nina's puzzled look out of the corner of her eye. Seth had given Morgan a play-by-play of Charisma's shenanigans at the bar the night it had happened, and she appreciated the way he'd handled it. It was her cousin's latest attempt to bait her, but she wasn't falling for it. She'd

THE BLAKE LEGACY 245

resolved to take the high road and let it go. Now the bitch was standing in her house as a dinner guest by default. Morgan's mind raced, trying to figure out a way to get her cousin out of there without performing dinner theater in front of Seth's colleagues.

She forced a smile. "Lamont, Charisma, we were sitting down to dinner. Please take a seat."

Lamont spoke first. "Nice to see you, Morgan. You look lovely as usual. I had no idea Charisma was your cousin. What a small world."

Morgan looked at Charisma. "It gets smaller every day."

Lamont and Charisma took their seats, and Morgan watched as Charisma's gaze roamed around trying to get the lay of the land. Morgan winked at Seth and managed another smile, hoping to defuse the tension she saw rising in his neck. Patton tried to pick up the dinner conversation where they'd left off but Nina interrupted him.

"So how did the two of you meet?" Nina's question crackled in the air like the snap of a whip.

Charisma took a long, dramatic pause and flipped her hair behind her shoulders. "We met at Club Six. Lamont was there celebrating his Super Bowl win. I asked him to dance and the sparks flew from there."

Lamont chuckled. "Yeah, Charisma surprised me with the direct approach. She definitely knows what she wants."

Seth tried to suppress a smile, while Morgan poured the wine.

"Lamont and I have been happily dating ever since. He even bought me this necklace I'm wearing." Charisma fingered the glittering piece of jewelry hanging off her neck.

Lamont continued, "I didn't notice it at first, but now that the two of you are together, I see the resemblance."

Morgan's hand slipped while pouring Patton's wine, and she almost spilled it onto the table.

"I wouldn't go that far, Lamont." Seth clenched his jaw.

Morgan had to hand it to her cousin; she was decked out and fit the part of the star football player's girl. It had been ages since she'd seen her. After that shouting match about Jason on the phone, Morgan had blocked her numbers and informed her family that Charisma was behind that attempted media smear campaign. The lockout was effective; the extended family supported her decision as well. But this new tactic, spending time with Lamont Brayer, was a bit creepy to her.

Charisma was trying to monopolize the conversation but Nina would butt in and steer it in another direction. The other guests stayed quiet, watching the train wreck unfolding. Morgan sliced her lamb like a surgeon in an operating room, opting to enjoy the meal she'd spent most of the day preparing. Seth kept playing with his fork, a sign he was getting agitated. Lamont, who happily chatted with his teammates, was the only person who was clueless about what was going on in front of him. After Nina shot down Charisma's third attempt to bait Morgan, everyone became eerily quiet.

After dinner they retreated back to the living room. Morgan glanced at the clock on the mantle, wondering how long it would take her cousin to start up again. Two minutes later Charisma opened her big mouth.

"Don't we get a tour?" Charisma said as she perused the room instead of taking a seat with everyone else.

"Morgan gave a tour to everyone who arrived on time," Seth said from the bar, making a Shirley Temple for Nina.

"Sorry about that. Charisma got hung up at the beauty salon." Lamont grinned.

"So, I still don't get a tour? I want to know what's so fabulous that has my family gushing about this penthouse all the time." Charisma smirked, playing with her necklace.

Morgan didn't realize her hand was shaking until she set her wine glass down on the table with a clink. "Charisma, I fed you and have shown exceptional control this evening. Don't push your luck."

Everyone looked at Morgan. Seth stood up but Morgan gave him a small nod, letting him know everything was OK.

Lamont wrinkled his brow, finally picking up on the tension. "Wow, you two sure don't sound like cousins."

"My cousin can be quite bratty at times. Been that way all her life." Charisma huffed.

Morgan stood. "Lamont, I don't know what my cousin has told you, but we do not have an amicable relationship. Never have. As a matter of fact, if it weren't for you, she would never have set foot in my home."

"Here we go. Playing Little Miss Victim again. It's always about somebody hurting Morgan." Charisma scoffed.

Morgan turned to Charisma, taking careful breaths. "*You're* the one who's always trying to hurt me. As far as I am concerned, we are not family. Family doesn't try to stab each other in the back and spread lies about them for money."

"You're just mad because you're not the only person in the family involved with a football star." Charisma clenched her perfectly manicured fists.

Morgan narrowed her eyes. "Don't you dare try to make my marriage sound like your pathetic attempt to land some celebrity with a big bank account."

Charisma's her eyes widened in shock. She started walking toward Morgan, but her jaw dropped when Lamont stood up and stopped her.

"Charisma, I think it's time to go. We've caused enough disruption to Morgan's dinner party tonight."

"But—"

"Walk out or get rolled out of here like a bowling ball. It's your choice." Morgan motioned to the door. Seth was standing there, holding it open.

Lamont uttered a low apology again to Seth as he ushered a muttering Charisma out the door. She threw one last incensed glare over her shoulder and stomped out as well as her stiletto heels would allow.

Morgan took a deep breath and addressed her guests. "I'm sorry you had to witness that. I hope you'll remember this night for my lamb and not the family feud."

There was a moment of silence. Then Nina smiled and rubbed her belly. "That lamb was pretty good. Do you have anymore?"

Morgan laughed, feeling ten times lighter. "Sure. I would never starve a pregnant woman."

The mood of the dinner party improved tremendously once Nina ate a second helping of the lamb, then everyone moved on to dessert. By the time everyone left it was after midnight. Seth carried Morgan out of the kitchen to deter her from doing the dishes and driving herself crazy over what Charisma had done. After all, tomorrow was another day.

Chapter Five

Teri-Lyn and John Jacob snatched their grandson out of Seth and Morgan's hands right after they walked off their plane at the private airport. It had been months since Jake's first visit to the ranch. John Jacob mentioned that he'd played a round of golf with T.K. last week and that brought up the subject of Seth's impending free agency. T.K. wasn't allowed to talk to Seth directly, but he was certainly reaching out like the hand of God and talking to everyone who knew him.

Seth and John Jacob unloaded the car while Morgan, Teri-Lyn, and Jake went inside.

"You know, the strangest thing happened when I played golf with T.K." His father snorted.

"What's that?"

"I think the son of a bitch let me win."

"Wow. T.K.'s the most competitive man I know." Seth ran his hand over his head.

"If he thinks golf wins are going to persuade me to convince my son to play for his team, he's got another thing coming. He can try all he wants. I think his assistant Ellen has invited your mother for coffee at least four times this month."

Seth slammed the door of the truck. "What do you think about all this?"

John Jacob looked him in the eye. "I think I raised you to make your own decisions. You'll know what's right for you and your family when the time comes."

Teri-Lyn happily volunteered to watch Jake while Seth and Morgan went for a ride. Bo had already saddled Reed's Fire for Morgan. Morgan had a heart-to-heart talk with the horse about why she hadn't been able to ride him for a while. Seth saddled Iris, and as they made their way around the property, he noticed how Morgan no longer needed direction about riding her horse, dismounting him, or gripping his reigns to guide him. She was turning into a country girl.

Later that evening when they prepared for bed, Morgan asked him questions about his impending free agency status.

"So there are rules in place so T.K. can't flat out seduce you into wanting to be on his team?"

Seth nodded. "Yes, there is a specific strategy involved but that's the gist of it."

"And you're having lunch with Ethan Thorpe tomorrow? And he's the governor?"

"Yes, ma'am. Ethan and I are old friends."

"Who happens to have been a Tomcat?" Morgan looked at herself in the mirror while brushing her teeth.

Seth turned on the faucet. "Yes, about fifteen years ago. And he's good friends with T.K."

"I smell a conspiracy." She stopped mid brush.

"Me too." He lathered the moisturizing bar and scrubbed his face.

"How long have you wanted to be a Tomcat?"

"Since my first visit to their stadium when I was ten years old." He splashed some water on his face.

"You talked about that in your book, didn't you?" She put her toothbrush back in the holder and poured mouthwash into a cup.

"I did." He smiled at her.

Morgan hesitated, cup in hand. "If things work out, you have a chance to fulfill a childhood dream."

"I suppose I would." He sighed.

Seth watched Morgan, who didn't say anything else while she put away everything on the counter. She was a neat person, but by the time she'd finished the bathroom could have passed a military inspection. He'd come to know that organizing things was her stress reliever.

Seth waited until he was sure Morgan was asleep to slip out of bed. He headed into the study, looking for something to occupy his mind. As he perused the library shelves Morgan kept meticulously alphabetized, his gaze fell upon a picture of him and his dad. He was suited up for a middle school game. It was one of the last times he'd played football just for the sheer joy of it.

Daddy, I'm going to play for the Tomcats one day.

I know you will son.

It seemed like it was only yesterday when Seth had gotten his first tour of the Tomcats stadium. He was ten years old and had gone with his father to pay his friend T.K. a visit. The feeling he got when he set foot on that football field remained with him still, and he got goose bumps when he thought about it. The Tomcats field was his first brush with his destiny. The feeling of awe and wonderment, even at the age of ten, was not lost on him. The stadium seated thousands, but from his tiny perspective, he thought millions could fit into the seats. Strangely enough it felt like home to him. When he'd come back from the tour, John Jacob had seen the look in his eyes.

"What's wrong son?"

"Nothing."

"Looks like Seth just got a glimpse of his future," T.K. had said with a wide smile.

That was twenty years ago. Now he was a legend in his own right, married with a son, but the gnawing attraction to the Tomcats remained.

* * *

Morgan and Jake helped Seth get ready for his lunch with Ethan.

"Babe, why are you wearing a suit for lunch with your friend? I know he's the governor but…"

"Ethan could invite you to play horse shoes and when you get there he'll have a tuxedo on. He always has to be the best dressed man in the room, and I cannot have that." Seth laughed.

"If it makes you feel any better, you will be the most handsome." Morgan kissed him.

"Have a good time with Momma." He kissed Jake, then Morgan, and headed out.

Morgan went into the kitchen, put Jake in his high chair, and gave him a cup of juice and his favorite toy while she cooked bacon and eggs. She was putting breakfast on the table when Teri-Lyn came into the kitchen with a big box.

"Good morning." Morgan kissed her mother-in-law on the cheek. "What's in the box?"

"I found some old home movies of the boys. I even have a few reels of Seth's football games." Teri-Lyn smiled as she took Jake out of his high chair.

"On film? Really?" Morgan scrunched her nose while trying to calculate exactly how old those movies were.

"Oh yeah. John Jacob refused to switch over to VHS camcorders for the longest time, so despite the appearance that it was the sixties, it was really the eighties." She laughed.

"Does the projector still work?" Morgan spied the projector in the box.

"Yes, it does."

"Maybe we can have a movie night outside? I'd love to watch these old things." Morgan beamed.

"Sounds like a good idea." Teri-Lyn kissed Jake's cheek. "I do confess I get misty when I look at those reels. Chasing after those hyperactive rug rats were the best times of my life."

Teri-Lyn continued to reminisce early days of the Blake family while they ate breakfast. With all the skinned knees, practical jokes played on one another, and football practices, Morgan was amazed at how Teri-Lyn had kept up with them all. But there was a formula to the calamity that Teri-Lyn described.

"That was a great breakfast, Morgan." Teri-Lyn put her napkin on the table.

Morgan put her coffee cup down and began cleaning Jake's hands. He loved his bananas so much he'd decided to wear them. "Thanks. Is my cooking getting any better?"

"Your cooking is just fine. Has my son been complaining about it?"

"No. He just seems to eat more when he's down here."

Jake was all cleaned up so she liberated him from his high chair and handed him to his grandmother.

"It's the country air," Teri-Lyn cooed at Jake as he grabbed onto her shirt and stood up. "You have a big appetite, just like your daddy did when he was a little boy."

"Where are you going mister?" Morgan said.

Jake responded with baby talk.

"You look just like your daddy when he was your age." Teri-Lyn kissed his cheek.

"Jake, where's daddy?" Morgan asked him.

"Da! Da!" Jake started wiggling.

"Say grandma!" Teri-Lyn squealed.

"Ga'ma!"

Morgan smiled. "You should hear him while he's watching sports with Seth. I think they have entire conversations."

"That's wonderful! I wish I could see you all the time. Grandma loves you and misses you every day." Teri-Lyn gave him a squeeze.

Morgan wanted to tell her that she may get the chance to see

him every day after all. But that would mean Morgan wouldn't get
to see her family as much anymore.

Teri-Lyn took a closer look at Jake's smile. "Morgan, is that a
tooth?"

Morgan gently squeezed Jake's cheek to get him to open up. A
small solitary tooth poked out from his gums. "My goodness."

"Look at that perfect tooth. Morgan, don't worry, he's going to
have a great smile. None of my boys ever had to wear braces."

"Your father is going to swear you're ready for a steak."
Morgan shook her head.

"I'll give you a bottle of whiskey to take home."

"Whiskey? For what?" Morgan gave Teri-Lyn a curious look.

"When they start coming in, he's going to get a little cranky.
Just rub some on his gums and he'll be alright."

"He'll be drunk." Morgan laughed.

"Just a dab on his gums. Trust me. You may want to take a
swig for yourself. It will save you many sleepless nights."

Morgan smiled, thinking how Teri-Lyn must miss seeing him
grow. "Would you like to babysit tonight?"

"Are you kidding me? I would love to! I have his room ready."

"He keeps to his schedule. So after his bath he'd probably be
out like a light. That will give Seth and me some alone time. I'm
sure Ethan bent his ear about the prospect of coming back to Texas
to play ball."

"What do you think about all of this free agency business?"
Teri-Lyn looked at her.

Morgan fidgeted with one of Jake's toys. "I know he's dreamed
of this for a long time. I also know we talked about moving here in
a few years."

"I won't lie to you. I am looking forward to the day I can see
the three of you all the time. But I know that means taking you
away from your family."

"It will all work itself out, Teri-Lyn." Morgan smiled, but it felt forced.

"I know it will." Teri-Lyn looked at Jake. "I would kidnap you from your momma and have you come live with me and grandpa." She turned back to Morgan. "So how was the transition back to the bookstore after being on maternity leave so long?"

"I missed Jake something terrible." Morgan pouted.

"It's hard being away from your kids. That's one of the reasons I decided to be a stay at home mom."

Morgan swallowed hard. "But Seth and I are managing well. I think the two of them spending time together when I'm at the bookstore has strengthened their bond."

Teri-Lyn rubbed Morgan's shoulder, a warm comfort soaking into her skin. "I think it's nice how the two of you find balance and make sacrifices for each other."

"It's what you do when you love someone." Morgan shrugged. "I have a present for you. I made a baby book of Jake. I know it's not like seeing him grow right before your eyes, but it's something." Morgan reached into a kitchen drawer and handed her the book.

"That's so sweet of you, Morgan. You don't know how happy the two of you have made me. I never thought this day would come. My boys are so content with having a good time, no one wants to settle down and start a family. Seeing Seth in a fulfilling, nurturing relationship is changing all of them. Thank you."

Morgan reached over and patted Teri-Lyn on the hand. "Tate's remodeling shocked me too."

"He deserves all the happiness in the world. He deserves much more than he thinks he does."

Morgan bit her lip. "I don't want to pry, but I can't help feeling Tate's childhood wasn't idyllic?"

Teri-Lyn shook her head, something flashing in her eyes. "It was downright rotten. Abusive alcoholic father. Neglectful mother. He came to live with us officially when he was sixteen, but he'd really been with us a few years before that. One day he stopped by and never went home."

Morgan tried to fight back the tears burning the corner of her eyes. "That sounds terrible."

"How someone could hurt such a lovely soul is beyond me." Teri-Lyn's eyes teared up too.

"So did you get legal custody of him?"

"Tate's dad showed up to one of his football games and made a terrible scene. The boys came home and told John Jacob what happened. Later that night John went to the McGill house with his shotgun. When he came back he said the matter was resolved. Two weeks later Tate's parents signed over custody of him and moved away."

Morgan nodded but didn't ask anything else. She didn't think she could speak without letting the cascade threatening to spill over her eyelids fall. She got up, put the dishes on the tray, and took them back to the kitchen from the veranda. She loaded the dishwasher, sadness pitting her stomach at the thought that Tate had experienced such horrific things in his life. Good thing the Blakes had found him. She could only imagine what her big, imposing father-in-law had said to make them leave town.

Teri-Lyn came into the kitchen with Jake. "How about we drive down to San Antonio? We can go to the River Walk. I think you'll like it. There are plenty of shops and restaurants there."

"Sure. It's time I know more about my new home state."

* * *

Seth drove home, thinking how nice it would be to drive back after practice to the serenity of the ranch. The first three years in Philadelphia had been rough for him. He'd missed the quiet life of the country and was often homesick. He'd spent so much time catching flights home during the off-season, buying a plane had seemed logical.

But there was a wrinkle in his perfect daydream. Morgan was already established in Philly. Sure she could start over in Texas, but what about the contacts and experience she'd already cultivated in Philadelphia? The bookstore was more to her than a place to sell books; it was just as much her child as Jake. She toiled away with the reading hour at the library, on her own volition, with the satisfaction that she was keeping kids interested in reading. She was also making great strides with Reading Builds Bridges. Doors were opening to her, providing her with unique opportunities to make a difference in the community. Even he, with all his money and influence in Texas, couldn't magically make an even better scenario appear for her there. He couldn't duplicate the friendships and family that were entwined with her life's work.

Seth waved at the ranch hands as he started down the long stretch of road toward his house. Morgan was standing outside with Teri-Lyn, who had Jake in her arms.

"Hey, Momma."

"Hey, baby. Jake's first tooth came in today. Kiss him goodbye, he's going with me." Teri-Lyn handed him his son.

"Your mom is babysitting for us tonight," Morgan said.

"Well, look at that." Seth inspected the tooth. "We didn't see that last night."

"It pushed through this morning. Your mom's going to give us a bottle of whiskey to take home." Morgan smiled.

"You handing over that baby or what?" Teri-Lyn took back Jake and secured him into his car seat.

Seth leaned in to say goodbye. "OK. Jake, you be good for grandma. Do you need any of his stuff, Momma?"

Teri-Lyn and Morgan both looked at him like he'd asked if she'd killed someone.

The back of his neck heated. "What did I say wrong?"

Teri-Lyn socked him in the arm. "I used to change your diapers, mister. I have everything Jake needs."

"Your mother has a baby arsenal at the house." Morgan laughed and shook her head at Seth.

Teri-Lyn got into the car, waved goodbye out the window, and headed down the road.

Seth pulled Morgan into his arms. "Why do I get the feeling we won't see him until he starts first grade?"

"I was thinking high school." She giggled.

Seth looked down at her. "You're taking this very well."

"I thought I was getting some action tonight after that kiss you planted on me this morning before you left. Or are you just a big ole six foot three tease?"

"I aim to please." Seth kissed her on her lips.

Seth's sensual smooch sent a pulsing firestorm to Morgan's clit. She pushed him against the truck and locked onto his head, a little bit more aggressively than intended, but Jake was riding off with grandma, and Seth looked so damn good today. She leaned in and explored his mouth thoroughly with her tongue, while trying to liberate him from the finely tailored suit. She ripped his shirt open, and Seth grunted when her hands moved to his pants. She slid her hand beneath the waistband of his briefs and began stroking him.

"Inside. Now," she breathed.

Seth picked her up, carrying her into the house, and made it just in time. As soon as he shut the door, Morgan dropped to her knees, pulled down his pants, and started pleasuring him.

"Morgan," he moaned.

Morgan took him deeper into her mouth, bracing her hands on his thighs for support. She pulled back, her tongue trailing the underside of his shaft only to cover him with her mouth again. Each time she repeated the motion she'd increase the pressure with her tongue, putting a death grip on his thighs. The sounds coming from Seth sent her to a blissful place in her mind. She thought she heard him tell her to stop, but she continued until he thrummed in her mouth.

Morgan looked up at Seth, who picked her up and carried her over to the couch. With one swift movement, he'd pulled her dress up around her waist, then ripped her panties off and tossed them onto the carpet. Without warning, Seth stopped and gazed into her eyes. The way he looked at her, she knew what was on his mind, and she loved him for it. Having Jake had redefined intimacy for both of them. It was more than just giving each other pleasure; it was knowing that the sensual heights they reached had the ability to bring a life into the world. She wiggled to get the momentum going, but he paced himself with a slow tortuous rhythm. He grew hard again and plunged deeper and deeper, hitting her clit with each stroke, pressing her further into the leather couch. Morgan locked her legs around his waist, her body contracting in response, causing them to tumble off the couch. Seth held out his climax until they came together on the floor, in a sweaty, heated frenzy.

* * *

Morgan and Seth lay on the floor of the living room panting hard, trying to get a second wind.

"I promise to replace that shirt." She held up two of the buttons in her hand.

"Replace it? Hell, from now on this is my favorite shirt." Seth let out a slow, devious chuckle.

"I suppose I could sew the buttons back on." Morgan put her arm over her eyes.

Seth turned on his side and nuzzled her neck. "Where the hell did that come from?"

Morgan giggled. "I decided to replace exercise with sex."

"I can get behind that." He kissed her.

She ran a hand through his hair. "How was lunch with the governor?"

"Great. Ethan's like a mentor to me." Seth rested his head on her chest.

"Did he ask you if you were receptive to playing for the Tomcats?"

Seth tickled her. "The one thing I like about Ethan is that you're never sure he asked you anything at all. He's a very savvy politician."

"Did he wink a lot while he was talking to you?"

"No, but he said we could have lunch more often if I were living in the state full time."

The doorbell rang.

"Who the hell is that?" Seth barked.

"Blake, language." Morgan laughed as she nestled closer to him.

"The whole damn state of Texas better be on fire." He got up to answer the door but Morgan grabbed his calf.

The doorbell rang again, repeatedly.

She coughed. "You might want to put on something to answer the door."

Seth grabbed his boxer shorts off the lamp shade and pulled them on while Morgan slipped on his shirt.

He wrenched open the door. "What?"

"I told you they were in there fooling around," Tyler said to Channing. Both of his brothers stood there with an expectant look, waiting to be let in.

"You two have been a pain in my ass since the day you were born." Seth made no attempt to let them pass.

"Hey, Morgan. How's my favorite sister-in-law?" Channing shoved his face through the opening.

"Hi, Channing. How's my favorite future attorney?" Morgan said.

"I'm fine. Came home to see my nephew."

"If that's all you want, he's at the house with Momma." Seth leaned against the door to obstruct his view.

"That's so sweet of you," Morgan said, coming up behind Seth. "Babe, let them in."

Morgan scurried around the living room picking up their clothes, then headed upstairs, probably to the bedroom. When Seth was sure she was out of sight, he opened the door and smacked both his brothers in the head.

"Ouch." Tyler grimaced. "What was that for?"

Channing smirked. "The man is standing in his living room in his boxers in the middle of the afternoon. What does that tell you?"

"I don't know. I go commando." Tyler shrugged.

"You would," Seth said, then smiled. His brothers were idiots, but they were still his brothers.

Morgan came back into the room, dressed in a blouse and a pair of jeans.

"Morgan, you are a sight for sore eyes." Tyler grinned as he moved toward her.

"You filled up your hug quota the last time you saw her." Seth stepped in his path. Channing slipped around him and hugged her anyway.

Morgan giggled. "What are you two handsome devils up to?"

"We came to take Jake out with us." Channing smiled as he looked at Seth. His arm was still draped around Morgan.

Tyler took a seat. "We're going to lunch at the Promenade and thought it would be nice to take Jake with us."

Seth ran his hand through his hair. "Hell no. You two are up to something."

The doorbell rang again. Seth, still dressed only in his boxers, sauntered over to the door. It was Tate.

Tate whistled as he entered. "This has got to be good."

"We interrupted a special moment." Tyler smirked.

"Can you believe he has no body fat? It's disgusting." Channing pointed at Seth and rolled his eyes.

Seth looked at Tyler. "I'm not letting you two chuckle heads take my son out."

"You don't have the only say. Morgan, can we take Jake to the Promenade?" Tyler said.

"Why do I get the feeling if Jake goes to lunch with his uncles, he's coming to come back smelling like regret and shame?" Morgan raised an eyebrow.

Tate wandered into the kitchen, yelling over his shoulder, "The owner Marco has seven daughters. One more beautiful than the next and these two go there every time they're in town, hoping to get lucky, but get shot down. It's pitiful to watch." He walked back into the living room with a bottle of water in his hand, shaking his head at Tyler and Channing.

Seth laughed. "Those girls aren't dumb."

"Jake is a babe magnet," Tyler said. "He's already got those eyes and the Blake charm. I showed his picture to some girls at a party last week, and I got asked out on two dates. Those girls get a look at how cute he is, and how his two doting uncles take such good care of him, we'll make some progress."

Seth shook his head. "You two are not using my son to help you get laid."

"But it's a Blake tradition," Channing said. "Morgan, you don't know how many times Seth and Tate—"

"Shut up, Channing," Seth barked.

"Mr. Blake, can I speak to you for a moment?" Morgan motioned for Seth to join her upstairs.

Closing the bedroom door behind her, Morgan turned to Seth. "It's clear they came here to spend time with you." She kissed him.

Seth slid his hands around her waist and guided her to the bed. "Morgan, Momma has Jake for the entire night. I'm still seeing stars from what we did in the living room."

"Why don't you grab a beer with your brothers? We can pick up exactly where we left off when you get home. I assure you I'll be ready to rip your jeans off with my teeth."

Seth let out a loud groan and his cock twitched between them. Morgan scooted out of the way and handed him the clothes she'd laid out for him on the bed.

* * *

Seth couldn't remember the last time they'd all been together. Channing and Tyler were behaving more like he was taking them for ice cream than for beers at the Bright Star. Tate's return was a bit of a surprise, but then again that was how Tate was. He would never say why, even if he had a day off in between tour dates, he would just come back to the ranch for a good night's sleep then take off again.

Morgan's observation about their union having a ripple effect on the boys made a lot of sense. Had he not gone on that vacation last year after his Super Bowl win, he would have rounded up Channing, Tyler, and Tate and gone partying for a month. When he'd returned to Philadelphia and pursued Morgan, he didn't let anyone or anything distract him from his mission: to convince his wife to live happily ever after with him.

On the ride over, Channing and Tyler grilled him about the prospect of playing for the Tomcats, while Tate remained quiet. They congratulated him on getting closer to his dream. Everyone agreed that him coming back home to Texas, playing for the Tomcats and raising his family, was a good thing. Channing was coming home after he graduated law school to pass the bar and get a job with a big firm in Dallas. The family would be together again, not scattered about the country. All seemed right in the world until Tate casually mentioned that Seth was also now a part of Morgan's family, which was based in Philadelphia. Seth shifted in his seat, cleared his throat, and asked to hear about Tyler's latest obsession instead: racing cars.

The Bright Star hadn't changed much since he was there last year after the Cinnamon Festival. Hell, it hadn't changed in the last ten years. The gruff décor and mechanical bull in the corner had long been a staple in his life. He'd spent his youth there and a few good fights there too.

Channing and Tyler were catching up with friends, so Seth went to the bar to get some food and another round of beers. Tate was talking to the owner, Cal, about an up and coming group, The Dirty Rascals. They were playing tonight and Tate agreed to talk to the band afterward about the music business as a favor to Cal.

Seth waved at an old friend while the bartender, Danny, went in the back to place his nachos order. Seth pulled out his cell phone and looked at Morgan's picture, intending to call and see how she was doing. She'd told him before he left she didn't want to horn in on Teri-Lyn's time with Jake, so she intended to read a book and have a bite to eat. Seth was poised to hit the call button when a loud and familiar voice carried across the Bright Star.

"Well, if it ain't the son of a bitch that broke my sister's heart."

The bar came to a standstill as Caine Winterbourne, Penny's brother, made his way across the room. So, Caine was back in town. Seth had heard he'd retired from the military and was moving back home. From the time Seth had picked up Penny for their first date, to their breakup a couple of years ago, Caine wore the same scowl on his face whenever he saw Seth. He'd always had a big, imposing stature and thought he could take on the world. Behind him stood three guys that Seth recognized as Penny's cousins. Well, at least it was an even number. By the looks of it, it was going to be a long night.

Seth put his phone back in his pocket and asked Danny to hold on to those beers. Tate ended his conversation with Cal and strolled over to the bar.

Tate shook his head. "I just bought this hat." He removed his Stetson and flung it past Danny. It landed on a bottle of vodka behind the bar.

Seth raised an eyebrow. "See, I knew you should have gone

pro."

Tate laughed. "Brother, we can talk about missed career opportunities later."

"Where's Horny and Randy?" Seth murmured.

"Right here."

Tyler and Channing walked up behind them.

Tyler inhaled deeply. "This brings back memories."

"The last time Cal banned us from here for two years." Seth rubbed the back of his neck.

"It was more like six months." Channing shrugged.

Caine walked up to Seth and got in his face. "I've been waiting for this day for a long time, Blake. It's about time someone took your pretty ass down a notch."

"Good to see you too, Caine. Did you miss me?"

"Sounds like you've been pining after the man." Tate laughed. "Caine, that break up was their business, why don't you be a good big brother and leave it alone?"

Caine grunted. "McGill, I always thought you talked too much."

"I did always have the gift for gab. The only time I didn't do much talking was when I was dating Chrissie." Tate winked at him.

Seth sighed while the rest of the patrons got a good chuckle. Tate had gone straight for Caine's sore spot, his wife Chrissie. She and Tate had dated briefly in high school, which drove Caine nuts. Any chance of coming to a diplomatic solution just went down the toilet.

"I told you a long time ago if you ever broke my sister's heart, I was going to beat you senseless," Caine said.

Seth's jaw clenched. "In all fairness, Caine, you told me that when I was fifteen. And like Tate said, our relationship was none of your business."

"You didn't deserve her anyway. Instead of marrying Penny

like you should have, you shacked up with some—"

Seth's punch packed a wallop, sending Caine to the floor. He didn't know what was at the end of his sentence, but he was going to make sure he wouldn't say it again. It was on.

Caine shot up and rushed Seth into a supporting beam. Seth was able to push him off and catch him in the jaw. Stools were flying, beer bottles breaking, and Cal was yelling for everyone to calm down. But a bar fight with Caine was small peanuts compared to what Morgan was going to do to Seth when he got home.

Chapter Six

After straightening up Jake's room and putting away the things she'd bought in San Antonio with Teri-Lyn, Morgan settled on the couch with a spy thriller she'd found in the library and fell asleep as soon as she cracked the spine.

The sound of the house phone ringing jutted Morgan out of her slumber on the couch. She looked at her watch. It was after midnight and there was no sign that Seth had been home. A lump rose in her throat, horrific images popped into her mind. Who called at this hour with good news?

"Hello," she murmured into the phone. The firm voice on the other end of the line rattled off a quick statement that brought her out of her sleepy state. "What? I'll be right there."

Morgan tried not to think about the massive size of the truck she was driving. She'd grabbed the vehicle parked closest to the garage, which she thought was Tate's, and was on her way to pick up Teri-Lyn. John Jacob's business meeting had run late, so he and Bo had stayed over in Dallas instead of making the trip home that night. She'd weighed her options: drive alone in unfamiliar territory with a GPS or ask her mother-in-law to dress Jake and take him along for the ride. The longer she drove, the more deliciously evil she knew it was to bring Jake to the police station. Now was a good time to teach every Blake male a lesson about setting an example for their children.

* * *

"Thanks, Cal." Teri-Lyn ended the call. "According to Cal, Caine Winterbourne came in looking to start a fight with Seth. He found one."

Morgan bit her lip. "Winterbourne? So he's related to Penny?"

"Yes, Caine is Penny's older brother."

Morgan would have closed her eyes if she weren't driving. Would Penny ever be out of their lives? "She's like a *bad* Penny. Forgive me. It's late, and I can't think of anything cleverer to say."

Teri-Lyn laughed. "Caine is a hot head. Penny didn't necessarily have to say anything to him. It's an ego thing. Seth and Caine never got along."

Morgan snorted. "The Seth and Penny story seems never ending."

Teri-Lyn looked back at Jake. "I hope this late night adventure doesn't disrupt his sleep pattern."

"Well, the good news is he's used to being up past his bedtime. Seth wakes him up, and they watch sports. He thinks I don't know about it." Morgan shook her head.

The inside of the police station was about as small as the town. After driving briefly down the Main Street, Morgan made a quick right, and they were at the Hanover Police Department. Teri-Lyn's phone rang—John Jacob was returning her call—so Morgan told her she would go in and get the delinquent Blake Boys.

Morgan marched into the precinct and up to the front desk, while juggling Jake on her hip. The officer on duty, who was reading a newspaper while sipping on a hot drink, barely looked up.

"I'm here to bail out my husband and his brothers."

The officer gave her a once over, then took his time folding his paper and even took another long sip of his drink. "And who exactly is your husband?"

"Seth Blake." Morgan moved back when the officer's cup

almost fell out of his hand.

The officer stood up straight. "Sure thing, Mrs. Blake. Would you like something to drink? We have coffee around the corner. You can have a seat right over there." He motioned for the chairs behind her.

"I'll stand, thank you." She glared at him.

The officer went into another room and started talking to an older man. Morgan instinctively rubbed Jake's foot, who giggled in response. He was wide-awake, considering it was hours past his bedtime.

"As soon as we get your jailbird daddy and uncles bailed out, you are going back to sleep, mister. No matter how much grandma plays with you." She kissed his outstretched hand. Jake responded by making agreeable sounds.

"He looks just like him," a high pitched, twanged voice said behind her.

Morgan tensed. She knew that voice. She turned to see Dr. Penny Winterbourne, dressed in hospital scrubs, her red hair pulled up into a wild bun on her head.

"Hi, Morgan."

Morgan exhaled. "Penny."

It was her wish that she never see Penny again, but she knew it was inevitable. If not now, then some time in the future when they settled in Texas permanently. Seth was still on the board of directors at the clinic, and although he didn't attend the meetings, he did sit in on the occasional conference call. They seemed to have a cordial relationship.

The last time they'd met, some pretty heated words had been exchanged. Morgan thought back to Penny's statement that he was just biding his time with her. It must have been greatly disappointing to her foe that they were still together and were doing just fine. What could Penny have possibly said to her brother to have him pick a fight a year after her talk with Seth in the stables?

It must have taken the good doctor some time to work through losing the love of her life. Morgan knew Seth meant a lot to Penny. Behind the cold eyes and bitter words she'd spoken the night of the banquet, Morgan could see the fear. She'd played a game a bit too long and lost him.

"You have your daddy's eyes. There's no shade of green quite like his." Penny cooed at Jake.

Jake made a whole lot of noise and reached out to her.

Both Morgan and Penny froze at Jake's gesture. Apparently, Seth had passed on his susceptibility to redheaded doctors to his son. When she didn't react, Jake reached for Penny again.

Penny looked at Morgan. "Can I?"

Morgan hesitated until she saw her son smile. "Sure."

Penny put her bag down and pulled Jake into her arms. "Look at you, Seth Blake Jr. You are such a big, handsome boy."

"The family nicknamed him Jake."

"Jake Blake, huh?" Penny gave her a curious look.

Morgan shrugged.

Penny smiled. "Has your daddy been feeding you table food? And putting barbeque sauce in your bottle?"

Morgan couldn't help but laugh. Penny did know Seth well. "It's a daily struggle."

"I apologize for my brother's behavior tonight. There will be a very loud conversation when we get home."

"Sometimes you just have to let men fight it out. I have three brothers, who fought all the time. A few punches and the world is back to normal again. Women could take a lesson from that simple, if barbaric, philosophy."

Penny shook her head. "Well, that wouldn't work. We'd be doing the right thing, duking it out, and some jerk will go and get some dirt and a hose and next thing you know we're mud wrestling, and they're being entertained." She laughed.

Morgan laughed with her. "True."

Penny caressed Jake's back, and he smiled at her. "Aren't you a healthy boy? You're gonna play football like your daddy?"

The officer returned. "Hey, Dr. Winterbourne. Your surly brother and cousins are back there. I suppose you want to bail them out too?"

"Want to? No. But I will never hear the end of it if I let those meat heads stay here overnight."

"Mrs. Blake, your bunch is coming out." The officer pointed down the corridor.

Morgan shook her head. "Don't I need to fill out some paperwork for the bail?"

Penny turned to her. "Sherriff Roberts is a friend of Seth's dad and mine. When the boys get into a scuffle, things are usually straightened out with a donation to the Hanover Emergency fund."

"And what's the going rate for four trouble makers?" Morgan reached into her bag.

Penny looked at her for a moment like she couldn't decide if she should say what was on her mind. Morgan stopped writing the check and turned to face her.

"Morgan, Caine's actions tonight may have been knee jerk from nights with me crying on his shoulder. He's just an overbearing big brother." Penny nervously tucked a loose lock of hair behind her ear.

"I see." Morgan blinked, taken aback at the sincerity in Penny's eyes.

Penny trudged on with her speech. "I said some harsh things to you last year, and I apologize. I was just hoping you weren't the *one*. I should have been more gracious and less childish about the situation."

Morgan didn't want to fully embrace the apology, but seeing Penny cuddling Jake in her arms weakened her resolve. How could someone who hated her guts hold her son like that?

"Thank you for saying that, Penny." Morgan smiled.

"I just wish so much damage didn't have to be done tonight. Poor Cal will have to close down for repairs."

"Maybe he won't. I think that if the eight of them can fight, they can put that bar back together." Morgan tapped the writing pen against her cheek.

Penny nodded in agreement. "Good idea."

* * *

When Seth rounded the corner, his stomach clenched, and he stopped dead in his tracks. Morgan was standing in the reception area with none other than Penny, who was holding Jake. The past, present, and an alternate future were playing out right before his very eyes.

"You can't catch a break today." Tate snickered, then slapped Seth on the back and pushed him forward.

Channing and Tyler burst out laughing. Seth shot them a deadly, silencing look.

As Seth got closer to the reception area, he locked eyes with Morgan. It looked like the women were having a civilized conversation.

Jake became animated when he saw him and started yelling out, "Da! Da!"

"What are you doing up?" Seth asked his son as he gently took him out of Penny's arms. Penny managed a regretful smile when he looked at her.

"He came to bail his father and wayward uncles out of jail," Morgan said.

Penny spoke up. "Hey, Blake. You and Caine work things out?"

"In a manner of speaking." Seth rubbed his neck.

"Good." Penny smiled again and touched the baby's arm. "It was good meeting you, Jake."

Jake lunged at her and gave her a kiss. Seth chuckled. He turned to Morgan. "Baby."

Penny rubbed Jake's head and moved to the other side of the counter to write her check.

Channing and Tyler both gave Morgan a grateful kiss on the cheek and kept moving in the direction of the finger-wagging Teri-Lyn.

"I'll take him." Tate grabbed Jake and went over to get his tongue-lashing from her as well.

"This ought to be so good I'm going to pop some popcorn when we get home and get ready for this whopper of a story." Morgan rubbed her hands together.

"Not as good as your chat with Penny." He gave her an expectant look.

"Did it scare the hell out of you seeing us talking? And Jake in her arms?" She laughed.

"I think I'd rather fight Caine again." Seth ran his hand along his jaw.

Morgan moved closer and looked him over. "Nothing looks broken. Just some slight bruising. Is the Blake name still intact?"

"Hell yeah." Seth put his arm around her waist and kissed her.

Caine appeared and stopped at the desk. Penny shook her head and gave him a hug.

Seth took a deep breath. "We good, Winterbourne?"

"Yeah, we good." Caine huffed.

Morgan chimed in, "I'm so glad everything is fine, because Penny and I were talking about it and it would be great if all of you helped Cal with repairs, starting tomorrow."

Penny laughed. "Exactly, so everyone should get a good night's sleep. I'll let Cal know to expect his construction crew."

Seth waited for the Winterbournes to leave, then he turned to his wife. "What exactly did you two talk about?"

"The same thing you and Caine discussed with your fists.

Forgiveness. Leaving the past in the past. New life. And maybe one day, friendship. Women are just more civilized about it." She smirked.

Seth pulled her close and kissed her on top of her head. He'd expected her to be mad at him for fighting. It still amazed him how she was able to see the good in things and not take their lives too seriously. Did he want her and Penny to become best buds? Hell no. He wasn't that evolved that he could live with the two of them being girlfriends. But they were two wonderful women who had the drive and ambition for helping others. Seth laughed to himself when Morgan finished writing the hefty check to the Hanover Emergency fund. She wasn't nearly as nervous as when she wrote that million-dollar check to the clinic last year. The money and being in the spotlight wasn't as worrisome to her anymore. She was still as grounded as the day they'd met.

* * *

By the time they made it to the ranch, it was late so everyone stayed at Morgan and Seth's house. The guys recounted their tale of how an innocent evening of fun turned into the brawl of the century. They all groaned when Morgan informed them that they were reporting to Cal in the morning to help with the repairs. Tate, Tyler, and Channing wandered off to guest rooms after taking some frozen veggies from the fridge and applying it on their sore spots. Teri-Lyn was sleeping in Jake's room.

Morgan tended to Seth, helping him get out of his clothes. Then her lips turned up into a wicked smile. "So did you see the way Jake acted around Penny? It's clear he knows she was almost his mother."

"That is not funny." Seth moaned as he leaned back onto the pillows.

"Or he has a thing for redheads. Take your pick. The fruit of your loins obviously has some of your tendencies. Hopefully fighting in bars won't be one of them." She punched him in the arm.

"That fight tonight was a long time coming for me and Caine."

Morgan nestled next to him. "Never liked you dating his sister?"

"Penny was only part of it. Caine was one of those guys who thought I led a charmed life and hated me for it." Seth pulled her closer and rubbed her back.

"I can't believe Tate made that remark about his wife." She giggled.

Seth burst out laughing. "I knew we'd have to fight our way out of there after that."

Morgan sighed. "After your little stunt tonight, I think we should lay down some ground rules. How about we come up with some things that we mutually agree not to do since we're parents now? That is what stopped me from beating Charisma's ass that night at our house."

"What do you have in mind?"

"Well, no fighting is number one. Unless you do it on the field for work."

Seth laughed. "Absolutely."

"Channing was right; you don't have any body fat." Morgan slid her hand along his side.

Seth gave her a wry smile. "I try to stay in shape."

"Which brings me to my next request. I went into this marriage knowing you took good care of your body, and I find it to be quite spectacular. So I have to request that you keep all this" — she motioned up and down his body — "in excellent condition. I don't think I could live with love handles or a beer gut on you."

"OK. I counter that with no more talk about weight gain. I think you're sexy just the way you are." He kissed her nose.

"When I start spontaneous fires because my thighs are rubbing together, you better be walking behind me with a fire extinguisher."

Seth shook his head. "Never going to happen."

Morgan ran her hand through his hair. "I know you won't keep your hair short forever, but I have to draw the line at you growing out something long with a feathered look."

"When have you ever seen my hair long?" Seth huffed.

"I haven't, but I don't want to wake up one day next to a seventies pop music star either."

He chuckled. "So Tate gets to be the only singer in the family?"

"Yes."

"Any more requests?" Seth rolled her over on her back and covered her body with his.

"No more shirtless, sexy magazine covers. I loved the cover of *Sports Page*. You have to be more dignified. You're somebody's father for heaven's sake." She tried to keep a straight face.

"OK, then you can't dress like a nun. I want to see some skin." He nipped her neck.

"I think this is the most counterproductive conversation we've ever had." She sighed.

"I'm surprised you didn't mention wearing a toupee if I went bald."

"Not worried about that. Your dad has a head full of hair, and if the gene deities are generous, so will you." Morgan smiled.

"Well, I have one last request. Once a year, I get to do something nice for you. No refusals. No balking at the cost. No negotiations."

"Deal." She shook his hand.

Seth kissed her long and hard. Morgan wrapped her legs around his waist.

"Think we could keep it down tonight? We have a house full of guests."

Seth pulled the covers over their heads. "I make no promises."

* * *

Morgan was still asleep when he left the house. He knew his big brother liked to get an early start on the ranch. Seth eased into his truck and drove down the main road to J.J.'s.

Like clockwork, J.J. was in the driveway loading up his truck.

"Hey, Big Brother," Seth said as he got out of the truck.

"Hey, yourself. Have fun at the Bright Star last night?" J.J. tipped back his hat to get a better look at Seth's face. "You look better than I expected."

"Morgan and I played doctor last night when we got home." Seth scratched at his temple, trying to suppress a smile.

"You know, we all have to set a better example for Jake." J.J. gave him an expectant look.

Seth sighed. "I know."

"But," J.J. added, grinning, "I am so happy you kicked Caine's ass. That was a long time coming."

Seth leaned against the truck. "I think so. Where's Eden?"

"Eden's been at her sister's house. She just had a baby and Eden's been helping her out." J.J. leaned against the truck too. "I'll be back around eleven. I have some things to do at the stables. How about a family dinner tonight? I miss my nephew."

"Good idea."

"See you tonight." J.J. got in his truck and pulled off.

J.J. wasn't the only Blake up at the crack of dawn. John Jacob, who'd returned from Dallas early in the morning, was in the stables saddling his horse.

"Morning, Daddy."

"Morning. I hear you had an interesting night."

"Yeah. I'm sorry about that." Seth looked away, rubbing the back of his neck.

"Sorry for whooping Caine's ass?" Bodine said as he emerged from a stable.

"Hell no." Seth turned and gave Bodine a hug. "Hey, Bo."

"Morgan speaking to you?" Bo laughed.

"Yes, thank goodness." Seth shook his head. "We're cooking out tonight at my house."

"I'll be there." Bo gave him a friendly punch to the shoulder and went into the office.

Seth's father looked at him. "Feel like riding out with your old man? I need to check on a fence."

"Of course."

They rode for a while, John Jacob pointing out the things that were going on around the ranch. His father kept a watchful eye over the property in Seth's absence. There was nothing major to be done, but it was good to keep on top of things. It was the quiet times like these with his father that Seth treasured. John Jacob was a country man who loved his land and his family. He'd done a fine job juggling them while building his empire. By looking at him, one would never think he was a millionaire several times over.

"So how's fatherhood treating you?" John Jacob smiled at him.

Seth thought about it for a long time, then gave his father a sidelong glance. "You want the truth?"

"And nothing but the truth."

"I'm scared out of my mind." Seth let out a deep breath.

John Jacob guffawed. "Welcome to the club."

Seth's cheeks reddened at his father's infectious laughter. "What's so funny?"

"If you're scared that just means you want to be a good father and husband. I was a nervous wreck when you kids started coming along."

"Really?" Seth asked.

"Yeah. I wondered if I was teaching you the right things. It was a wild and crazy ride but it was the best years of my life. Being with the woman I love and raising our children."

"Thanks, Daddy. Everything I've accomplished in my life, I owe that to you."

"I'm proud of each and every one of you. Just like you will be proud of Jake."

Seth smiled at his dad.

"So, did Ethan give you a hard sell at lunch?"

Seth exhaled. "You know Ethan, he didn't say anything. That said it all."

John Jacob gave Seth a hard look. "What do you want, son?"

"I've been thinking about retiring soon. I want to spend as much time as I can with Morgan and our kids." Seth tipped his hat back.

"Kids? Do I hear a plural?"

"We negotiated. Five kids or until Morgan gets a girl."

John Jacob slapped him on the back. "It's a nice change of pace, a young couple who actually want to have more than two kids. I welcome all the grandkids you can give me."

"And I want all of that to happen here, on the ranch. Sooner than later. I think the Tomcats can help me do that."

"Then you know what you have to do."

* * *

Morgan stared at the directions on the back of the box of grits, trying to decide if she should cook the entire contents. Knowing how much the Blake men could eat, the last thing she wanted to do was run out of food. Seth joked with her at home that she only cooked just enough for one meal, and he liked to go back and nibble on leftovers until the next meal was ready. She'd already put the bacon on the griddle, mixed the batter for the pancakes, and started the coffeemaker.

She reached for her coffee, hoping the caffeine would push her brains cells along. The sound of yawning coming from the living room brought her out of her cooking stupor.

"Hey, Morgan." Tyler gave her a lazy smile.

"Good morning, Tyler. Want some coffee?" She held up a mug.

Tyler took a seat at the kitchen table. "I would love some."

"Let's see, you take it with cream and two sugars."

"I'm impressed. You remembered."

Morgan smiled and prepared his coffee. "Of course I did. I had your mug ready. I remember you being an early riser."

Tyler accepted the brew with a wink and a grin. "Seth still asleep?"

"No, he went out a little while ago. I think to see J.J." She took the bacon off the griddle.

"J.J. was missed last night. Eden probably wouldn't let him out." Tyler chuckled.

Morgan scrunched her nose at him. "Why is Eden such a sore spot with everyone?"

"Eden is the exact opposite of you. She's selfish, materialistic, mean as a lion with a splinter stuck in its paw, and she lives to spend my brother's money."

"Then why did J.J. marry her?"

"The phrase starts with the letter p and ends with whipped."

Morgan giggled. "Tyler!"

Tyler shrugged and scratched at his five o'clock shadow. "Sorry to be so blunt, but that's how I see it."

"And what about you? Ever have a woman lead you around by the nose?"

"Hell no." Tyler snorted. "I have an undefeated record in the game of love."

Morgan cleaned the griddle and began pouring the pancake batter. "And you're very proud of that."

"I'm sure Seth and my momma have told you I am the odd ball. I don't commit to work or women." He folded his arms over his chest.

"I've heard choice words from both of them. They worry about you."

"I know." He sighed.

"Seth told me you thought about driving a racecar."

"It was a thought. A buddy of mine races. I've spent some time behind the wheel. It's exhilarating."

"Looking for a rush?" She waggled her eyebrows.

"Something like that." He grinned.

"I'm sure you'll figure it out. Just be safe. I'm sure Jake would be very upset if something happened to his Uncle Tyler." Morgan hoped a little guilt would make him think carefully about career decisions.

Morgan retrieved the last pancake from the griddle. She picked up the box of grits again and studied the instructions for a minute. But Tyler huffed and walked over to the stove and took it out of her hands. He filled a pot with water and turned on the fire. Morgan blinked. Standing next to Tyler sometimes felt like she was standing next to Seth. The physical similarities were there, but when one of them opened their mouths, it was no mistaking which Blake was her husband.

"Were you and my friend Michelle flirting at the Super Bowl?" She glared at him.

Tyler smiled, his eyes crinkling. "We were feeling each other out."

"Just out and not up, right?"

Tyler howled. "I hate to tell you, Morgan, but your water breaking was a bit of a mood killer. Thanks to you I didn't want to have sex for a month after Jake was born."

Morgan crossed her arms and gave him a steady look. "I can get nosey when I care about people. And I care about both of you."

He hugged her with one arm. "Of course you do. Tell you what. If Michelle and I pick up the flirting where we left off, I promise I will think before I do anything."

"Don't you hate having another sister-in-law?" Morgan patted him on the back.

"Actually, I like having an interactive sister-in-law. Eden and I stay far away from each other. And unlike her relationship with J.J., you've made Seth a happy man. You two make me believe marriage isn't a constant struggle."

"Do you think you will get married one day?"

Tyler's eyes widened. "Baby steps, Morgan. Baby steps."

Tyler and Morgan laughed.

He made the grits and poured them into a giant serving bowl while she set the table. Channing was the next person to come down, followed by Tate. There was no surprise at all that Jake was bathed and dressed when Teri-Lyn brought him downstairs. Morgan sent a text to Seth telling him they were eating breakfast, and she would save him some food. She placed Jake in his high chair but let Teri-Lyn feed him. Morgan looked around the table at the Blakes, knowing it would make Seth extremely happy to live in Texas full time. She wished she felt that same happiness instead of being wrought with conflict over a no-win situation. Tyler's comments about Eden echoed in her mind. It seemed the root of J.J.'s unhappiness was his constant appeasement to his wife. If Morgan made a big deal about moving so soon to Texas, would Seth give in to her to make her happy? And at what cost to his heart and his career? Resentment had a way of sneaking in when no one was looking.

* * *

Hung over and stuffed from a big breakfast, Seth and the boys made their way to the Bright Star. After assessing the damage Seth sent Channing and Tyler off to the hardware store for supplies. The Winterbournes arrived on time as well, and Caine was kind enough to bring coffee for everyone. Seth and Tate opted to see Caine take the first sip before they'd drink. Caine uttered a curse and took a walk around and then out the door to appraise the outside.

Once all of the repair work was singled out, the crew of eight men began to work. Channing was the first to break the ice with one of the cousins, and slowly but surely a friendly dialogue had started. They even came up with a few ideas to spruce up the place, like a new railing for the outside and replacing a few of the planks on the handicap access ramp. Someone found a ladder, and Tyler and Peter Winterbourne whitewashed the Bright Star sign.

Seth offered to go for a food run so the cook wouldn't have to fire up the oven while they were working on repairs. He got the shock of his life when Caine volunteered to go with him.

"I'll help you with the food. It's only fair we split the bill," Caine said.

"Sure." Seth looked at Tate, who nodded in response.

They picked up some barbeque from a popular restaurant. While waiting for the order, Seth and Caine took a seat at a table.

"You out of the military for good?" Seth sipped on the beer Caine had bought him while they waited.

"My family would like that. But I think there's still some good I can do over there," Caine said.

"I hear that. I always admired your dedication to the military."

"Well, I've always excelled at stirring up trouble." Caine smirked.

"Don't I know it."

Caine shifted in his seat. "Listen, you know I had to come and clean your clock, right?"

"Did you really?" Seth looked him in the eye.

"My baby sister called me up last year crying because you didn't love her anymore. I know she's a grown woman, and she knows what mistakes she made. Still, it does something to my heart when she hurts. So, I decided to hurt you as much as she was hurting."

"That doesn't exactly sound rational."

"You have a family now. Wait until you have a daughter. I'm expecting to see you on the news, often." Caine laughed.

"Probably." Seth laughed too.

The order was ready so they headed back to the bar. The Dirty

Rascals were playing a set for Tate, who had apologized for the ruckus cutting their performance short. Everyone was in a good mood as they took a break for lunch.

"Everything OK with Caine?" Tate said as he heaped coleslaw onto his plate.

"Yeah. Penny cried. He reacted. He told me to wait until I have a daughter to see his side."

Seth and Tate looked at each other for a while.

Tate finally said, "We're going to need to build a moat around the ranch."

"Exactly. How did it go with the Dirty Rascals?"

"I like their sound. I'm going to make a few calls to my manager," Tate said. "Man, I love coming home."

Seth patted Tate on the back. "Me too."

* * *

That evening Bo and John Jacob tended the grill while the brothers kicked back, drinking beers and talking about all the hard work they'd done for the Bright Star, which looked better than it had in years. With Channing's help Morgan had the projector set up and aimed at the broad wall on the side of the house as a mock screen. When the sun began to set, she turned it on and sent everyone back in time. The Blake boys appeared on screen. They were a handsome brood of rowdy, hyperactive boys. She immediately knew which one was Seth; those eyes popped right off the wall at her. They were the eyes of her son, filled with kindness and sincerity.

It was easy to see the pattern: Seth followed J.J., Tyler followed Seth, and Channing followed Tyler. Tate popped up from time to time, meshed in the middle. He was part of the family back then as he was now. Morgan noticed a few shots of Teri-Lyn giving him hugs. It seemed to do young Tate a world of good to get affection from her. The love, friendship, and closeness they all shared now was years in the making. Morgan glanced over at Seth, who was smiling and laughing while giving commentary to Jake.

She loaded the next reel, marked S.J.'s Greatest Hits. As soon as the footage started, Seth's fresh face appeared on the screen. He looked about twelve, his hair styled in a shaggy bob, and he was just developing that legendary million-dollar smile. The football game began, and she could see how much of a natural he'd been on the field even back then. There was no hesitation when he played. When he had the ball, all that mattered was the execution leading to the next play. His reflexes hadn't changed. He still had a lightning speed precision that surprised her on many occasions.

He'd won that game. Seth took off his helmet and ran toward the camera to talk to John Jacob. Teri-Lyn took over the filming and zoomed in on father giving his son a pep talk. Morgan wished she could hear what he'd said, because little Seth smiled and rejoined the team. The reel continued for a while with shots of the boys playing on the now empty field as the sun was setting. The last shot was of a little Tyler and Channing holding up a homemade sign that said Texas Tomkats. Morgan laughed at the misspelling and at how the boys were barely big enough to hold it up before falling on the grass. Seth rubbed them both on the head, and the reel ran out as the boys were walking off the field.

Jake's applause at the end of the movie tugged at her heart. He was cheering for his dad. She asked Channing to load the next reel while she retrieved some more food from the house.

"Woman, what are you doing?" Seth leaned against the doorframe.

"Just getting some more potato salad. Tyler confiscated the bowl I put out and won't let anyone near it." Morgan took the dish out of the refrigerator.

"Can I help?" Seth sauntered over to the sink.

"Want to tell me what's on your mind?" She smiled.

Seth ran a hand through his hair. "I've been concerned about global warming. The polar ice caps are melting at a rate of—"

Morgan threw a kitchen towel at him. "What a smart ass. How about what you were thinking when you had Jake in your arms a few minutes ago? You were pointing to something in the home movie."

"I was just telling him about some boyhood escapades. Stories his Momma won't want me telling him." Seth looked at her for the longest time before he asked, "How would you feel about me joining the Tomcats next year?"

She took a deep breath. "I want you to do whatever makes you happy."

"And I want to make you happy." Seth came over and took her into his arms.

Morgan rested her head on his chest and took a breath. "It's sooner than we talked about. I thought we would have more time."

"I know. And I know it's a lot to ask, taking you away from your life in Philadelphia."

Morgan's eyes teared up. "You and Jake are my life."

"Maybe there's a way we can split the time like we do when we come here. Or if you want, you could stay in Philadelphia and—"

"I don't want a part time marriage. That wouldn't be fair to Jake or to us." She sniffed.

"I don't know how to fix this," Seth said quietly.

She looked up at him, wiping away her tears. "Some things can't be fixed. Sometimes we have to make decisions and accept the consequences of those decisions. If you have a chance to follow your dream, you have to try."

Chapter Seven

As soon as they touched down in Philly, life for the Blakes resumed full speed. The talk they'd had at the ranch had lit a fire under Seth. He made an appointment with his agent, Luke, for the following day to develop a game plan for his future. Going home had given him the clarity he needed to move forward. He was taking his father's advice and going with instincts that had never failed him so far. Morgan insisted that she agreed with his decision, but he saw the look of sadness in her eyes.

He wanted to kick himself for suggesting they have a long distance relationship. It would kill him if he didn't wake up and see his wife and son in the morning. She was right; being apart was never good for a marriage, no matter what the intentions were. For the first time in his professional career, he had to think about someone other than himself. It was scary taking a gamble when the woman he loved seemed so conflicted about it.

He'd sworn to himself that his career would never get in the way of his marriage or her happiness, and here he was turning her life upside down. He was going to chase a lifelong dream and hope he didn't jeopardize his future with Morgan.

* * *

Morgan's heart did a happy flip to see the teen book club meeting for the fifth time. Avery and her friends loved spending time at the bookstore. Michelle's enthusiasm didn't wane when the club got underway, and she was officially the facilitator of the group. Morgan spied the signup sheet and saw five new names.

She cleaned the café tables and straightened the magazine racks, anything that would keep her busy while she waited for Seth and Jake to pick her up.

"Hi, handsome." Morgan beamed as Seth and Jake entered the bookstore.

"Hey, baby." Seth kissed her.

Morgan shook her head. "I was talking to my son."

Seth laughed. "What, I'm just an afterthought now?"

Jake lurched at Morgan, but she caught him just in time. She hugged him close and looked back up at Seth. "What have you two been doing today?"

"Went shopping for your dad and Sydney's anniversary present. We found some nice things, and Jake and I got new suits for their party."

"Aw." Morgan smiled. "My baby's first suit. I bet its precious on him."

"It comes with a little tie, which I don't think he'll keep on, but he will make a grand entrance." Seth rubbed Jake's head.

"Well, if anyone can teach him how to do that, it's you. I like it when you wear a suit." Morgan eyed him up and down. He had a great sense of style. Today he looked like a catalogue model dressed in jeans, a nice pair of brown shoes, a scarf dangling around his neck, and a khaki jacket. He often found complementary clothes for Jake to match his wardrobe color scheme. No one believed her when she said she wasn't responsible for father and son wearing matching clothes.

The book club meeting in the cafe was ending. Michelle closed with a few notes about the book and the girls were busy packing up their things. Avery looked up, spotted Seth, and came over.

"Hi, Uncle Seth." Avery smiled, showing off her braces.

"Hey, pretty girl." Seth winked at her. "How was the book club meeting?"

"It was great." Avery blushed, then turned to Morgan with her cell phone. "Aunt Morgan, my dad is on the phone."

"Hey, Robert." Morgan chatted with her brother for a few minutes. "Not a problem at all." She hung up and turned to Avery. "Avery, you will be spending the night with us. Your dad got a lead on a case he's working on and your mom will be back tomorrow from her work retreat."

Avery jumped up, her eyes wide with excitement. "Cool!" But then she frowned. "Dad was supposed to drop off three of my friends."

"Babe, Avery and I can drop off her friends. I'll leave Jake with you. When I come back the four of us can go to dinner. Avery, you choose the cuisine." Seth smiled.

"OK." Avery floated off in the direction of her friends.

Morgan let out a deep, sinister chuckle. "You don't know what you just did."

"What? Was I not supposed to offer?" Seth frowned, puzzled.

"We'll talk when you get back from your excursion. Jake, do you want to ring up customers or stock the inventory?"

Michelle came over, shaking her head. "What are you doing?"

"He doesn't know." Morgan smirked.

"Can one of you tell me?" Seth said.

Michelle looked at him like he was crazy. "Every girl in my book club went mute when you walked through the door. They were so flustered I thought the sprinklers were going to go off."

"Remember that cheerleaders-in-the-locker-room story Tate told that night around the bonfire? Think of them as little cheerleaders in training." Morgan laughed at Seth's clueless gaping.

"Oh." Seth blushed.

Morgan shook her head. "Avery doesn't give a crap about

having dinner with *me* tonight."

Seth paled as Avery and her three friends giggled by the door.

Michelle patted Seth's shoulder. "Try to belch or something, a fart wouldn't hurt either."

"Michelle," Seth drawled.

"Yeah, don't do that sexy southern accent thing." Michelle shook her head.

Morgan pushed him toward the door. "We'll be ready when you get back. Try not to break any hearts."

* * *

The small article in *New Day* magazine turned into a full spread feature. Morgan wanted to run for the hills when they asked if she would grace their cover.

She called Nina, hyperventilating. "Why the hell do they want me on their cover?"

"Because you're pretty." Nina laughed.

"Nina, I can't do this. I am a nobody. The magazine will have their lowest-selling issue ever."

"Remind me to slap you when I see you. I know Seth probably tells you that you're beautiful all the time, but it's the truth. You would look great on that cover. The article would be a great piece on your life and that non-profit you hold so dear. If you don't want people peering into your life, then tell them you won't answer invasive questions. You can highlight that you're married to a great guy who happened to be a quarterback, you have a beautiful son, and you are a crusader for literacy. It's not about you, it's about getting a platform to sell the ideal that everyone is entitled to read, and get enjoyment from it, and what a valuable tool it is."

"I hate when you're right." Morgan moaned.

"I'll go along with you. This is so cute that you, Seth, and Jake have magazine covers this year. That pic of the two of them on the *Sports Page* cover is too adorable. It's my screen saver. All you need is a family cover."

"Nina!" Morgan yelled into the phone.

"Well, it would be."

* * *

Morgan attended the African American festival every year, but unlike the previous years where she'd attended alone, the entire Reed clan was there. They were walking around, enjoying the activities, while she manned her booth with the help of Sydney. The book sales were more than decent this year, although she suspected some people just lingered around the table for a glimpse of Seth, who was walking around the grounds with Jake and Avery. Seth appeared back at the table an hour later, bearing lunch.

"Ladies, this is baked chicken and steamed vegetables. Avery, Jake, and I are going to get something to eat while we listen to the jazz quartet perform." Seth set down the food on the table.

"Does he need changing?" Morgan spied her son, who was rummaging through bookmarks he'd picked up off the table.

"Nope, we're good."

"Blake!" Patton yelled out about a half mile away. After saying hello to a few fans, Patton made his way to the table. He gave Morgan and Sydney a kiss on the cheek.

"Patton, glad you could make it." Seth gave his friend a pat on the back.

"You know I'm ready. I did my stretches and everything before I came here." Patton rubbed his stomach.

"You stretched to eat?" Morgan said.

"Yes, Ms. Morgan, I did." Patton pinched her cheek. "You know I'm mad they didn't add the eating contest. I put that in the suggestion box last year."

Morgan laughed. "Nina sent me a text and wants to know if you overeat. So I'll be watching."

"Snitching ain't cool, Morgan." Patton took Jake from Seth and walked away. "I'm going to show my godson how you do it."

Seth gave her a quick kiss on the lips. "We'll be back in an hour or two."

"OK." Morgan turned to her niece. "See you later, Avery."

Avery waved but didn't speak. She simply tightened her grip on Seth's hand and left with him.

"I don't think she heard a word I said." Morgan laughed.

"When Seth gave her friends a ride home, that's all they talked about for weeks." Sydney chuckled.

Morgan and Sydney ate their lunch while people watching. Morgan's dad sent a text saying he was on his way with Jared. There was a lull in the foot traffic in the giant tent so Morgan told Sydney to take a break and enjoy the festival.

"I want to catch the art dealer. There is a painting I think would look nice in the study." Sydney slid her purse on her shoulder.

"Take your time. If I get a crowd I'll call you on your cell phone."

"This has been such a nice day. I see why you enjoy doing this every year."

"Yes, it has." And it would be one more thing to miss. "Now get out of here. If you see a nice pair of silver earrings you don't think Jake will pull out of my ears, let me know."

Morgan took a seat in a chair, content knowing her family was scattered around the festival. For so many years she'd come here, set up her booth, and spent her day reading and daydreaming. Today, seventy percent of the merchandise she'd brought with her had already been sold and it was still early. Sydney was happy they were doing something together. Seth was probably feeding Jake something crazy.

She picked up the book she'd been trying to read for the last three months, finally cracking the spine when a familiar voice called out her name.

"Hey, Morgan." Lamont Brayer stood at her table.

Morgan waved at him from her chair but didn't get up. "Hi, Lamont. Seth and Patton went to get some barbeque. If you follow a trail of rib or chicken bones, you should be able to catch up with them."

Lamont took a deep breath. "Actually, I was hoping to talk to you."

Morgan's back stiffened against her chair. She had made great strides to avoid Lamont after the scene at the dinner party. She didn't want to be involved with him or Charisma. There had been a few team events since where he'd attended alone, but she still kept her distance.

"OK. What do you want to talk about?" Morgan walked over to the table.

"This thing with you and Charisma. I apologize for bringing her to your home. I thought it would be a nice surprise to see your cousin."

"You don't have to keep apologizing."

Lamont went to turn away but stopped. "A producer approached Charisma about doing a reality show."

"I couldn't imagine a person more suited to have a camera following her around." Morgan sighed.

"It's a show about women who date athletes. Sounds like they want to document her eventually marrying me." Lamont chuckled but there was a dark look in his eye.

"Oh, I didn't know you guys were that serious," Morgan said.

"We're not. Your cousin is like a runaway freight train. She's got us married, and I just want to have fun." He folded his arms across his chest.

"I am the last person to give you advice on her, if that's what you're looking for?" Morgan hunched her shoulders.

"There's a hitch to the reality show deal. They will only do if they can get you too. They wanted to do a family angle. She's alluded to people that you two don't get along and apparently that's good television."

Morgan erupted in laughter. Now the calls from her aunt and Charisma's blatant flirting with Seth at that bar were becoming clear. "There is a better chance of seeing an actual dinosaur roaming downtown Philadelphia than it is of me and Charisma being on a reality show together."

Lamont smiled. "I figured as much. You're one tough cookie, Morgan. You want to tell me why you and Charisma don't get along?"

"You want to tell me why you didn't ask her yourself?"

Lamont shrugged, head down. "I wanted to hear your side of the story."

"She's your girlfriend. You shouldn't want to hear *my* side."

Sydney came back to the table with a painting. Lamont helped her set it near a chair behind their display.

He squared his shoulders and shifted on his feet for a moment. "I'm off to find Patton and Blake."

Morgan nodded, her jaw tight. "Good bye, Lamont."

Lamont slowly walked away as if he was hoping Morgan was going to call him back to the table.

Sydney studied Morgan's face. "What did I miss?"

"An episode of *The Twilight Zone*. My cousin has her eye on a reality show. Lamont says they won't do it without me."

Sydney eyed Lamont as he walked out of sight. "You've got to be kidding me. Charisma brought him by the house and tried to introduce him to us as if we cared. Curtis didn't ask him one question about the Titans. I think that pissed her off. While she was going on about how happy they were, Lamont was walking around the living room looking at pictures of you. I thought that was odd and was amazed Charisma didn't think that was peculiar."

"That girl's got tunnel vision and she's hoping there's money and status at the end of it." Morgan rolled her eyes.

"Well, I put them out. Nicely, but I put them out all the same.

Then Debra had the nerve to call me and ask if she could come over the next time I was watching Jake. She said you were too busy to visit the family, and she wanted to see him."

"What did you say?" Morgan bit her lip.

"I told her it wasn't going to happen. If you wanted her to see your son, you'd visit her. That mother and daughter are two peas in a pod. No one is going to use me to hurt to you."

Morgan almost couldn't speak, shock and affection warring inside her. "Thanks, Sydney."

* * *

Morgan had never felt more loved by her brothers than when she invited them to Seth's private suite to see the Titans play their home games. Being among the testosterone driven mania reminded her of the noisy Sundays of her youth. She made sure there was plenty of beer and greasy snack foods for her brood. Jake, who loved the excitement of his crazy uncles, managed to stay awake the whole game.

Her brother Jared arrived first.

"Hey, Squirt and Lil Squirt." Jared kissed her.

"Hey, how's work? Any new projects?"

He scratched at his beard. "Working on a waterfront office building right now."

Morgan laughed. "I remember your first project. That house you designed for my dolls one summer."

Jared laughed too. "I remember you made me give you a homebuilder's guarantee before you would let them move in."

"How's the love life?"

"I still have the stench of a new divorce on me. There is no love life to speak of at this time." Jared shifted in his seat.

"I don't believe that."

"I've been busy with work." Jared flashed her a cheesy smile and pulled Jake onto his lap. "Is Jake signed with a team yet?"

"Ha ha. No, but he has a Blake jersey."

Jared bopped Jake's nose. "My nephew has some big shoes to fill."

"I prefer that he find his own way in life. Who says he's not going to be an architect like you? Or a construction worker? Or a scientist?"

Jared gave her an expectant look. "You do know who you married, right?"

Morgan sighed. "I think he's teaching him stats instead of the alphabet."

Jared burst out laughing. "That kid doesn't stand a chance."

"Don't I know it." Morgan handed Jake a toy.

Jared looked at her for what seemed like an eternity.

"Why the hell are you staring at me?" Morgan said.

"It's nice having you back in the family fold. I missed you." Jared smiled at her.

"Are you saying that because you're in a private suite at the Titans' stadium watching your favorite quarterback, who happens to be your brother-in-law?"

"Partly, yes." Jared laughed.

"Jerk." Morgan laughed too.

"Love you too, squirt." Jared kissed her on the cheek. "Sydney and Dad's anniversary is at Palazzo's in a private dining room. You up for that?"

Morgan thought about it. "Sounds like fun. We already got them a present."

"I got a yes on the first try!" Jared squeezed Jake. "Nephew, I do believe you have softened mommy up a bit."

The rest of the family arrived just in time for kick off. Morgan's stomach clinched the second the game started. No matter how good a player he was, she worried that Seth would break a bone or suffer a concussion. It seemed like the opposing team always made a beeline for him and it frustrated her. She covered Jake's eyes whenever Seth got hit as they watched him on television. By the third quarter, it looked like the Titans were going to win this one.

Jared's comment was ping ponging in her head as she watched the game. Morgan looked around the room to see the happy smiling faces of the men in her life. Sydney, Michelle, Nina, and Avery were sitting in the back talking. Jake had somehow made his way to her father and was taking a nap in his lap. It was funny how football had brought them all back together again. Maybe their new bond was strong enough to withstand a move to another state.

Chapter Eight

Morgan hustled into the library to get out of the torrential rain. She'd wanted to reschedule the meeting, but it would have been the third time she'd cancelled. These days going to the library left her feeling melancholy knowing in a matter of months she wouldn't be there. She'd begun packing some boxes at the house, mostly unessential items she didn't need. For her, it was a practice run for when Seth's announcement was made, and they were bound for Texas. It was even more agonizing because she couldn't tell anyone what she was going through. The risk of the information leaking would have dire consequences for Seth. The formality of a player being traded or becoming a free agent had rules that needed to be followed in accordance with the football association. She loved Michelle, but she couldn't risk her loose lips blurting out the news one day in front of the wrong person, or even worse, within earshot of the media. Nina wouldn't keep a secret like this from Patton, who would directly be affected by Seth's decision to leave.

"Hi, Harriet." Morgan hugged her.

"Hello, Morgan. Sorry to make you come out in this rain." Harriet took her raincoat.

"That's OK. I apologize for cancelling so many times. I hope Maura isn't mad." Morgan bit her lip.

"I was trying to reach you. Maura had an emergency about

twenty minutes ago. Her son got injured at school. I hope *you're* not mad, coming all this way."

"I hope her son's alright. Now that I'm a mom I know you have to dash off and apologize later."

Harriet nodded. "Let's take a walk." She linked her arm with Morgan's.

Harriet led her around the first floor, then ascended the marble steps to the next. Morgan knew where Harriet was herding her: to the picture of her mother.

"I know why Maura wants to meet with you." Harriet stopped by a display case, where a picture of Morgan's mother sat on the top shelf.

"Maura likes feedback about the programs. I assumed she just wanted an update."

Harriet shook her head. "Maura was so impressed with your creative efforts to keep reading hour going, she asked me about your Reading Builds Bridges. I told her about the book clubs you have at the bookstore and the book fairs you coordinated in the community centers. She wants to offer you a job."

"What?" Morgan eked out, her throat tightening.

"She wants to make you the head of the volunteer services. You would oversee the Reading Hour volunteers and take the reins on some new ideas that have been floating around. You sparked a renewed interest in literacy. Your mother would be proud of you."

"I already have my family, the bookstore, and…"

"It wouldn't be full time. You could make your own hours," Harriet assured her.

"Well, this is unexpected."

"When you do good things, opportunities sprout up. Forgive me for being so sentimental, but just had to tell you this near Elizabeth's photo." Harriet squeezed her tight.

"Thank you for giving me the heads up." Morgan smiled.

"You will pretend to be surprised when Maura talks to you?"

Harriet whispered.

Morgan winked. "Of course."

That evening when she returned home, Seth and Jake were playing on the floor with his Tiny Tots farmhouse. Seth was explaining to his son the names of the little plastic farm animals and even had horses the same color as Iris and Reed's Fire. Seth smiled at her when she walked in.

"Hey, babe, I was just giving Jake a tour of the stables."

"I see." She knelt on the floor and picked up a cow.

"How was your day?"

"My day was good."

She wanted to tell him that her day was great. Harriet had told her a juicy secret that she didn't have the luxury to be excited about. She wanted to ask him if he'd be willing to stay with the Titans for a little while longer, while she chased her dream. But instead she gave a kiss to both of them and headed to the bedroom to change for dinner.

* * *

Seth said goodbye to his teammates and loaded himself into his Range Rover. The days on the road were getting harder. Video chat just wasn't as satisfying as being there. But when he wasn't there, he still kept his head in the game. Surprisingly having a family had made him more focused. He knew they were safe, happy. When he needed reassurance he'd ask Channing and Tyler or one of Morgan's brothers to pop in on them. He would laugh to himself when she would call, telling him about some unannounced visitor that spent the day with her and Jake. She was sharp, he knew she suspected what was going on, but she let it alone like she knew it made him feel better.

As he winded through the streets, he noticed the subtle changes in the landscape. He loved Philadelphia in the fall. The air was crisper, the people began dressing up in their heavier attire, and the city would slow down a bit in anticipation for winter. It had taken him some time to get used to the snow and the occasional blizzard but that was the cost of signing with the Titans.

Soon he would be back in Texas, feeling the warmth of the hot sun year round. He hoped the occasional cold snap or periodic rain would be enough to soothe Morgan's fondness for the less torrid temperatures. He'd have someone come in to give the central air system in the house an overhaul, to make sure she'd be comfortable.

He knew his mother would keep her busy when they moved, but he also knew she needed something of her own to pursue. He never figured her for a full-time housewife, so he anticipated she would open another bookstore or get involved in something educational.

Finally he was home. The entrance to the Ashcroft had never looked so good to him. He said hello to a few of his neighbors in the lobby, then got on the elevator. He was exhausted and needed a long shower to soothe some tight muscles, but all he wanted to do was see how his two favorite people were enjoying their day.

"Stop right there," Morgan said as she ran into the hallway to greet him and gave him a quick kiss.

"OK." Seth closed the door and dropped his duffel bag. "What's going on?"

"Give me one minute." Morgan flitted into the living room. A few minutes passed, and Morgan called out to him. "OK, come in and stop at the doorway."

Seth turned the corner to see the living room in disarray. She was on her knees near the coffee table with Jake, who should have been asleep. He was holding onto the table for dear life, when Morgan came up behind him and took his hands.

"OK, Jake, go to daddy," Morgan said.

The second Morgan let go of Jake's hands, Seth saw a flicker of sadness in her eyes. Jake sprinted clumsily toward him, and Seth knelt down just in time to catch him. Morgan cheered and clapped while Seth held him in his arms, unable to speak for a moment.

"I think he broke your yardage record." Morgan laughed.

"I think he did too. I am so proud of you, Jake. Want to walk back to Mommy?" Seth set him down, and Jake took off like a rocket into Morgan's arms.

Morgan and Seth followed behind their son as he took his new walking tour of the living room. Each time he looked like he was going to fall, Morgan would lunge behind him but Seth would stop her. The concept of letting him go was foreign to him, but he knew his son needed freedom. Jake walked around the room until he was tired. He turned, arms outstretched, waiting for Morgan to pick him up. She obliged and smothered him with kisses. Finally they all settled on the couch.

"Here you go." Morgan replayed the video she'd captured of Jake's first steps.

Seth looked at the video while Jake tried to climb into his lap.

"Now to send to everyone we know." Morgan's hands flew over the keys as she sent Jake's debut to everyone in her phonebook.

"Morgan," Seth sighed.

"One more thing." Morgan picked up the remote off the coffee table and turned on the flat screen. It was paused on the game Seth had played the day before. "Jake, look at daddy on the screen."

"Watch him," Morgan mouthed to Seth.

Jake looked at the screen like he was trying hard to decipher what was going on. Seth made a pass and a tight camera frame came in on him. The number twelve on his jersey could be seen.

"Bla' sco's!" Jake yelled.

Morgan jumped up off the couch with Jake in her arms, running around and whooping it up. They collapsed back on the couch after a minute.

Seth raised an eyebrow. "So this is what you do while I'm at work?"

"Yes. We wear our Blake jerseys and have snacks. Jake takes a nap during the game. If you're not on the screen he gets disinterested quick." She smiled.

"Morgan," Seth said as the video started again.

"I know." Morgan leaned closer to kiss him. Jake popped his head up and caught a kiss from both his parents. "Can you believe he'll be one year old in a few months?"

Seth tickled his son. "Yes, he has a big milestone coming up. My dad wants to throw a big birthday party at the ranch. And he wants your family and our friends to come down."

"I expected that. Speaking of big milestones. How does it feel to be undefeated this season?"

"It feels good." For a moment he'd forgotten what he'd been doing before he walked through the door and saw a new chapter in his life unfolding. Soon Jake would be running around the house, getting into everything, and Seth couldn't wait to chase after him.

Morgan's phone started pinging with responses to Jake's first steps while Seth's rang. It was his mother calling. Seth and Morgan looked at each other, knowing it was better to vet the calls than ignore them. Morgan started cleaning up while Jake played with the building blocks on the coffee table.

Seth hit the answer button. "Hey, Momma. I know, isn't he something?"

* * *

Morgan could hardly believe that was her face on the cover of *New Day* magazine. The issue had finally come out and she'd been in agony waiting for it. They'd offered to send her a proof, but she had Nina look at it and approve it. Thanks to Nina's angelic cosmetics skills, she was so transformed on the magazine cover, she hardly recognized herself. Jocelyn called her and congratulated her on the article, reaffirming that she'd done a good job covering all the bases with the primary focus on her work life, not her personal one. She'd talked in detail about interracial relationships with the reporter, offering insight on her perspective of what was deemed her mysterious relationship with Seth. The magazine had wanted a picture of Jake, but she'd declined. Her son being on the cover of one magazine was enough for a year. That issue of *Sports Now* was the magazine's highest selling ever. She had to admit the picture they went with, Jake asleep on Seth's shoulder while he held his football helmet in one hand and a bottle in the other, was quite endearing. It was hanging in their living room. To her it symbolized the infusion of his family into his football life.

Michelle snuck up behind her at the bookstore counter. "Can I have your autograph?"

Morgan put the magazine behind her back and tried to act natural. "What are you talking about?"

"I want to be the first person to get your autograph. I'm going to whine until you do it, so just do it." Michelle dangled a Sharpie marker in front of her.

"Here, and you're paying for this magazine." Morgan scribbled on the cover.

"Thank you!" Michelle kissed her on the cheek. "By the way, don't you have somewhere to be?"

"Right." Morgan headed for the backroom to get her coat.

She walked out the door, on her way to the library to meet with Maura and pretend to be surprised about the job offer that she had to turn down.

* * *

Seth sat in his chair in his study, staring at the cover shot of Morgan on *New Day* magazine. Morgan's bright smile illuminated the page as she perched on a chair wearing a satin red dress Nina had chosen for her that accentuated those curvy hips he loved so much. The caption, The Perfect Play: Morgan Blake Literary

Crusader, jumped off the cover.

He became engrossed in the article, impressed with the way she'd steered it. It was personal in a reserved way. She'd kept her responses to the fluffy questions very concise and nicely stated she wasn't divulging any personal information about him.

New Day: "You are a very busy lady. You own a bookstore, have a son, and run a non-profit. How do you do it all?"

Morgan Blake: "Lots of energy and a great husband. We made a commitment to being great working parents whose priority is family first."

ND: "What do you attribute to your success?"

MB: "The love and support of my husband, Seth, who encourages me to follow my dreams. He inspires me to keep trying, even when doors are slammed shut in my face, and he has faith in me, even when I lose faith in myself. He makes me feel that I have an inner strength that's just as immense as the physical strength he has as a football player. He is a great husband, father, and friend. I am grateful to have him and our son in my life."

Seth smiled to himself. She was no longer Seth Blake's wife. She was Morgan Blake, literary philanthropist and bookstore owner. Seth found himself drifting into the background more and loved it. The woman he loved was capable of so many things. She was even willing to give up her life in Philadelphia so he could pursue his dreams...

* * *

Morgan buttoned her coat as she slid out of the Range Rover and made her way up the stairs. She was in unchartered territory today. Sydney was hanging a decorative fall wreath on the front door. It was almost Halloween. The leaves were turning and the weather was getting crisp. It was her favorite time of the year. When he didn't have a game, she and Seth would cuddle up in the living room and have long leisurely days watching movies, taking naps, or just talking.

"I didn't think I'd be seeing you today. Where is Jake? I bought him the cutest pair of boots the other day." Sydney smiled at her.

"I thought I'd drop by. Seth is home with Jake, and Michelle has things covered at the store." She hunched her shoulders and passed Sydney a scarecrow from inside the house. Morgan shook her head. Sydney's decorating was getting more elaborate each year.

"I'm hoping Jake doesn't find this too scary. I want him to enjoy his first Halloween." Sydney sighed.

"I think he'll like the colors."

"Did you get him a costume yet?"

"No, I was hoping we could go shopping together this weekend." Morgan smiled.

"Let's see, maybe he could be a bunny or a pumpkin! How cute would that be?"

"That would be too precious."

Sydney positioned the last scarecrow. "There. What do you think?"

"Looks great."

They went into the house. Morgan took off her coat and joined Sydney in the kitchen. Still at a loss for words, she took a seat at the kitchen table to stop herself from pacing the floor. She could do this.

"This must be important," Sydney said, her back to Morgan as she fixed them both a cup of tea.

"What?"

Sydney laughed. "Yes, it is important."

"Why do you think that?"

Sydney placed a teacup in front of Morgan and sat down.

"When you are nervous, you do that. Say 'what?' Or 'excuse me?' It's your defense mechanism."

Morgan thought for a moment. "I guess you're right."

Sydney patted her hand. "In my experience I find it best to just let it rip."

Morgan took a deep breath. "The library offered me a job. They liked the proposal I submitted to get help with the reading hour so much, they want me to be their director of volunteer affairs."

"Congratulations!" Sydney beamed. "I know you have a lot going on, but you're very good at juggling things. I will help out any way I can."

Morgan let her shoulders droop. "Seth's contract with the Titans ends in March. If things go well he wants to join the Texas Tomcats. The owner is a friend of his dad's and has wanted Seth to play on his team for a long time."

"Wow." Sydney swallowed.

Morgan stared hard at the table. "I love him. I am happy for him, but sad at the same time. I feel guilty because I'm not supporting his decision one hundred percent like I should."

"You're entitled to your feelings. You would be giving up a good opportunity."

Morgan closed her eyes. "He's dreamed of this most of his life."

"I know. He wrote about it in his book."

Morgan opened her eyes and looked up at her. "You read his book?"

"Of course I did. Just like I bought a copy of *New Day* magazine. I'm proud of both of you. You're my kids." Sydney smiled.

Morgan bit her lip, wondering how Sydney did it. Taking the time to care about her and she'd always been a cold fish to her. "Can I ask you a question?"

"Sure."

"Why have you always been so nice to me? I haven't exactly

been…friendly to you over the years."

Sydney reached out and touched Morgan's hand. "I know you miss your mom."

"I worried that you would somehow make me forget her." Morgan's eyes teared up.

"It was never my intention to take your mother's place. I couldn't if I tried. You having Jake and asking me to look after him gave me hope that we can have a relationship." Sydney wiped away a tear running down her cheek.

"When my dad started dating you, he became happy again. Even if I didn't respond to it well at the time, thank you for that," Morgan said quietly.

"*Thank you* for trusting me with your son."

"You have a loving way about you. I've side stepped it long enough to know you are a warm, caring person and that Jake would be in good hands." Morgan smiled despite a tear streaming down her cheek.

"So, what are you going to do about your dilemma?"

Morgan threw up her hands. "There isn't one, is there? I love Seth and I don't want to be the reason he derails his football career."

"I'm going to miss you when you move." Sydney gave her a hug.

Morgan leaned into Sydney's body and accepted the warmth. She held on to her for a bit, sorry she'd missed so many opportunities to be loved by this kind, gentle woman. "I'm going to miss you too. Please don't tell anyone about the Tomcats situation. No one's supposed to know."

"I won't say a word." Sydney opened a kitchen draw and pulled out the magazine. "But before you go, I want you to autograph my cover."

"Good grief," Morgan moaned at seeing herself for the second time that day.

"I read the article. You look stunning on this cover."

Morgan laughed. "Prettier than Seth?"

"Almost." Sydney chuckled and hugged her again.

The sound of the front door opening meant Morgan's dad was home. He came into the kitchen grumbling about his day and how cold it was getting outside, but he stopped in his tracks when he saw Morgan and Sydney in an embrace.

"Am I dying?" he asked.

Morgan laughed and kissed her father on the cheek. "No, Dad, you're fine. We're all going to be fine."

Chapter Nine

The Titans had a hell of a season, and although they'd made it to the playoffs, they weren't going to the Super Bowl this year. The team played hard and, despite injured players, they achieved twelve wins and two losses. Lamont was injured in game seven and sat out the rest of the season.

Patton, however, was on cloud nine. Nina had delivered a healthy baby girl. He was on the road when she went into labor but was comforted knowing Morgan was right there with her in the delivery room. When Nina's water broke while visiting the bookstore, Morgan hustled her to the hospital and coached her through her labor. As each labor pain hit, Nina cursed and screamed for Patton's head on a platter for knocking her up. Morgan couldn't help but laugh, knowing all Nina had been through to have her baby. Eight hours later Gabriella Hawkes came into the world. Morgan stepped out into the hallway and cried after seeing Nina give birth. Suddenly she got Seth's enthusiasm for adding to their family.

* * *

Morgan was trying, in vain, to pack Seth's bags for his away game. Seth was getting dressed while she had her hands full looking for his lucky boxer shorts and keeping Jake from climbing into the bag. She hated it when he had to leave but opted to make it as light hearted as possible so Jake wouldn't get sad every time he saw his father's bags by the door.

"I found your shorts." She closed the dresser drawer with her hip. "Promise me you'll wear your hat if it's cold there."

"Will do." Seth kissed her. "Jake, I need you to look after your momma while I'm gone, OK?"

Jake smiled and gave him an affirmative nod.

Morgan's cell phone rang. "Hey, Michelle, what's up?"

"Are you near a television?" Michelle said over the phone. "Turn on channel one eighteen."

Morgan held her breath, hoping whatever was on wasn't going to ruin her night. It was the celebrity gossip talk show Talk of the Town. Morgan avoided that show like the plague.

"Michelle, this better be good."

"Oooh! It's starting! Be quiet and listen!"

The host of the show stared into the camera and said, "Last night police were called to Club Serenity after a heated argument occurred between Philadelphia Titans wide receiver Lamont Brayer and his now ex-girlfriend Charisma Reed. Ms. Reed was in the social hotspot looking for Brayer, who was in a VIP lounge canoodling with another woman. A shoving match ensued between the two women, and Ms. Reed was escorted out of the nightclub, where she continued to make a scene until police arrived to quiet her down. Sources close to the couple say Charisma had her heart set on marrying the Super Bowl champ, but he was only interested in a fling. She was courted for a prospective reality show, but it seems the producers would only do it if she could get her cousin to be part of it. Charisma Reed is the cousin of Morgan Reed-Blake, the wife of quarterback Seth Blake. It's rumored the cousins do not get along and had a falling out at a dinner party at Morgan's house. Friends of Brayer say they're surprised it lasted this long and that he had tired of her flashy, obnoxious ways, a complete contrast to her elegant, humanitarian cousin, who is the darling of

Philadelphia."

As soon as Morgan hung up with Michelle, her phone began
pinging with text messages. Apparently a lot of people she knew
watched that show.

Morgan sighed. "The signs were there. Sydney said the family
was trying to get Charisma to put on the brakes and take it slow,
but she wanted to go faster with Lamont."

Seth shrugged. "He mentioned something at practice one day. I
tuned him out. It was none of my business."

The text messages continued to pour in, but she didn't respond
to them. The platform in which her cousin suffered her latest
humiliation couldn't have gotten any bigger, but Morgan was
through talking about the never-ending saga of Charisma.

* * *

Jake's first birthday party would be at the ranch and all family
members were attending. Morgan tried to get a sympathetic
shoulder to lean on about the huge event Teri-Lyn was planning
from Sydney when she dropped Jake off at the house on the way to
the bookstore. But Sydney shut down her pity party and scolded
her too. Teri-Lyn had already called her and together they were
making plans.

The Blakes arrived a week early to help prepare for the party.
Sydney, who was part of the planning committee, flew down with
them as well. Morgan smiled at Sydney's appreciation of a private
plane with a stewardess, a small conference area, a kitchenette, a
bedroom, and a shower. Seth kept her busy gazing out the window
at the cloud formations while Morgan went through educational
flashcards with Jake, which included team positions and facts
about the game of football. Eventually Jake informed her that he
wanted to take a nap by tugging on her pants leg.

They touched down early in the afternoon, giving everyone
time to wind down before Teri-Lyn revealed the big birthday bash

schematic. Morgan squeezed Seth's hand when Teri-Lyn rolled the blue prints across the dining room table after dinner. There were going to be carnival rides, games, horseback riding, food, and even a sound stage. The Dirty Rascals had volunteered to play to thank Tate for the help he'd given them. They were slated to record their first album in the spring. When Morgan saw the card for a local clothing retailer on the table, she decided to speak up.

"Ladies, this all sounds nice, but why is this clothing store coming?"

"Every guest will get a pair of cowboy boots." Teri-Lyn smiled.

"When Teri-Lyn told me that I thought it was too precious," Sydney said.

"But—"

Seth kissed her before she could finish. "Ladies," he drawled, "we'll leave the planning to you. Morgan and I will get Jake settled."

Teri-Lyn and Sydney waved them off as Seth pulled Morgan out of the dining room. The kitchen was clean and their bags had been unpacked. Seth led her to the veranda, sat her in a swing chair, and put Jake between them.

"They're insane." Morgan huffed.

Seth chuckled. "Quite possibly."

"You didn't tell them to scale down anything."

"Why should I? They're happy to be planning his first birthday. It means as much to them as it does to us."

Morgan closed her eyes. "Am I the party pooper in the family? Michelle already calls me the s-e-x deterrent."

"Babe, I don't think Jake knows what that word means yet."

"Well, I don't want him yelling out s-e-x at his birthday party and add to his already colorful vocabulary. I think damn it and jack ass are enough for now." She looked at Seth.

He suppressed a smile and turned his head. "I don't know where he heard that language."

"The possibilities are endless. His foul mouthed uncles, your foul mouthed friends."

Seth coughed. "Excuse me, Michelle and Nina could make a fleet of sailors blush."

'True." She bit her lip.

* * *

The ranch was a flurry of activity. Work crews had begun assembling rides and building booths days earlier. When the guests arrived on Friday, Teri-Lyn and Sydney hosted a cocktail party that evening. The guest of honor made an appearance for thirty whole minutes before he was put to bed. Jake's party looked more like a state fair than a simple happy birthday for a one-year-old. But Morgan let it go and took Seth's advice to pick her battles with the family. By the day of the party, everyone was in a festive mood, especially Nina. She was finally able to travel with the baby. When she emerged from the clothing tent decked out in jeans, cowboy boots, and a hat, Morgan thought she had finally gone over the edge. Nina detested hats that ruined her hairdos.

"You look great!" Morgan said.

"Thank you. What do you think?"

"Elegant, country chic. I like it." Morgan laughed.

"I was going for that look." Nina twirled around.

"As usual, you've put your own fashion stamp on something."

"I can see why you like being down here." Nina beamed.

"Well, we don't dress like this all the time." Morgan had donned her favorite pair of jeans, which were back to fitting the way she liked, a comfortable shirt, the pair of pink cowboy boots Teri-Lyn had bought her the first day they had lunch together, and a hat.

"I know that. You just look…like you're in your element here. Natural. Country. Beautiful. If we'd never met before I would swear you were born here."

"Th-thanks," Morgan said. "Did Patton have any trouble finding boots?"

"No, they had his size." Nina looked back at the tent. Morgan looked up and saw her niece Avery riding Reed's Fire. Bo was walking beside them with the reigns while she got acclimated to the horse.

"Avery's riding your horse, isn't she?" Nina squinted up at her.

"Yes, she is. I hope you like your riding lesson."

"Bo is going to give me a refresher. I used to ride when I was a kid."

"Maybe we can take a ride together before you leave. I can show you the rest of the ranch." Morgan locked arms with her friend.

"The rest?"

"It's a pretty big stretch of land."

"Damn."

"Later Bo's going to break out his moonshine; it will knock you on your ass."

"Thank goodness I brought my nanny."

Morgan laughed, thinking of Nina's nanny, Britta, an elderly woman who looked like she could bench press Patton. "Enjoy your lesson." She released Nina's arm and pointed her in the direction of the stables.

From a distance Morgan saw a pair of long, muscled legs wearing jeans and leaning into the cab of a truck to get something, and she knew it was Seth. He looked good in his red plaid shirt and his favorite pair of cowboy boots. He hadn't had time to shave so he had a bit of stubble on his face. Not so much that anyone would notice, but she did. Living here full time meant she'd see him dressed like that more, and she could get behind that. When he donned his favorite hat, it made her skin tingle. He must have sensed her lusty thoughts, because he turned around when he finished with the truck, tipped his hat, and smiled.

"Have you seen our son?" Morgan asked as she approached Seth.

"Daddy was showing him off to some of his friends." Seth gave her a bear hug. "Don't worry, this will all be over soon."

Morgan looked around at all of their family and friends having fun and shrugged her shoulders. "Everybody's having a good time. I don't want to rush it. As obnoxious as all this is, it's sweet too. I can't believe my brothers are riding horses."

"Wait until I tell you about the poker game we had last night." He whistled.

"I probably don't want to know what happened."

"Probably not, but we all had such a good time. Your dad and mine talked for hours. Patton drank three mason jars of Bo's moonshine. Robert apparently knows how to play the guitar, he and Tate played together. J.J., Channing, and Tyler have a surprise for Jake. They'll have to pick it up in a few hours." Seth smiled.

"Why do I get the feeling that our family and friends got to have that wedding reception they were all so pissed about missing out on?"

"You know what? You're absolutely right."

Morgan squeezed him tight. "All we women did last night was complain about you men."

"Really?"

"No, not really. Sydney mixed drinks, and they all got hammered. Eden stayed for all of thirty minutes then made up an excuse to leave. Michelle got drunk and asked your mom how she managed to have such hot sons. Nina admitted that your dad was the most handsome man she'd ever seen in her life. And my sister-in-laws asked me some raunchy stuff about you."

"Like what?" Seth waggled his eyebrows.

"They wanted to know if you had the same stamina in bed as you do on the field. I think that's the most I've ever talked to Alicia and Janice." She laughed.

The Dirty Rascals exited the stage when John Jacob approached it, requesting a few minutes with the microphone.

"What is your father up to?" Morgan looked up at Seth.

"You'll see." He put his arms around her and turned her in the direction of the stage.

John Jacob began his speech. "Thank you all for coming out here today to celebrate my grandson's birthday. One year ago today my son Seth and beautiful daughter-in-law Morgan made my wife and I two of the happiest people in the world. My grandson Jake has been a joy to have in our lives. I know he will grow up to do great things, just like his father and mother. It gives me great pleasure to say that in three months we will open Jacob Springs, a new golf resort and spa project in Arizona. Jacob Springs is my gift to him."

Morgan looked up at Seth. "You knew about this?"

"Daddy wanted it to be a surprise."

John Jacob and Teri-Lyn descended the stage with Jake. He reached out for Morgan as soon as he saw her.

She pulled Jake into her arms.

John Jacob smiled. "Morgan, I hope you don't mind about my gift to Jake."

"It's a wonderful gesture. Thank you."

Morgan's cell phone vibrated in her pocket, taking her by surprise. Everyone she knew was here on the ranch, who could be calling her? She looked at the display to see that it was a call from Maura at the library. She'd been putting the poor woman off for weeks, not ready to verbalize that she couldn't take the position. Her neck tensed, and her smile must have slipped, because she could feel the heat of one of Seth's concerned stares on her.

* * *

The party was in full swing and everyone was enjoying the festivities, but Morgan could see Jake's energy waning, so she and

Seth cut the birthday cake early. Everyone gathered around as Seth
plopped their son on the table and let him grab two fistfuls of
birthday cake. Channing and Tyler were off to retrieve their
present. After everyone was served, she informed Seth she was
going to get Jake cleaned up.

"I am going to change your clothes and then you'll have a
quick nap."

Jake was fighting sleep, but she knew once he settled down
with his favorite stuffed animal, he'd be out like a light. Truth be
told, she needed a nap herself. She walked into the dining room,
eyeballing the table filled with presents. A new gift had been added
to the pile. She looked at the card on the elegantly wrapped box
and saw that it was from Penny. The corners of Morgan's mouth
turned up as she looked at it again, to make sure she'd read it
correctly. But John Jacob had provided the biggest present of all—a
golf resort and spa in Arizona. Her son was the owner of a multi-
million dollar property on his first birthday.

It looked like they'd be unwrapping presents for weeks. They'd
have plenty of time to do it, since their move was imminent. The
idea of being at the ranch fulltime was both exciting and
depressing. She knew she'd love it here, but her life in Philadelphia
was pretty awesome too. Sydney wasn't the boogeyman anymore,
and Morgan enjoyed seeing her brothers. She needed more time to
set up her projects for the non-profit. Michelle was capable of
taking over the store, but it was an appendage to her. Her adult life
had begun with that store, and in time maybe she would be able to
let go, but it all seemed too soon right now.

Morgan walked past the library to see Avery sitting in one of
the overstuffed leather couches reading a book.

"Hi, Avery. What are you doing in here?"

Avery smiled and stretched out her legs to show off her new
cowboy boots. "Just catching up on my book club reading."

"You picked a nice pair." Morgan smiled; Avery's boots were

pink like hers.

"Thanks. I liked yours, so I asked for a pair that looked similar." Avery swung her feet back and forth.

Morgan plopped down on the couch next to her and took the book out of her hand. "Well, you are on a ranch filled with horses and there's a carnival right outside. I demand you go have some fun and some more cake."

"Thanks for the riding lessons. I enjoyed riding Reed's Fire. He's a beautiful horse."

"I'm glad you're having a good time. You know, you can come here in the summers when you're on your school break."

"Really?"

"As long as it doesn't conflict with something your parents want you to do, you always have a room here."

Avery jumped over and hugged her. "That would be awesome!"

"I thought you'd like that." Morgan kissed her on the cheek. "I'm putting Jake down for a nap. Now go and have some fun. That book will be here when you get back."

Morgan watched as Avery skipped out of the house. Then Morgan turned to Jake. "Your cousin reminds me of me when I was her age."

Jake looked at her in disbelief.

"Honest." She laughed and climbed the stairs.

Morgan lay beside her son in the middle of the bed, stroking his hair, enjoying the soft sounds of his breathing. He was growing up so quickly. It was only a matter of time before he'd be taller than her and going off to college. He was almost down for the count when Seth appeared.

"Daddy!" Jake said, seeing Seth.

"Hey, baby. Are you OK?" Seth said from the doorway.

"I'm fine, but your son needed a nap." Morgan motioned to Jake. "Or at least he did until he saw you."

"Looks like his Momma is tired too." Seth smiled. "I brought you something." Seth pulled a piece of birthday cake from behind his back and placed it on the nightstand.

"Thank you."

"You want to tell me what's wrong? Your mood changed from day to night out there when you looked at your phone." Seth rubbed her cheek.

Morgan hitched a grin onto her face. "What makes you think something is wrong?"

"Morgan Blake, you can flash that beautiful smile at everybody else, but I can see past that particular defense mechanism."

Morgan sighed. "I got a message from Maura at the library. They offered me a job at the library months ago. Director of Volunteer Affairs."

"Wow, that's great. Why didn't you tell me?"

"Because I know I can't take it. And I didn't want you to feel guilty about your decision. I accept that I can't do everything I want to do in life. There are some opportunities that will pass me by. But it did make me a little sad that I couldn't take it."

"But—"

"Seth, I don't want to talk about it. Maura's call just took me by surprise. I want to enjoy our son's birthday. One year ago today, our lives changed forever. He is our love manifested. How cool is that?"

"That is very cool." Seth grinned. "Have you had any fun today?"

"Of course I did." She smiled back.

"I meant non-organizational fun."

She shrugged. "You know how I get."

"Jake, it's time for your momma to have some fun." Seth opened the door to their bedroom terrace and the soft sounds of love a ballad the Dirty Rascals were playing filtered into the room. He took Morgan's hand, pulled her into a tight embrace, and rocked in time with the music.

"I still don't know how to dance." She leaned into him and swayed with his body.

"Just follow my lead." He kissed the top of her head.

Morgan smiled and held him tighter, thinking about that night at the Bright Star. Jake lay on the bed watching, the gentle rocking of his parents lulling him to sleep.

Morgan looked at her son. "Jake, promise me you won't use these cheesy moves when you get older."

"Hey, these cheesy moves work." Seth laughed.

She rubbed his back. "I know."

A few minutes later Morgan did a silent cheer when Jake fell asleep. Seth led her to the chaise lounge by the window. Morgan sat back in his arms while he fed her cake. Neither said a word for a while.

"If you're not OK with my dad's present, we can give it back," Seth said against her ear.

"I know your family does things a bit differently than I'm accustomed to. That was a generous thing John Jacob did for his first grandson. It's his way of looking out for Jake's future." She sighed. "I've been thinking."

"About?"

"I want to make another baby with you. Our lives are going to change in a hundred different ways soon, and I want to make another baby with you." Morgan looked up at him.

"Is that right?"

"That's right."

"Morgan." Seth covered her mouth with sweet kisses that grew more passionate with each stroke of his tongue.

"Wait, we can't have sex in the room with the kid." Morgan stopped his hand from unzipping her jeans.

"Hang on." Seth jumped up and went into the walk-in closet. He started moving things around.

"Shhh," she said. The sound of his banging and clanging would wake up Jake.

Seth emerged from the closet. "Come on."

Morgan walked into the closet to see Seth had laid out a sleeping bag on the floor and had fashioned several pairs of jeans into makeshift pillows. She closed the doors behind her.

"Very classy." She giggled as he pulled her down on the floor on top of him.

Morgan nipped Seth's neck as he unbuttoned her shirt. The camisole she wore underneath was no match for his nibble fingers. He slid it off her with ease. She returned the favor by unbuttoning his shirt, careful not to tear the buttons off this one. As she slid the fabric down his sculpted arms, she caressed every muscle and moved to his back as he shrugged off his shirt. Seth flipped her over on her back and liberated them both from their jeans. He braced himself on his knees, and Morgan opened wide to welcome him. He looked at her for a moment and didn't say a word, but she knew what he was thinking. The culmination of this intimate act, in a walk-in closet on a floor no less, would result in creating another life. Just like the perfect one that was spread out in the middle of their bed taking a nap during his first birthday party.

Seth raised her hips up a bit and plunged into her. The feel of that first contact of him inside of her never failed to take her by surprise like it was the first time they'd made love. Each moment with him was a series of first times that never got old. After all, his body was made for a rigorous, full body contact sport like football. He once told her that he used every muscle in his body when making love to her, just as he did on the field. He gave it his all, in pursuit of the lusty victory of claiming her as his and his alone.

The muscles tightened in his chest as he found the rhythm with her body. He pulled her up to meet him, and Morgan tightened her legs around his waist and anchored her arms around his neck. The satin and lace of her demi cut bra created a scintillating friction between them. Seth trailed kisses down and between her breasts, and he pulled at the bra with his teeth to expose a nipple. The feel of his breath so close made her skin tingle. He licked and sucked her nipples, and she shuddered—they'd become more sensitive since she'd had the baby. Morgan sighed as Seth rocked back, manipulating her buttocks to meet his thrusts halfway. The friction of sliding up and down on his steel rod was making it hard to stop the orgasm building inside her. Seth's sweat mixed with hers, his hair plastered to his head. Morgan leaned back to give in to the feeling ripping through her body, but he pulled her forward and covered her mouth with his to smother her climactic moans and followed her into rapturous oblivion.

Jake repositioning himself on the bed brought them out of their lust-filled haze. Morgan and Seth slipped into the bathroom and cleaned up before he could fully wake.

"What time is it?" Morgan grabbed Seth's wrist and spied his Rolex. "Crap, we've been gone for two hours!"

Seth laughed and tried to kiss her again, but she ducked and headed for Jake's bedroom for a change of clothes. Once Jake was up and ready to return to the party, they walked out of the house as casually as possible. No one said anything but the look on Tate's face said everyone had been discussing their absence. Seth shook his head while Morgan tried to slink back into the house. She didn't get too far. Teri-Lyn and Sydney were waiting for her at one of the tables. Channing and Tyler were back at the party with Jake's present: a border collie puppy named Rowdy. Jake clutched awkwardly at the puppy at first, but when Seth showed him how to pat Rowdy, they became the best of friends. Morgan smothered J.J., Channing, and Tyler with kisses for coming up with such a wonderful present.

The photographer was ready for a group photo. It took almost an hour to wrangle everyone together and get them perfectly placed before the picture was taken. When the camera flash started going off, Morgan teared up, knowing all of the Blakes and Reeds and their friends were in the photo. No matter where they lived, she would always have that memory of the day they were all together. The photographer finished up and everyone retreated back to their party spots. After disappearing for hours, Morgan handed Jake over to Sydney and Teri-Lyn without a fuss. The Dirty Rascals began to croon another slow tune. That was her cue to keep moving again even though her life was changing. Morgan went in search of her husband. It was time for another dance.

Chapter Ten

Seth told Morgan he wanted to take her and Jake to the Titans stadium to get one last look at the place. Since their return from the ranch, the wait for the free agency window to open was interminable. She went through the emotional wringer while Seth showed very little reaction at all. She went to work, he took care of Jake. They'd even planned a vacation to take after he made his announcement.

Today was the day he'd announce to the whole world that he was leaving the Titans and would become a Tomcat. He'd spent all morning talking to his agent, Luke. As expected, the Tomcats made an offer to Seth, which was communicated to the league and to the Titans. Seth had had a meeting with the Titans three days ago.

There was an eerie silence in the stadium as they made their way to the field. She laughed to herself, thinking how funny it was that this giant building felt like home to her. The first time she'd seen that larger than life banner they had of him on the outside of the building, she had a better understanding of what the sport of football and its heroes meant to fans.

Seth would stop and show something to Jake, who listened like he knew what his father was talking about. She liked the relationship that was developing between the two of them. She'd been around Seth and John Jacob enough to know they had that same bond. Seth listened to his dad and enjoyed spending time with him. Now that Seth was a dad, they talked more about life and family.

Once on the field, a bittersweet feeling took over. He'd helped change the course of a football dynasty. He'd won three Super Bowls with this team. No easy feat in the history of the sport. Now he was off to accomplish a new dream. She was rooting for that ten-year-old boy who'd made the declaration to his dad that he would be a Tomcat one day.

Seth stopped at the fifty yard line, pulled a mini football out of Jake's bag, and gave it to him. "OK, Jake, throw a pass to Daddy."

Jake ran for a bit then threw the ball at Seth and yelled, "Touchdown!"

Morgan got out her cell and snapped pictures of the two of them. "Jake, this is where all the magic happens. Your daddy did some good work here."

Seth picked up Jake and put him on his shoulders. "The first time I set foot on the field, I was terrified. I'd just left a defunct team, the Titans were in a slump, and I didn't know if this was the right move despite the money they were paying me. Philadelphia was so foreign to me."

"What changed?"

"Patton Hawkes." Seth smiled. "The first words Patton ever said to me were 'So, you're here to save the world.' Then he laughed."

"What did you say to him?"

"I told him I didn't know about saving it, but I brought my shovel to help the Titans dig themselves out of the hole they were in." He sighed. "Patton told me he was here to dig with me."

"And the budding bromance of Seth Blake and Patton Hawkes begins." She giggled.

"I guess you could say that. I didn't do all of this by myself. Patton and the other guys all made an effort."

"I think you gave them inspiration."

"I like to think I did." He nodded.

She rubbed his cheek. "I know you did. That's why it's been hard for some of them to see you go. I've been on the receiving end of one of your speeches. You have a way of inspiring people to want to reach their fullest potential. How do you think I've trudged along with my reading programs? You believed in me, even when there were days when I didn't believe in myself. You didn't try to buy a solution for me; you helped me find a way through them. Obliterate an obstacle, and you won't have to worry about seeing it again."

"You are always in my corner." Seth kissed the top of her head.

"That's what you do when you're crazy in love with someone." Morgan gave him a squeeze.

"Even give up everything you love and move to another state?"

"Well, we've been living in two places for over a year now. We'll just be spending more time in Texas."

"What about the bookstore? The job offer? Your non-profit? I know they're more than jobs to you. It's a part of who you are."

"Just like being a professional football player is part of yours. Concessions will be made, but we'll adjust. Life will go on, just a bit differently."

Seth put Jake down and reached in the bag for a juice box and an apple slice. Jake took it and walked down the field.

"Joining the Tomcats has been my lifelong dream. I never wanted anything so badly in my life. It was what drove me to become a football player. It was the most important goal in my life."

Morgan smiled. "Your dream is coming true. Congratulations."

Seth looked into her eyes. "You're going to miss your life? Your family?"

She nodded. "Who would have thought I'd grow closer to those lunkheads. Or have a relationship with Sydney? Just when I stop running from everything, it's time to go."

Seth pulled her to him. "Having you in my life will always be the best thing that has ever happened to me Morgan. I love you."

Morgan put her arms around his waist. "Love has a way of changing a person's life. You've changed mine in every way imaginable."

Seth ran his hand through her hair. "Morgan, I renewed my contract with the Titans."

Morgan froze. "What?"

"The good things you achieve with the bookstore and your charity are just as important as my football career. You're making great strides and keeping you away from it isn't fair. This is about more than my legacy as a pro athlete. It's about our legacy as a family. The Titans have been good to me, and I want to continue to play for them while you continue following your dreams."

Morgan shook her head. "I-I can't let you do that."

"I'm invoking my get out of anniversary jail free card. So you can't object to my decision." He laughed.

"Is that why you didn't do anything crazy this year for our anniversary? Because you were saving your card for this?"

Seth grinned. "Yes. I am crafty."

"This would be using up all of your cards for a lifetime."

"That's not fair," he drawled.

"Why are you doing this?"

Seth put his finger under her chin and lifted her face to meet his gaze. "I want our kids to know that we are partners in our life journey. I want them to know that a man's legacy is greater than what he achieved in his career. It's about being a good husband and father."

Morgan stared up at him, tears burning her eyes. "I love you so much, Seth Blake."

"I love you too." Seth kissed her long and hard. "The new contract is for five years. After that I'm thinking about retirement."

"Retirement?"

Seth laughed. "You do remember that I have another job? Blake Enterprises, the company I own with J.J. and my dad?"

"Yes, I vaguely recall my son inheriting a golf resort last month," she quipped.

Seth caressed her cheek. "You should talk to Maura at the library and see if that position is still available. I think it would be a great fit for you."

"My personal spy Harriet came into the store the other day and said she hadn't filled it yet." Morgan smiled.

"And don't worry, we'll work it all out. Look at how well we're doing with Jake."

Morgan looked around. "Where's Jake?"

It took a minute for her statement to register. "He's at the twenty yard line."

"How did he get all the way down there?"

Seth looked on in amazement. "That boy takes off like a rocket."

"Can you believe how much he's grown?" She sighed.

Seth kissed her again. "Yes, and he's a very independent toddler."

Morgan smiled at him. "I'm late."

"What?"

"I was thinking it was the stress of your impending decision, but I feel it. I had this feeling when I was pregnant with Jake, I just didn't know what it was at the time."

"What does it feel like?" Seth touched her tummy.

Morgan thought about it for a minute. "It feels like love is growing inside me."

"Let's go to the doctor now," Seth said.

"How about I call and make an appointment? In the meantime, we can get one of those pregnancy tests at the pharmacy after we grab a bite to eat." Morgan looked down at Jake pulling on her jean pocket. "See, he's hungry."

"No, he just loves tugging on his momma." Seth laughed.

Morgan gathered her bag, and they made their way off the field. Jake took his place back up on Seth's shoulders, giggling.

"Did the Titans match T.K.'s offer?"

Seth winked. "Sure did."

"Did you talk to him?"

"Yes. He was formally notified, but I called him and we talked."

"What did he say?"

"He said he was disappointed, but there was a new Blake he had his eye on." Seth patted Jake's knee.

"T.K. is too funny."

Seth shook his head. "T.K. doesn't joke around, especially when it comes to football."

Morgan took his hand in hers. "Thank you for changing your dreams for me. For us. For our family."

"Thank you for giving me something new to dream about." Seth kissed her.

"So where do you want to go on vacation? What do you think about going back to the island? You know they named bungalow twelve, the Blake bridal suite."

"Is that right?"

"We can make sand castles, think of baby names, and discuss your retirement in five years."

Seth walked off the field with Morgan beside him and Jake on his shoulders. They were going to have another baby, and Seth was ready. Five years seemed like a lifetime, but he was sure it would all fly by in a whirl of laughter and love.

~ About the Author ~

Rhonda Laurel is a contemporary interracial/multicultural romance writer whose two great loves are writing and landscape photography. She uses both as a vehicle to convey the complexity of the human spirit and the beauty of the world around her. *Ebb Tide, For the Love of the Game* and *Masquerade* were released in 2012. *Shutter, Memories of You, Star Crossed, MVP* and *California Bored and Tourism* in 2013. The print anthology, *The Rhonda Laurel Collection*, featuring *Ebb Tide, For the Love of the Game* and *Shutter* released June 2013. The author is happily building her backlist.

Discover more about Rhonda Laurel here

http://www.rhondalaurel.com

http://www.facebook.com/authorrhondalaurel

http://www.twitter.com/rhondalaurel

http://www.goodreads.com/RhondaLaurel

http://pinterest.com/rhondalaurel/

~ Available Now from Etopia Press ~

Shutter

Photographer Antonio De Soto's life is out of focus. Everyone in his family thinks it's time for him to settle down. He doesn't want to be strong-armed into domesticity, even if he does feel the bachelor lifestyle is starting to wear thin. So when his friend invites him to do a pictorial on the community theater, Antonio's prepared to do his thing and follow his normal womanizing M. O. Instead, he finds himself sparring with the resident artist, Lucy Marceloni. Lucy's dime-store analysis of his love life—and him—leaves him angry and shaken, but it's too close to the truth to dismiss. The quirky artist is not his type, but their passionate fights generate a deeper heat between them he can't ignore…

Lucy wants a man who's sensitive and intellectual, the exact opposite of Antonio De Soto. The moment she meets the handsome photographer she pegs him as arrogant and self-centered, but that doesn't protect her from the sizzling chemistry between the two of them. Being drawn to the rogue's charm and subtle seduction tactics is the last thing she wants. Working with him on the community theater fairytale production could prove to be more than she can handle...

~ Available Now from Etopia Press ~

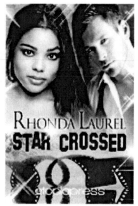

Star Crossed

When Hollywood's sexiest secret explodes, stars are born.

Music mogul Kate Garrison's husband is a leading Hollywood director. He also happens to be a cheat. When he's caught having an affair with an actress, Kate becomes the talk of the town—and not in a good way. So when she stumbles into Hollywood's new golden boy, Chris Cavanaugh—in the men's room, of all places—the gossip mill starts working overtime. Especially since Chris is starring in her husband's next film.

Chris Cavanaugh couldn't imagine a woman would have such an effect on his life. But amid the gossip and Hollywood politics, his only option is to ride out the media storm and play house. He never expects to actually fall for her, but when illusion begins to look more and more like reality, Chris has his hands full keeping his career intact and his eye on the target of making the Hollywood A-list. So why does spending time with Kate suddenly seem more important?

CPSIA information can be obtained at www.ICGtesting.com
Printed in the USA
BVOW05s1308161114

375331BV00001B/111/P